SPILL ZONE

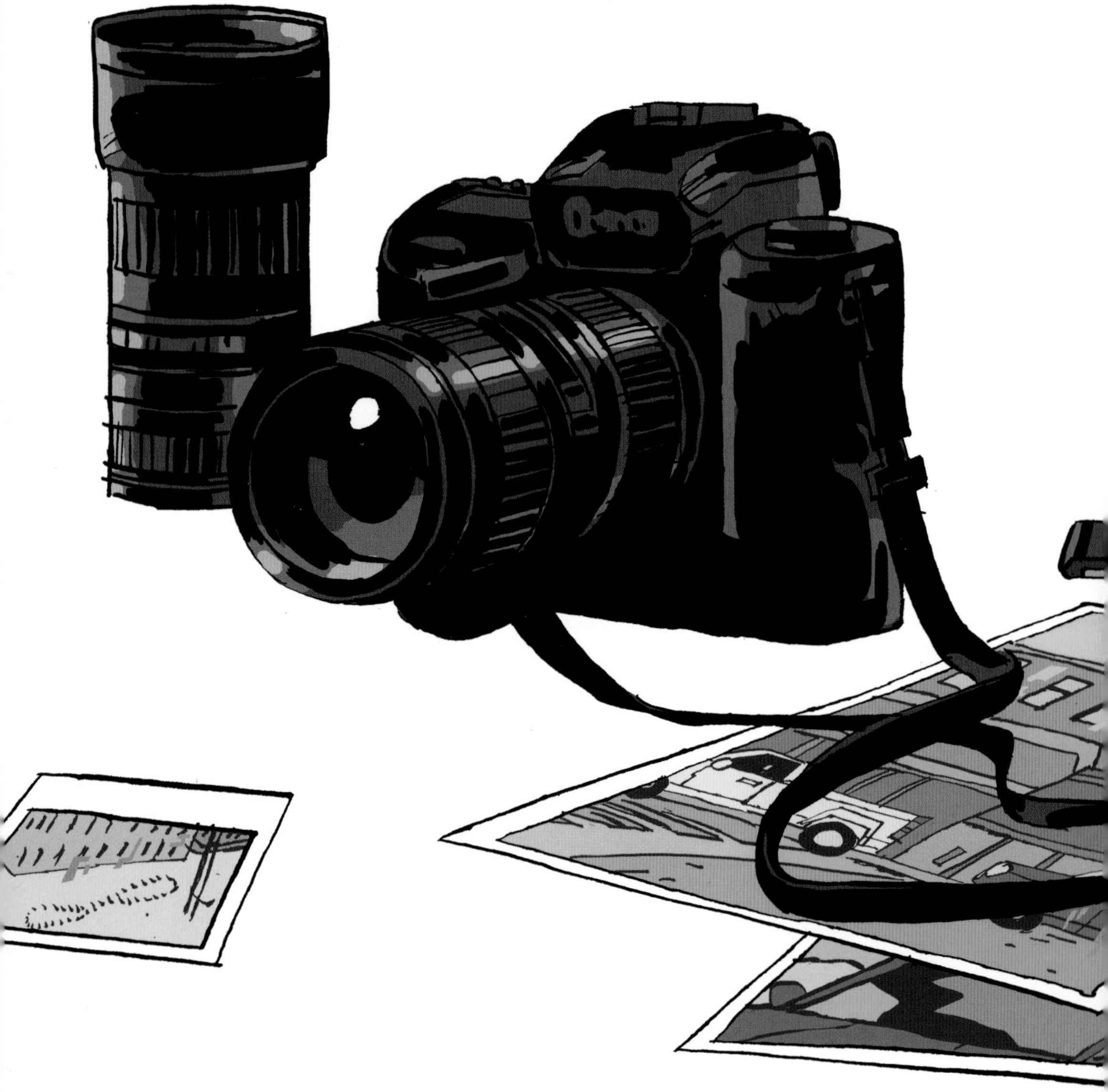

SPILL ZONE

SCOTT WESTERFELD
AND ALEX PUVILLAND

Colors by
HILARY SYCAMORE

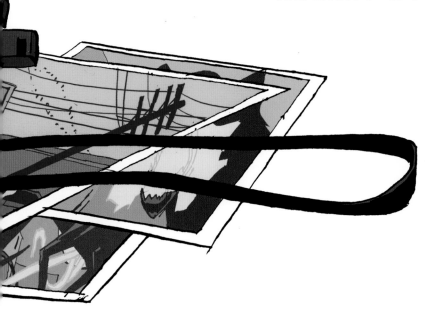

First Second
NEW YORK

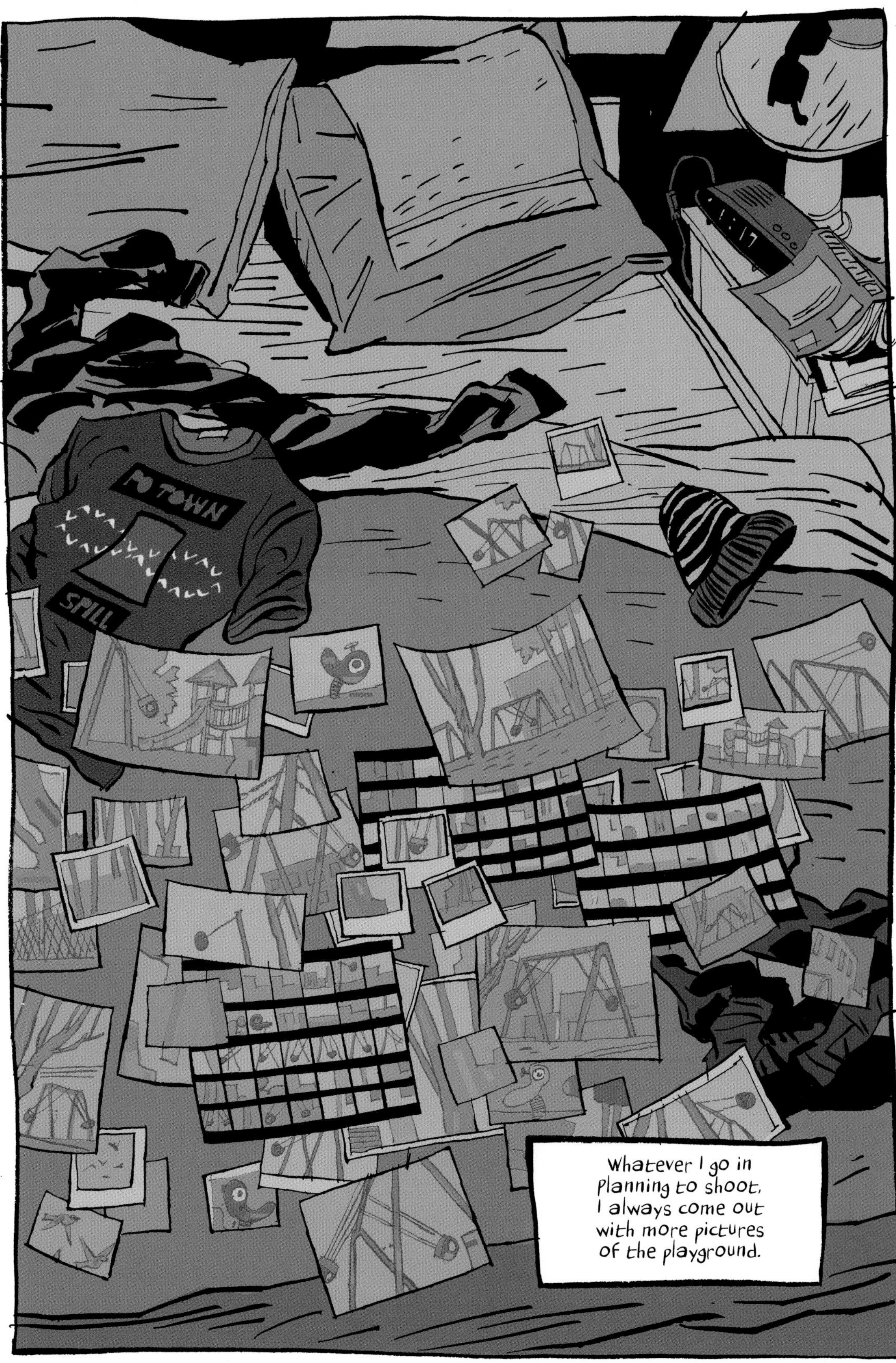
SPILL
Whatever I go in planning to shoot, I always come out with more pictures of the playground.

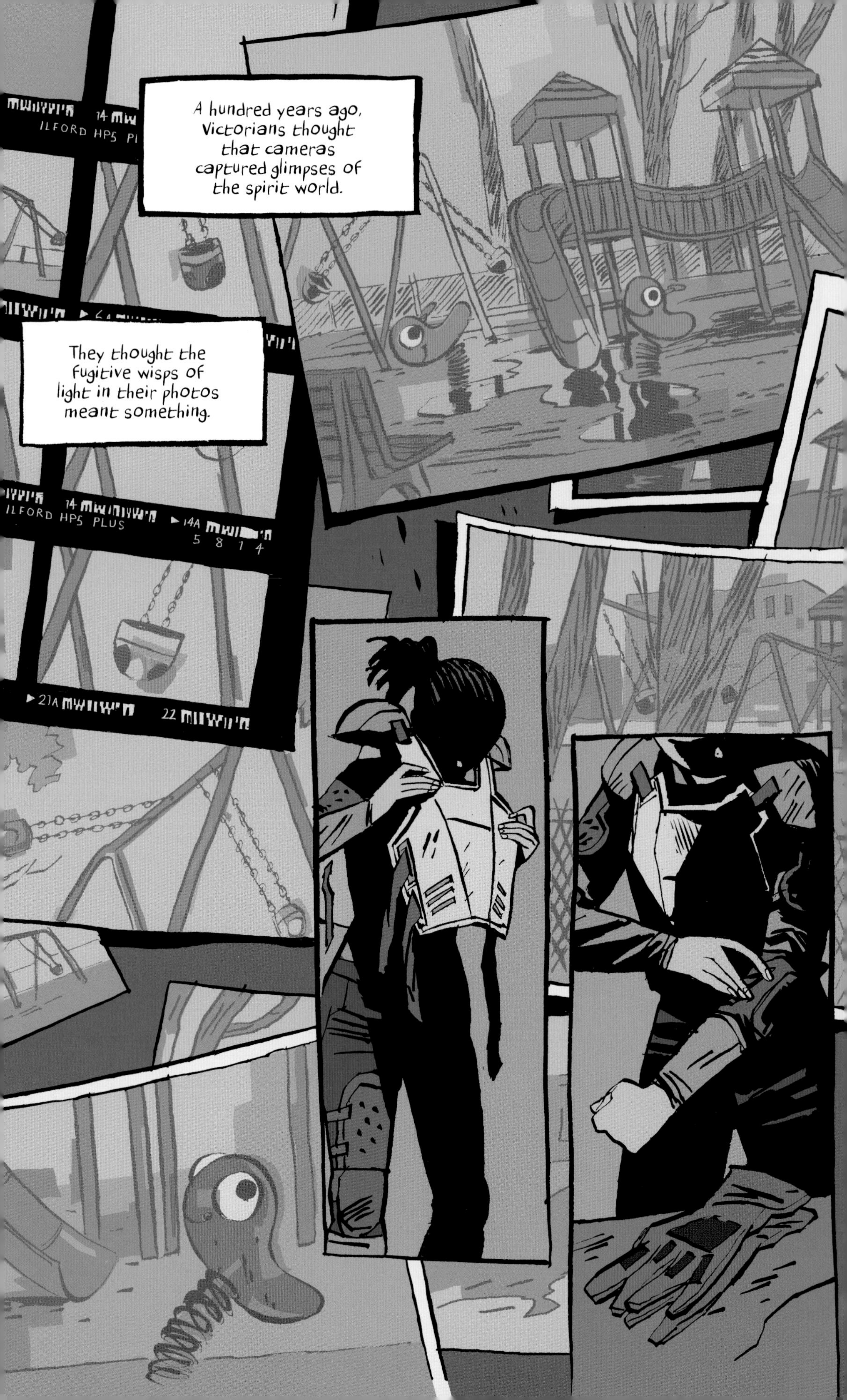
A hundred years ago, Victorians thought that cameras captured glimpses of the spirit world.
They thought the fugitive wisps of light in their photos meant something.
ILFORD HP5 PLUS
14A
5 8 7 4
21A
22

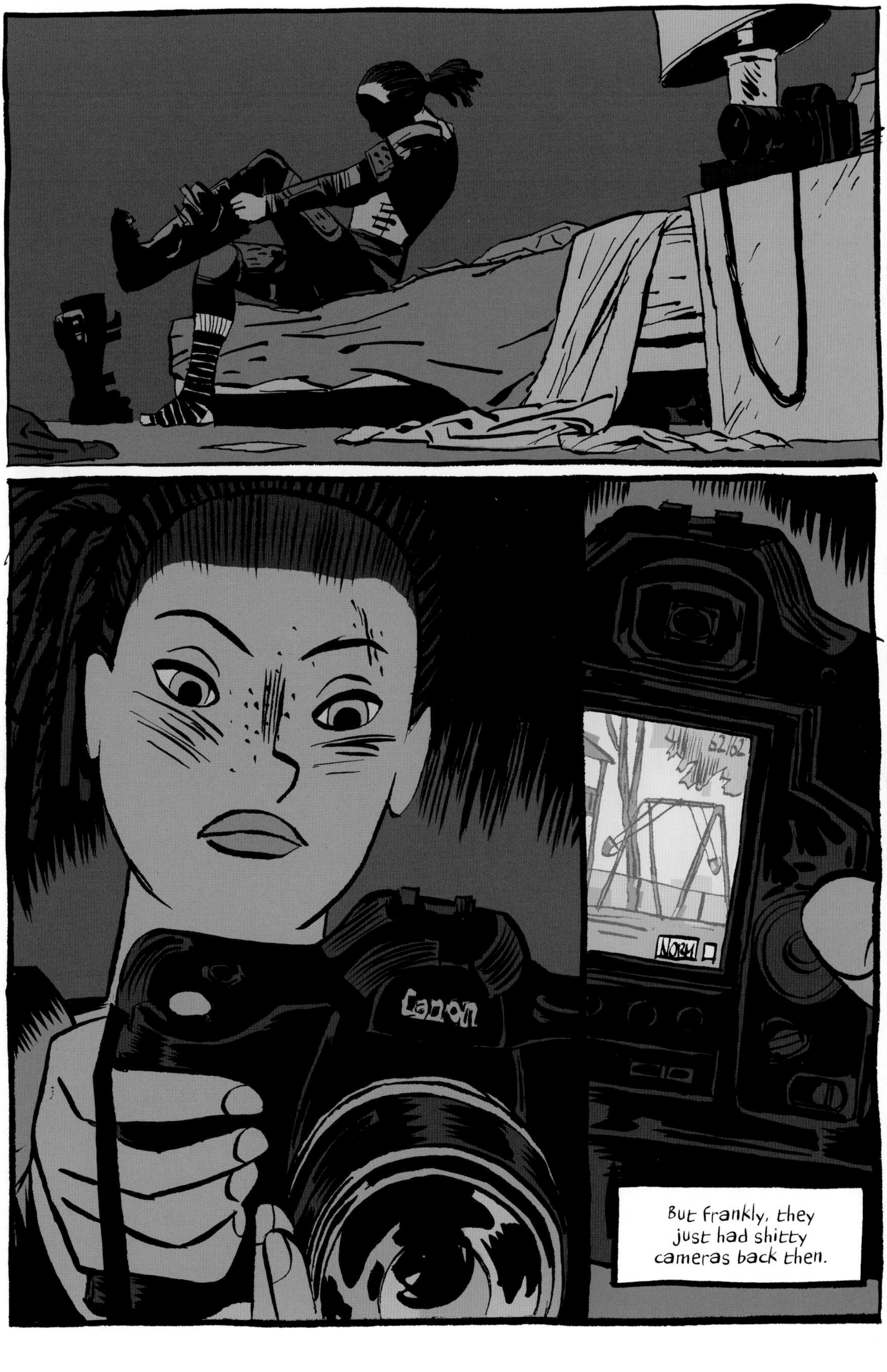
Canon
But frankly, they just had shitty cameras back then.

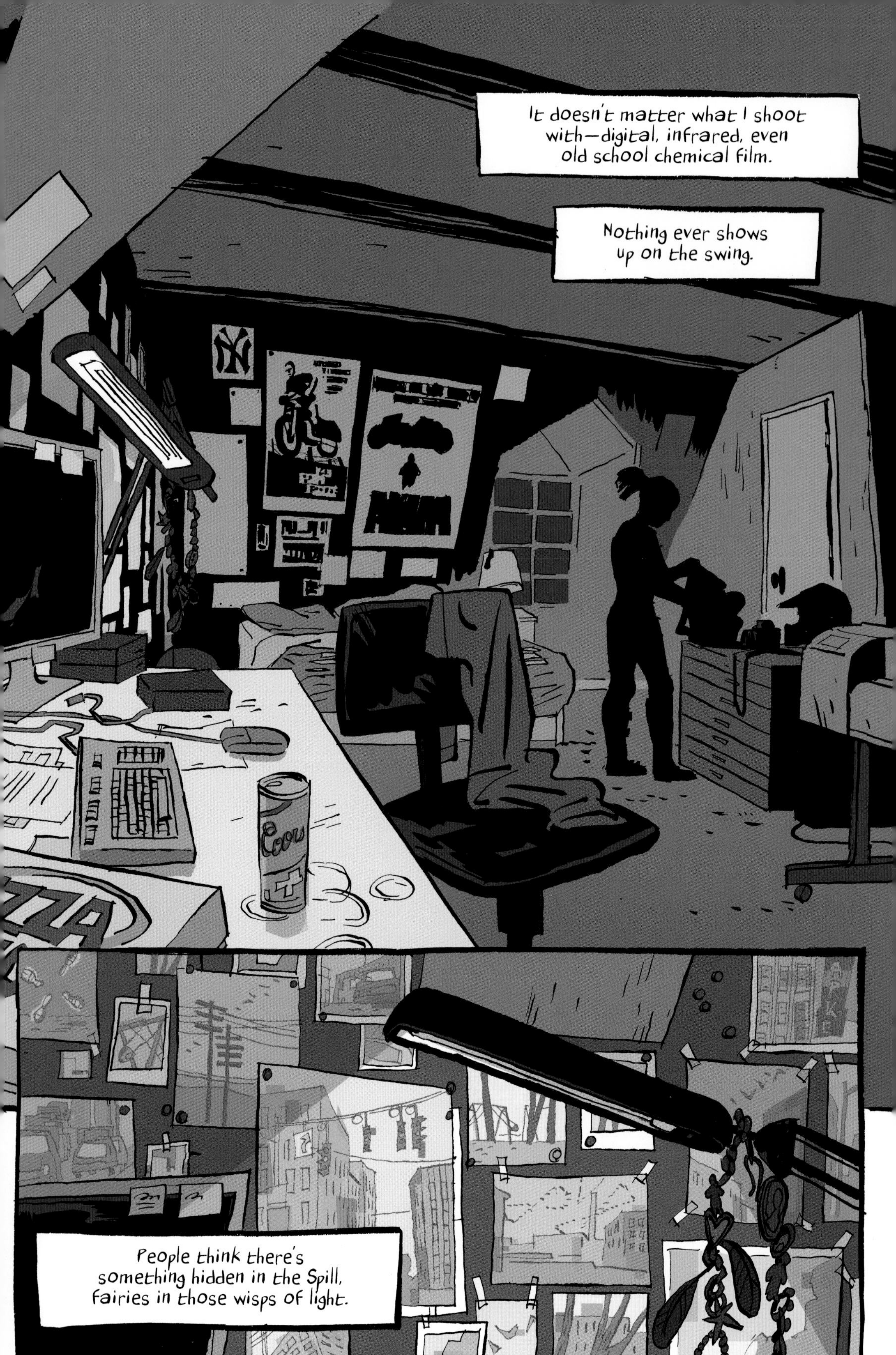
It doesn't matter what I shoot with—digital, infrared, even old school chemical film.
Nothing ever shows up on the swing.
People think there's something hidden in the Spill, fairies in those wisps of light.

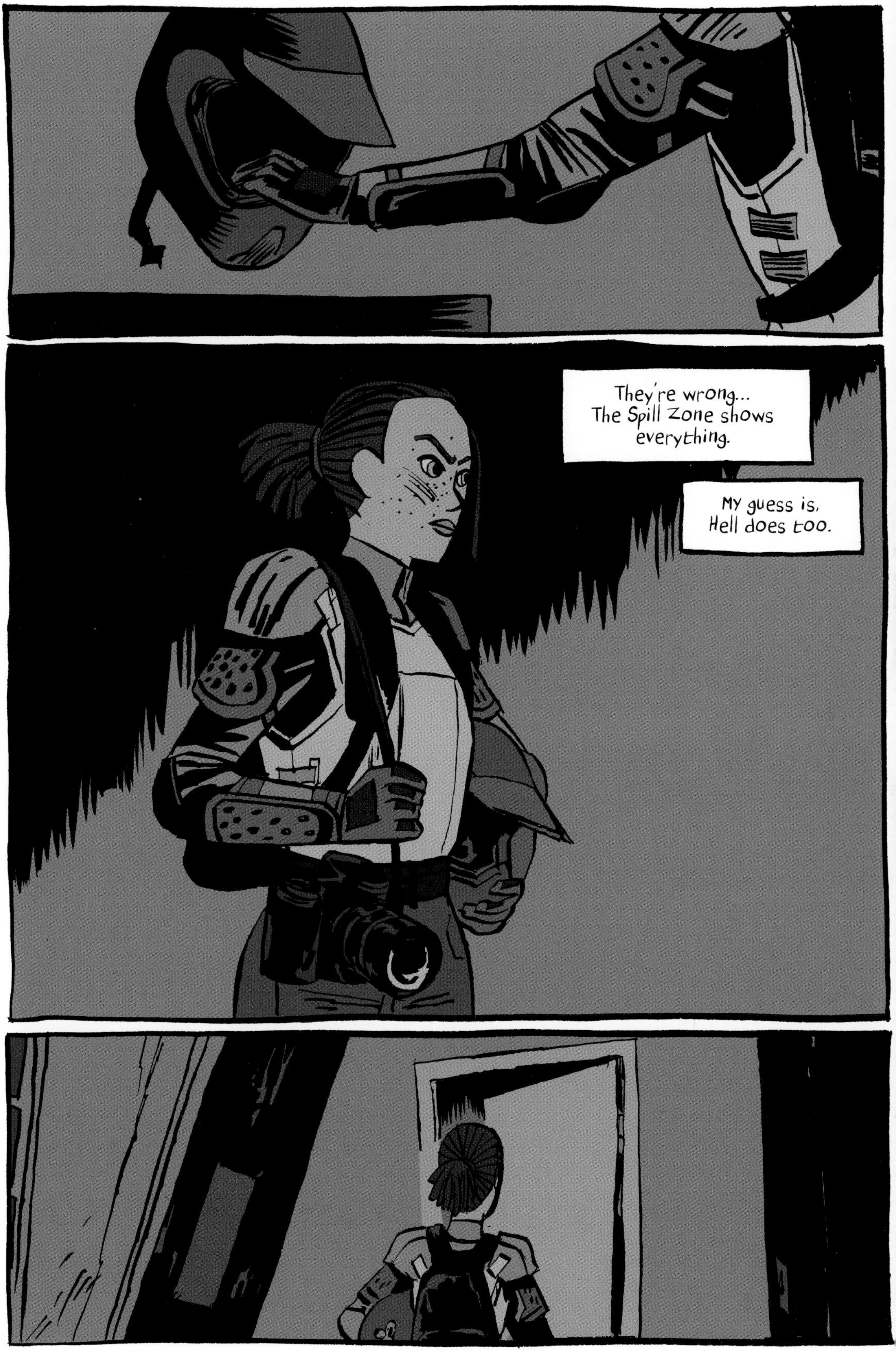
They're wrong...
The Spill Zone shows
everything.
My guess is,
Hell does too.

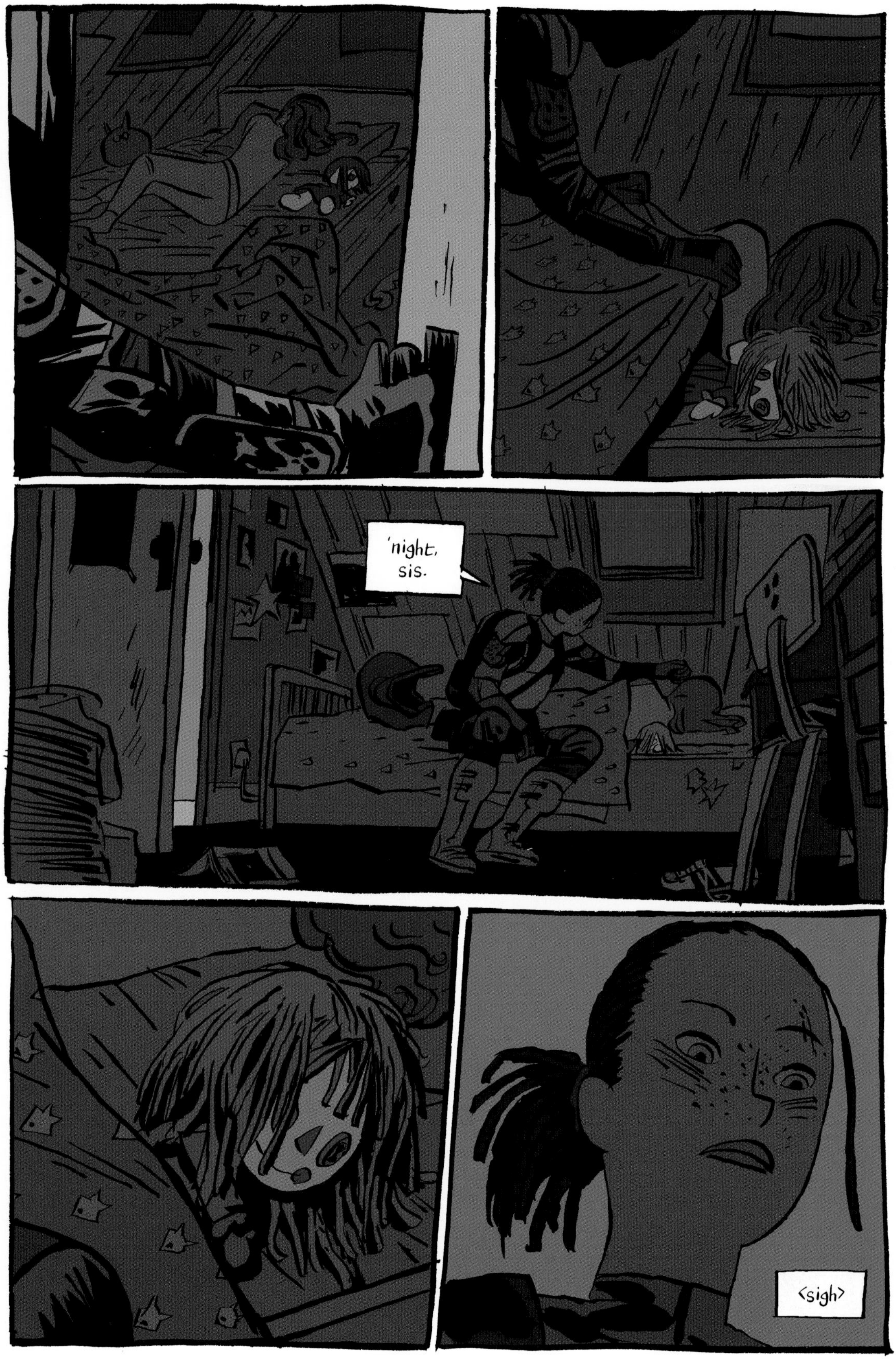
'night, sis.
<sigh>

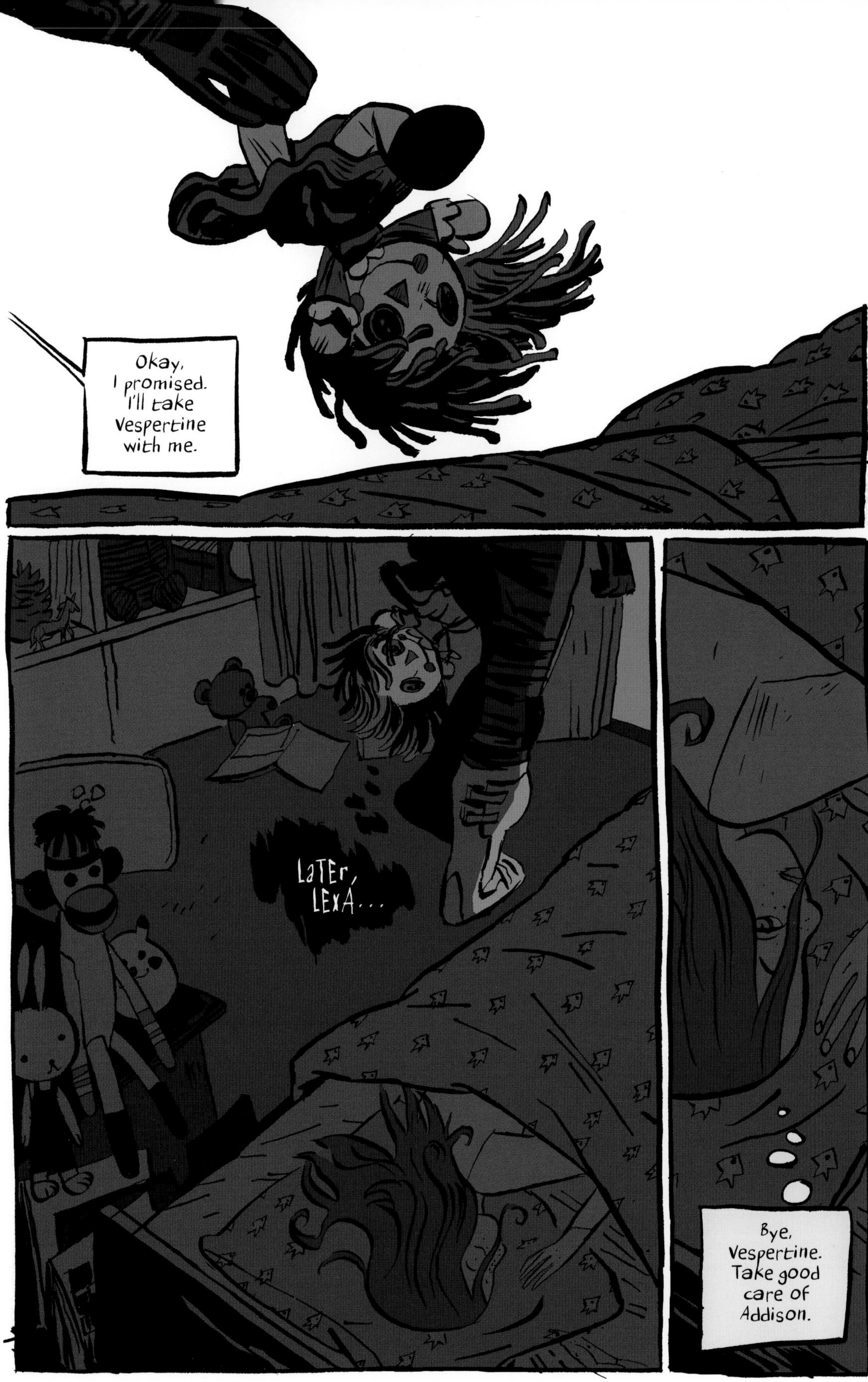
Okay, I promised. I'll take Vespertine with me.
LaTEr, LExA...
Bye, Vespertine. Take good care of Addison.

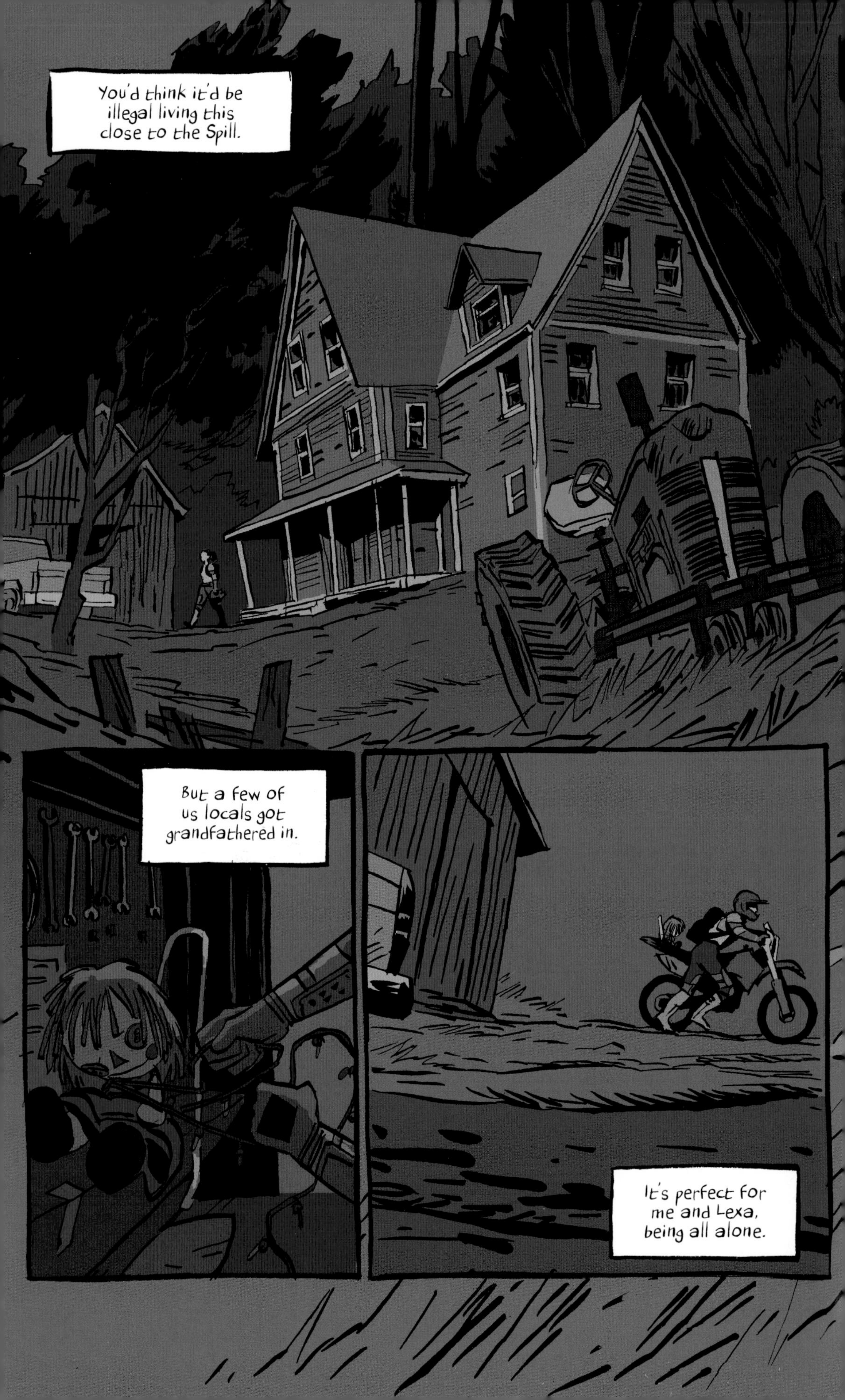
You'd think it'd be illegal living this close to the Spill.
But a few of us locals got grandfathered in.
It's perfect for me and Lexa, being all alone.

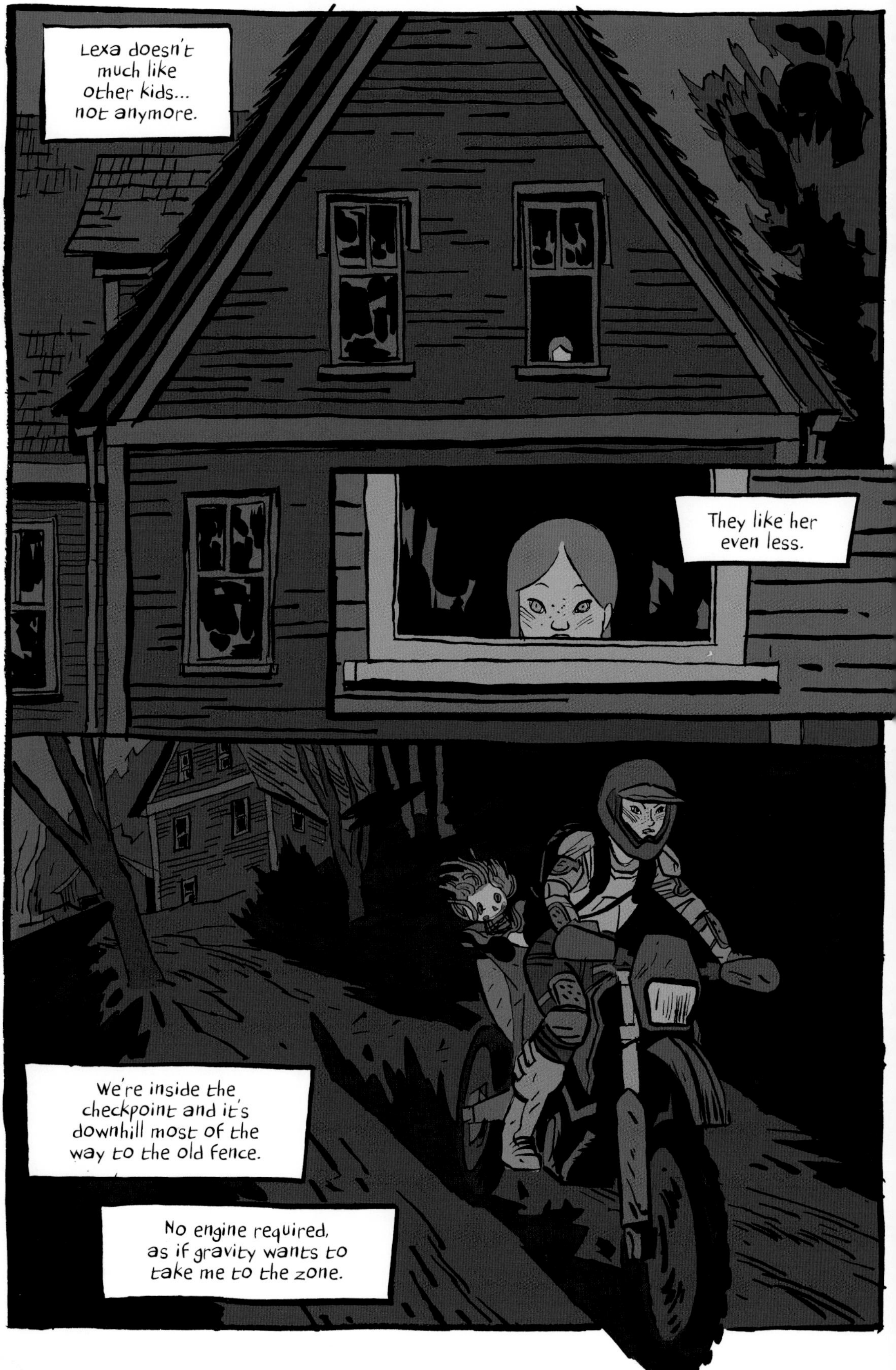

Lexa doesn't much like other kids... not anymore.
They like her even less.
We're inside the checkpoint and it's downhill most of the way to the old fence.
No engine required, as if gravity wants to take me to the zone.

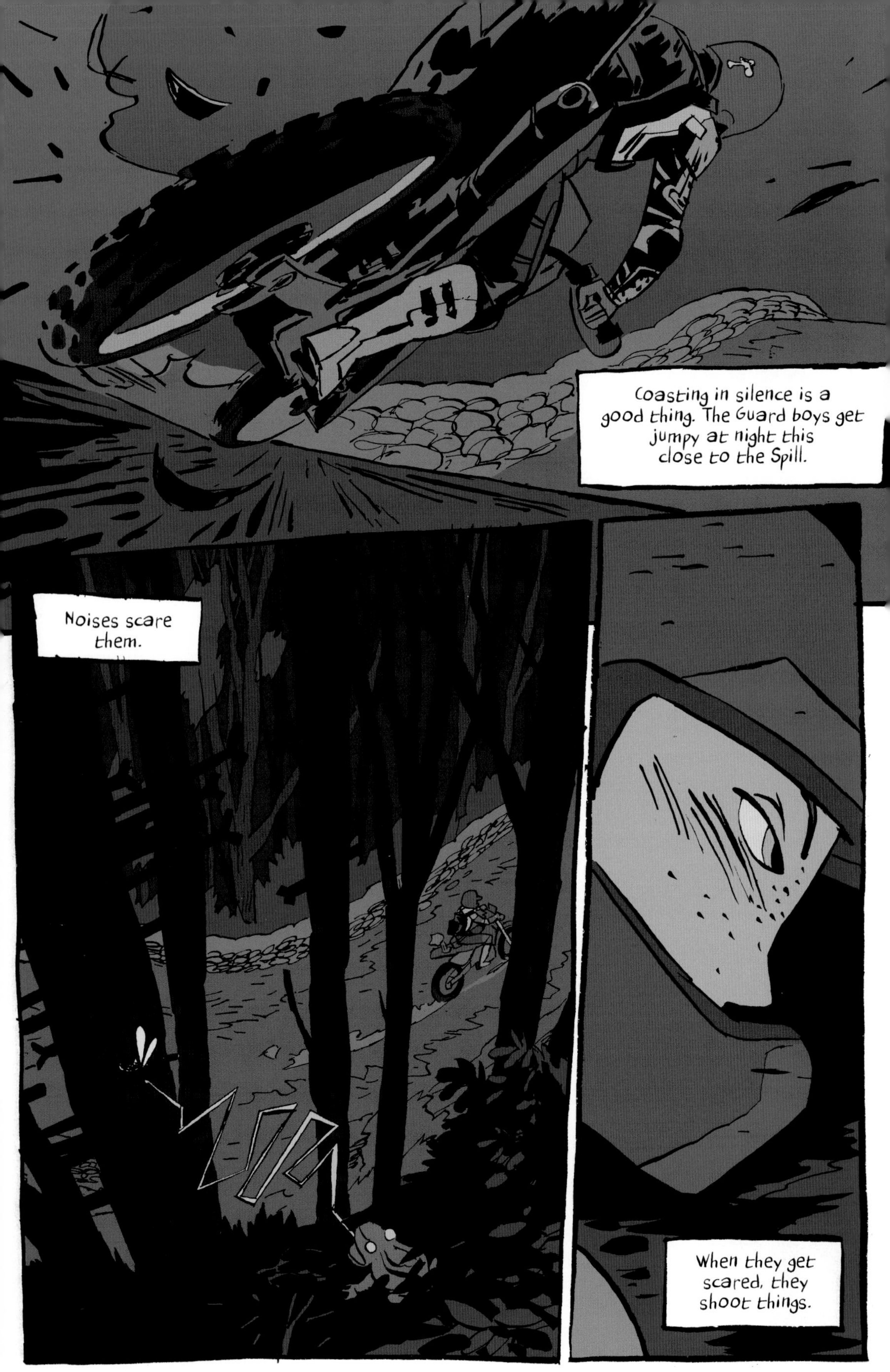
Coasting in silence is a good thing. The Guard boys get jumpy at night this close to the Spill.
Noises scare them.
When they get scared, they shoot things.

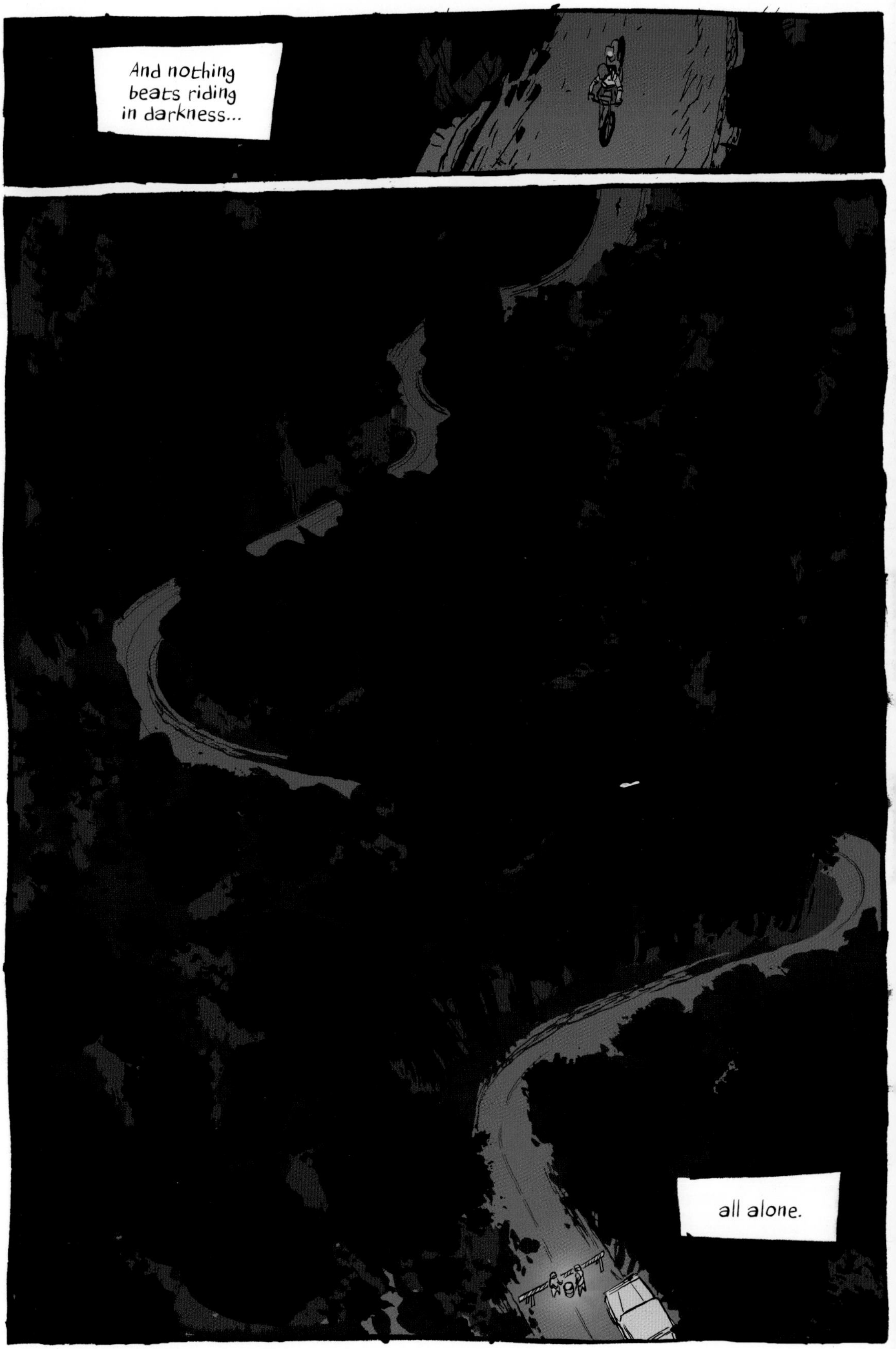
And nothing beats riding in darkness...
all alone.

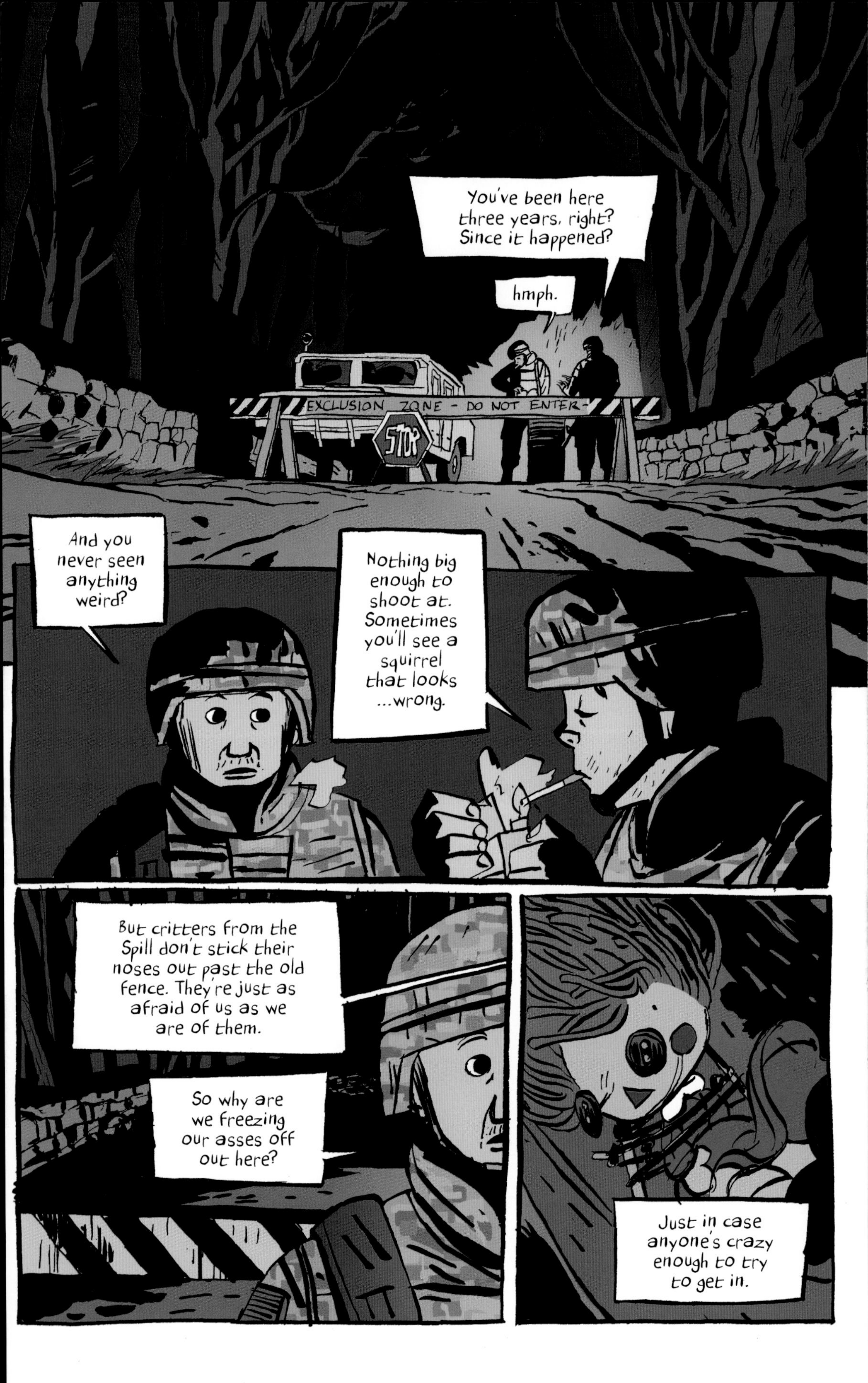
You've been here three years, right? Since it happened?
hmph.
EXCLUSION ZONE - DO NOT ENTER
STOP
And you never seen anything weird?
Nothing big enough to shoot at. Sometimes you'll see a squirrel that looks ...wrong.
But critters from the Spill don't stick their noses out past the old fence. They're just as afraid of us as we are of them.
So why are we freezing our asses off out here?
Just in case anyone's crazy enough to try to get in.

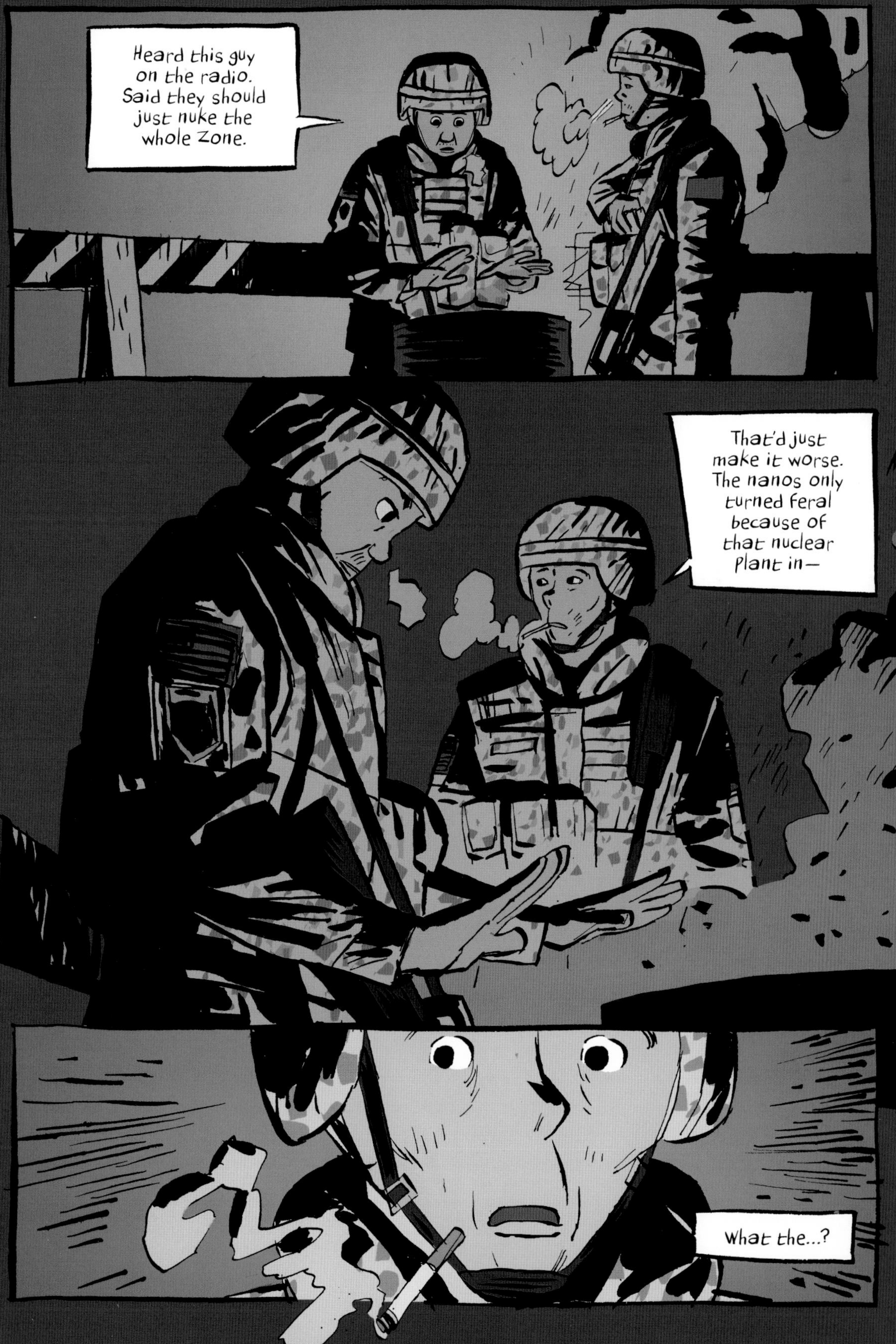
Heard this guy on the radio. Said they should just nuke the whole Zone.
That'd just make it worse. The nanos only turned feral because of that nuclear plant in—
What the...?

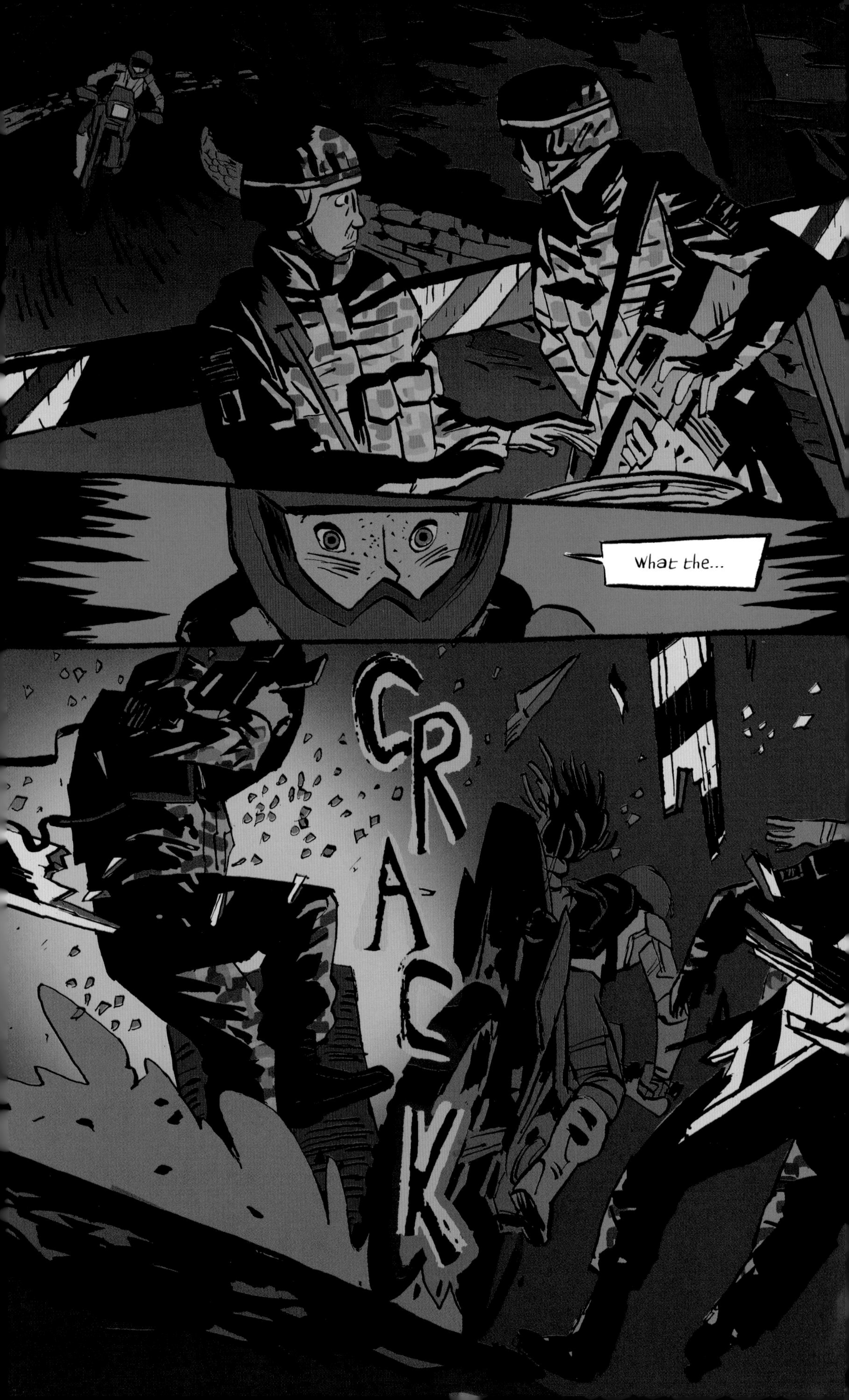
What the...
CRACK

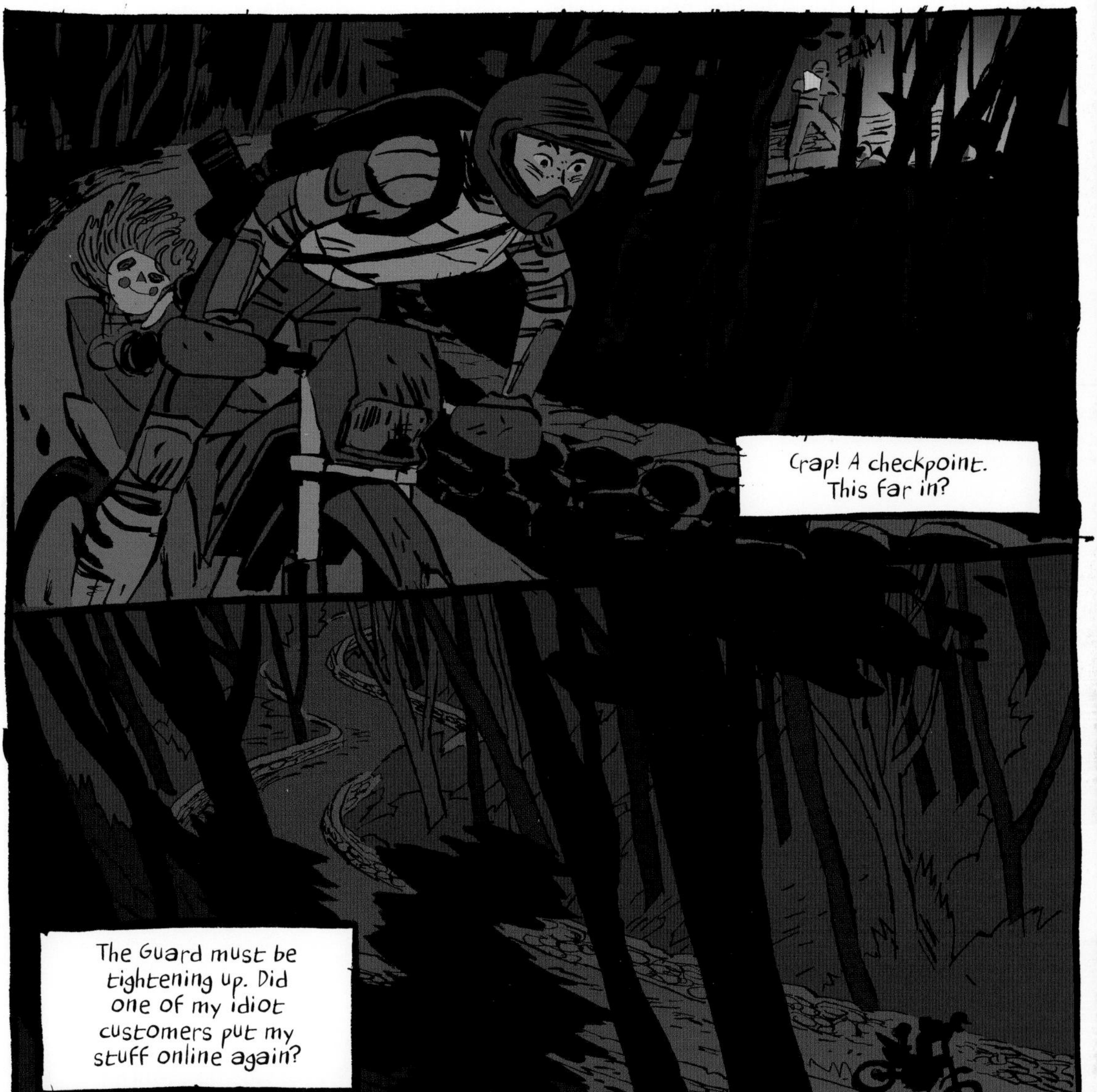
Crap! A checkpoint. This far in?
The Guard must be tightening up. Did one of my idiot customers put my stuff online again?
SUMMIT ROAD
Sooner or later they'll put up a real wall. Seal off all hundred miles of perimeter.
Then I'll be screwed.

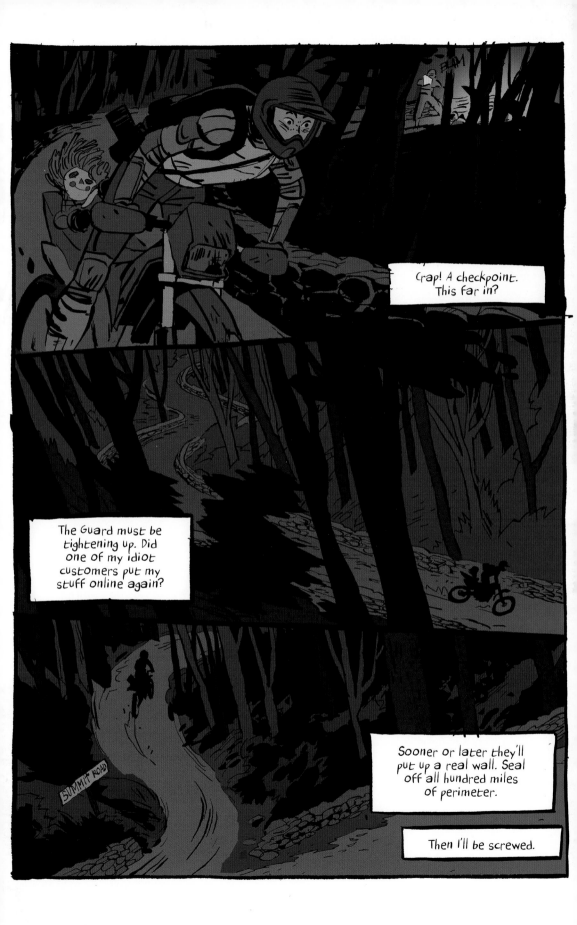

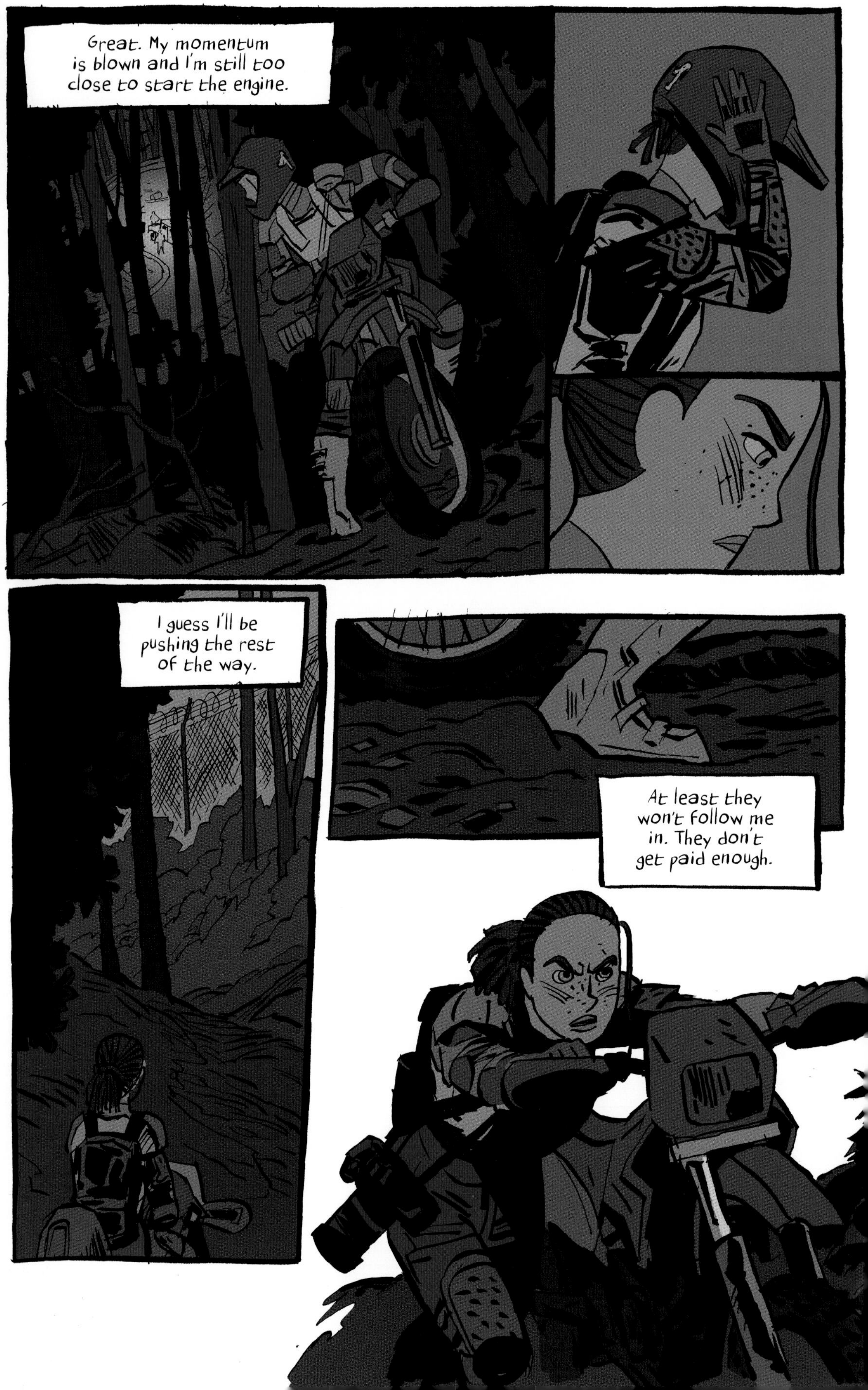
Great. My momentum is blown and I'm still too close to start the engine.
I guess I'll be pushing the rest of the way.
At least they won't follow me in. They don't get paid enough.

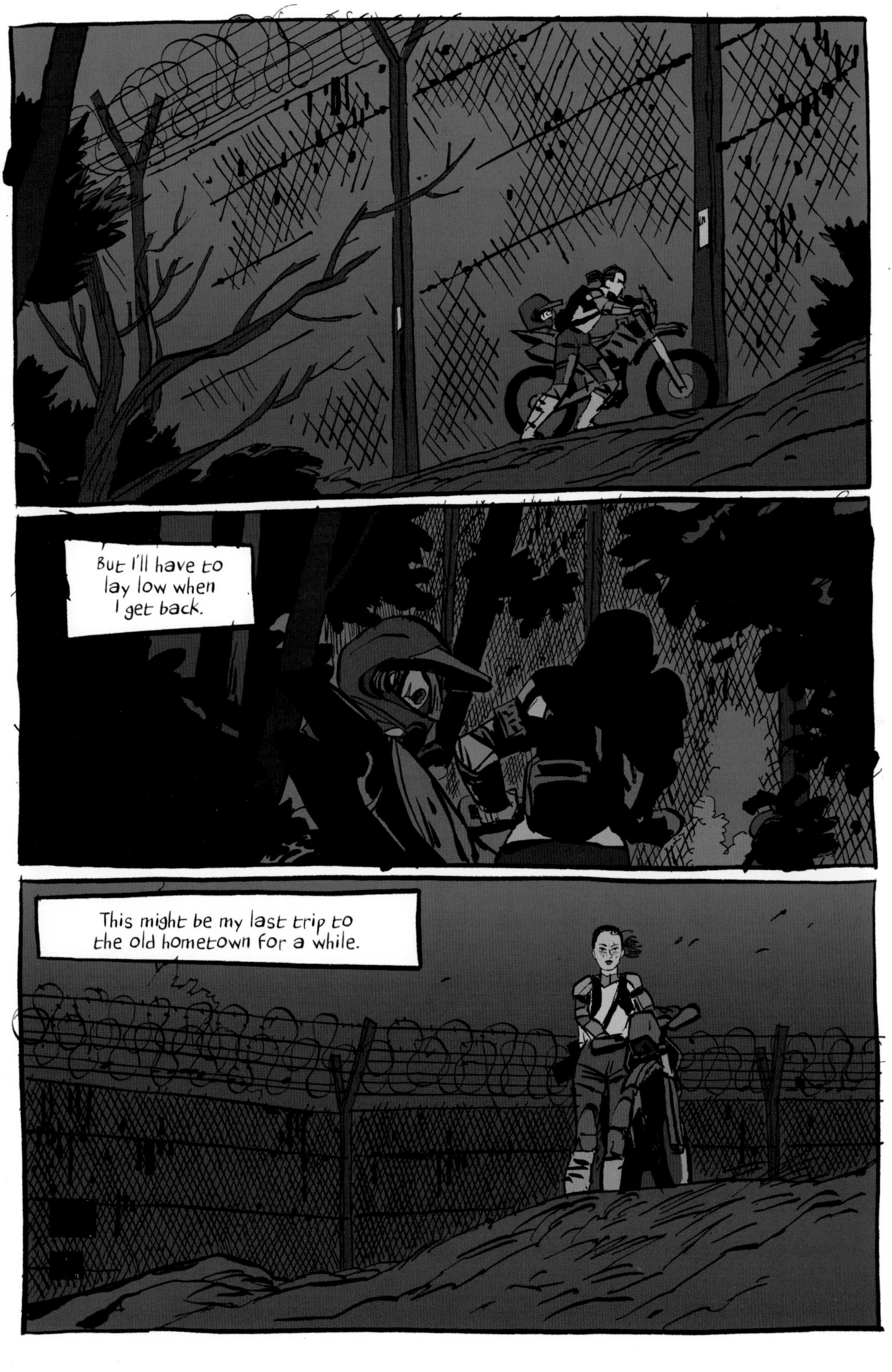
But I'll have to lay low when I get back.
This might be my last trip to the old hometown for a while.

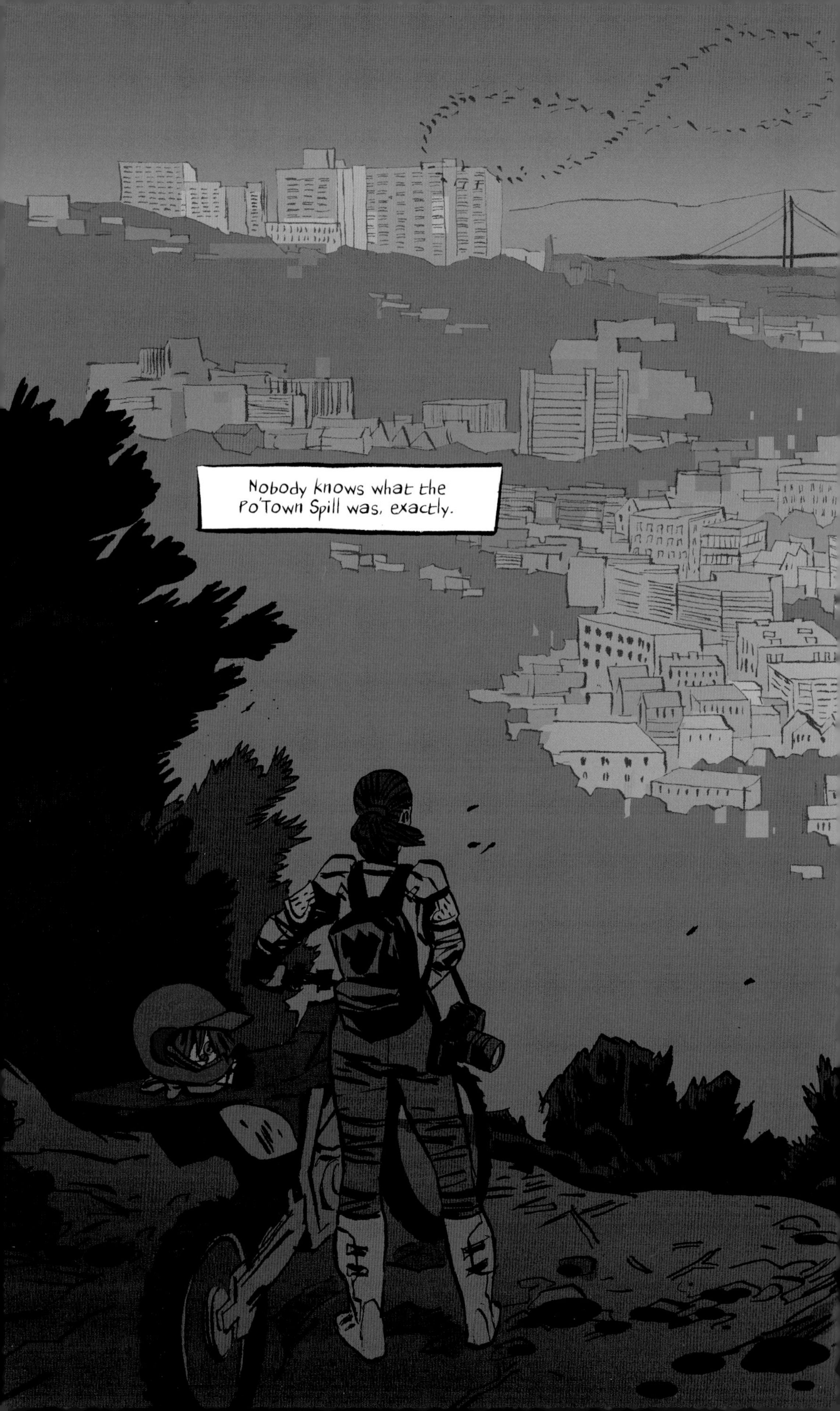
Nobody knows what the Po'Town Spill was, exactly.

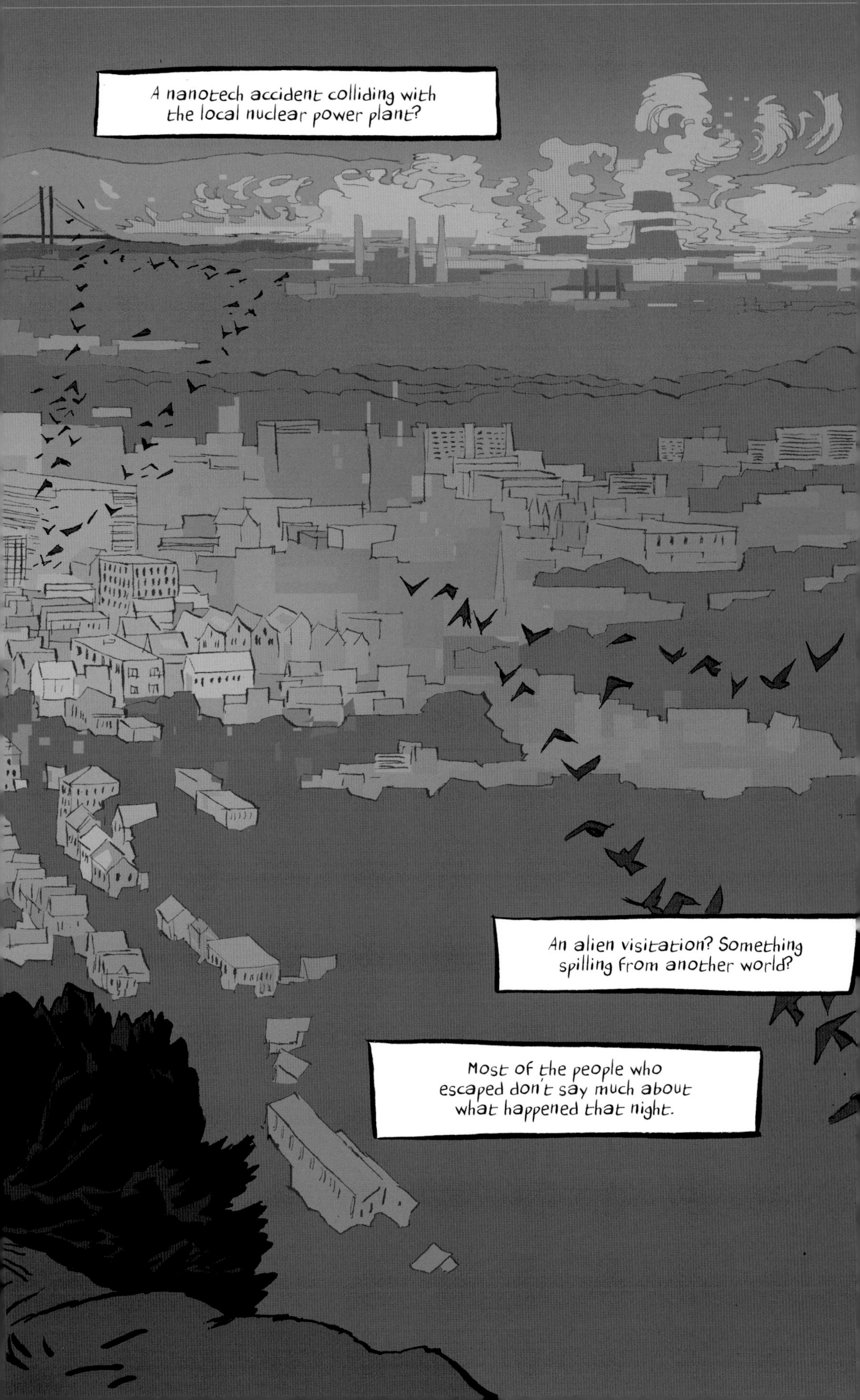
A nanotech accident colliding with the local nuclear power plant?
An alien visitation? Something spilling from another world?
Most of the people who escaped don't say much about what happened that night.

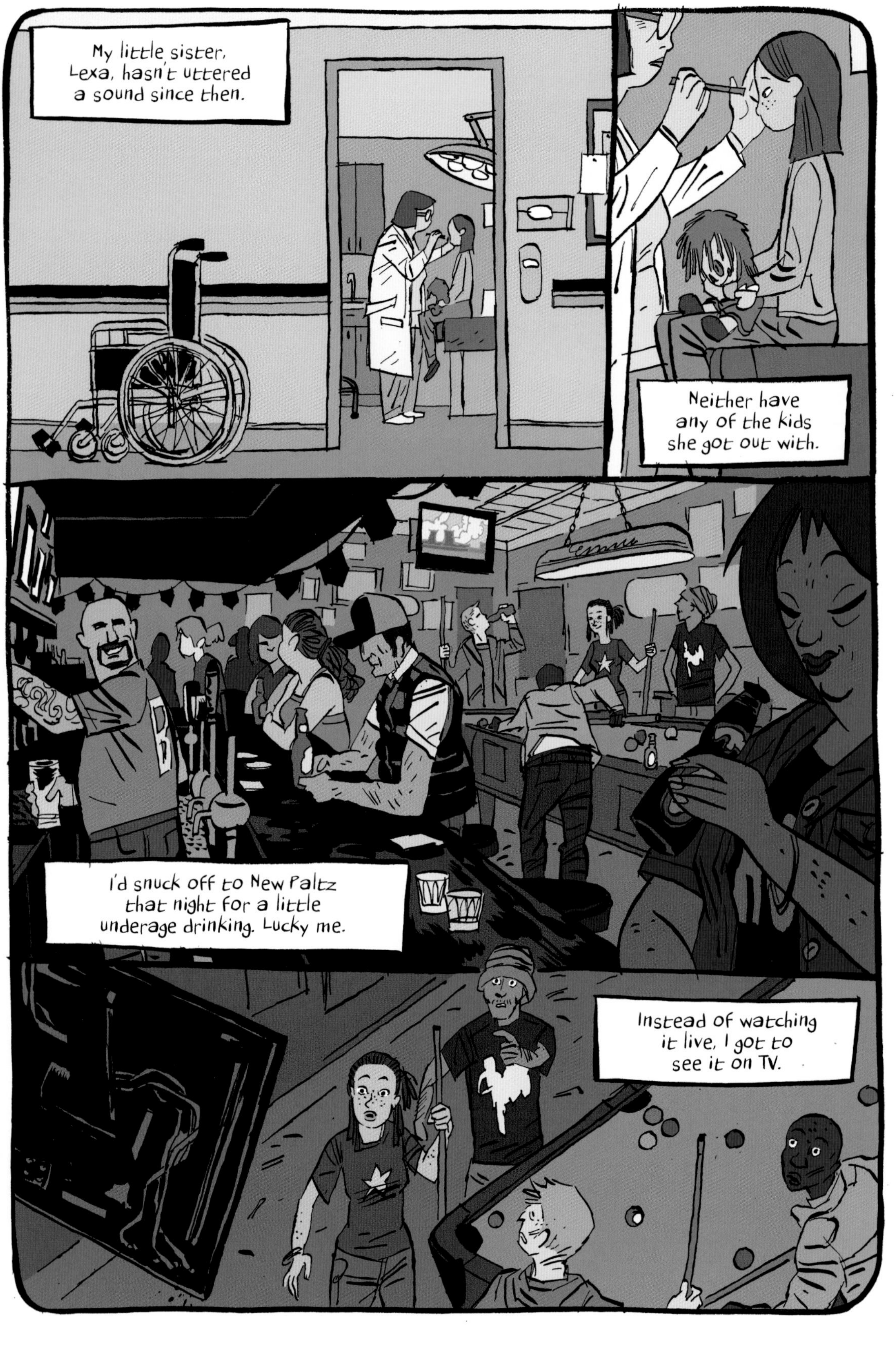
My little sister, Lexa, hasn't uttered a sound since then.
Neither have any of the kids she got out with.
I'd snuck off to New Paltz that night for a little underage drinking. Lucky me.
Instead of watching it live, I got to see it on TV.

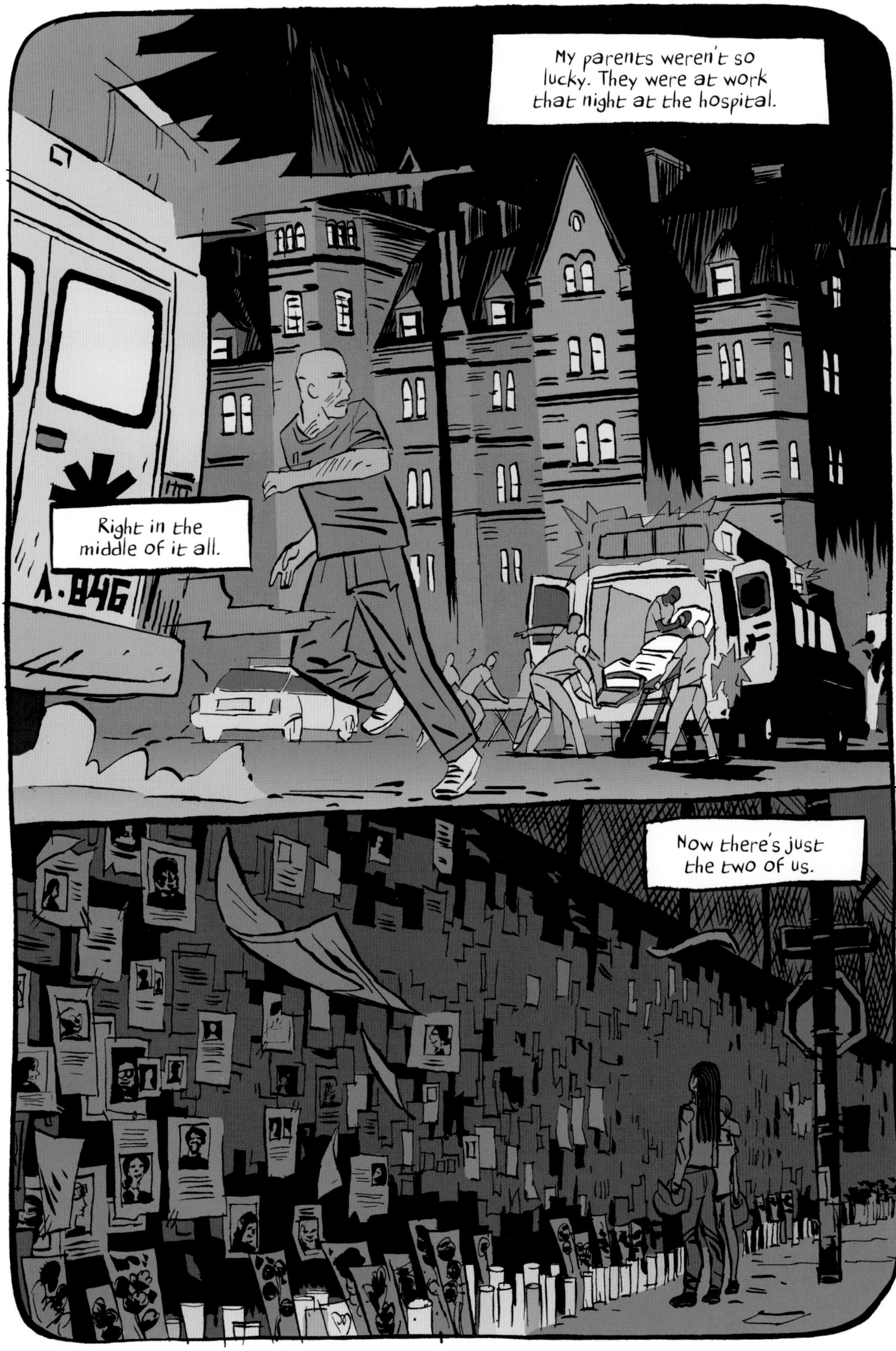

My parents weren't so lucky. They were at work that night at the hospital.
Right in the middle of it all.
A-846
Now there's just the two of us.

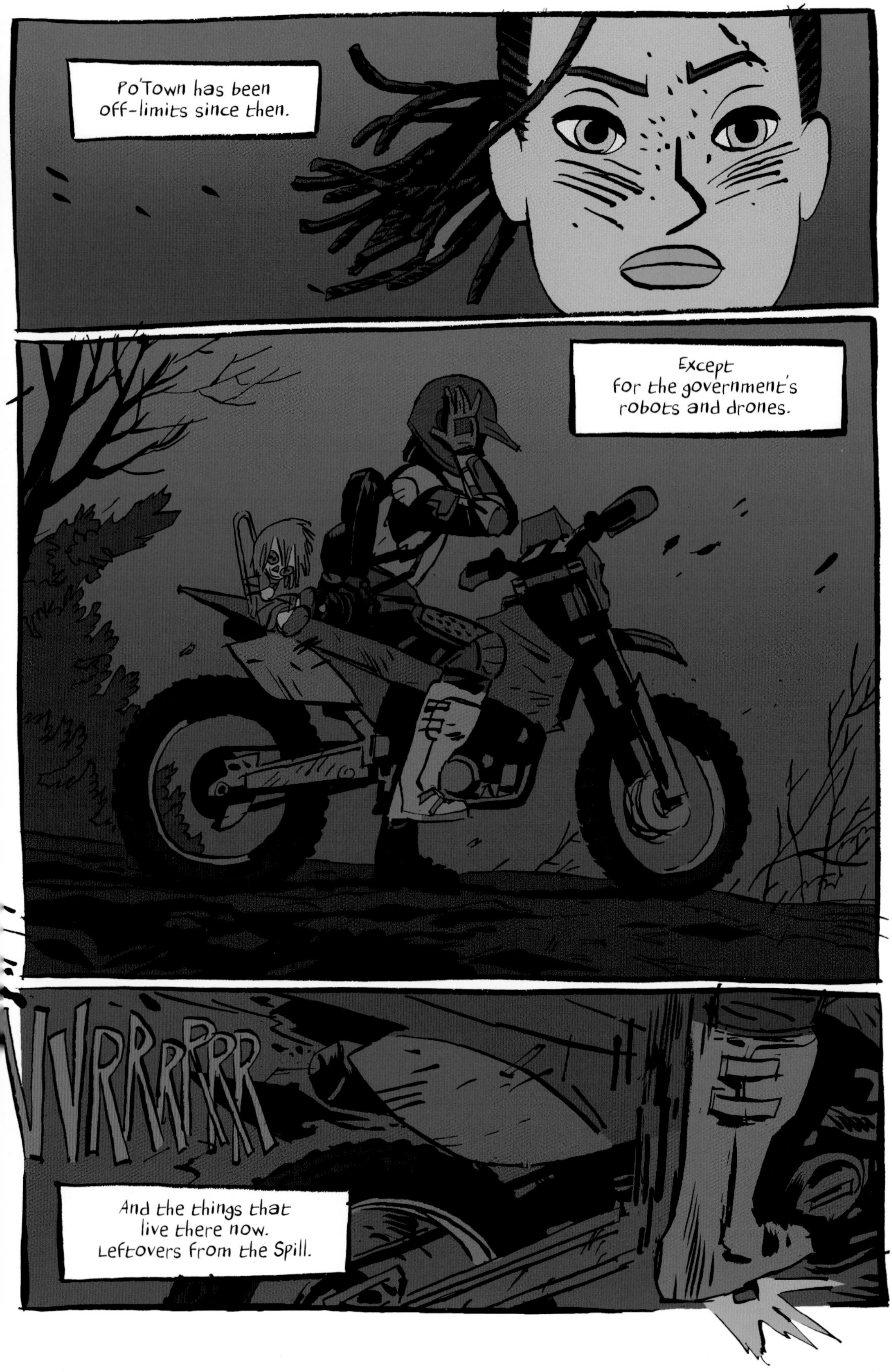
Po'Town has been off-limits since then.
Except for the government's robots and drones.
VVRRRRRR
And the things that live there now. Leftovers from the Spill.

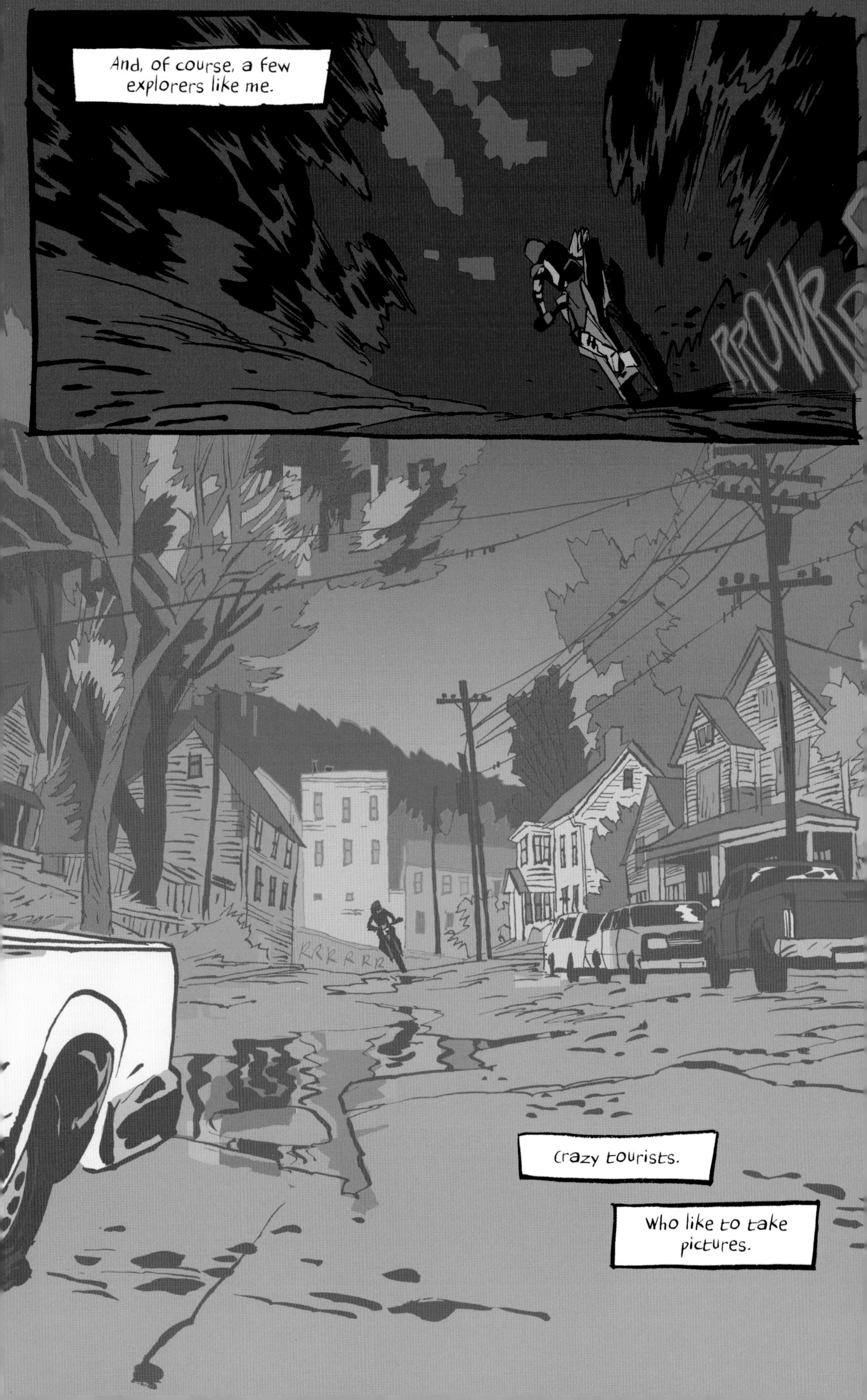
And, of course, a few explorers like me.
Crazy tourists.
Who like to take pictures.

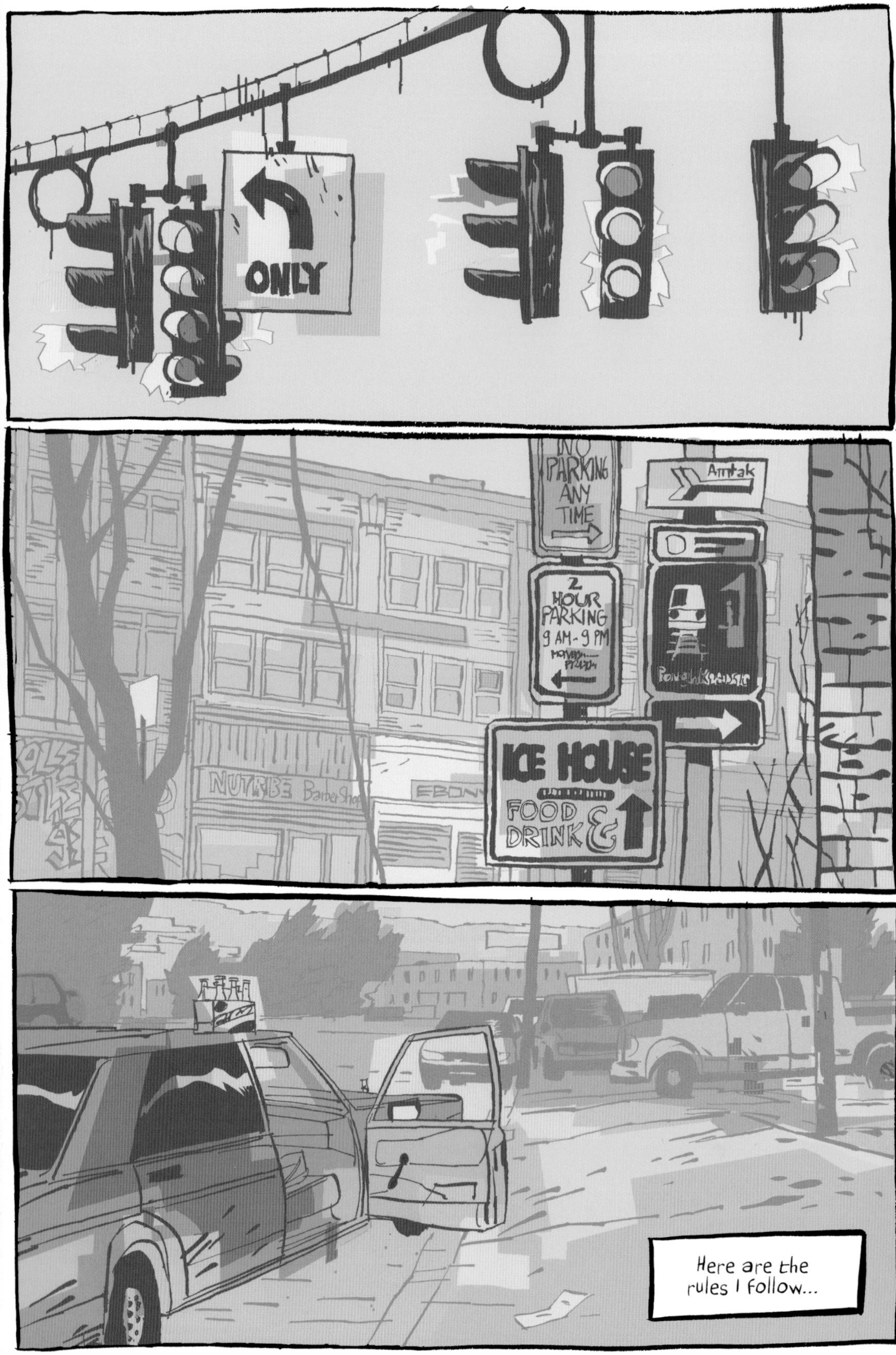
ONLY
NO PARKING ANY TIME
Amtrak
2 HOUR PARKING 9 AM - 9 PM
ICE HOUSE
FOOD & DRINK
Here are the rules I follow...

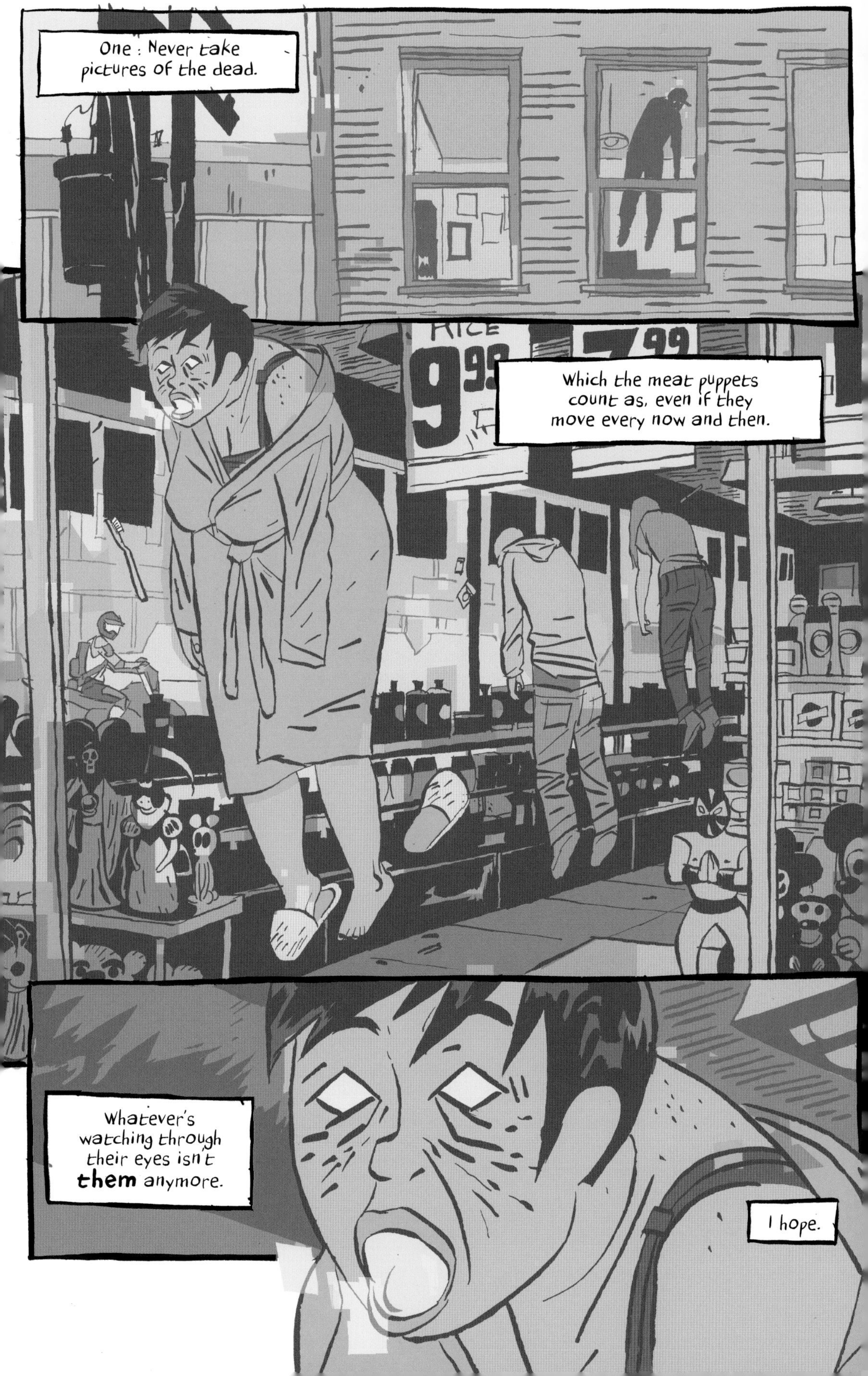
One : Never take pictures of the dead.
Which the meat puppets count as, even if they move every now and then.
Whatever's watching through their eyes isn't **them** anymore.
I hope.

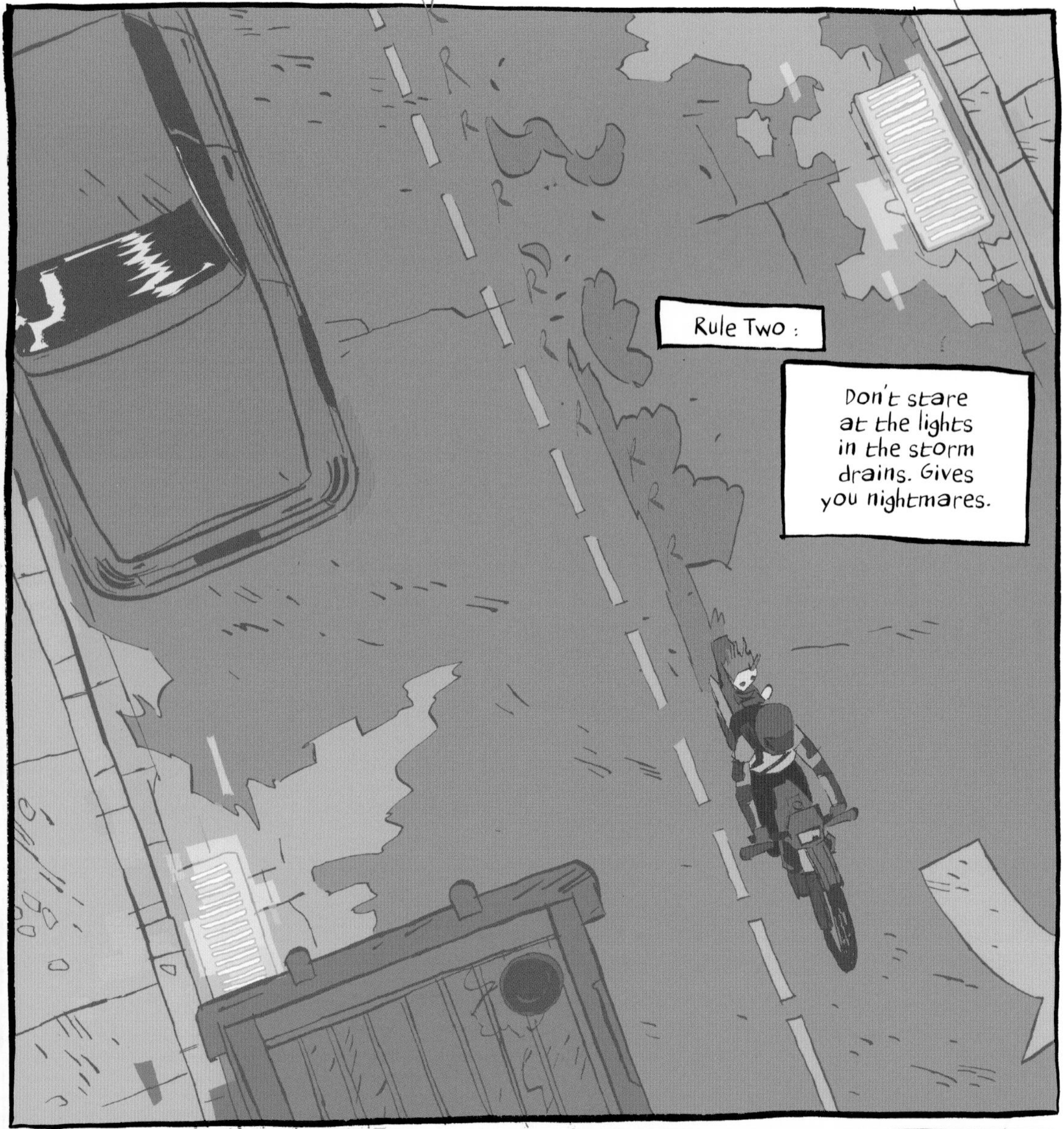
Rule Two :
Don't stare at the lights in the storm drains. Gives you nightmares.

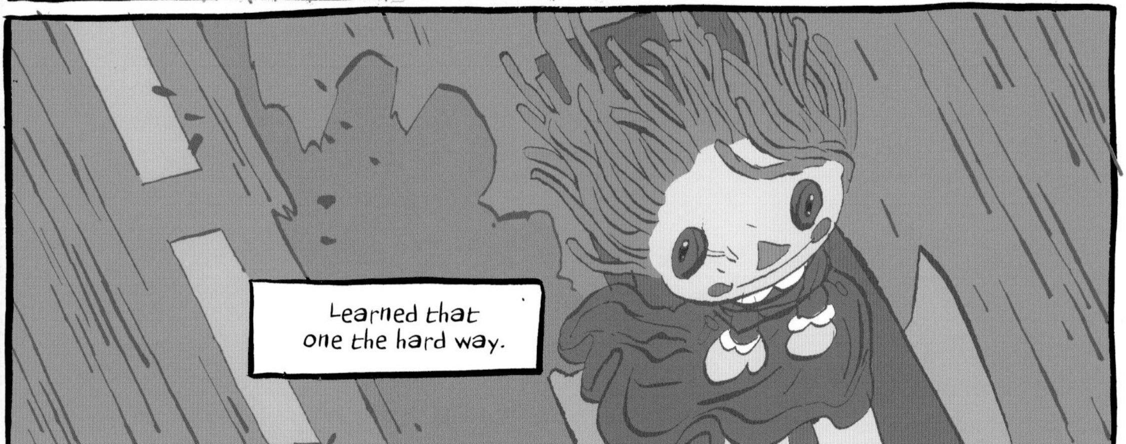
Learned that one the hard way.

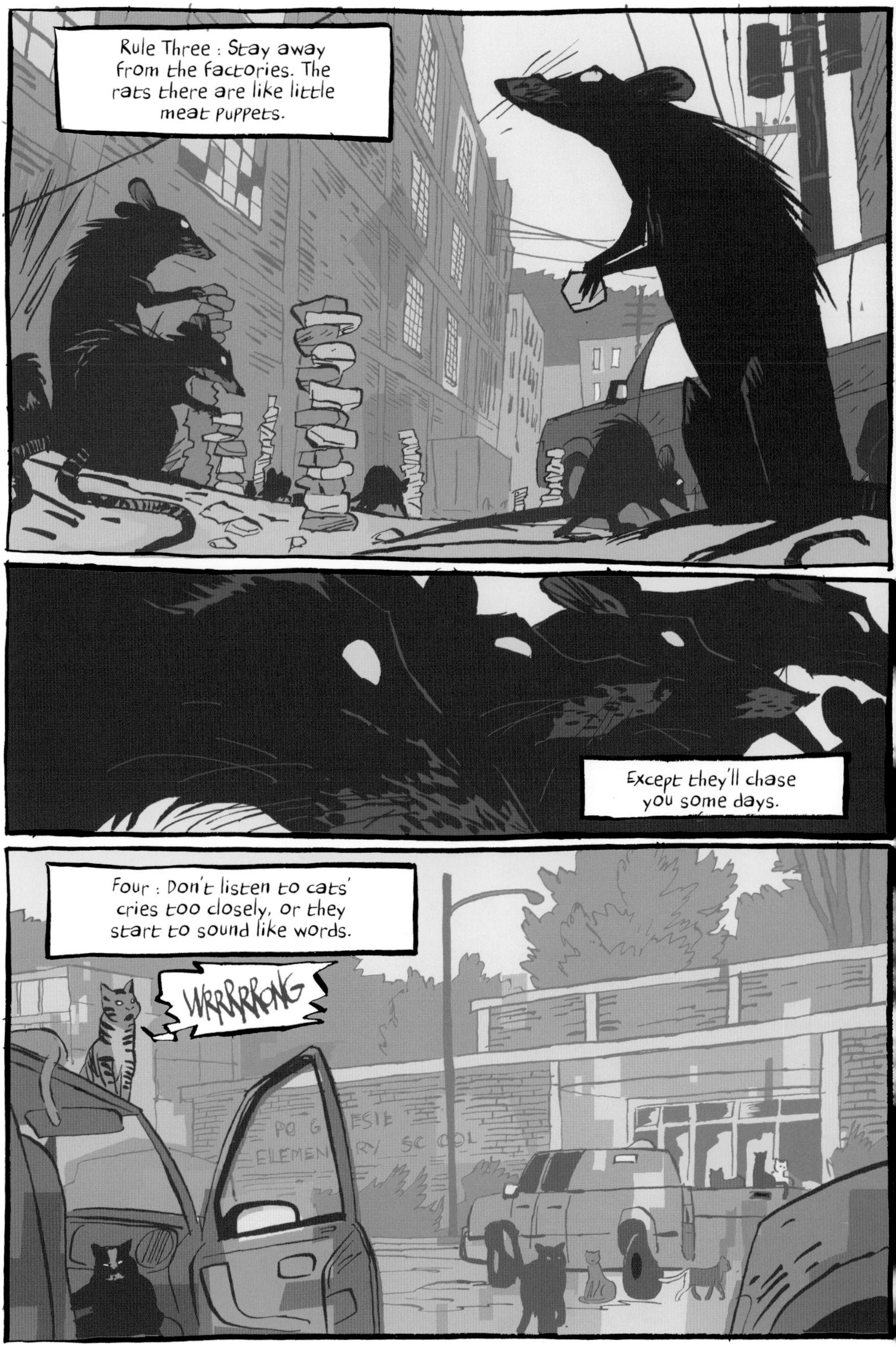
Rule Three : Stay away from the factories. The rats there are like little meat puppets.
Except they'll chase you some days.
Four : Don't listen to cats' cries too closely, or they start to sound like words.
WRRRRRONG

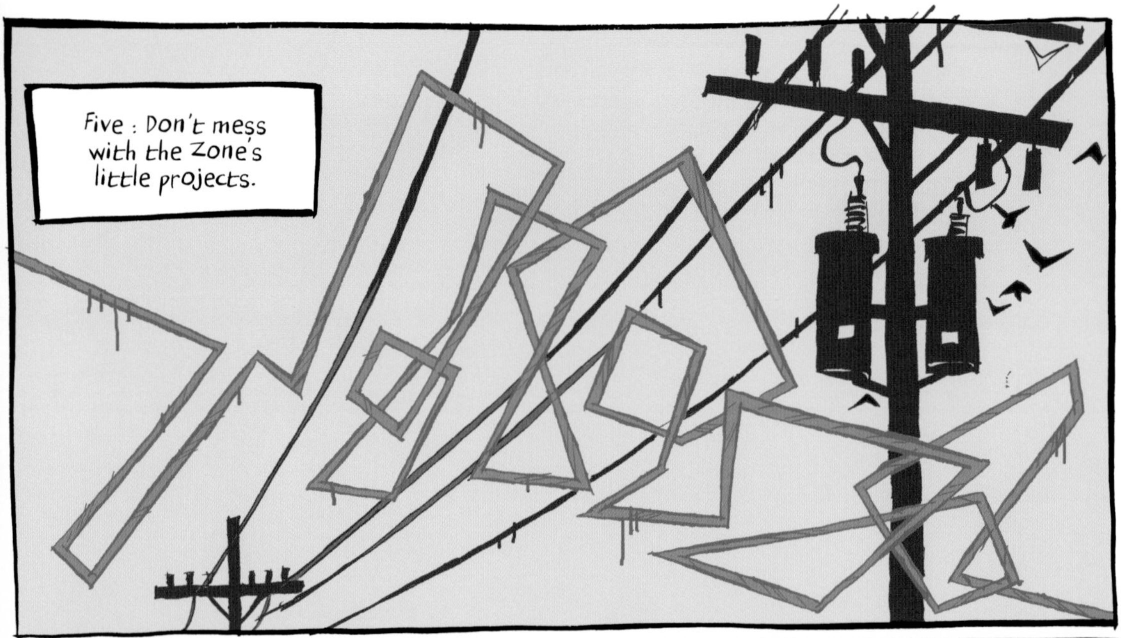
Five : Don't mess with the Zone's little projects.

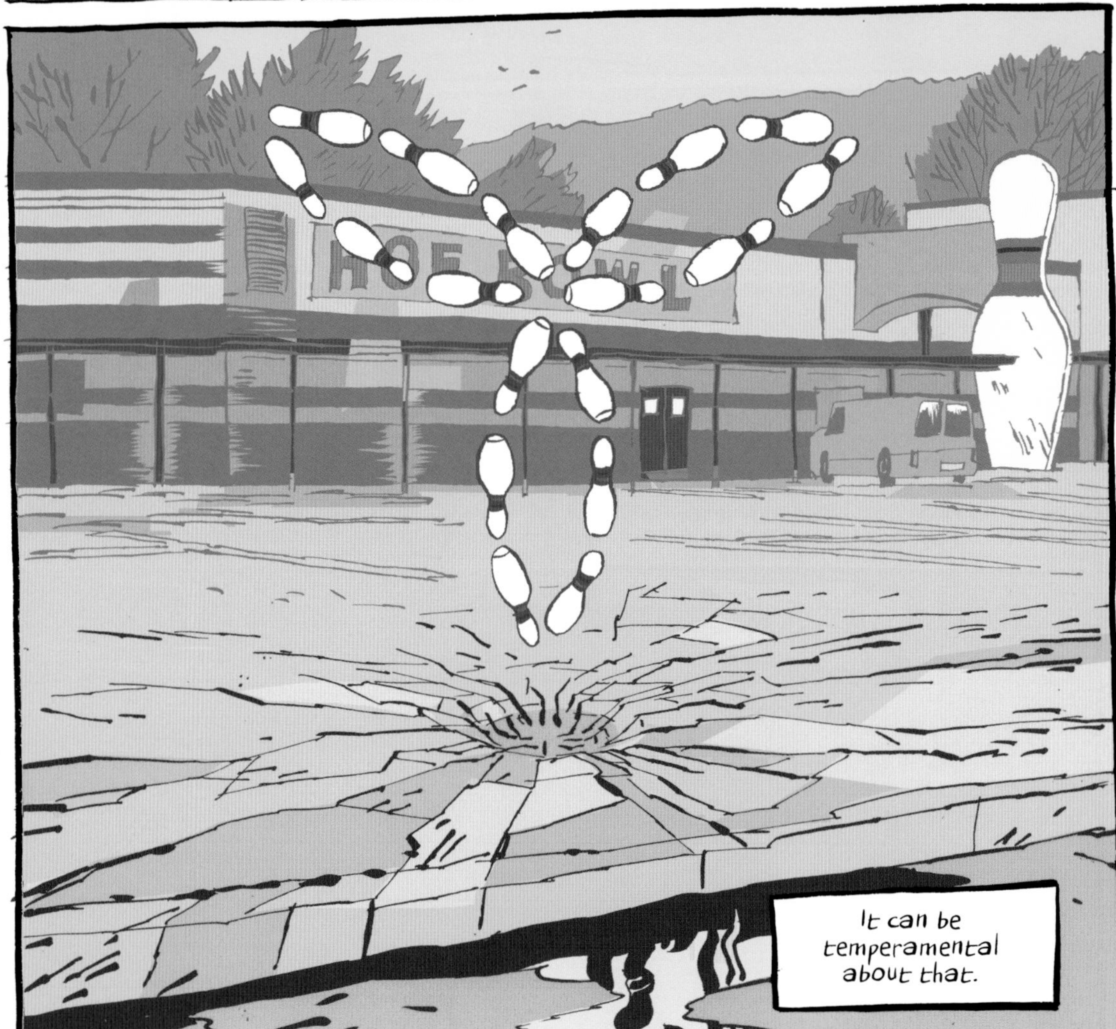
HOE BOWL
It can be temperamental about that.

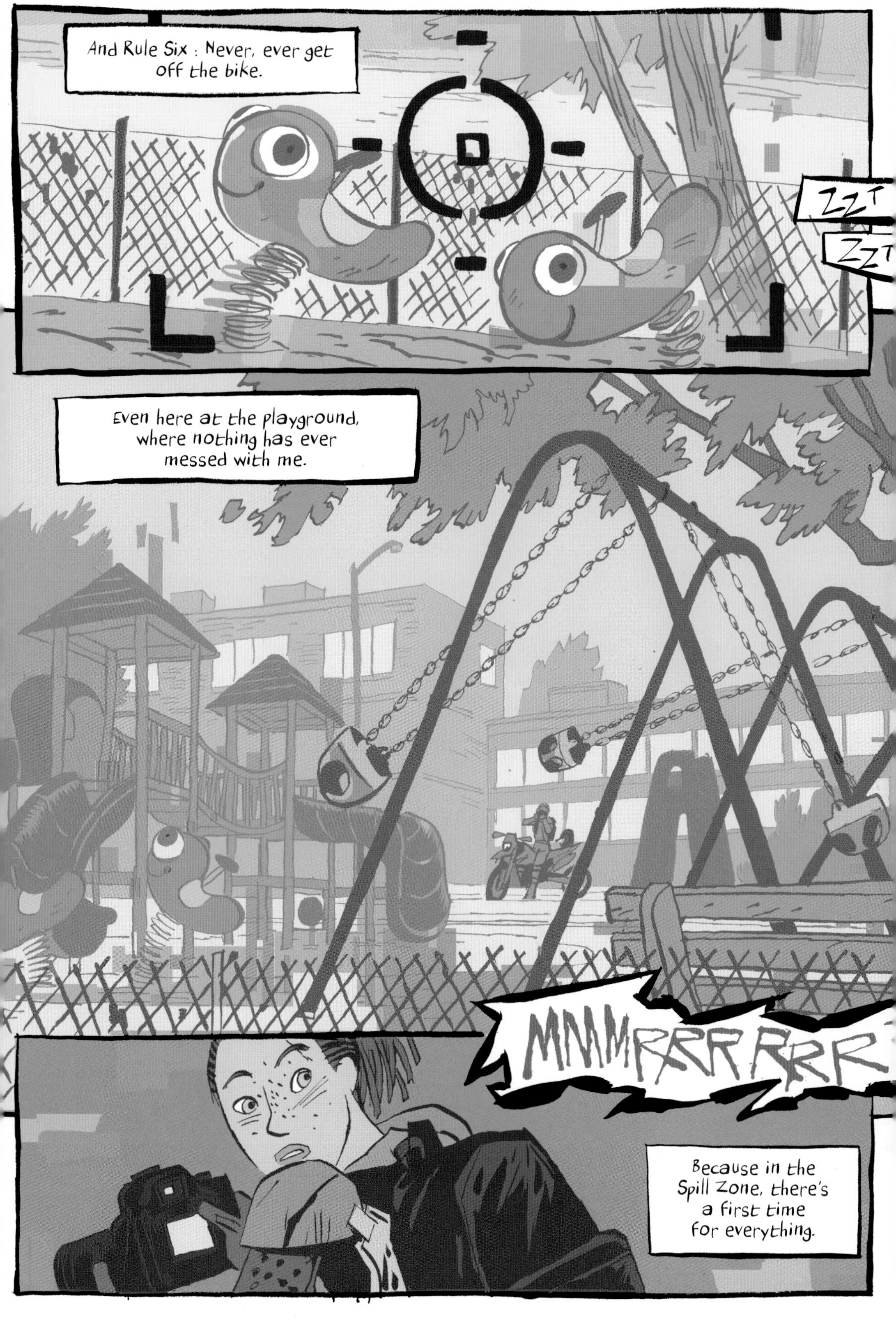

And Rule Six: Never, ever get off the bike.
ZZT
ZZT
Even here at the playground, where nothing has ever messed with me.
MMMRRRRRRR
Because in the Spill Zone, there's a first time for everything.

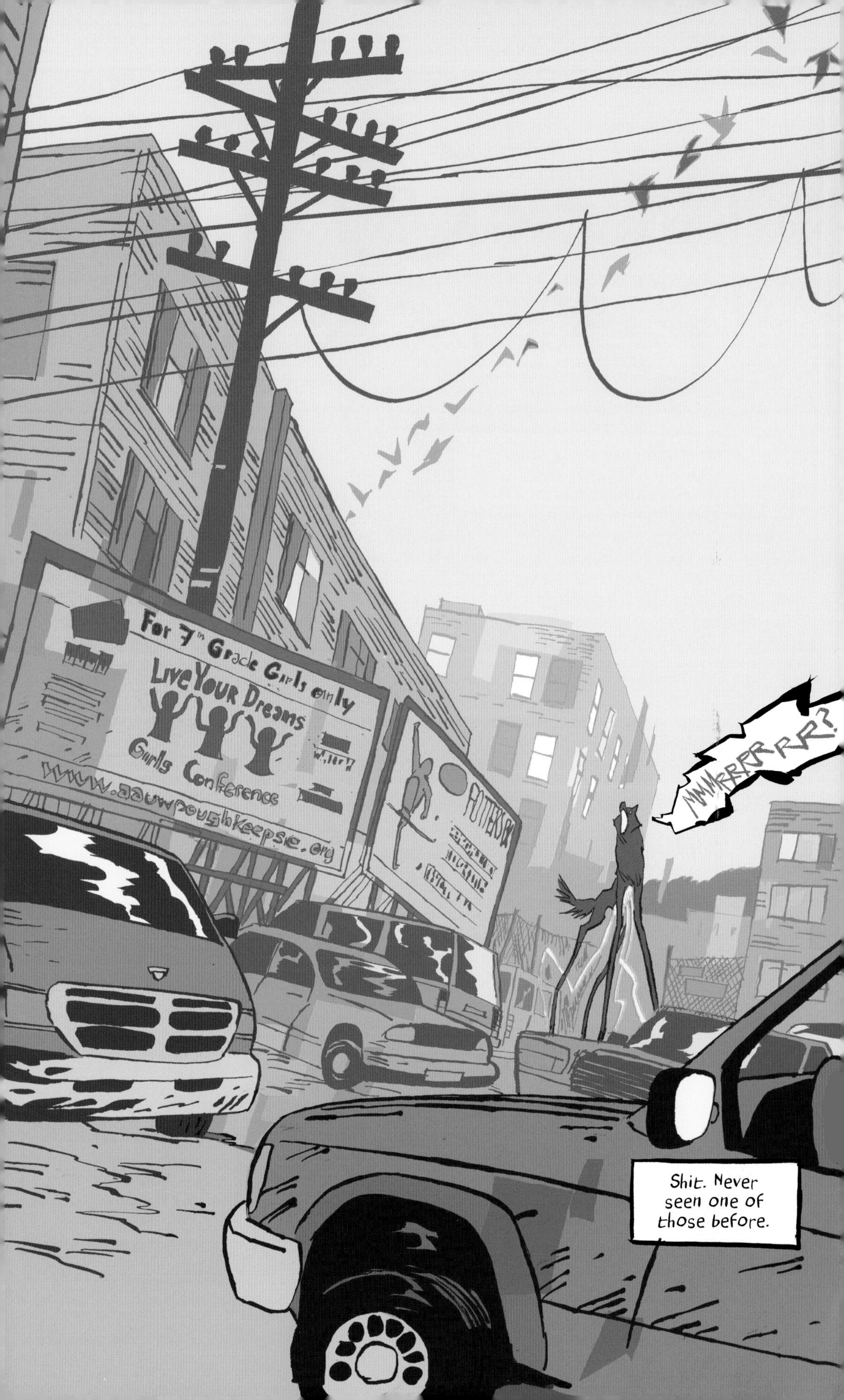
For 7th Grade Girls only
Live Your Dreams
Girls Conference
www.aauwpoughkeepsie.org
MMMRRRRRRR?
Shit. Never seen one of those before.

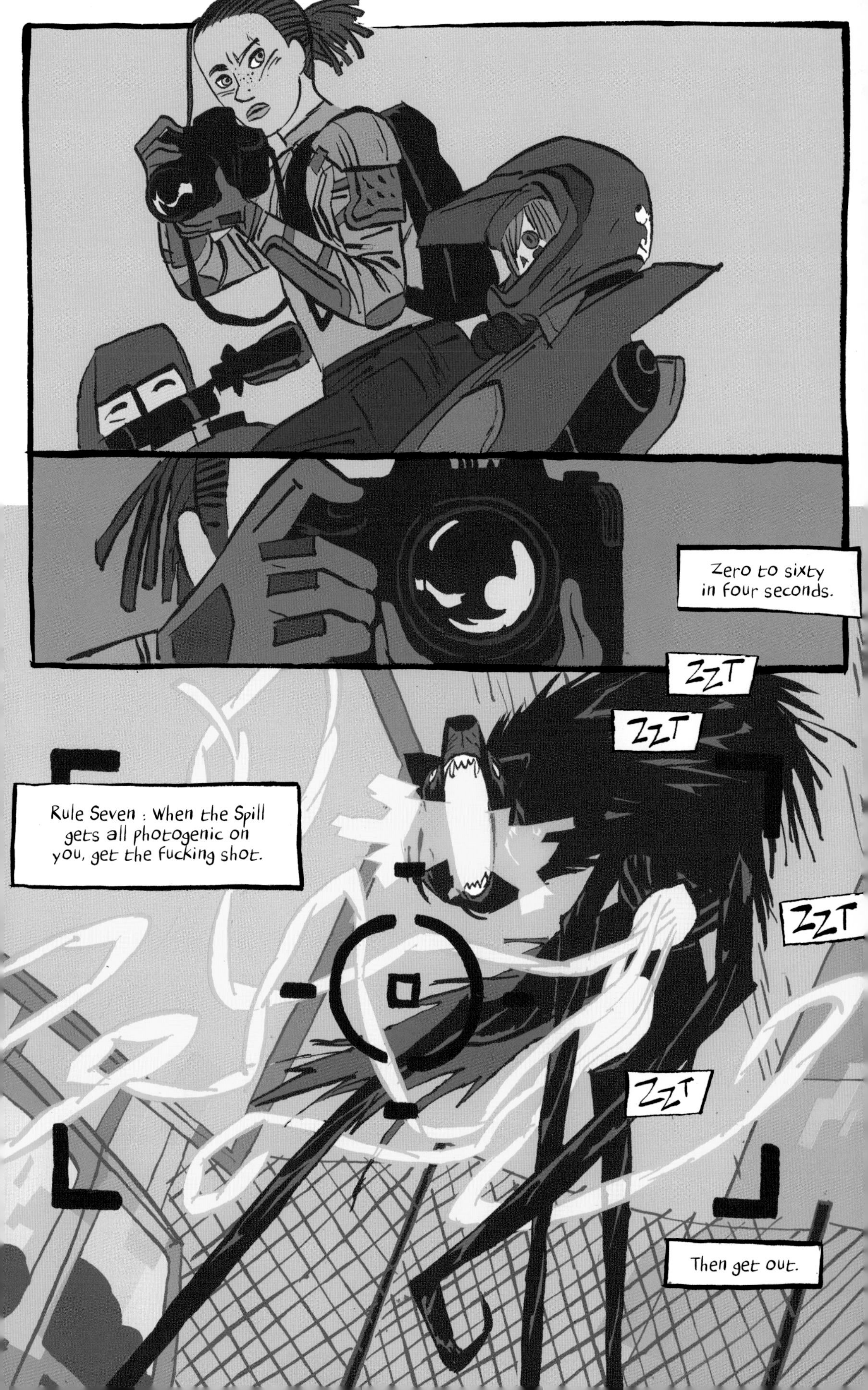
Zero to sixty in four seconds.
ZZT
ZZT
Rule Seven : When the Spill gets all photogenic on you, get the fucking shot.
ZZT
ZZT
Then get out.

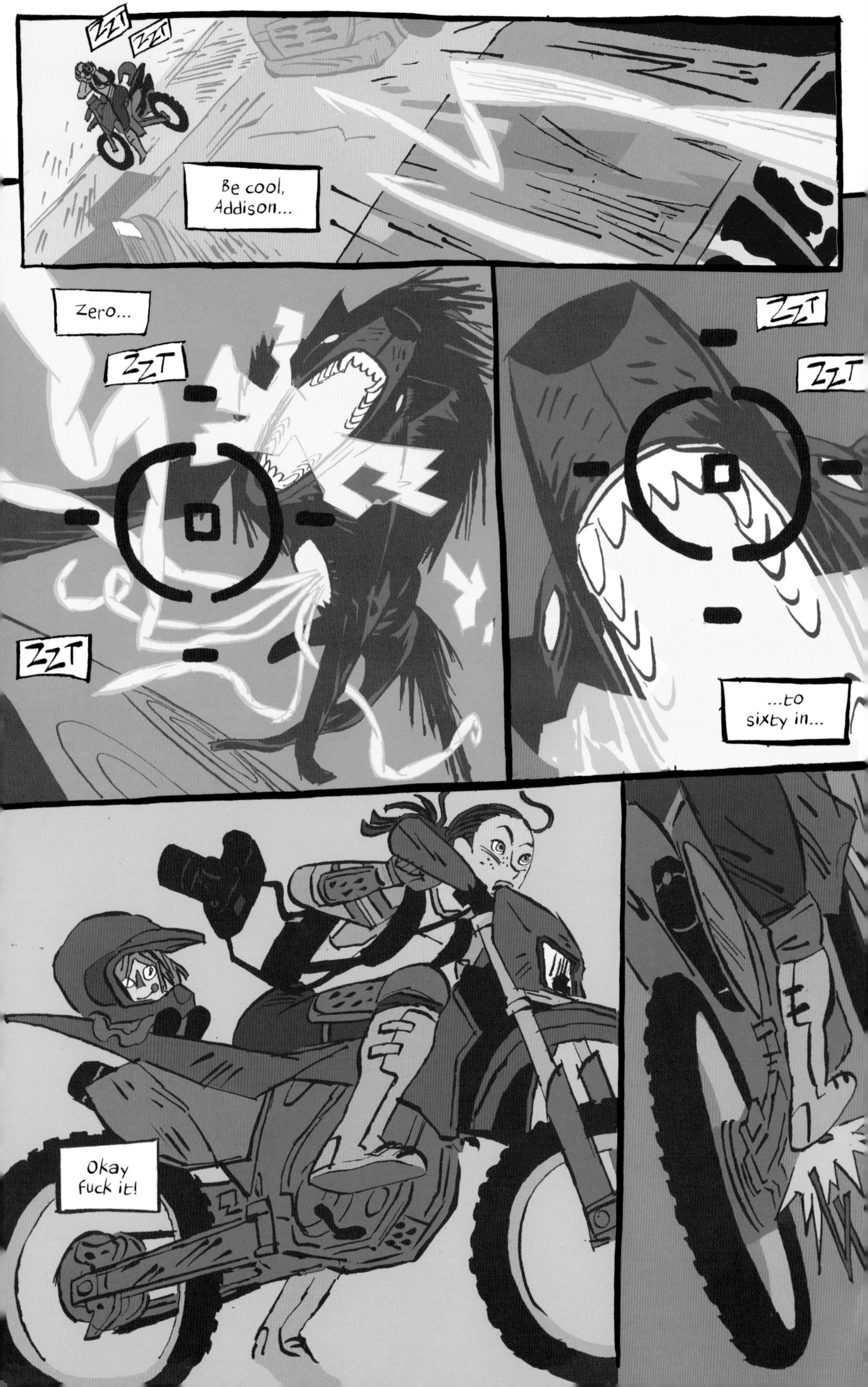
ZZT
ZZT
Be cool, Addison...
Zero...
ZZT
ZZT
ZZT
ZZT
...to sixty in...
Okay fuck it!

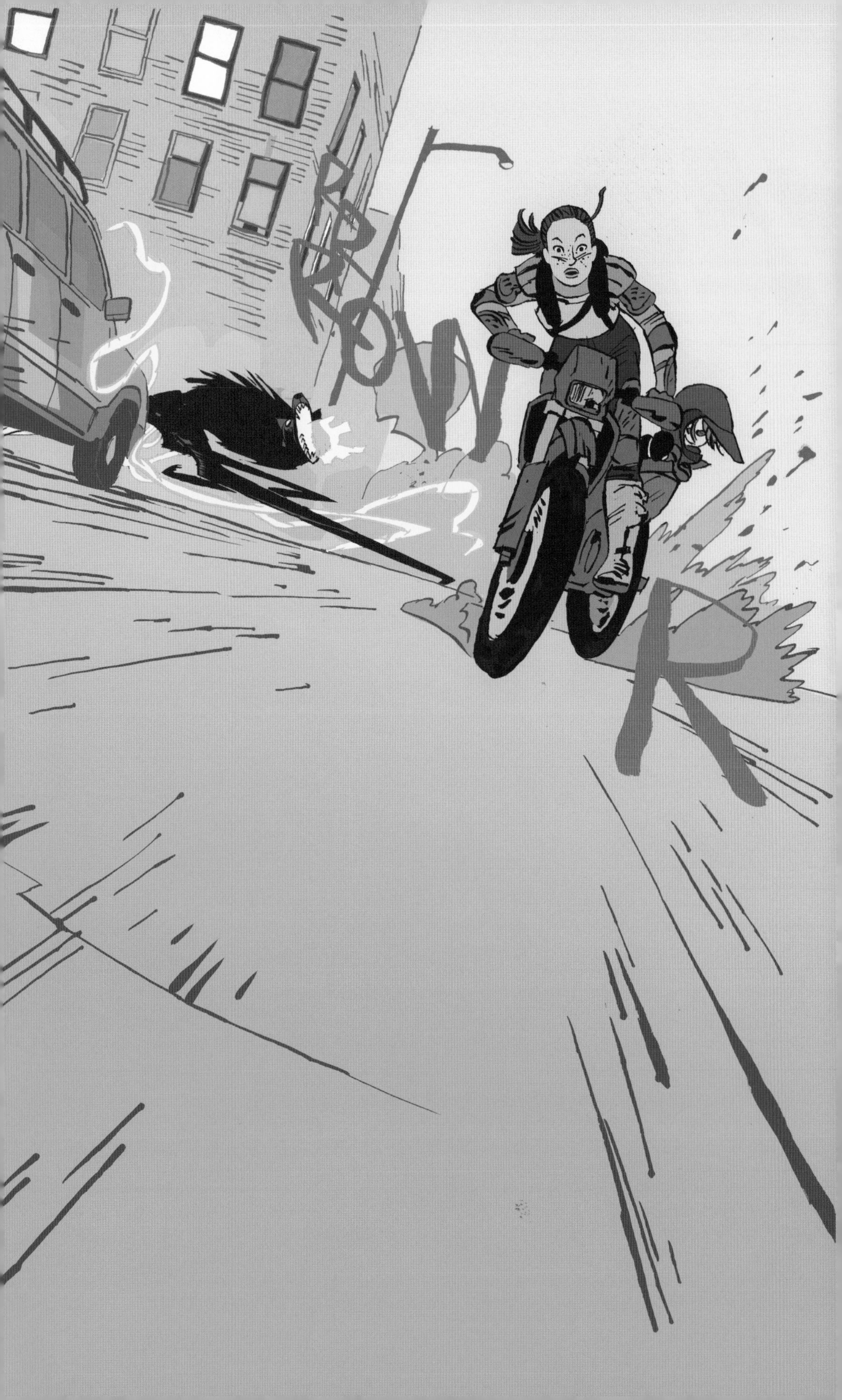

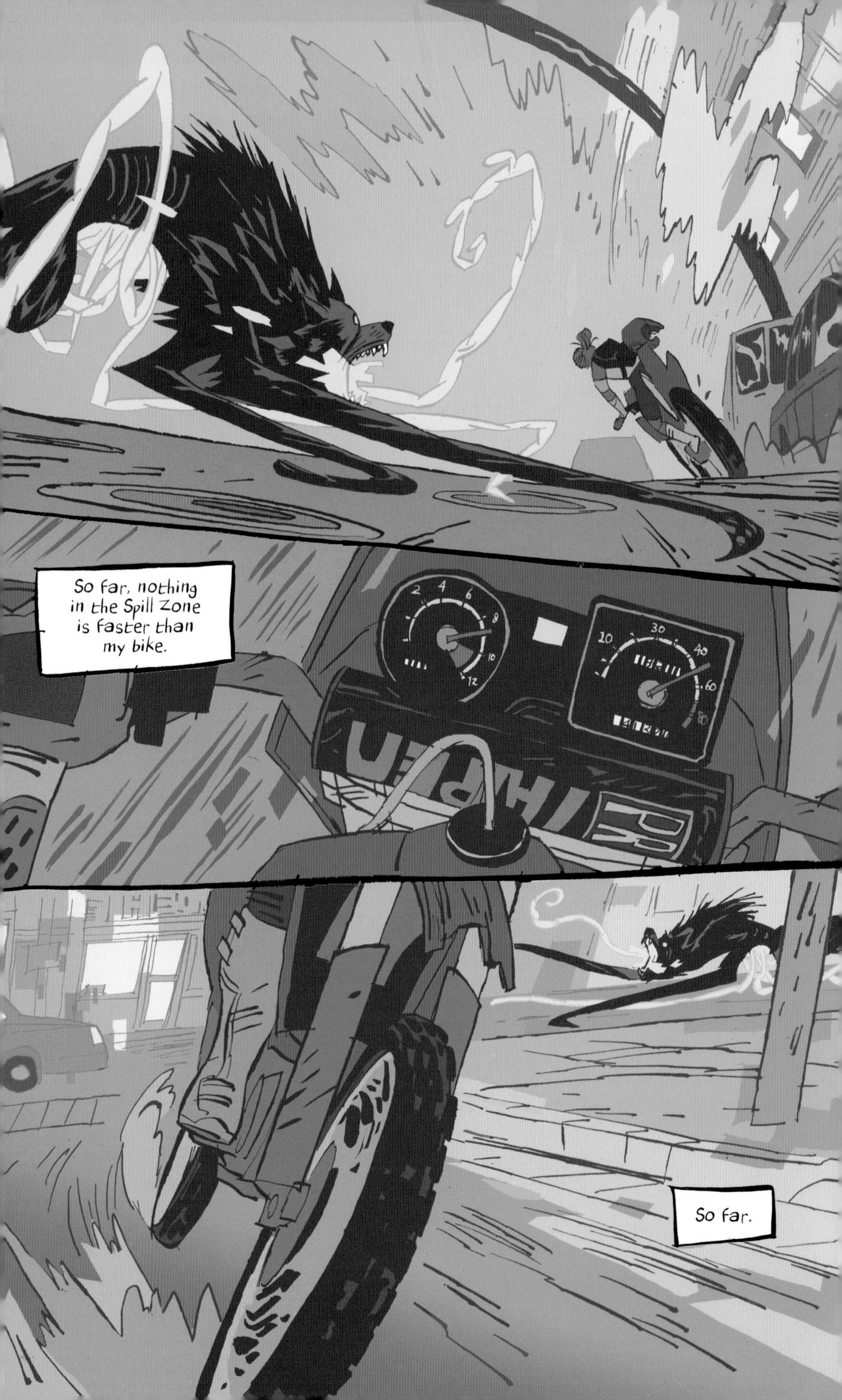
So far, nothing in the Spill Zone is faster than my bike.
So far.

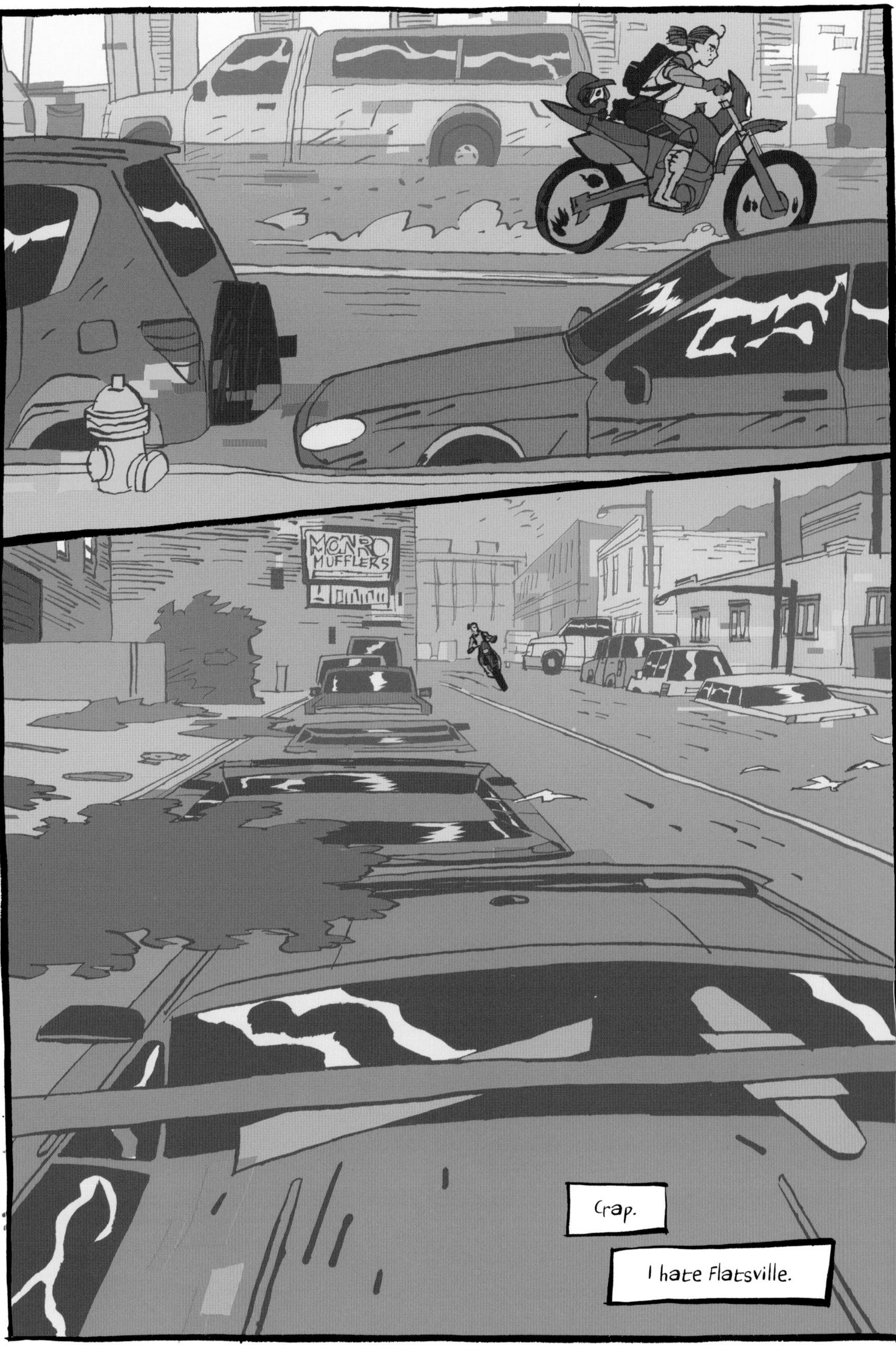
MONRO MUFFLERS
Crap.
I hate Flatsville.

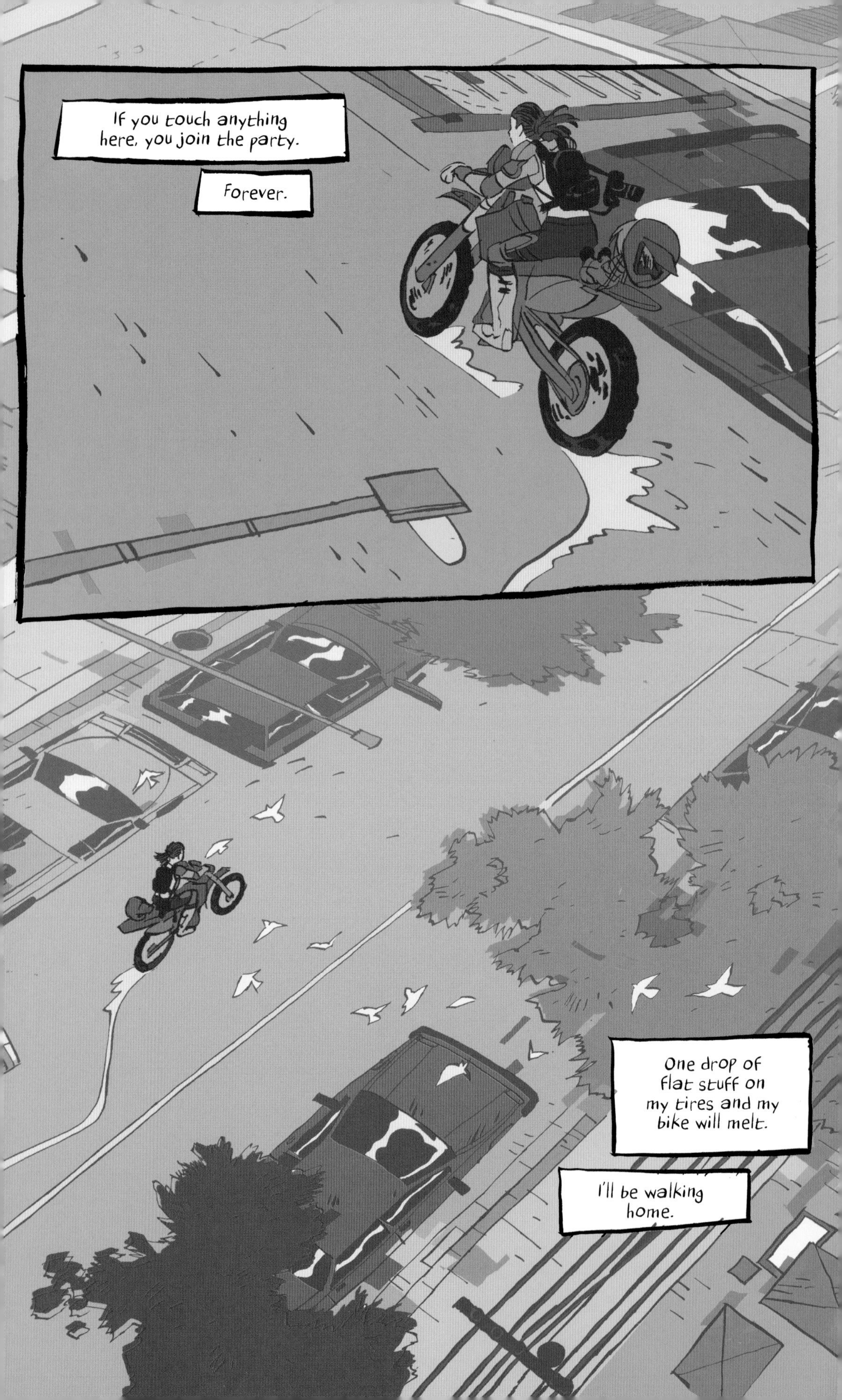
If you touch anything here, you join the party.
Forever.
One drop of flat stuff on my tires and my bike will melt.
I'll be walking home.

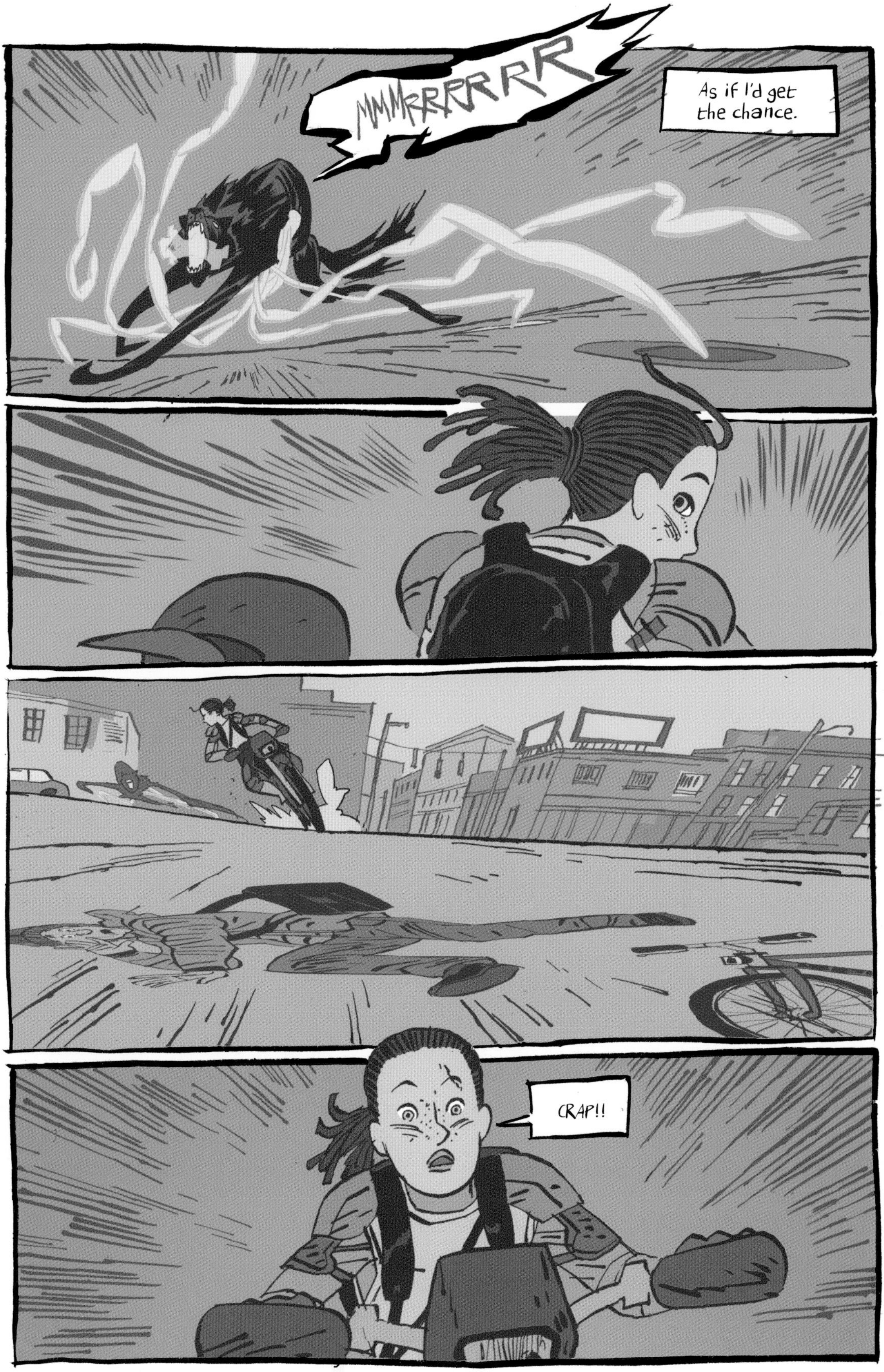
MMMRRRRRRRR
As if I'd get the chance.
CRAP!!

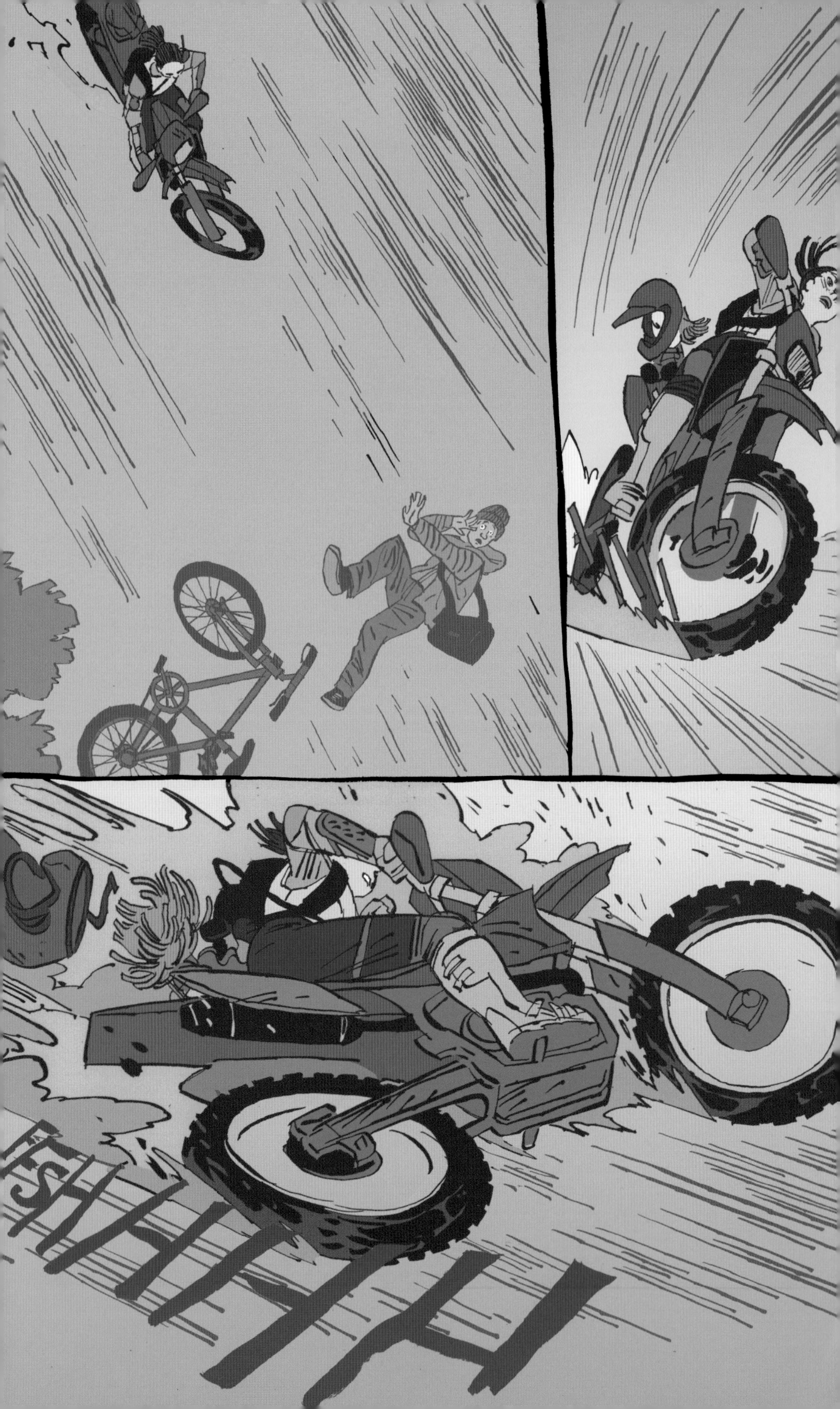
FSHHHH

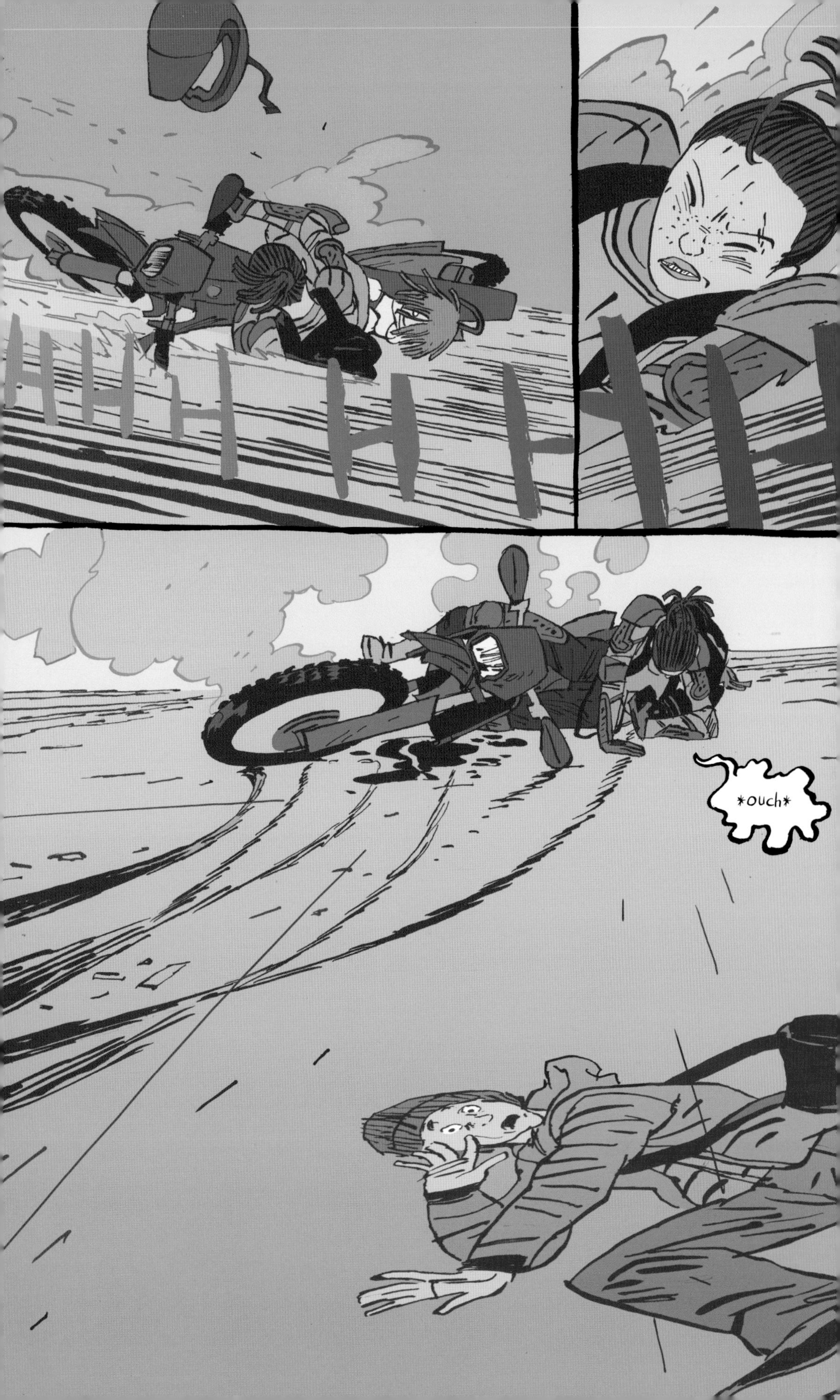
ouch

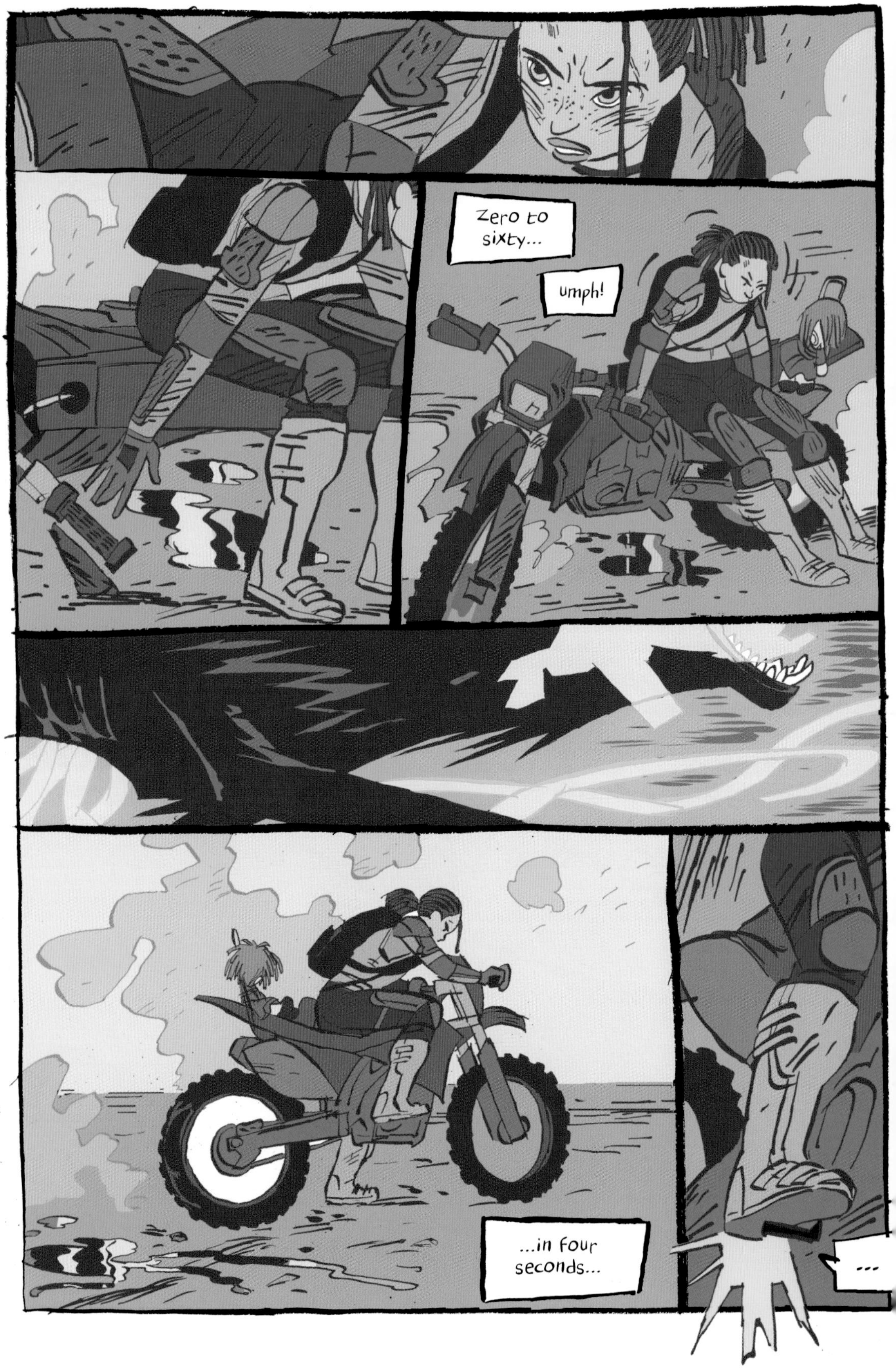
Zero to sixty...
umph!
...in four seconds...
...

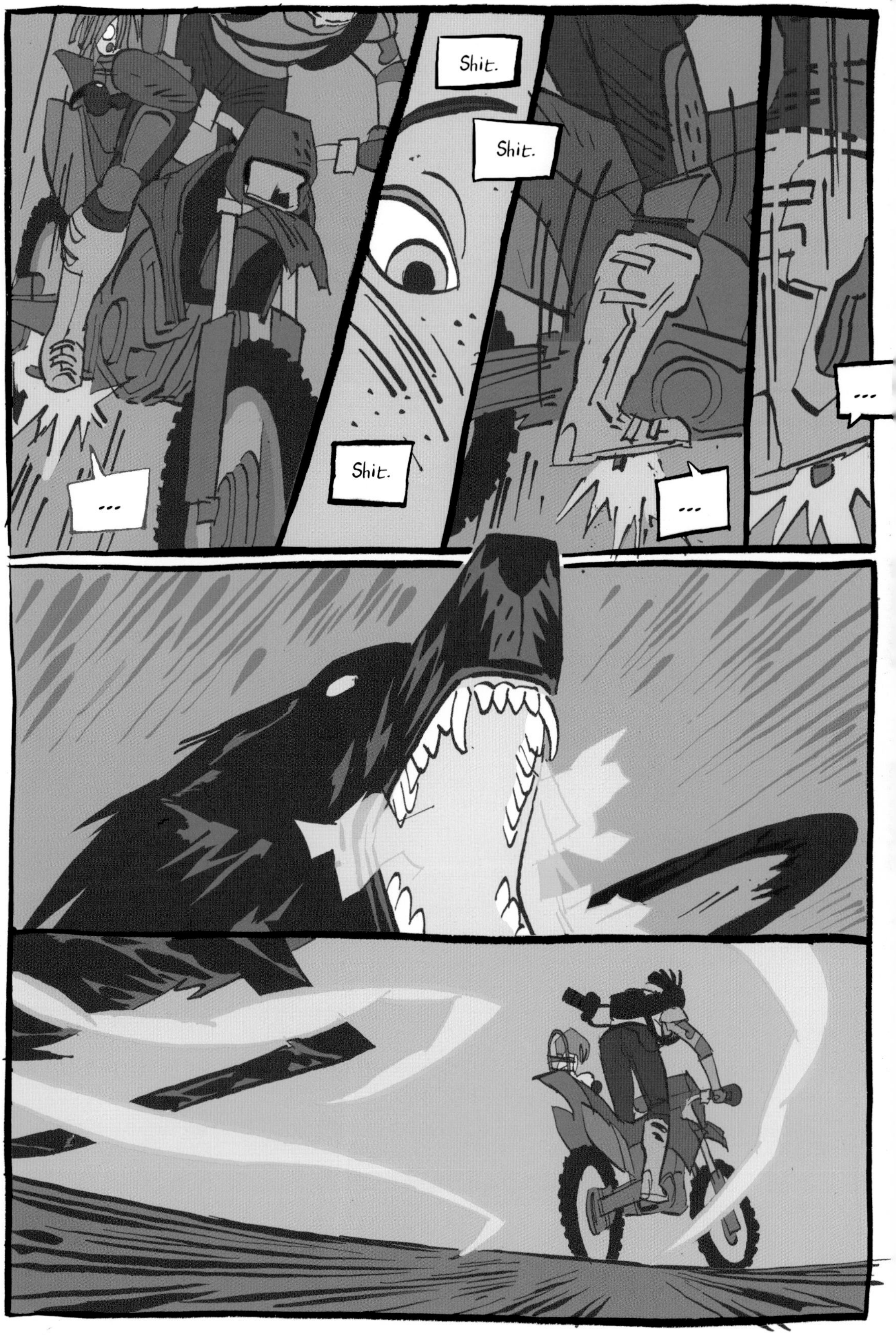

...
Shit.
Shit.
Shit.
...
...

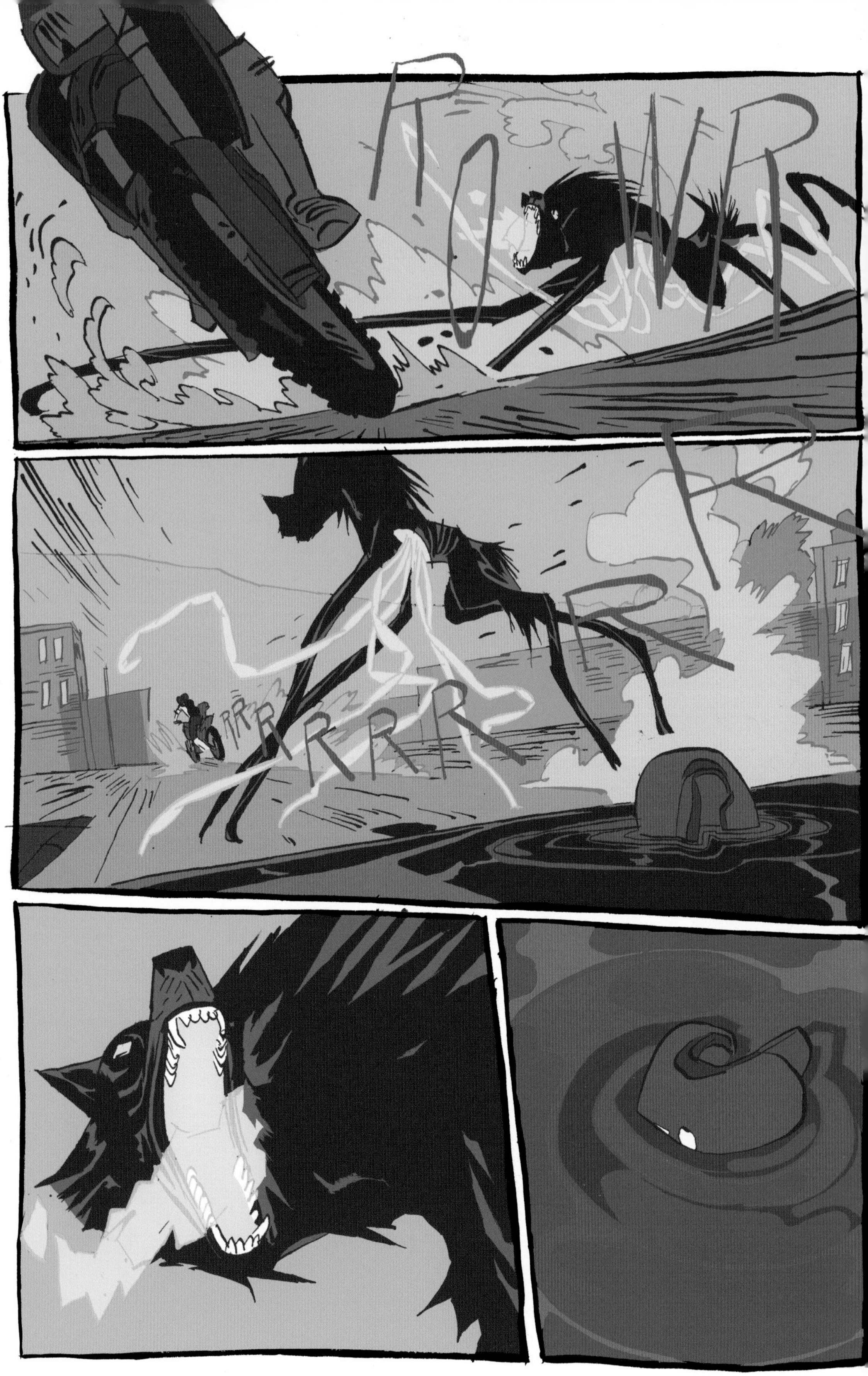
ROWR
RRRRRR

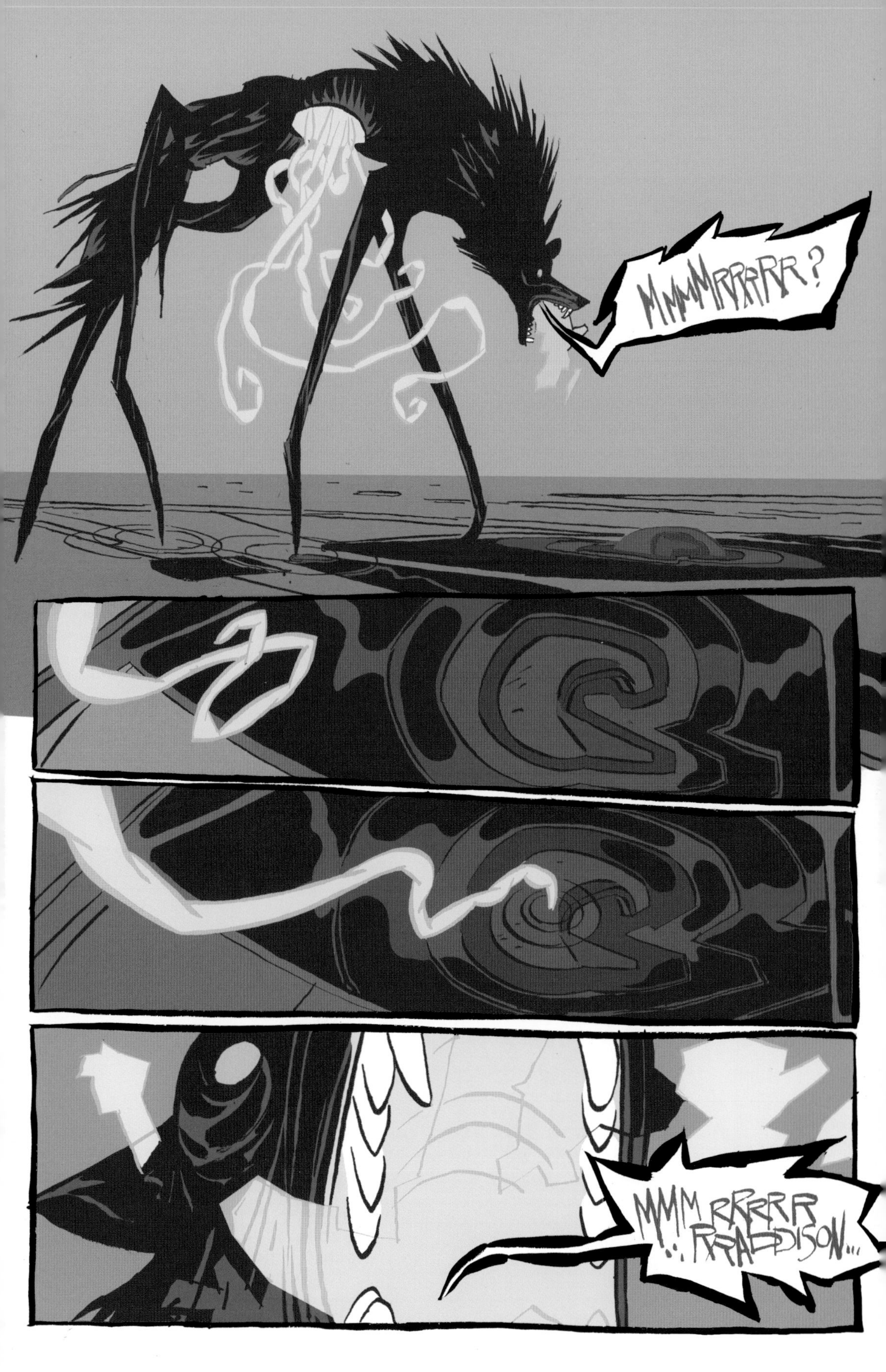
MMMMRRRRRR?
MMM RRRRR RRRADDISON...

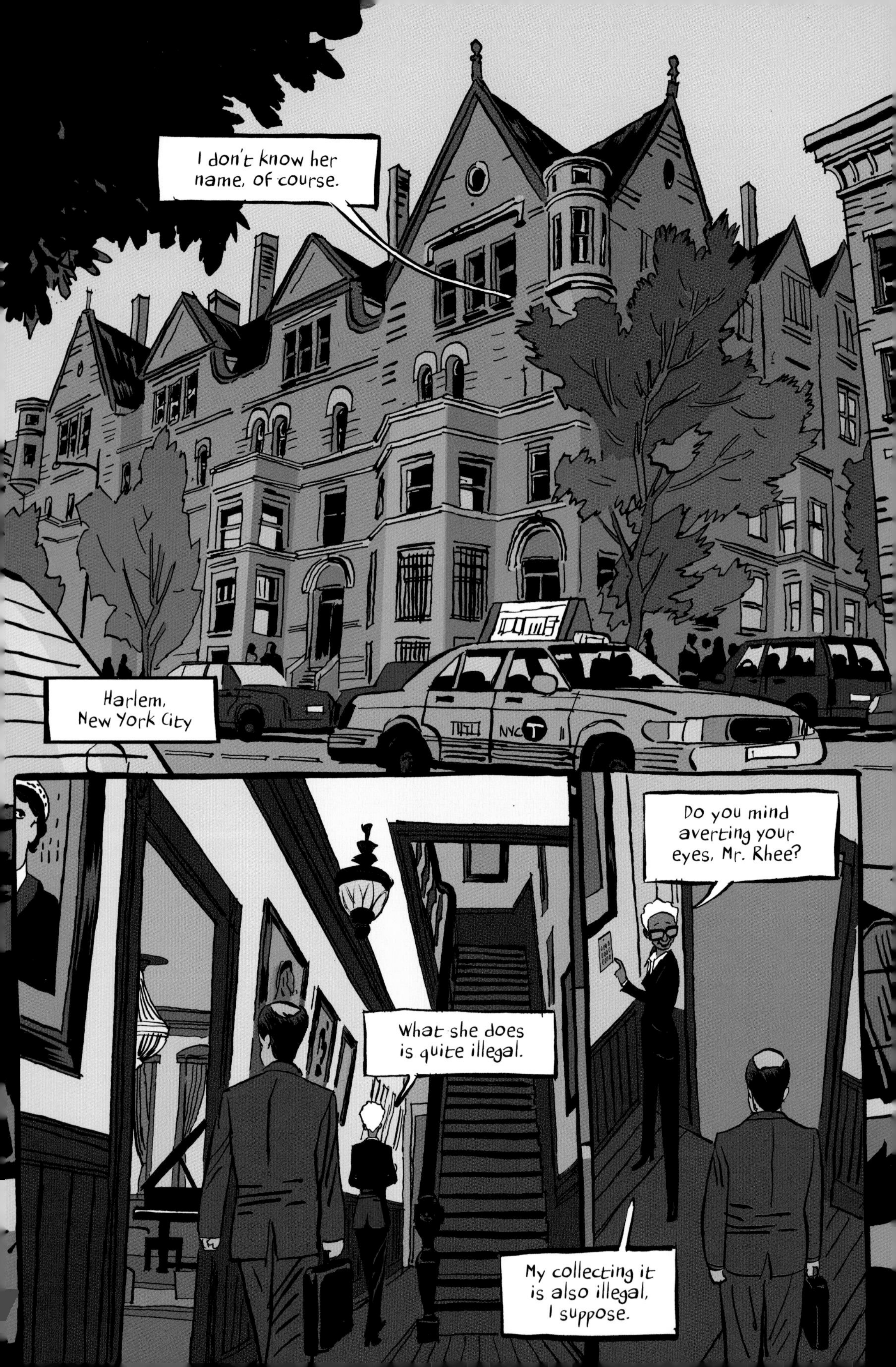
I don't know her name, of course.
Harlem, New York City
Do you mind averting your eyes, Mr. Rhee?
What she does is quite illegal.
My collecting it is also illegal, I suppose.

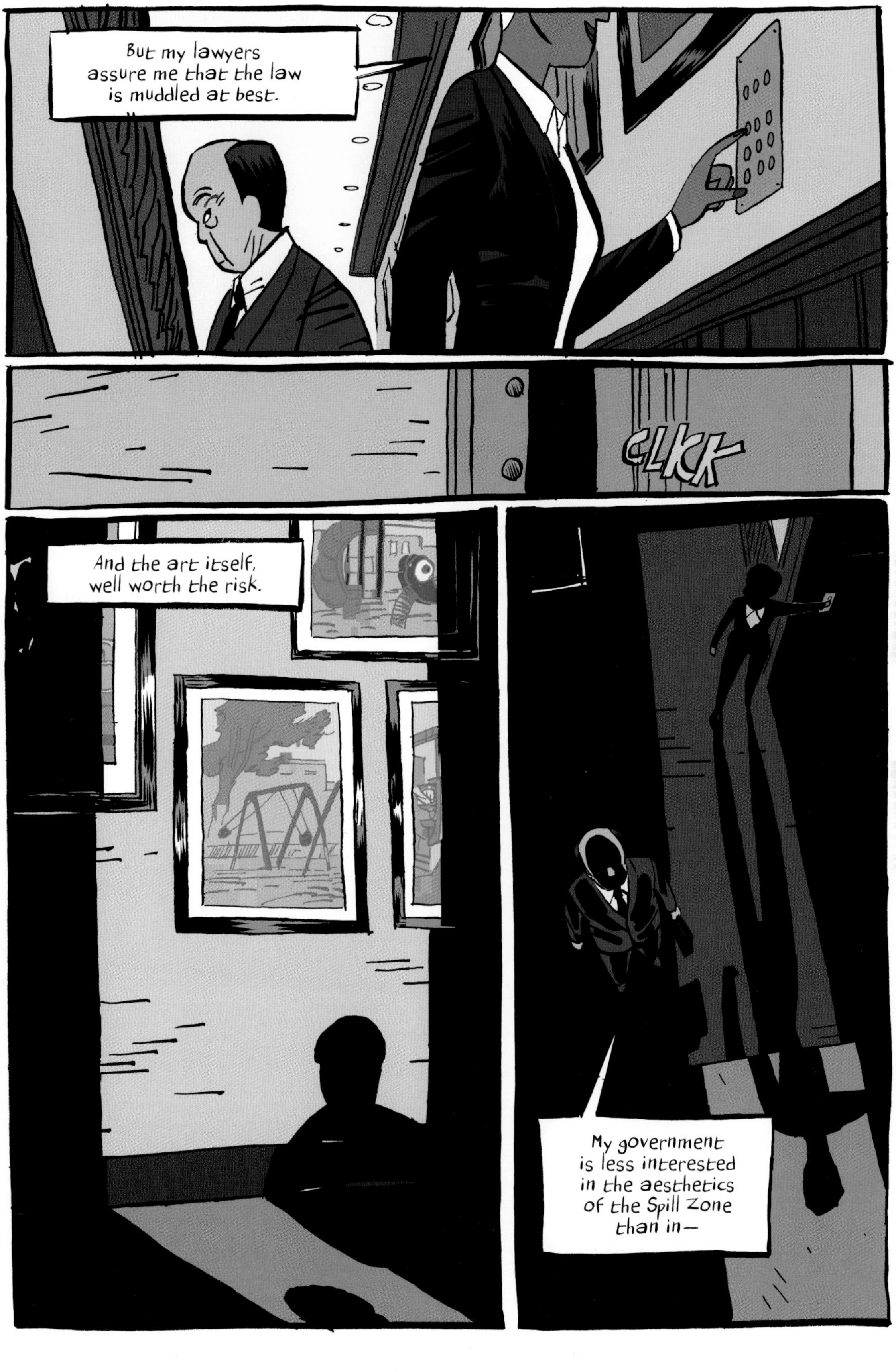
But my lawyers assure me that the law is muddled at best.
CLICK
And the art itself, well worth the risk.
My government is less interested in the aesthetics of the Spill Zone than in—

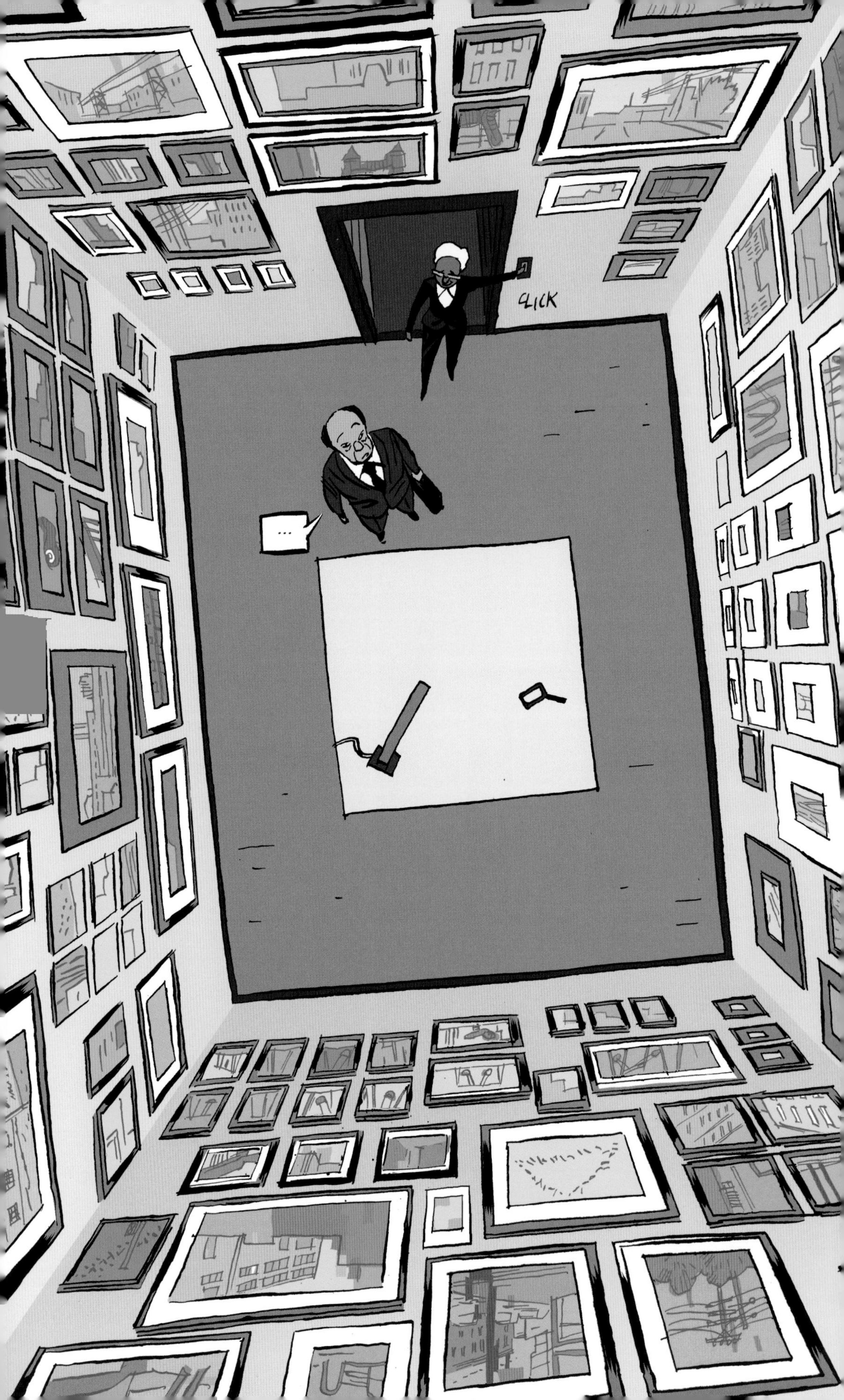
CLICK
...

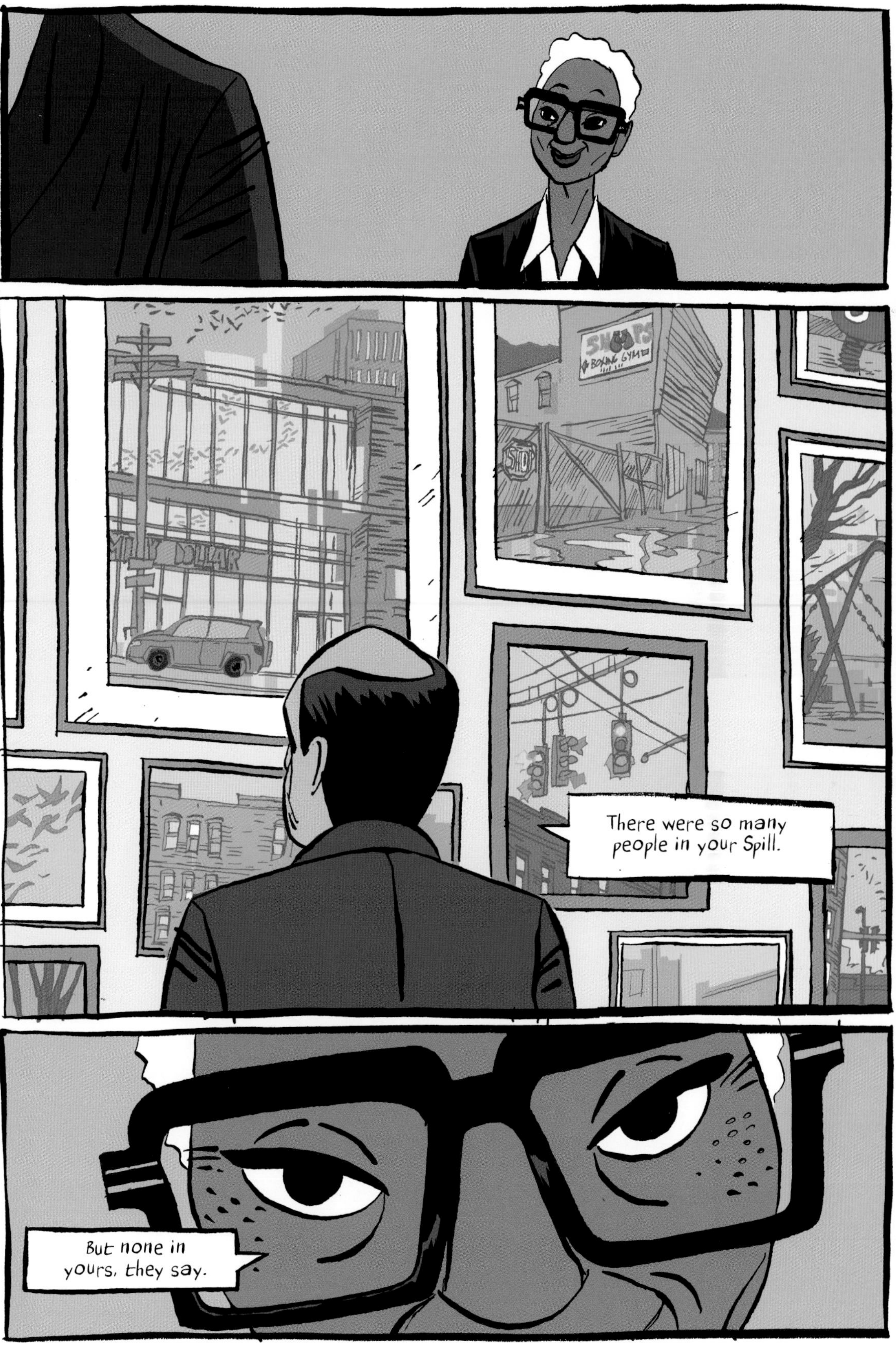
There were so many people in your Spill.
But none in yours, they say.

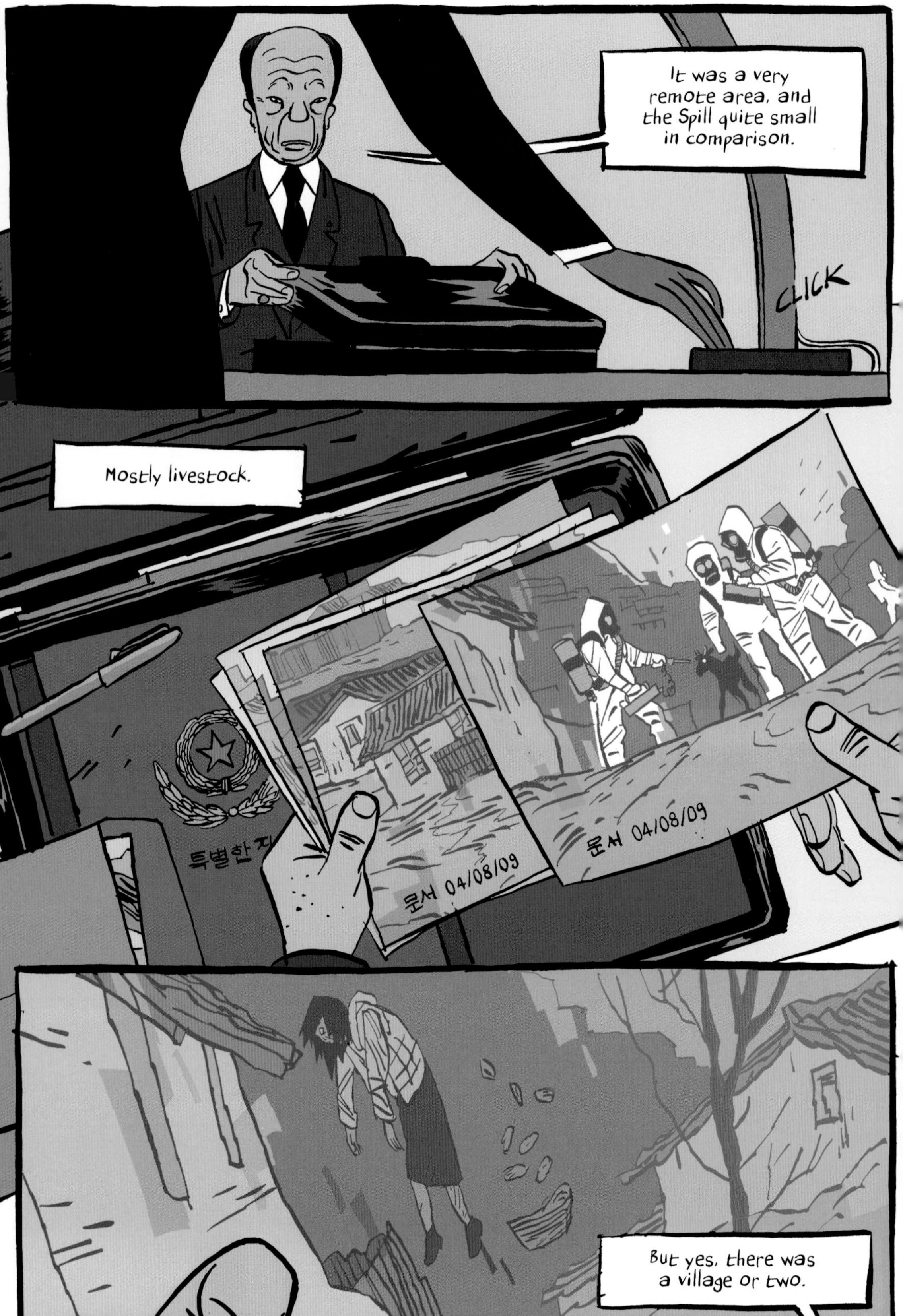
It was a very remote area, and the Spill quite small in comparison.
CLICK
Mostly livestock.
특별한 지
문서 04/08/09
문서 04/08/09
But yes, there was a village or two.

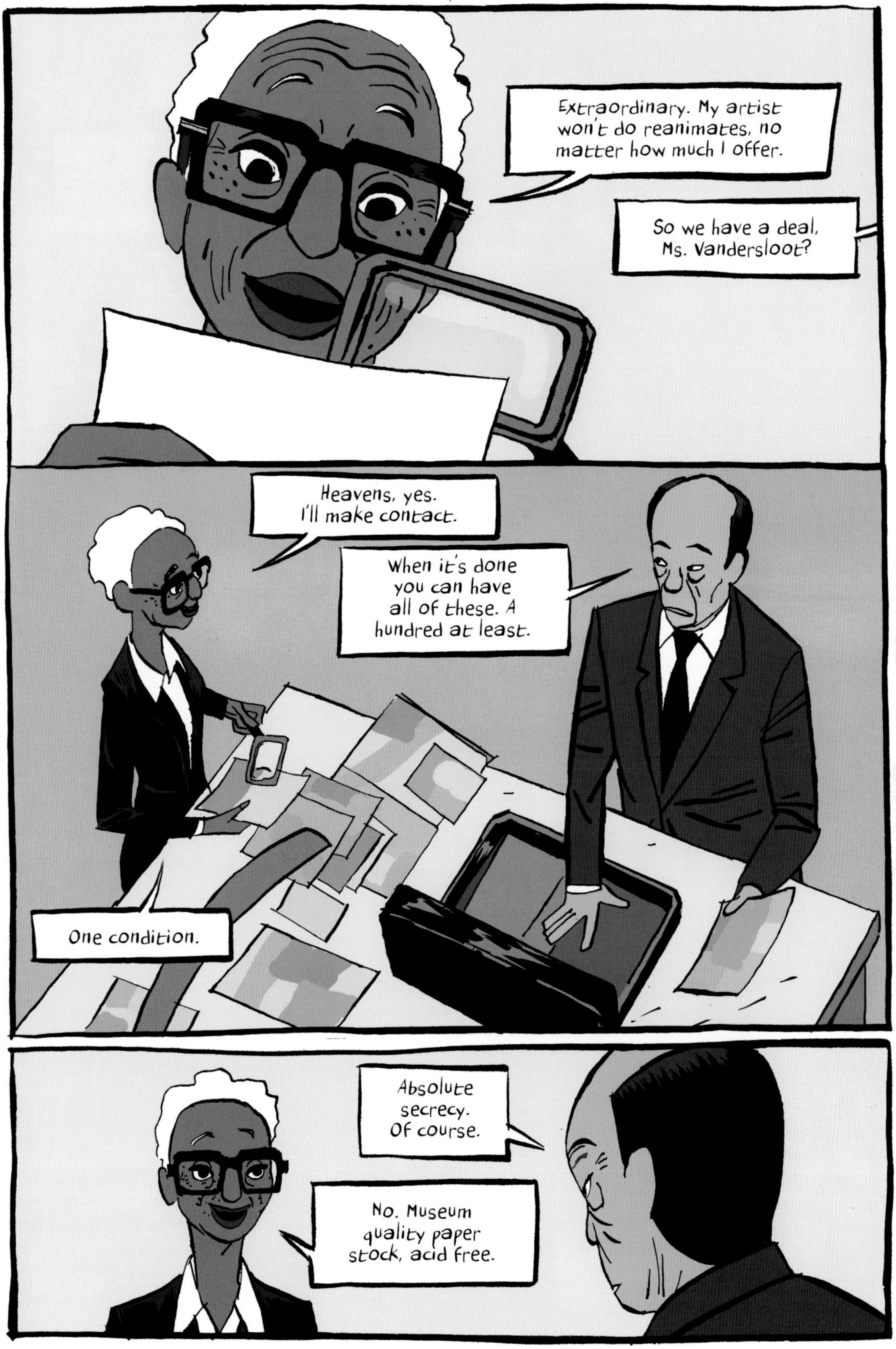
Extraordinary. My artist won't do reanimates, no matter how much I offer.
So we have a deal, Ms. Vandersloot?
Heavens, yes. I'll make contact.
When it's done you can have all of these. A hundred at least.
One condition.
Absolute secrecy. Of course.
No. Museum quality paper stock, acid free.

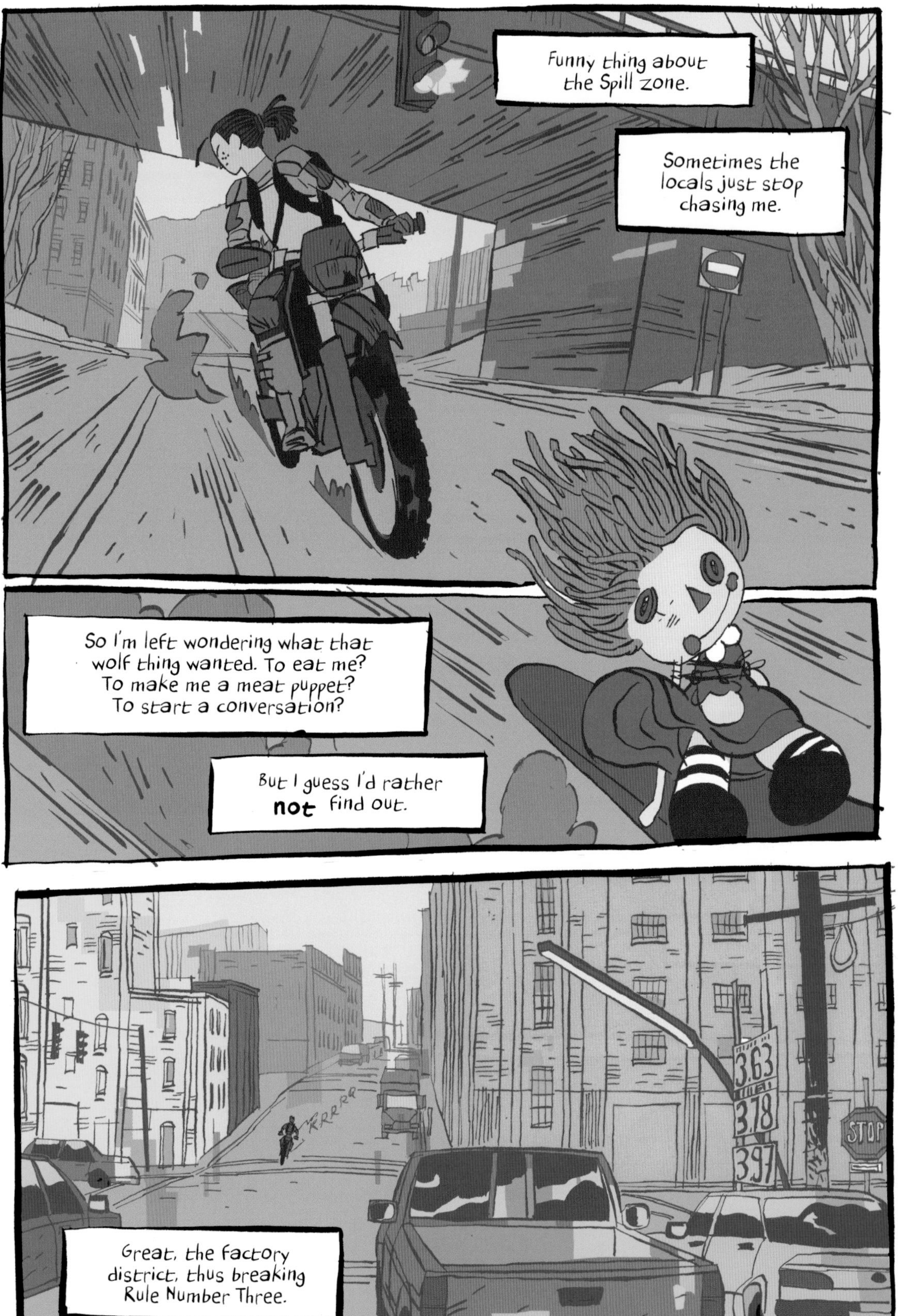

Funny thing about the Spill zone.
Sometimes the locals just stop chasing me.
So I'm left wondering what that wolf thing wanted. To eat me? To make me a meat puppet? To start a conversation?
But I guess I'd rather **not** find out.
RRRRR
3.63
3.78
3.97
STOP
Great, the factory district, thus breaking Rule Number Three.

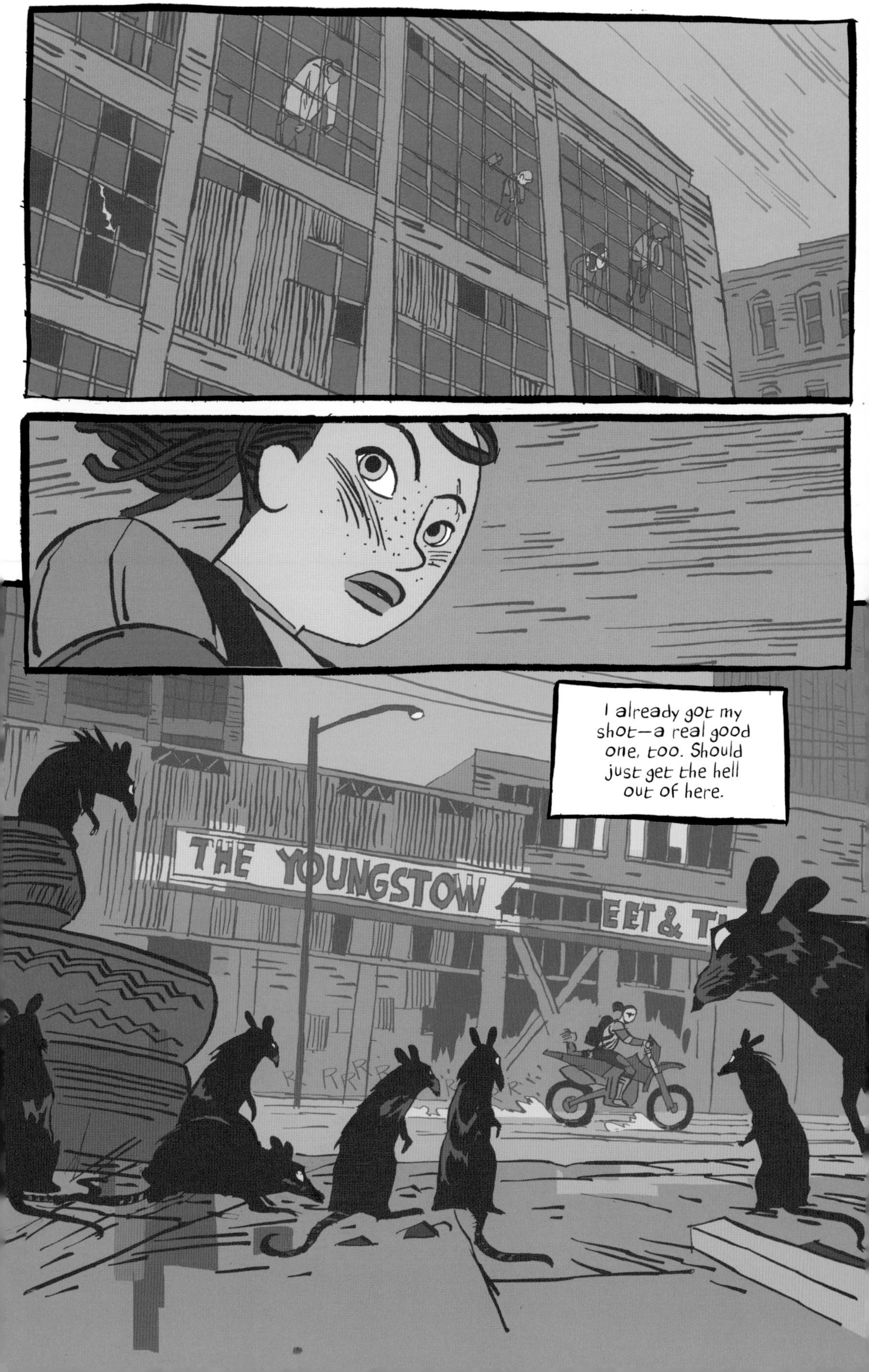
I already got my shot—a real good one, too. Should just get the hell out of here.
THE YOUNGSTOW
EET & T

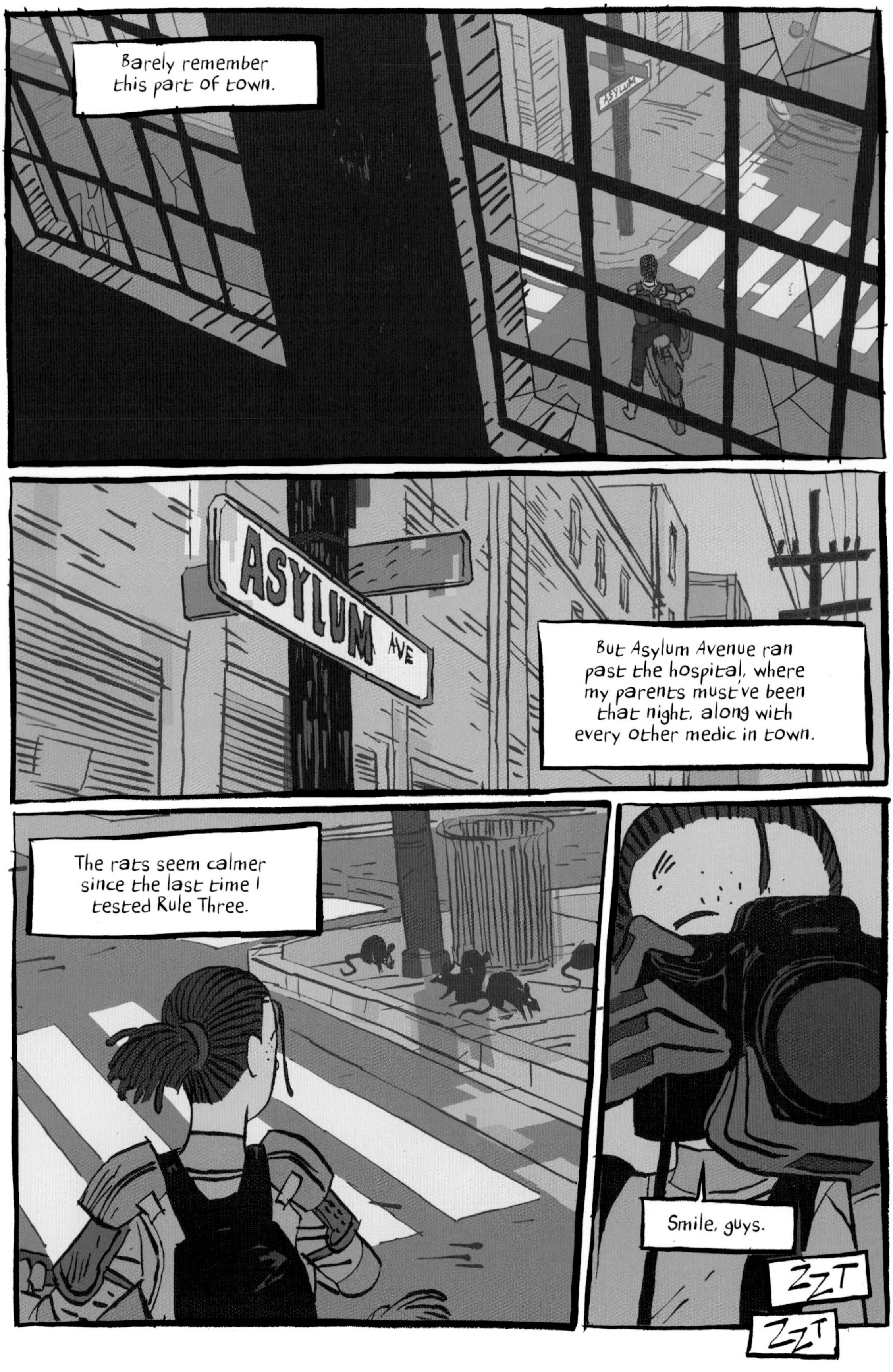
Barely remember this part of town.
ASYLUM
ASYLUM AVE
But Asylum Avenue ran past the hospital, where my parents must've been that night, along with every other medic in town.
The rats seem calmer since the last time I tested Rule Three.
Smile, guys.
ZZT
ZZT

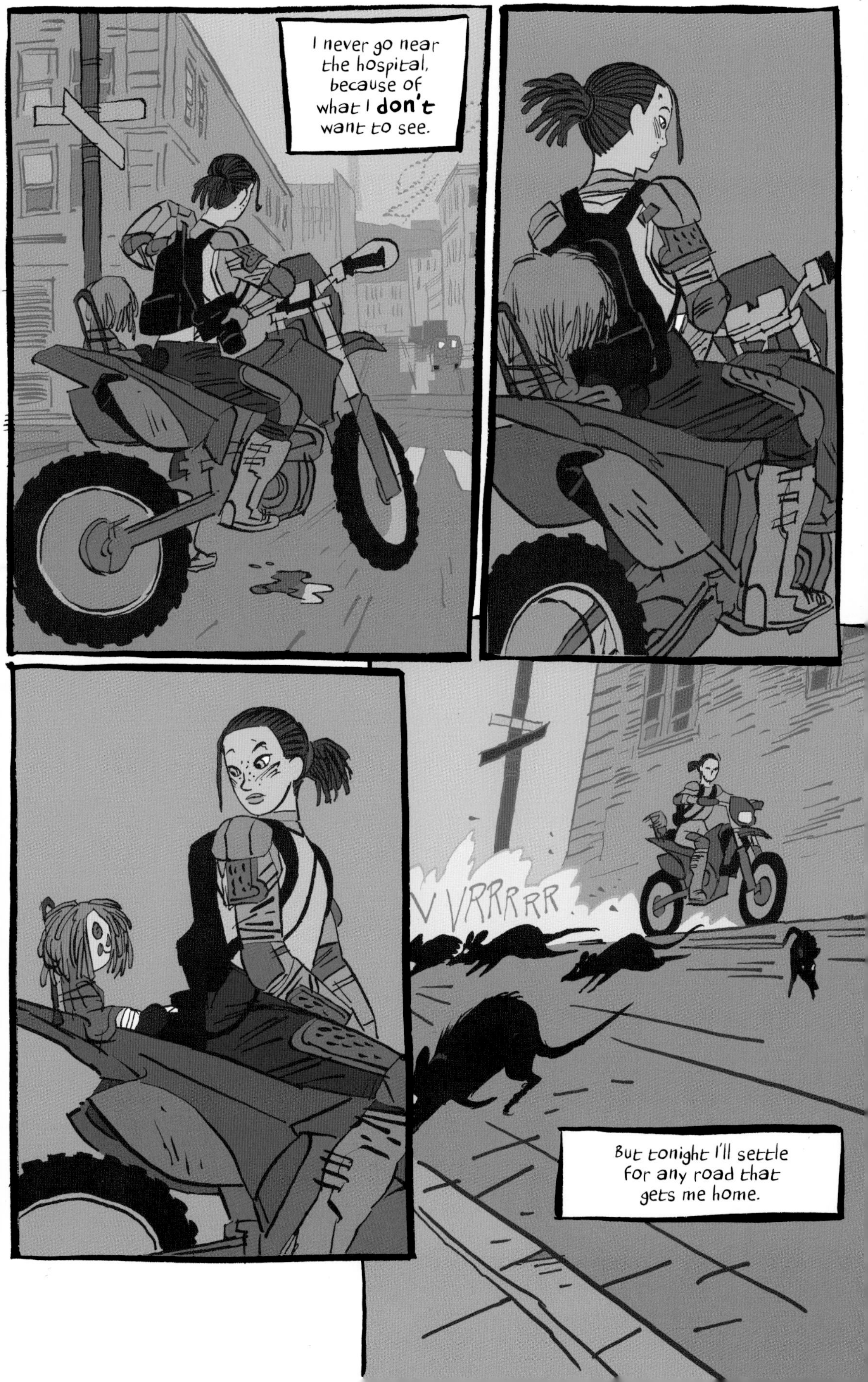
I never go near the hospital, because of what I **don't** want to see.
VRRRRR
But tonight I'll settle for any road that gets me home.

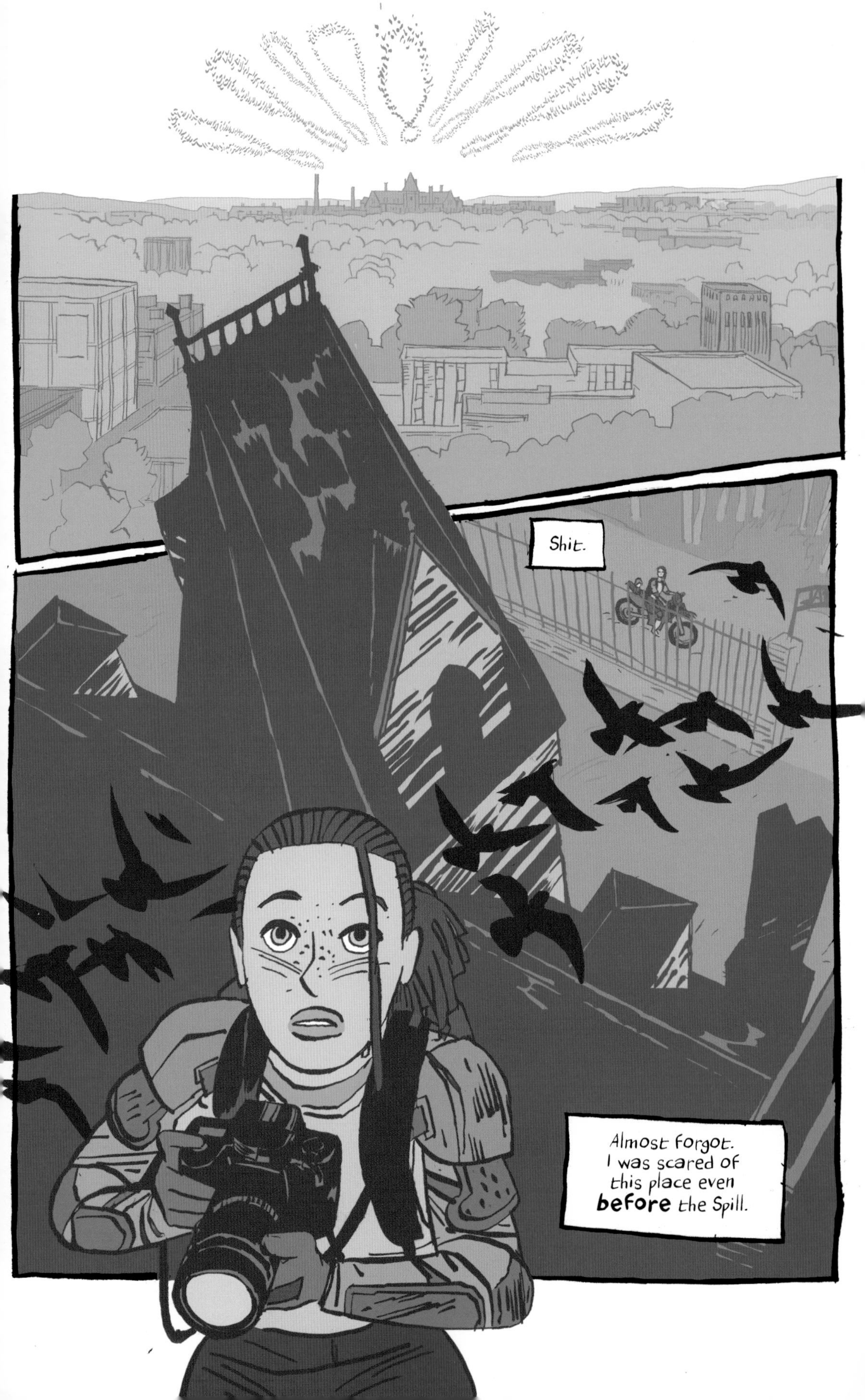
Shit.
Almost forgot. I was scared of this place even **before** the Spill.

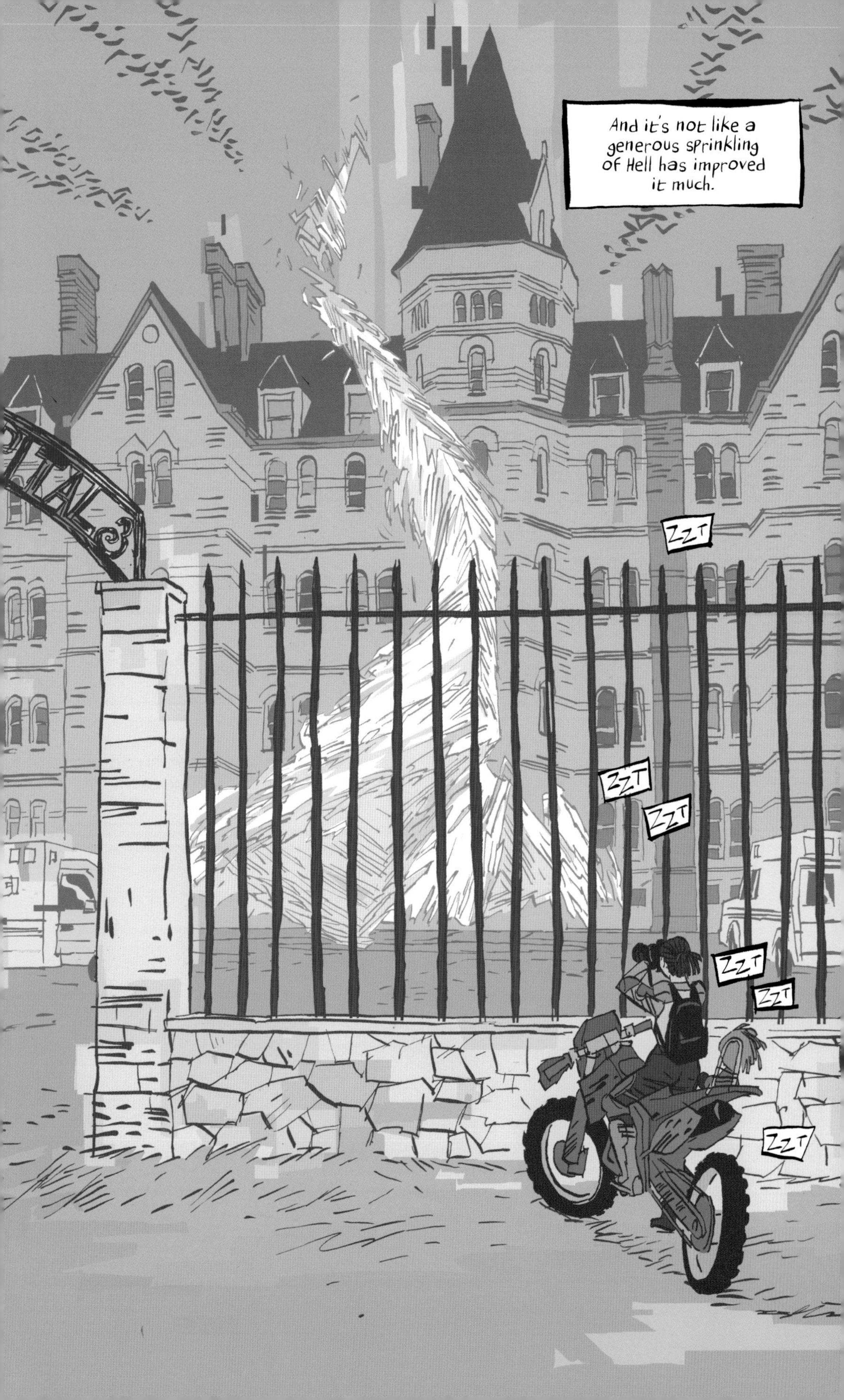
And it's not like a generous sprinkling of Hell has improved it much.
ZZT
ZZT
ZZT
ZZT
ZZT
ZZT

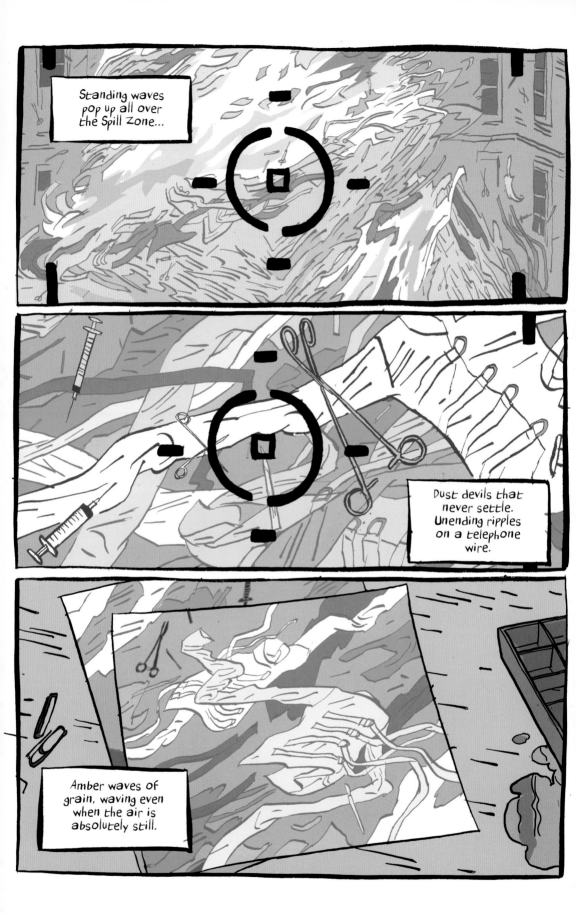

Standing waves pop up all over the Spill Zone...

Dust devils that never settle. Unending ripples on a telephone wire.

Amber waves of grain, waving even when the air is absolutely still.

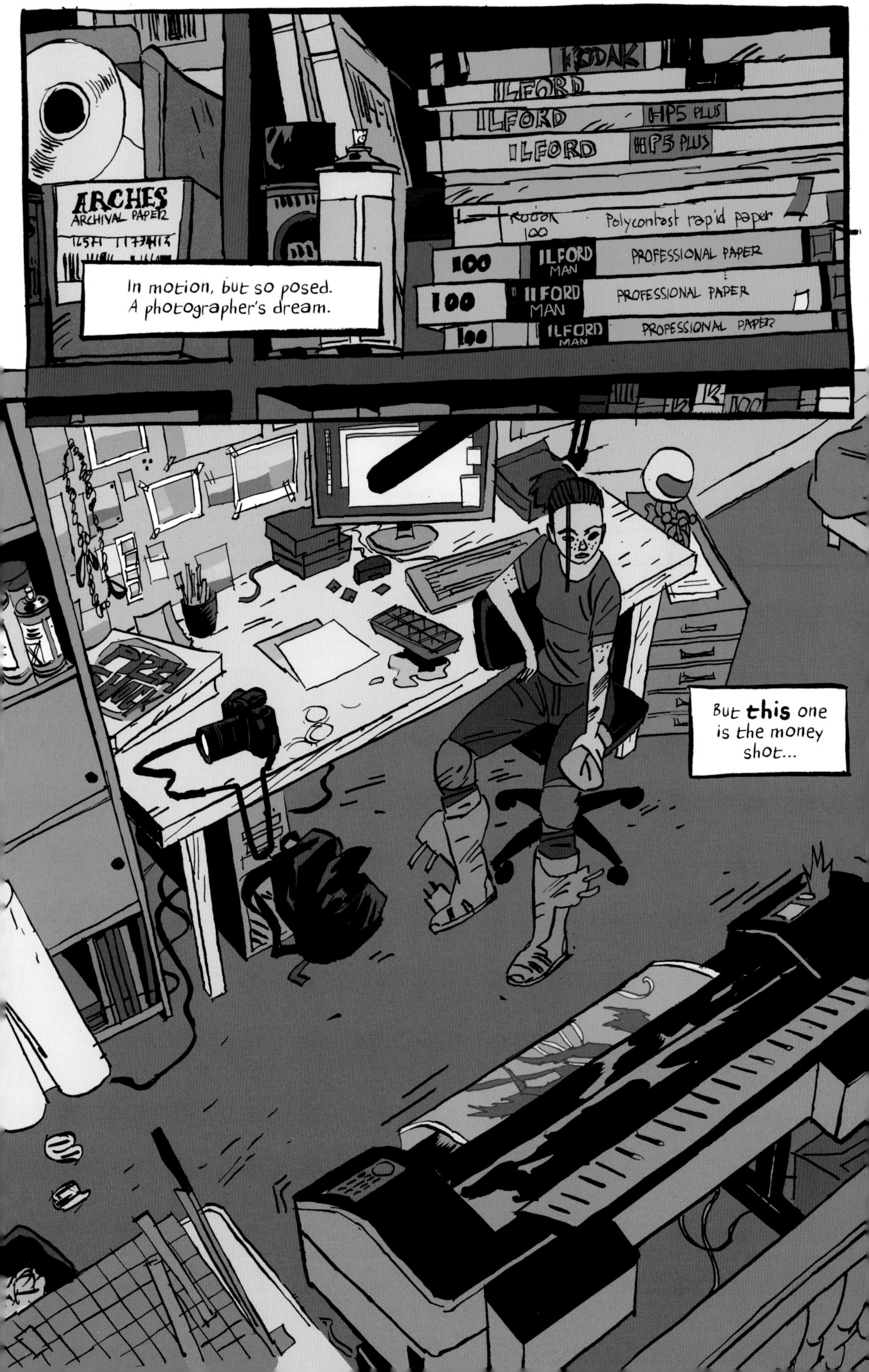
ARCHES
ARCHIVAL PAPER
KODAK
ILFORD
ILFORD HP5 PLUS
ILFORD HP5 PLUS
Polycontrast rapid paper
100 ILFORD MAN PROFESSIONAL PAPER
100 ILFORD MAN PROFESSIONAL PAPER
100 ILFORD MAN PROFESSIONAL PAPER
In motion, but so posed.
A photographer's dream.
But **this** one
is the money
shot...

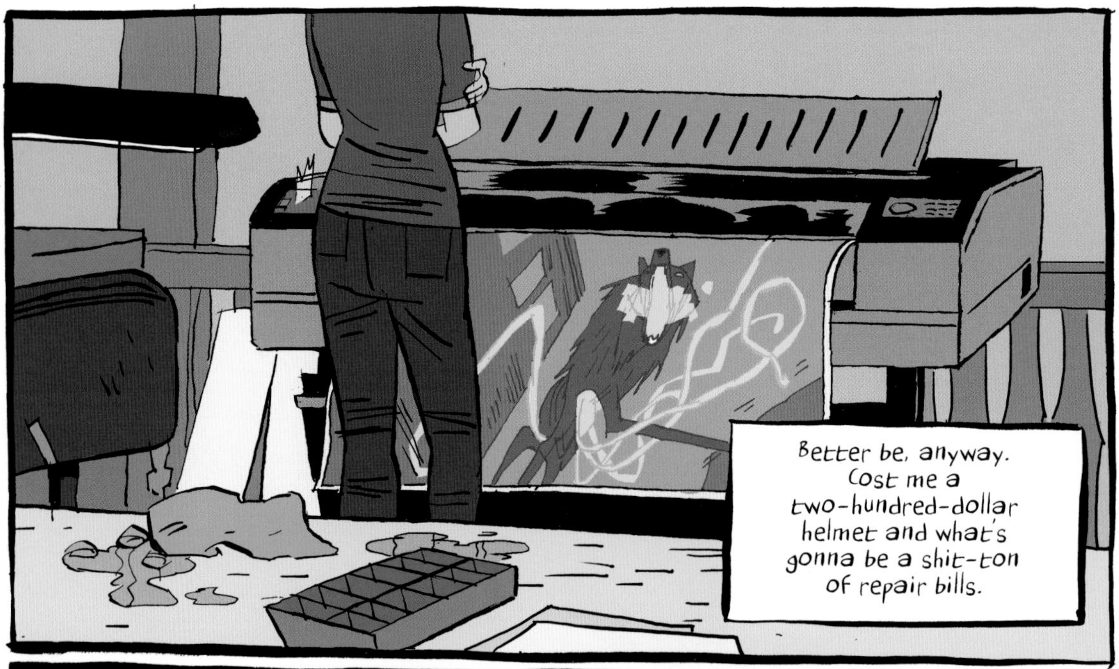
Better be, anyway. Cost me a two-hundred-dollar helmet and what's gonna be a shit-ton of repair bills.

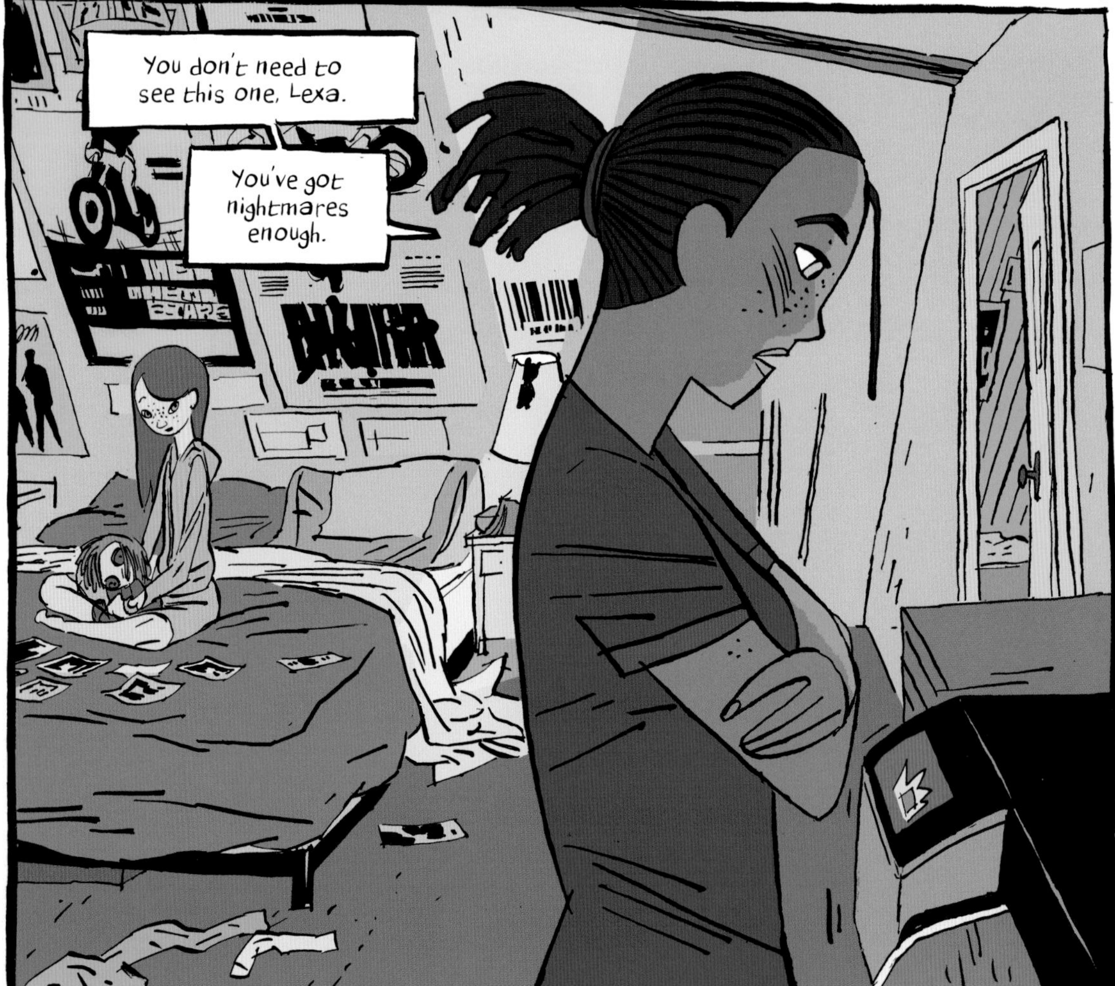
You don't need to see this one, Lexa.
You've got nightmares enough.

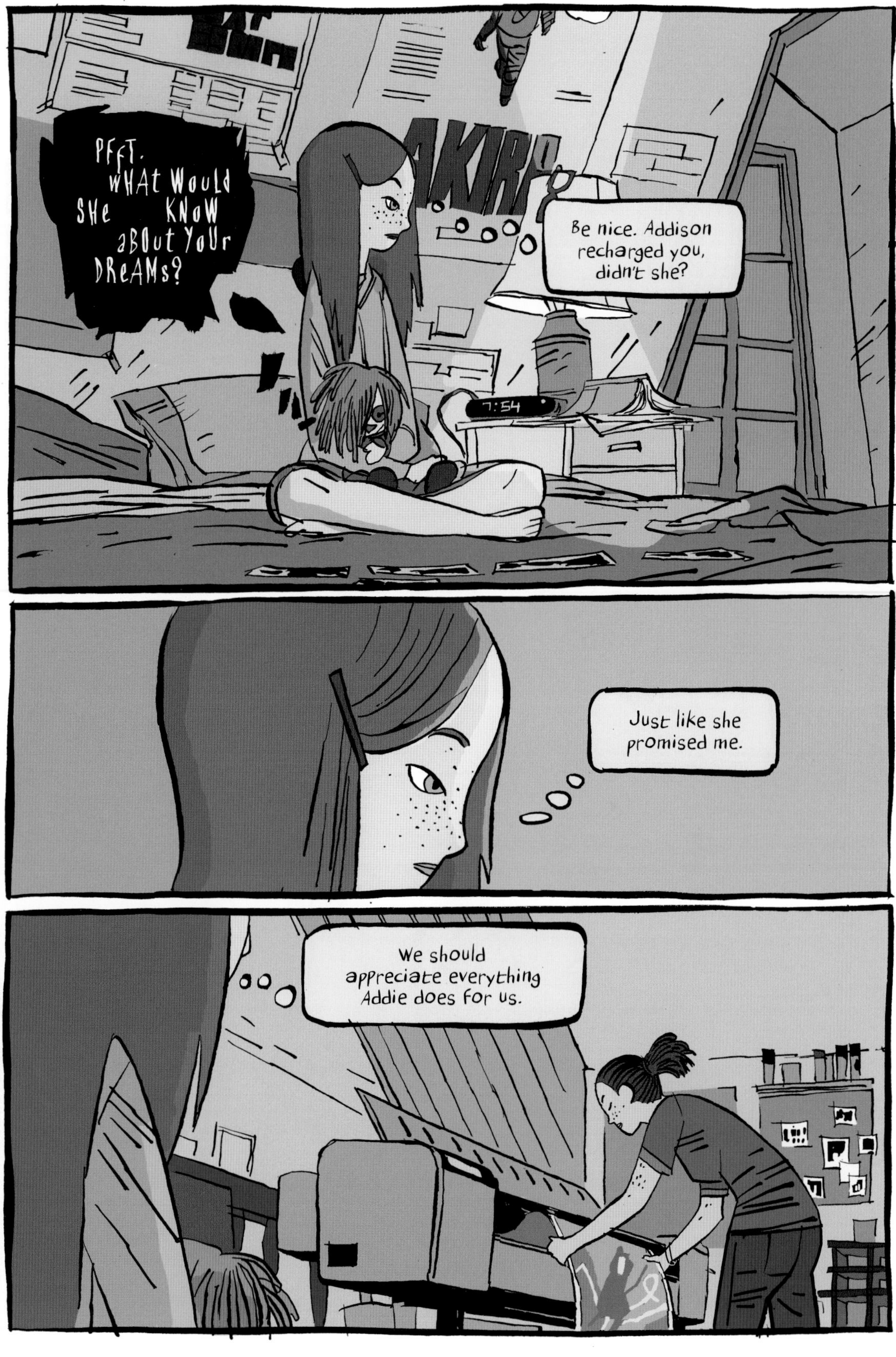
PFFT. WHAT WOULD SHE KNOW ABOUT YOUR DREAMS?
Be nice. Addison recharged you, didn't she?
7:54
Just like she promised me.
We should appreciate everything Addie does for us.

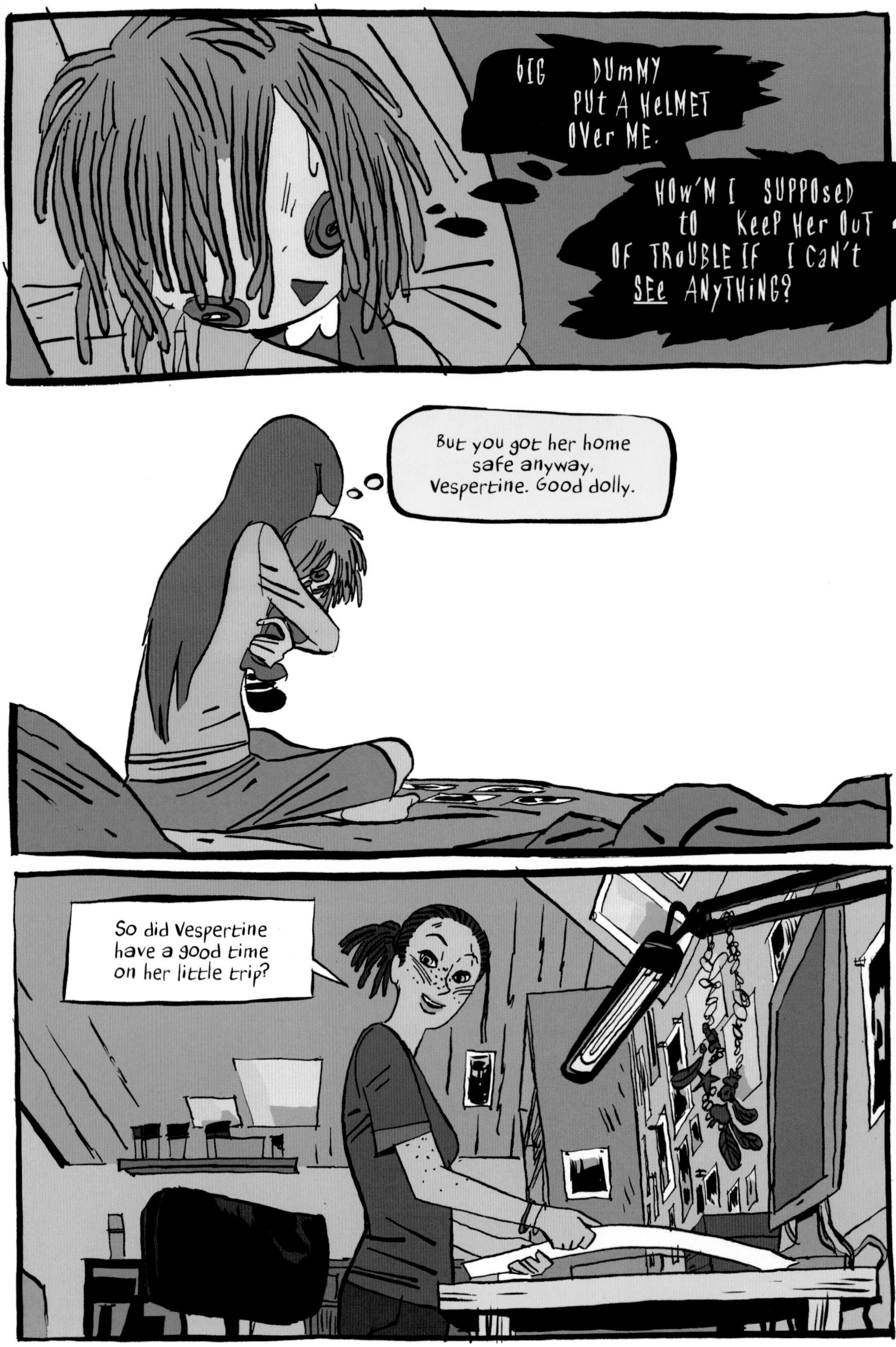
BIG DUMMY PUT A HELMET OVER ME.
HOW'M I SUPPOSED TO KEEP HER OUT OF TROUBLE IF I CAN'T SEE ANYTHING?
But you got her home safe anyway, Vespertine. Good dolly.
So did Vespertine have a good time on her little trip?

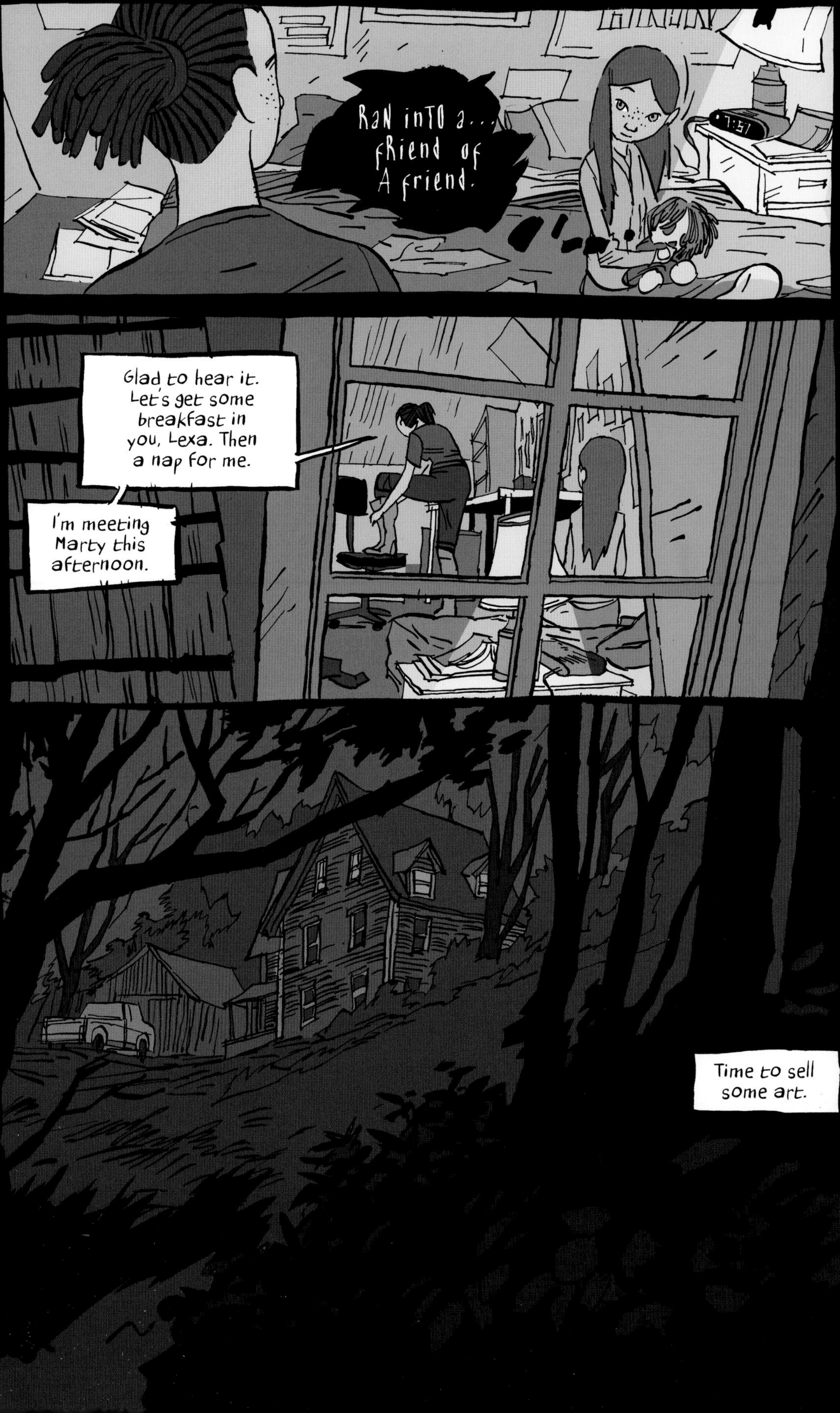
Ran into a... friend of a friend.
Glad to hear it. Let's get some breakfast in you, Lexa. Then a nap for me.
I'm meeting Marty this afternoon.
Time to sell some art.

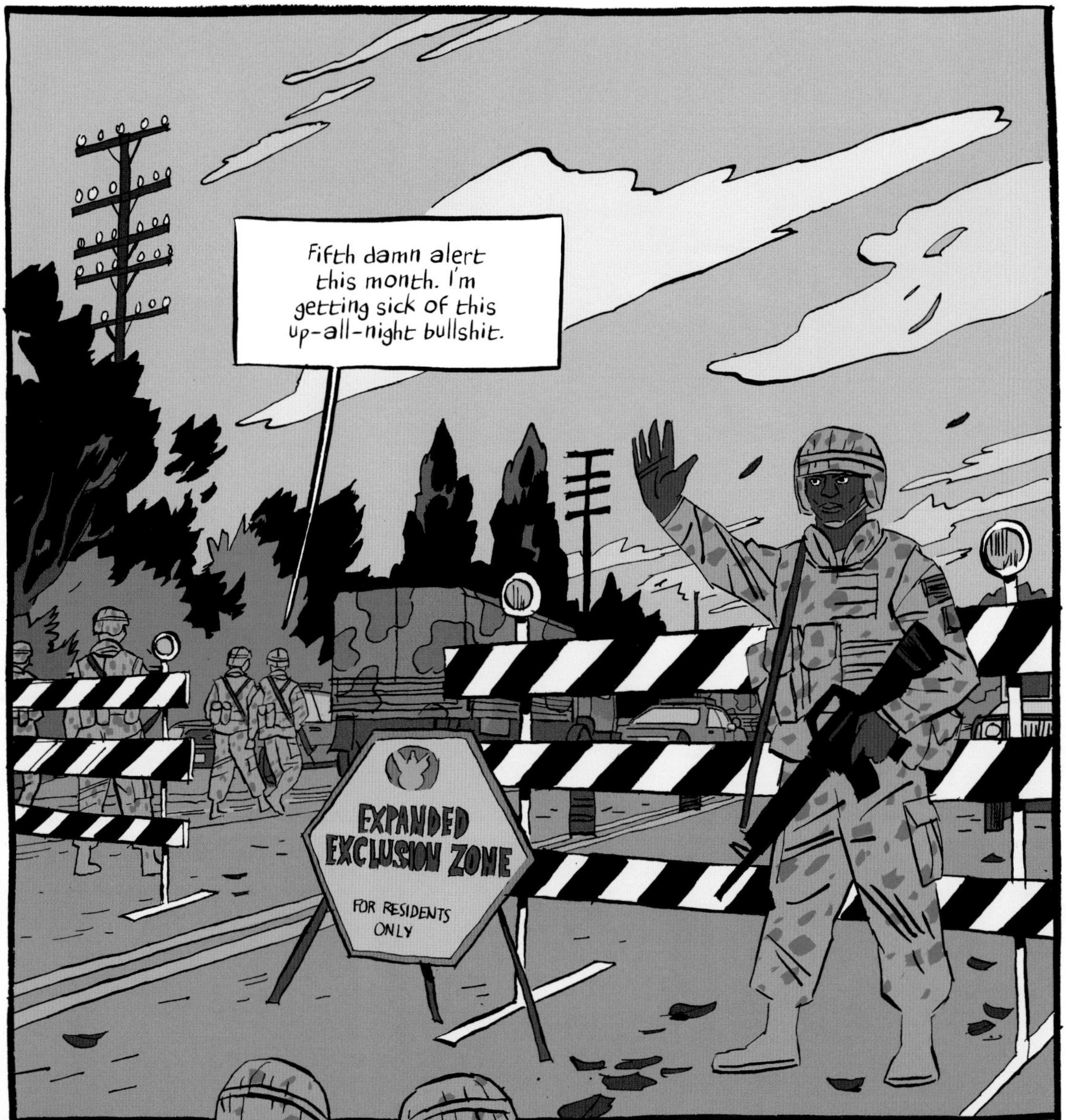
Fifth damn alert this month. I'm getting sick of this up-all-night bullshit.
EXPANDED EXCLUSION ZONE
FOR RESIDENTS ONLY

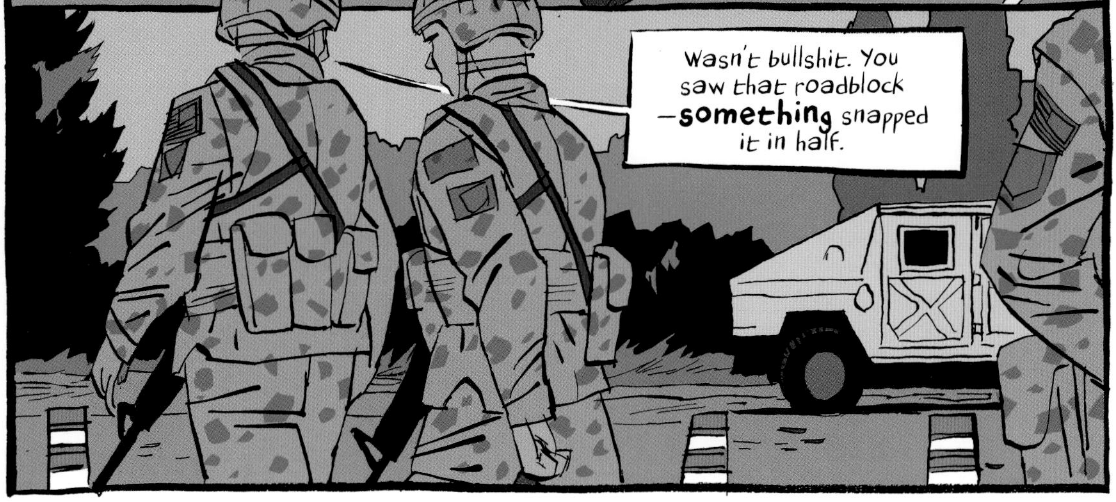
Wasn't bullshit. You saw that roadblock —**something** snapped it in half.

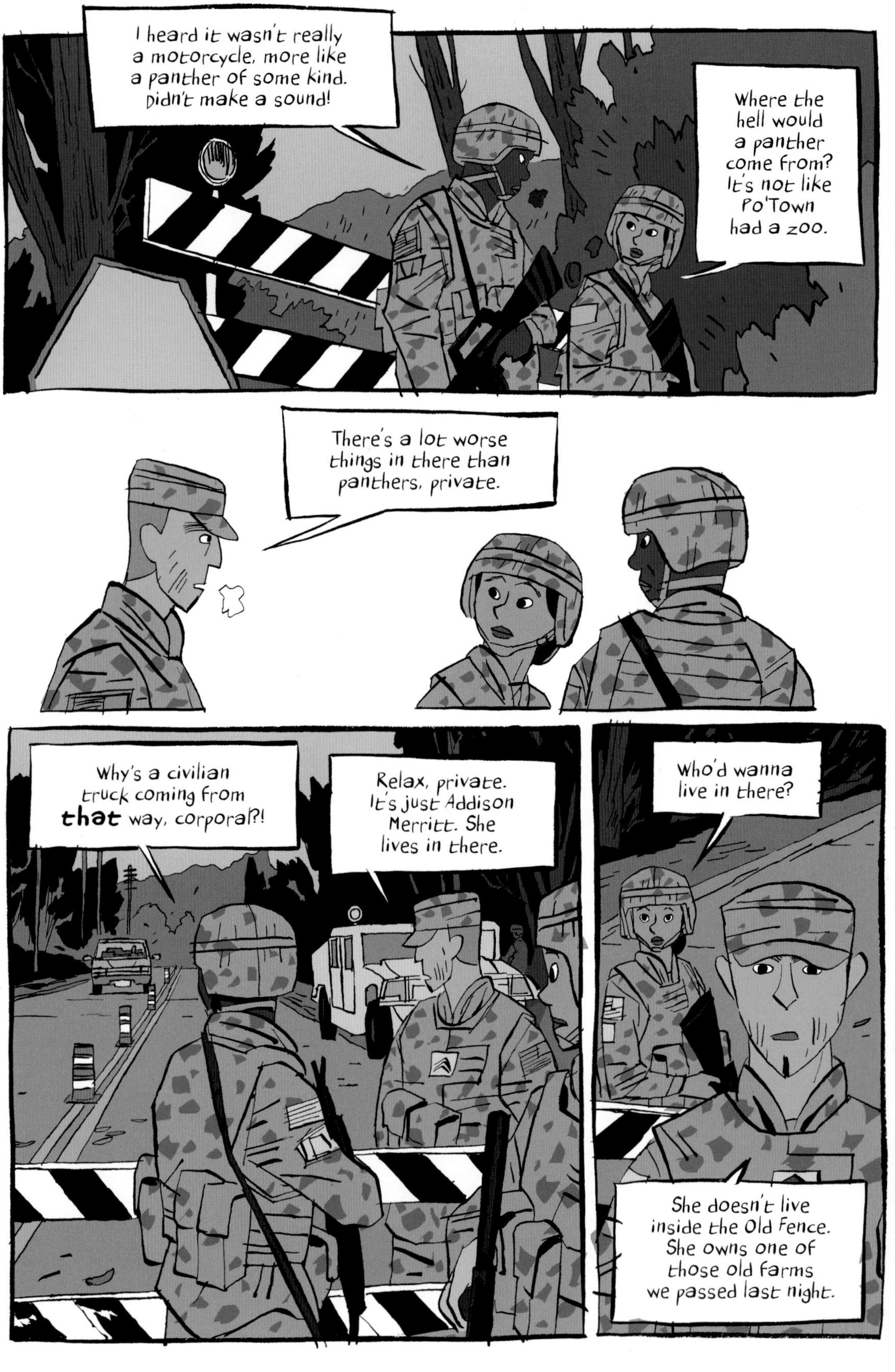
I heard it wasn't really a motorcycle, more like a panther of some kind. Didn't make a sound!
Where the hell would a panther come from? It's not like Po'Town had a zoo.
There's a lot worse things in there than panthers, private.
Why's a civilian truck coming from **that** way, corporal?!
Relax, private. It's just Addison Merritt. She lives in there.
Who'd wanna live in there?
She doesn't live inside the Old Fence. She owns one of those old farms we passed last night.

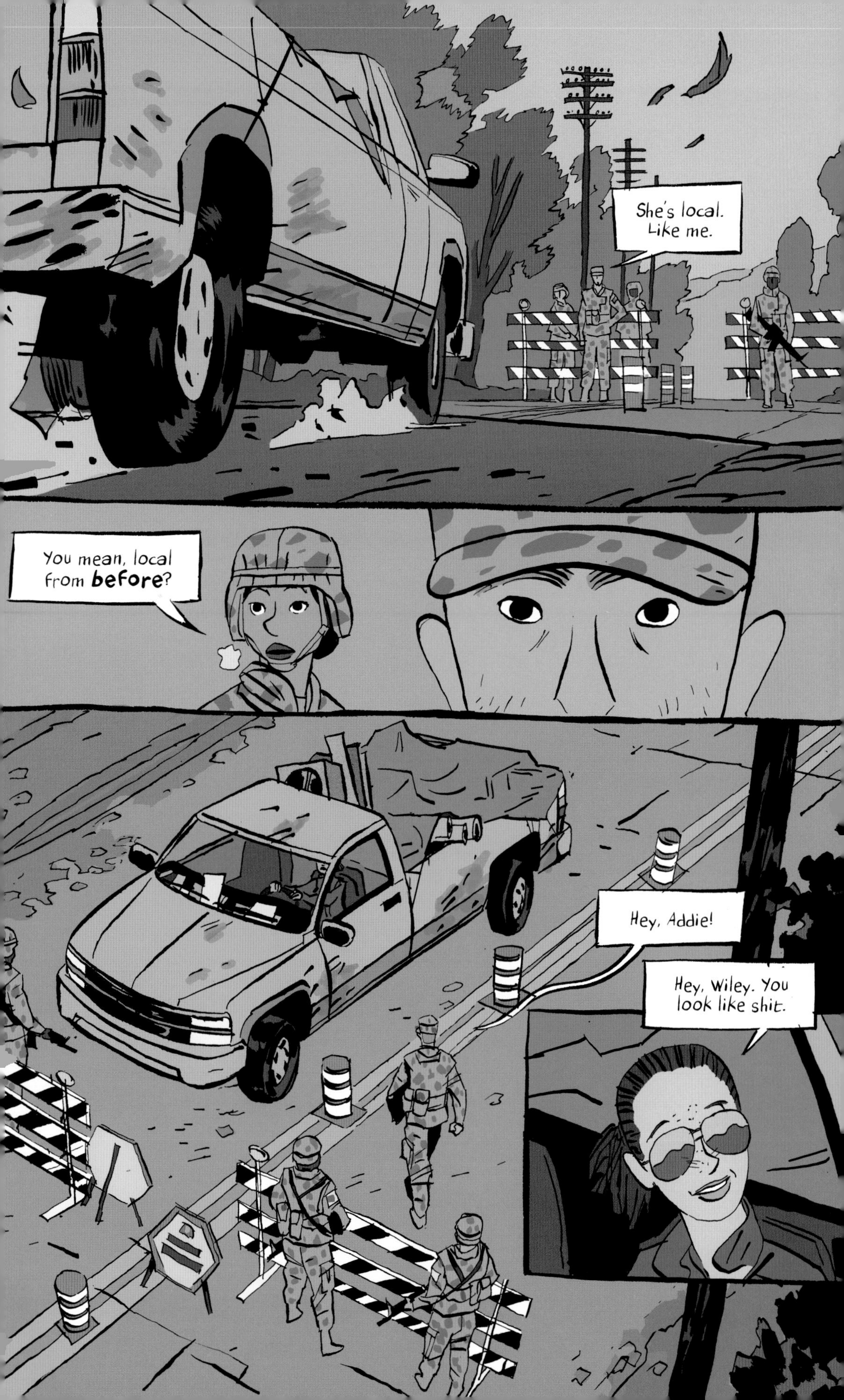
She's local. Like me.
You mean, local from **before**?
Hey, Addie!
Hey, Wiley. You look like shit.

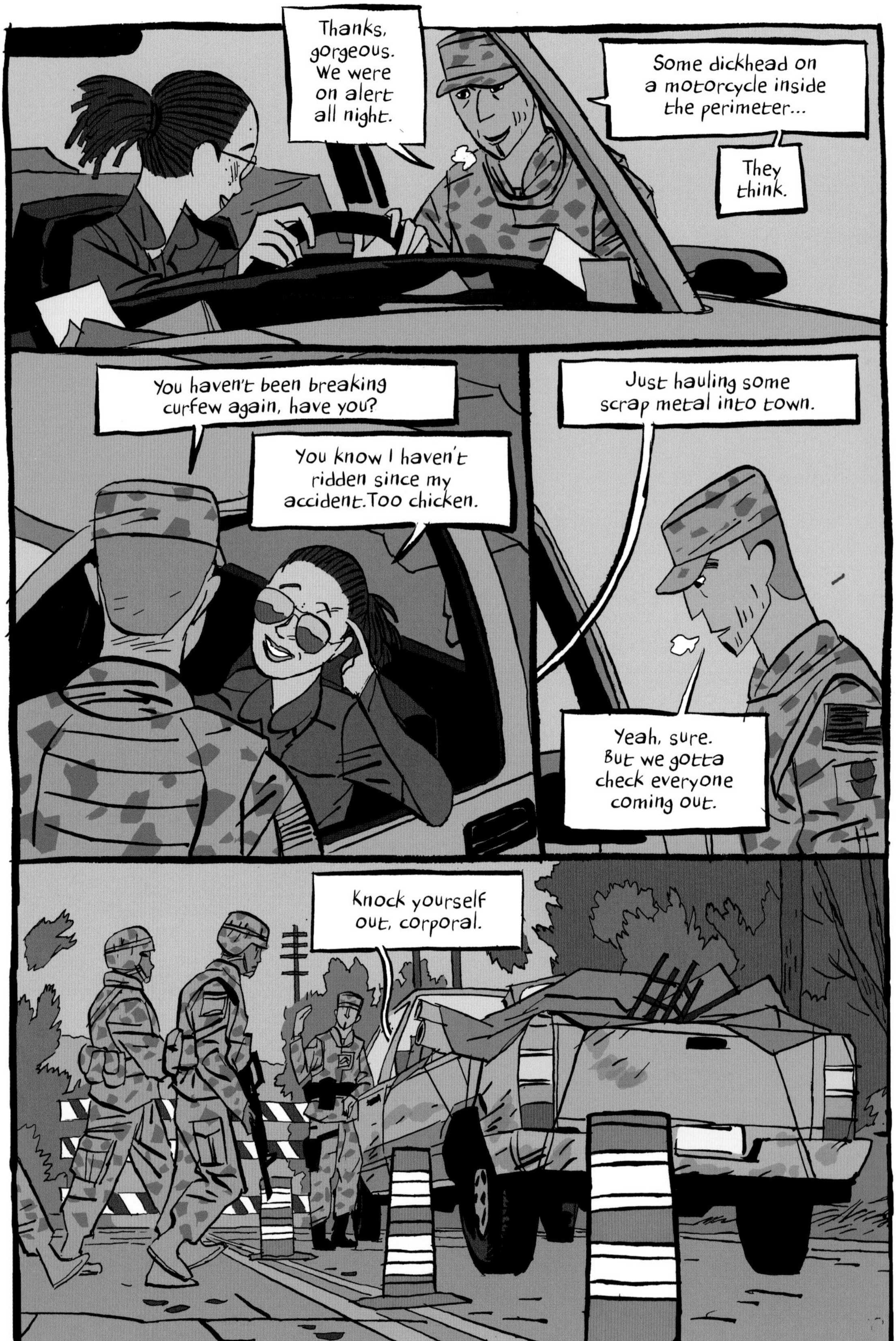
Thanks, gorgeous. We were on alert all night.
Some dickhead on a motorcycle inside the perimeter...
They think.
You haven't been breaking curfew again, have you?
You know I haven't ridden since my accident. Too chicken.
Just hauling some scrap metal into town.
Yeah, sure. But we gotta check everyone coming out.
Knock yourself out, corporal.

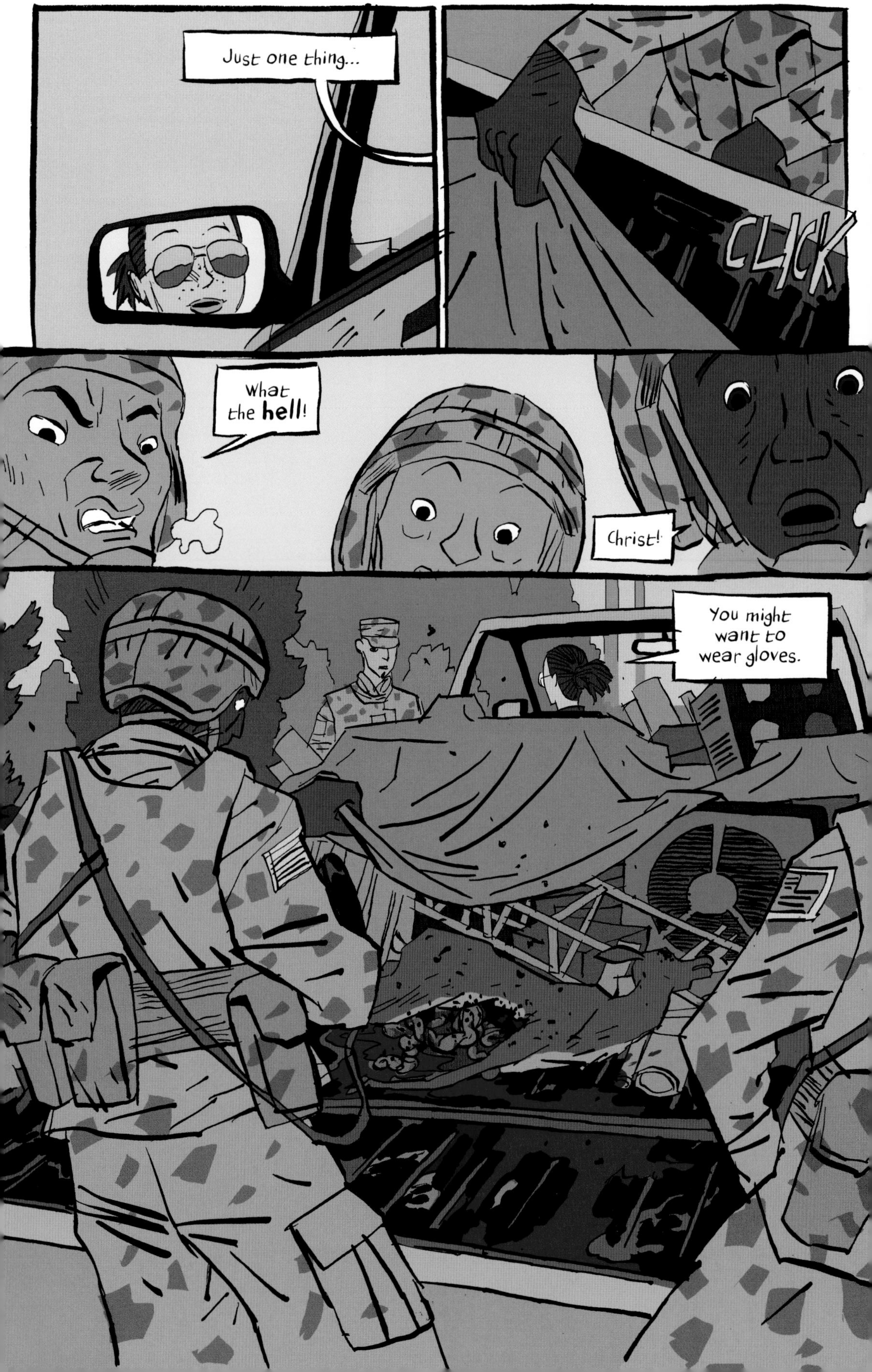
Just one thing...
CLICK
What the hell!
Christ!
You might want to wear gloves.

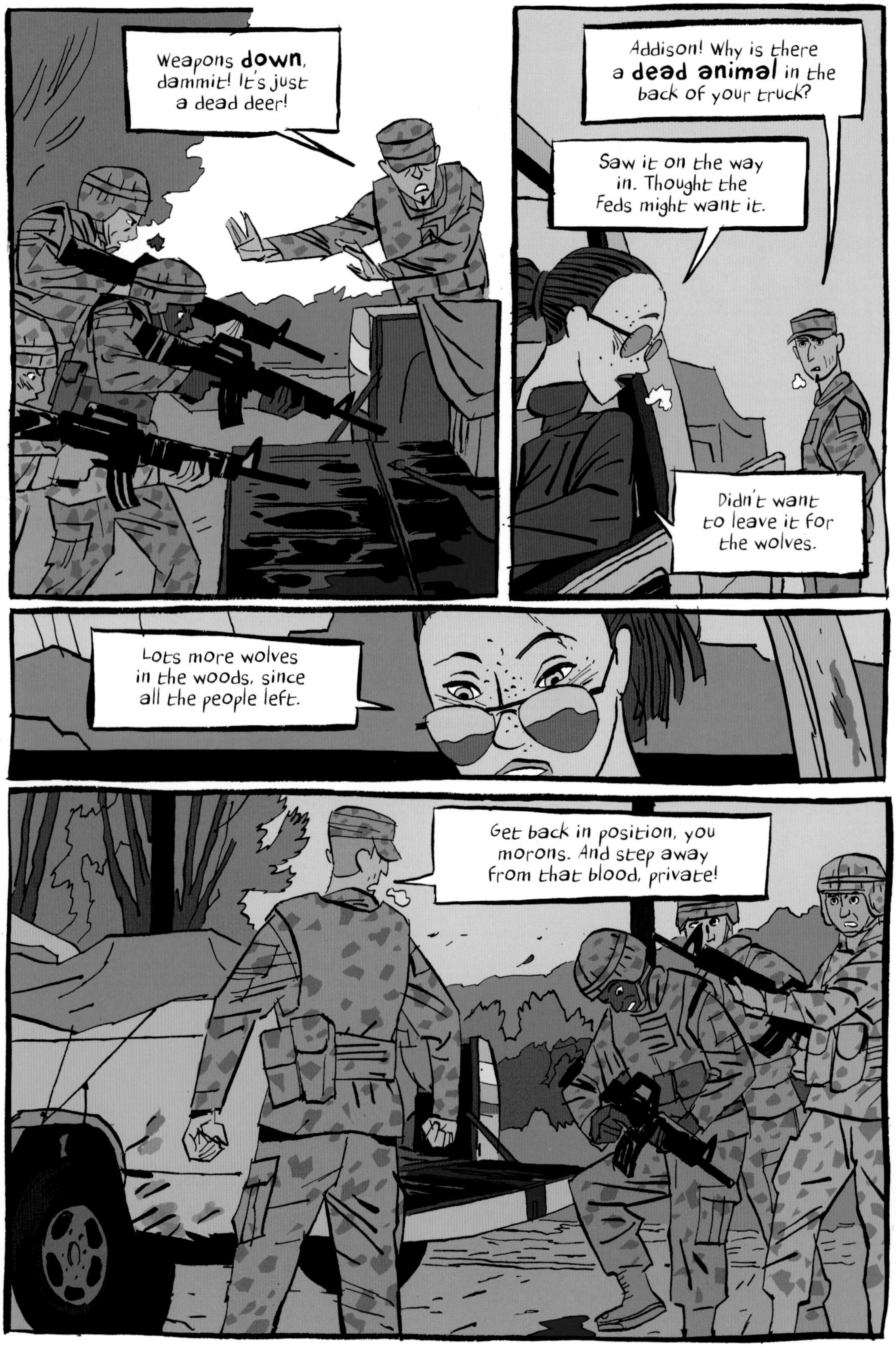
Weapons **down**, dammit! It's just a dead deer!
Addison! Why is there a **dead animal** in the back of your truck?
Saw it on the way in. Thought the Feds might want it.
Didn't want to leave it for the wolves.
Lots more wolves in the woods, since all the people left.
Get back in position, you morons. And step away from that blood, private!

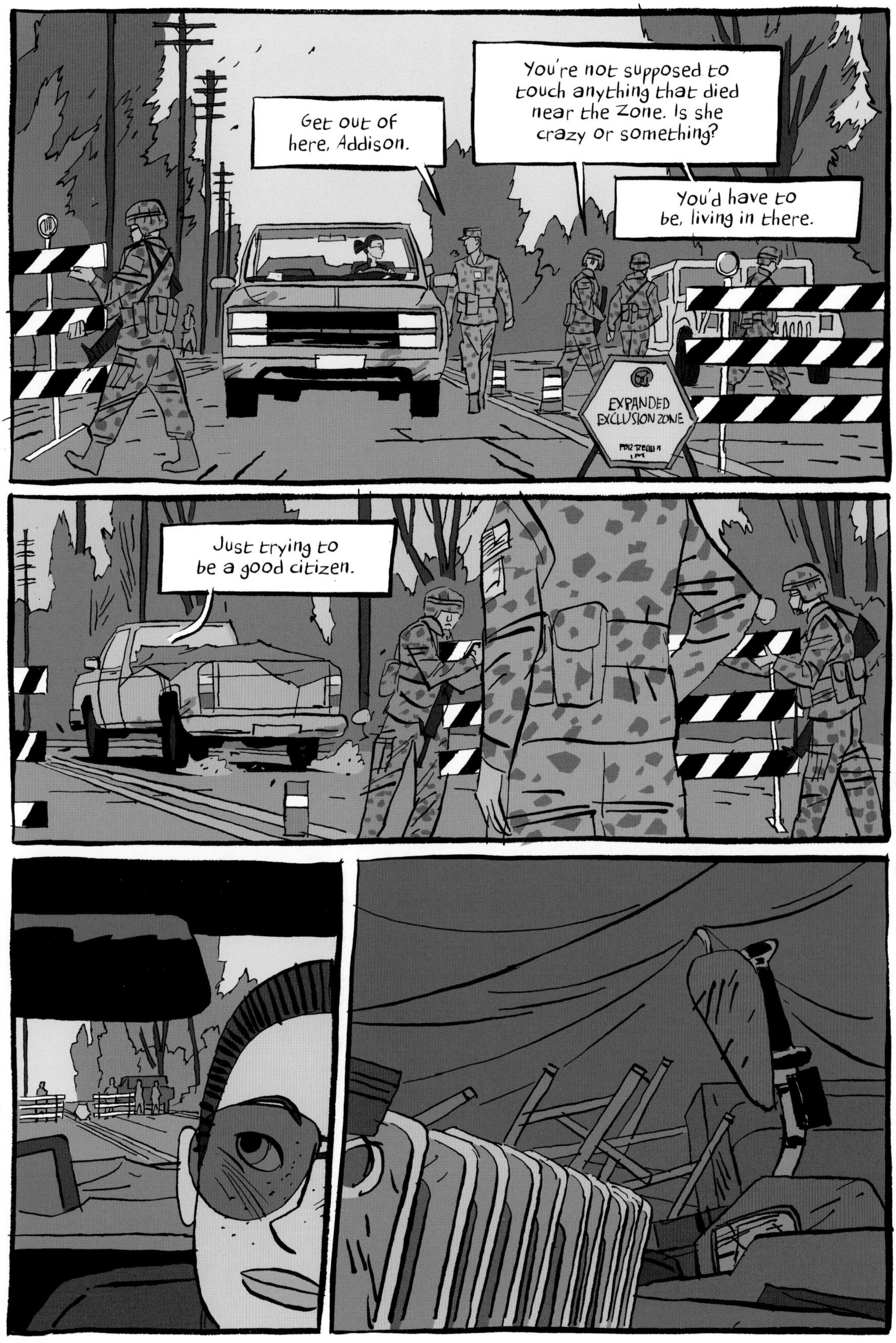
Get out of here, Addison.
You're not supposed to touch anything that died near the Zone. Is she crazy or something?
You'd have to be, living in there.
EXPANDED EXCLUSION ZONE
Just trying to be a good citizen.

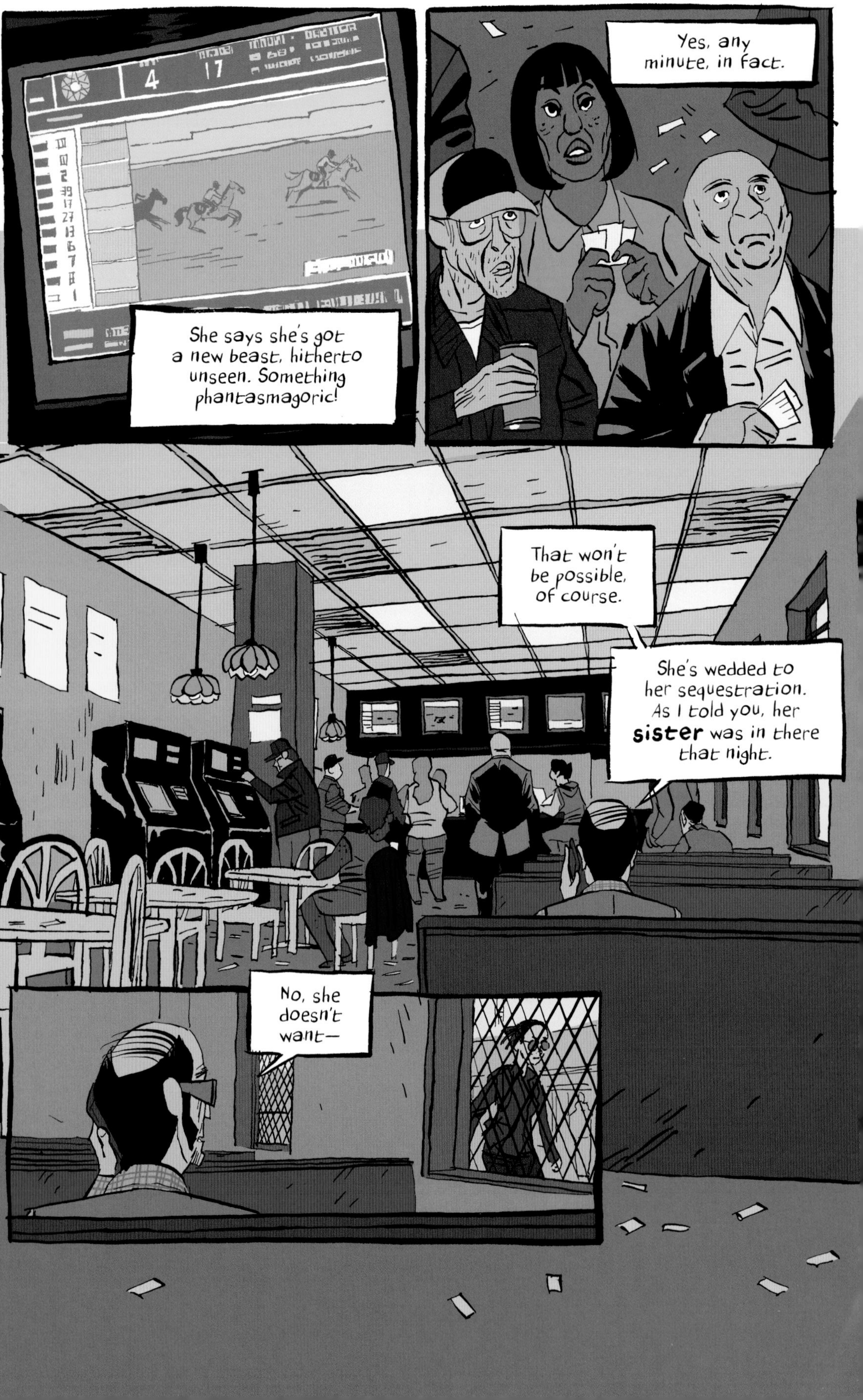
She says she's got a new beast, hitherto unseen. Something phantasmagoric!
Yes, any minute, in fact.
That won't be possible, of course.
She's wedded to her sequestration. As I told you, her **sister** was in there that night.
No, she doesn't want—

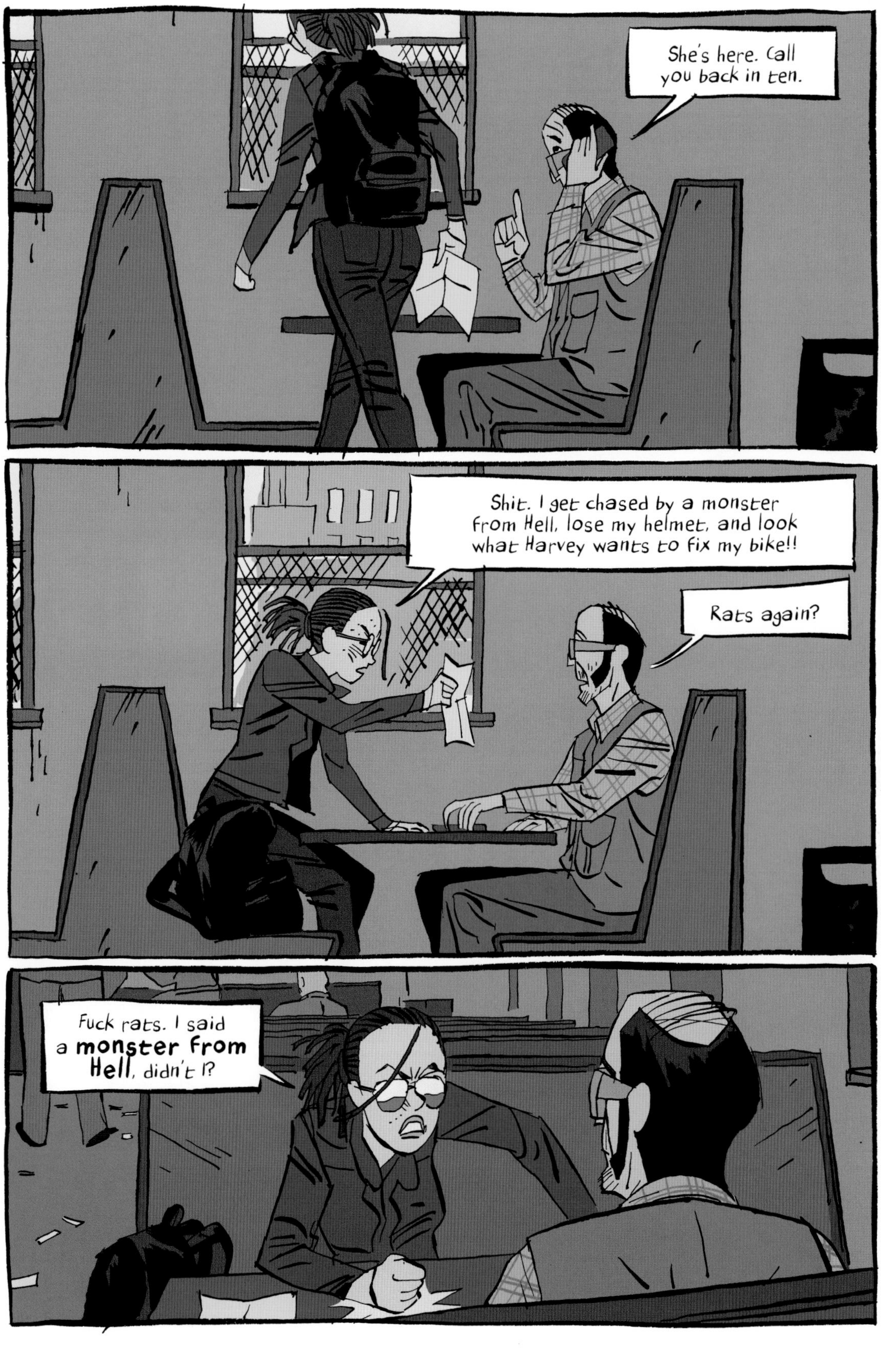
She's here. Call you back in ten.
Shit. I get chased by a monster from Hell, lose my helmet, and look what Harvey wants to fix my bike!!
Rats again?
Fuck rats. I said a **monster from Hell**, didn't I?

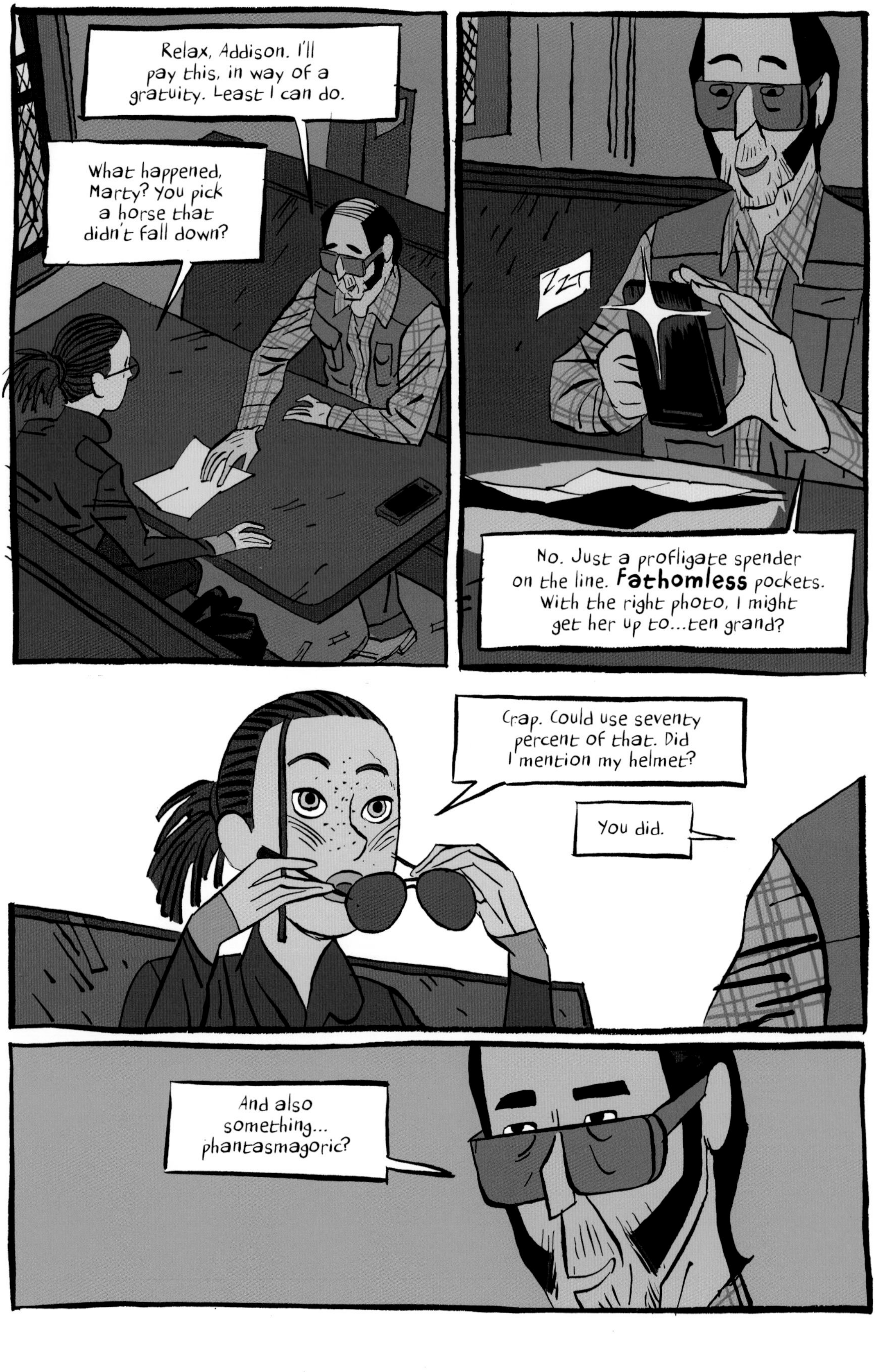
Relax, Addison. I'll pay this, in way of a gratuity. Least I can do.
What happened, Marty? You pick a horse that didn't fall down?
ZZT
No. Just a profligate spender on the line. Fathomless pockets. With the right photo, I might get her up to...ten grand?
Crap. Could use seventy percent of that. Did I mention my helmet?
You did.
And also something... phantasmagoric?

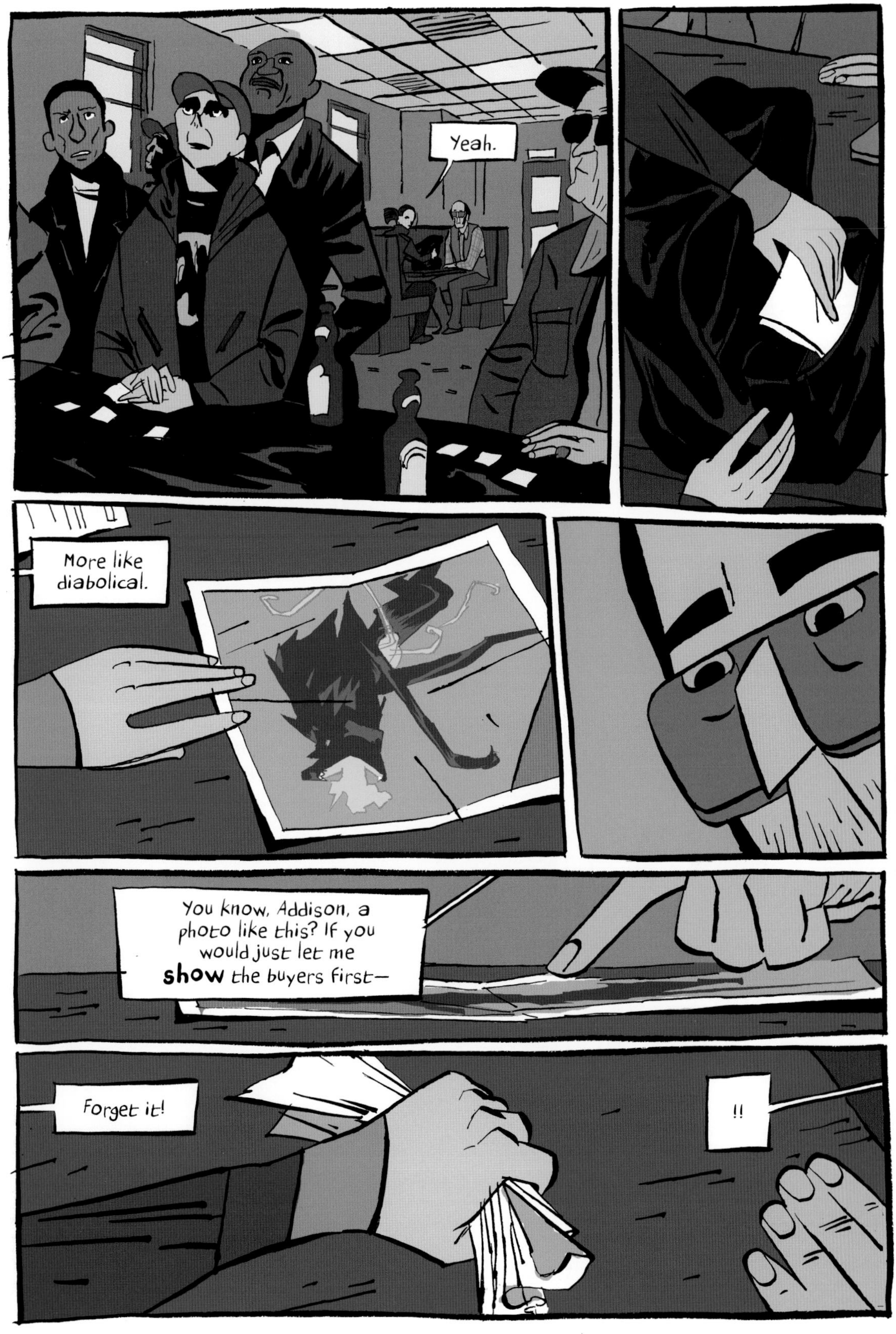
Yeah.
More like diabolical.
You know, Addison, a photo like this? If you would just let me **show** the buyers first—
Forget it!
!!

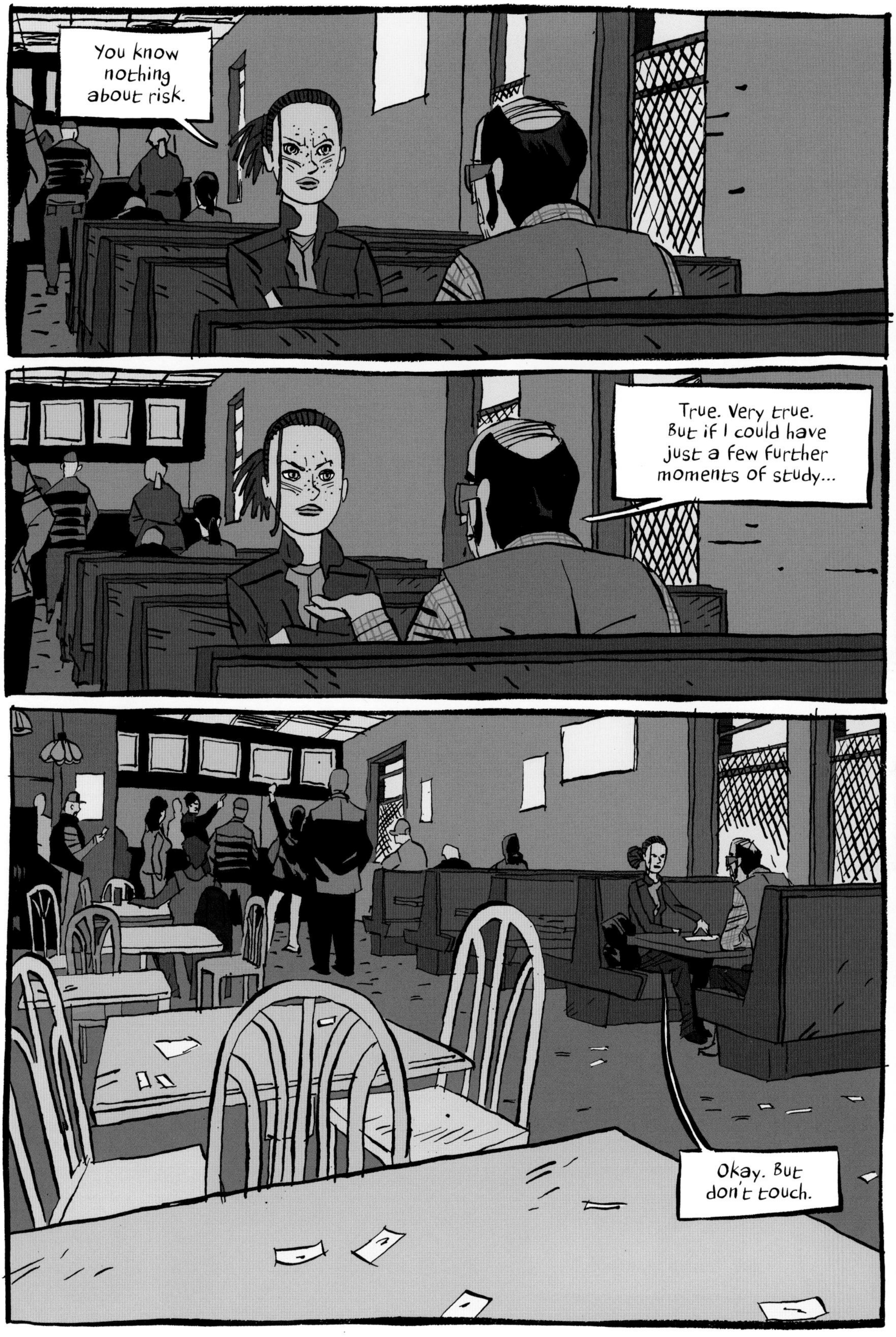
You know nothing about risk.
True. Very true. But if I could have just a few further moments of study...
Okay. But don't touch.

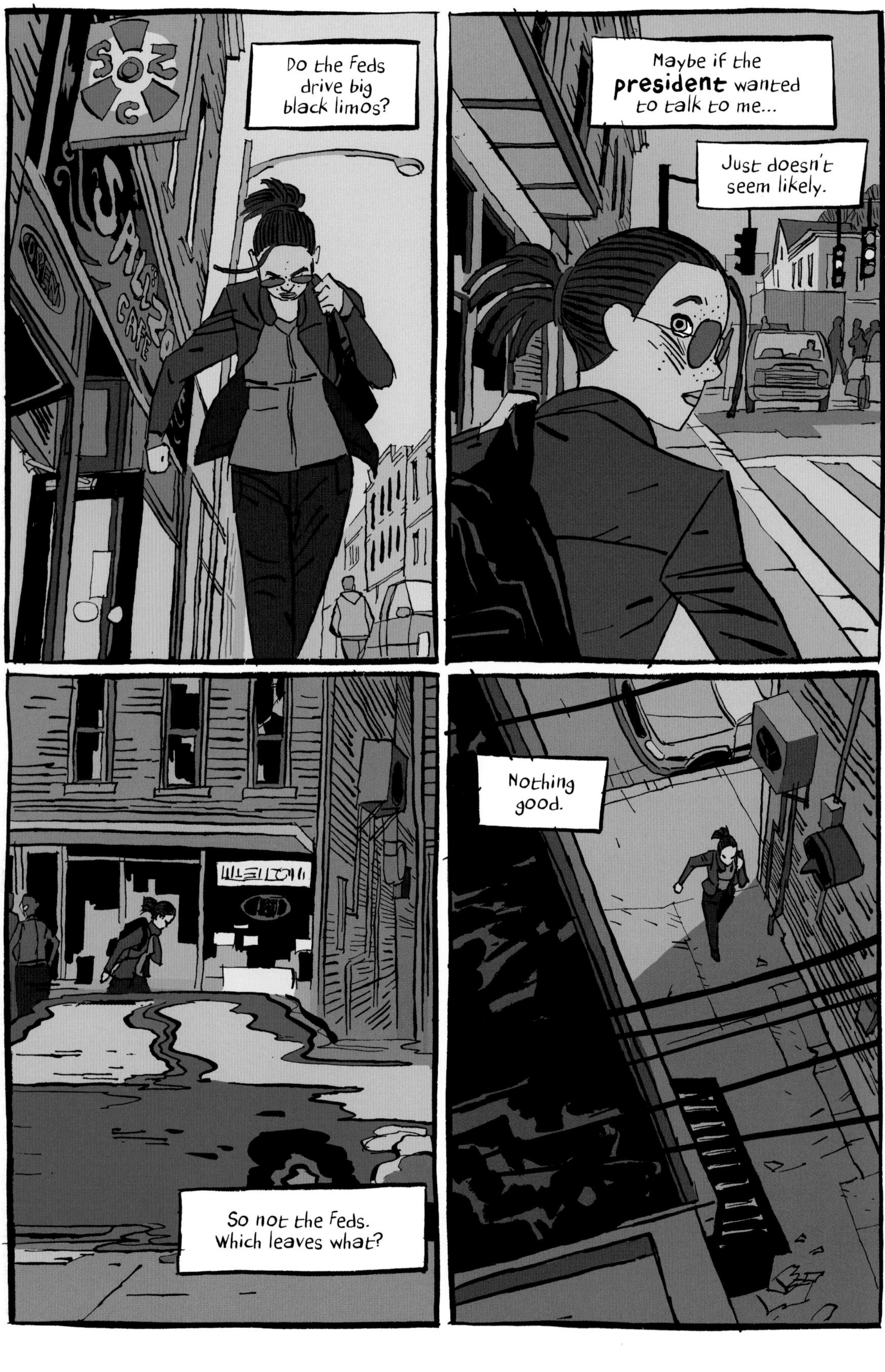
Do the Feds drive big black limos?
Maybe if the **president** wanted to talk to me...
Just doesn't seem likely.
So not the Feds. Which leaves what?
Nothing good.

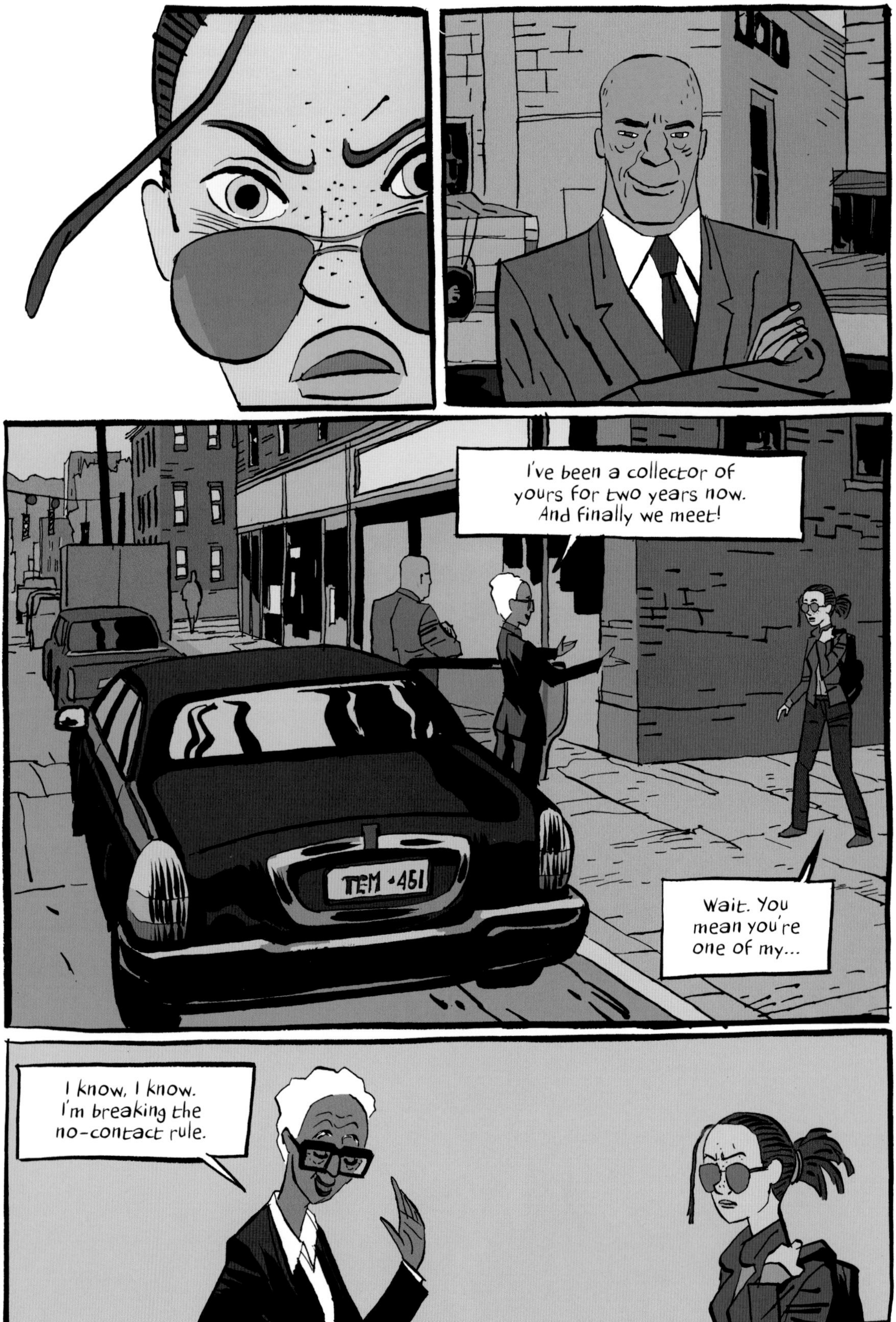
I've been a collector of yours for two years now. And finally we meet!
TEM 461
Wait. You mean you're one of my...
I know, I know. I'm breaking the no-contact rule.

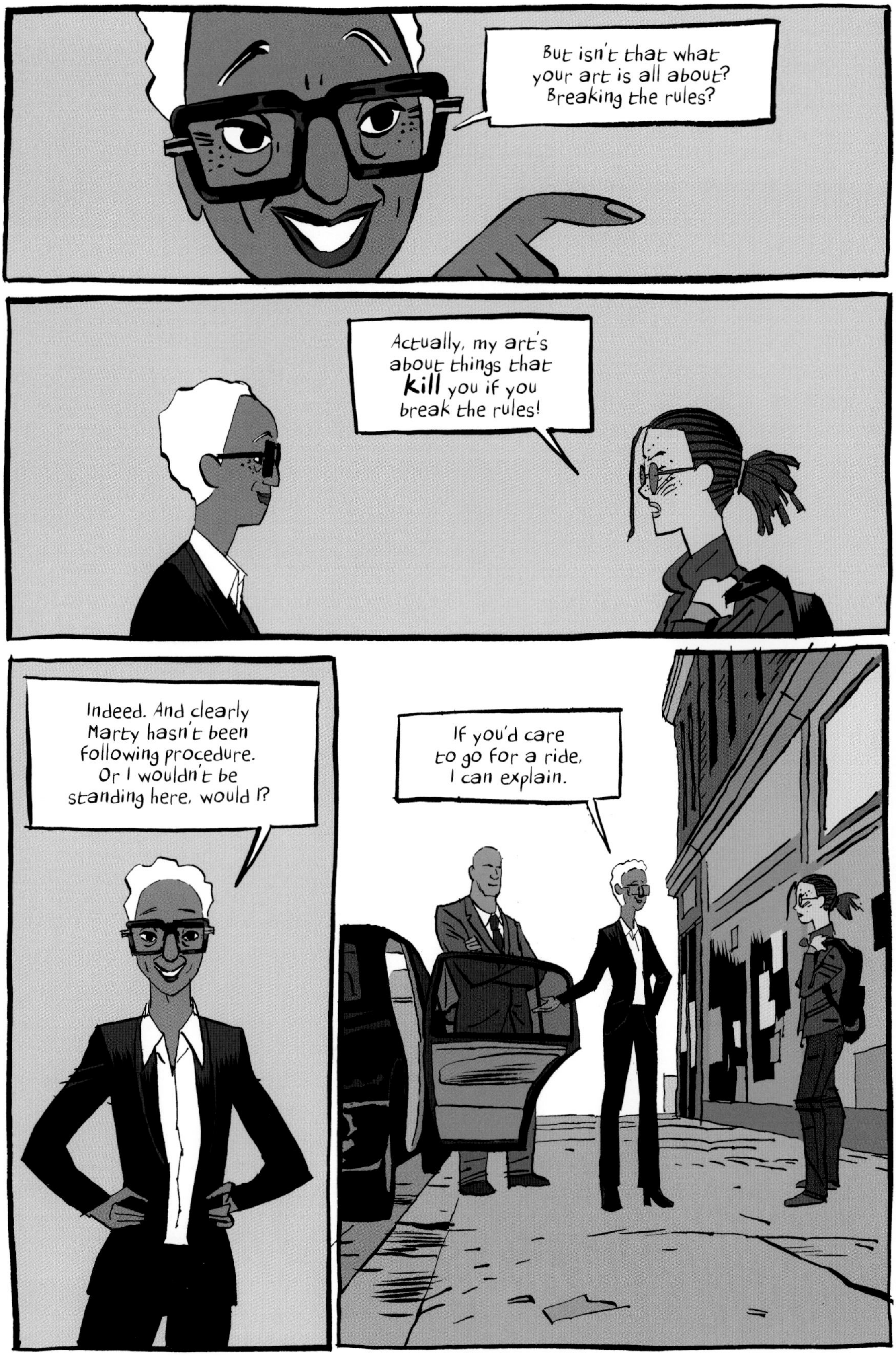
But isn't that what your art is all about? Breaking the rules?
Actually, my art's about things that **kill** you if you break the rules!
Indeed. And clearly Marty hasn't been following procedure. Or I wouldn't be standing here, would I?
If you'd care to go for a ride, I can explain.

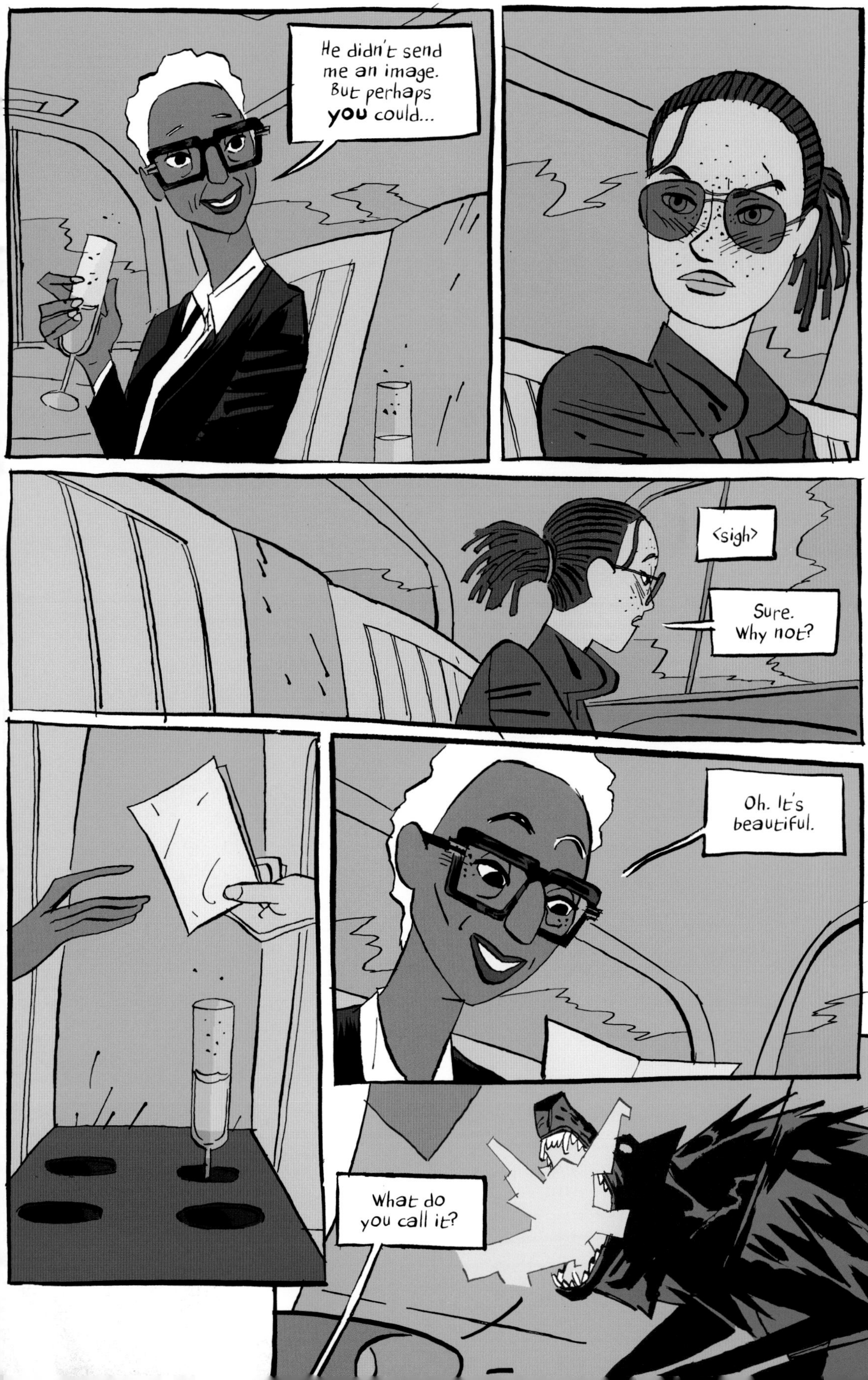

He didn't send me an image. But perhaps **you** could...
<sigh>
Sure. Why not?
Oh. It's beautiful.
What do you call it?

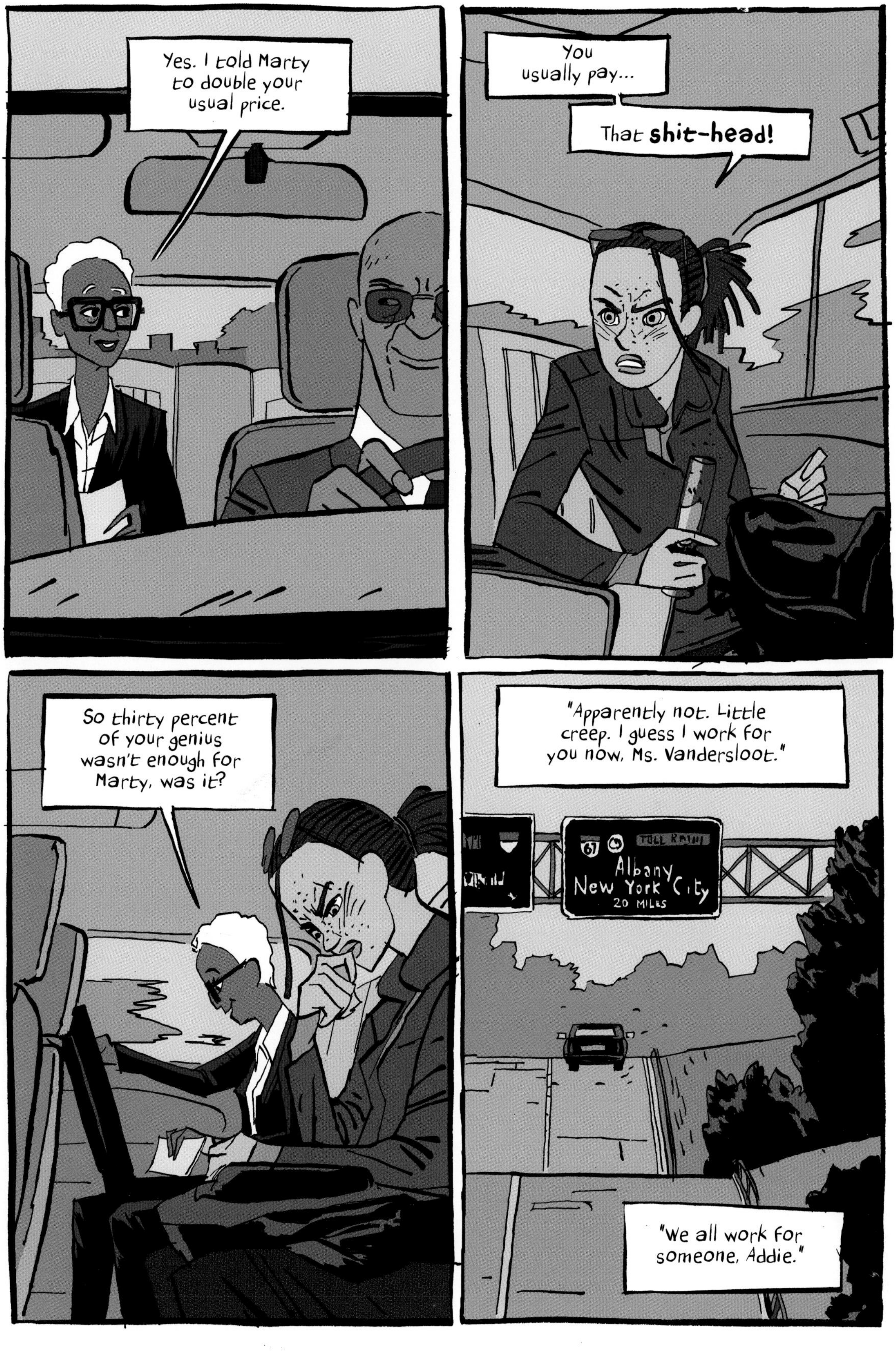
Yes. I told Marty to double your usual price.
You usually pay...
That **shit-head!**
So thirty percent of your genius wasn't enough for Marty, was it?
"Apparently not. Little creep. I guess I work for you now, Ms. Vandersloot."
Albany
New York City
20 MILES
"We all work for someone, Addie."

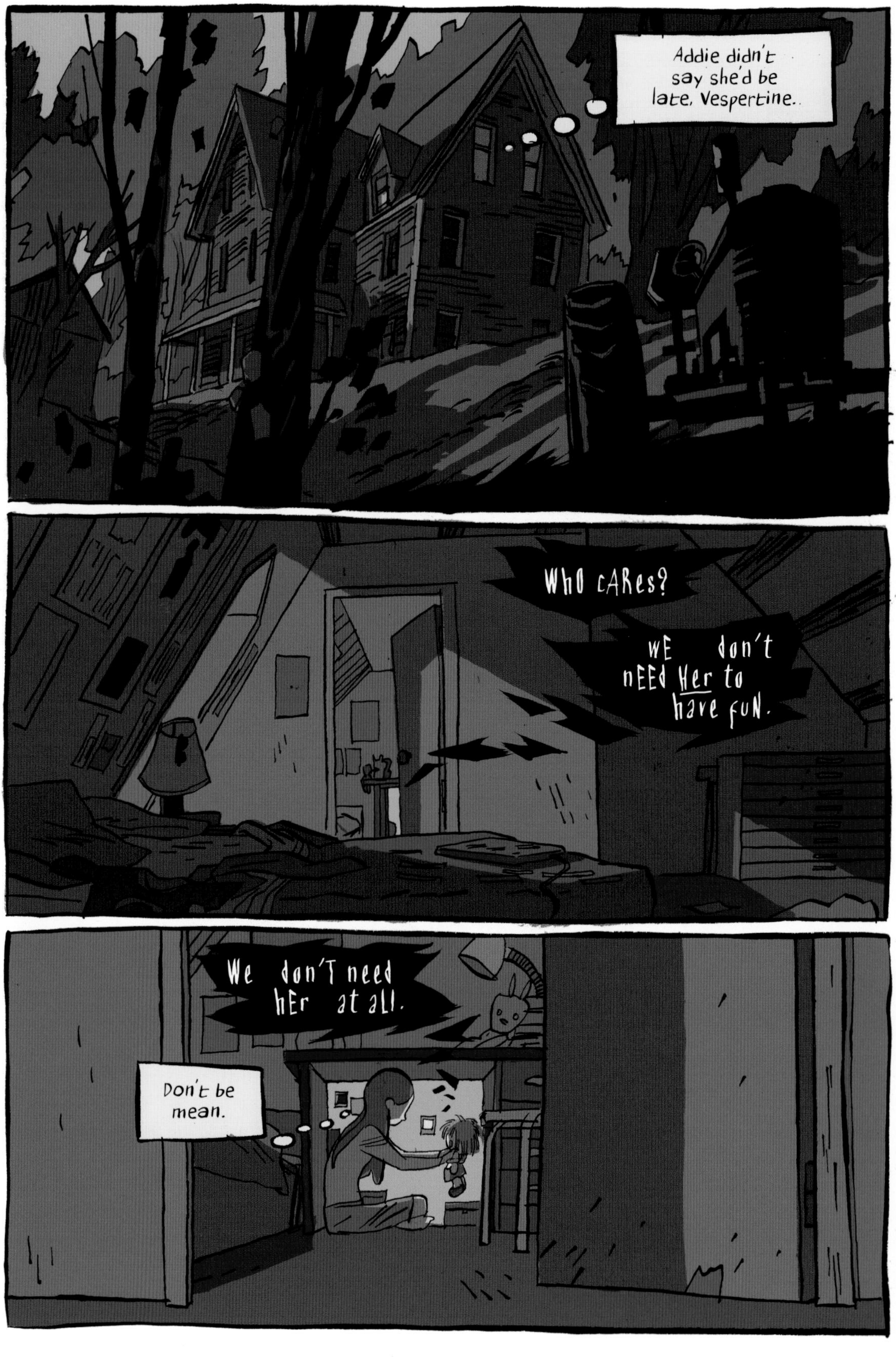
Addie didn't say she'd be late, Vespertine.
Who cares?
We don't need her to have fun.
We don't need her at all.
Don't be mean.

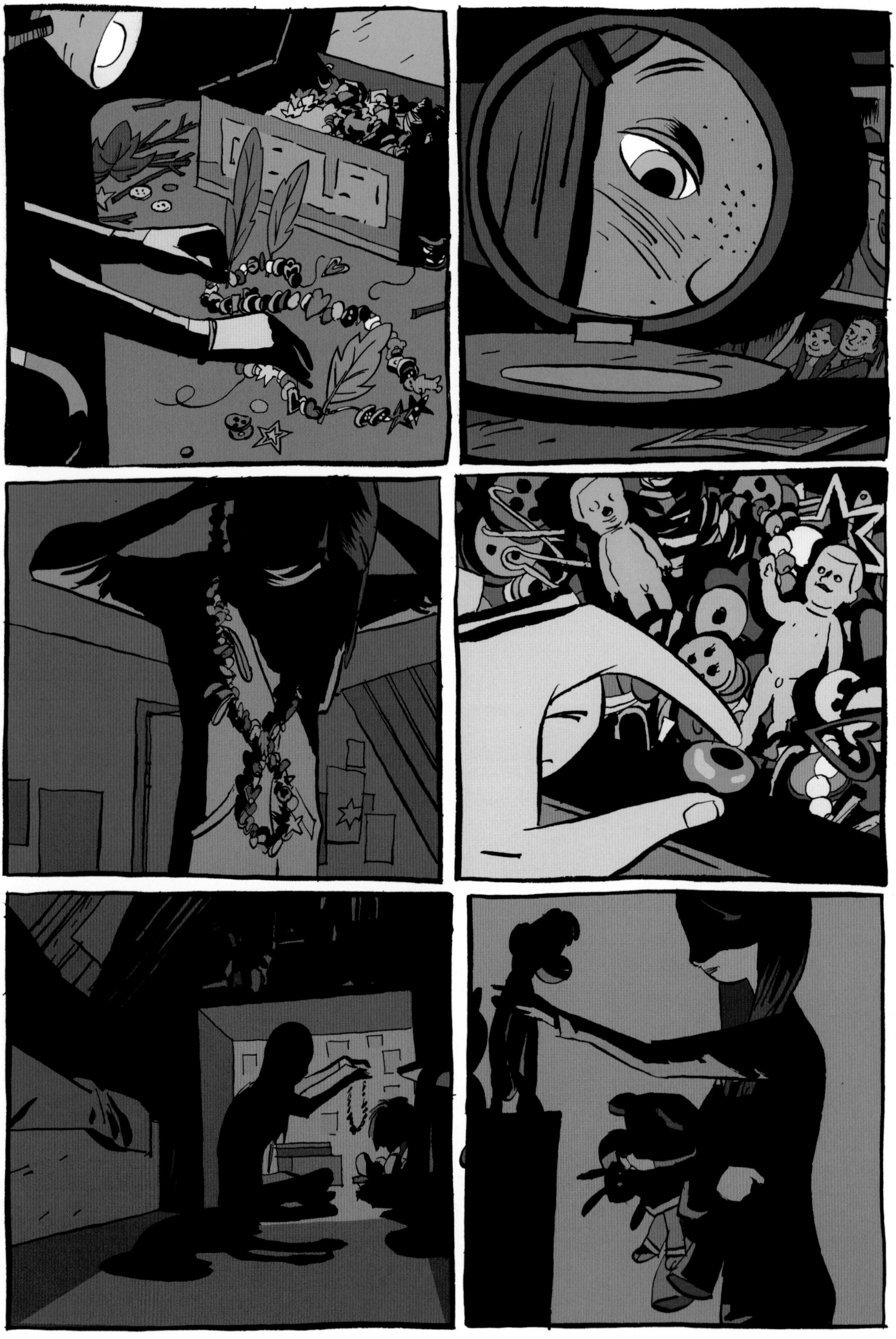

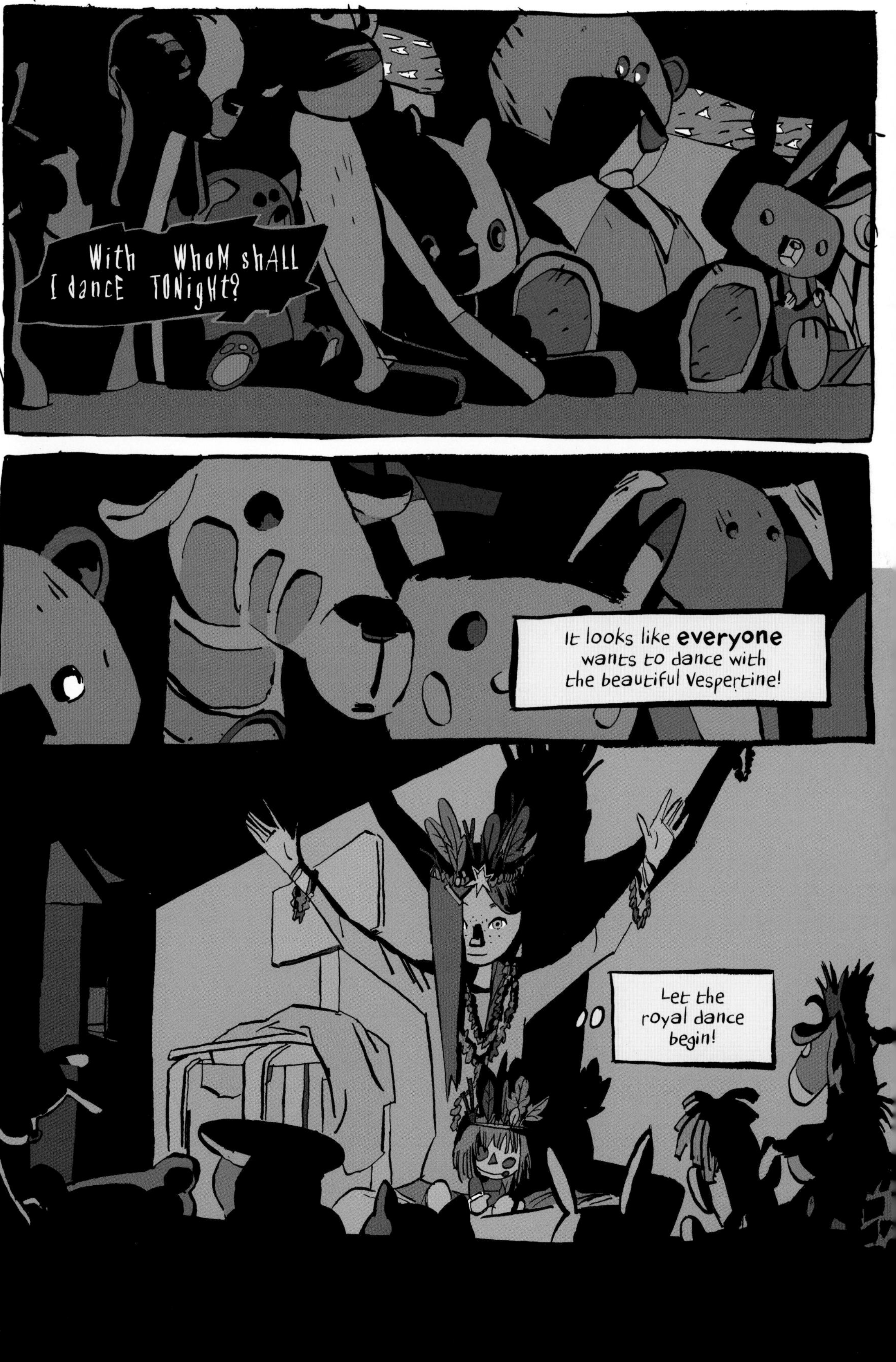

With whom shall I dance tonight?
It looks like **everyone** wants to dance with the beautiful Vespertine!
Let the royal dance begin!

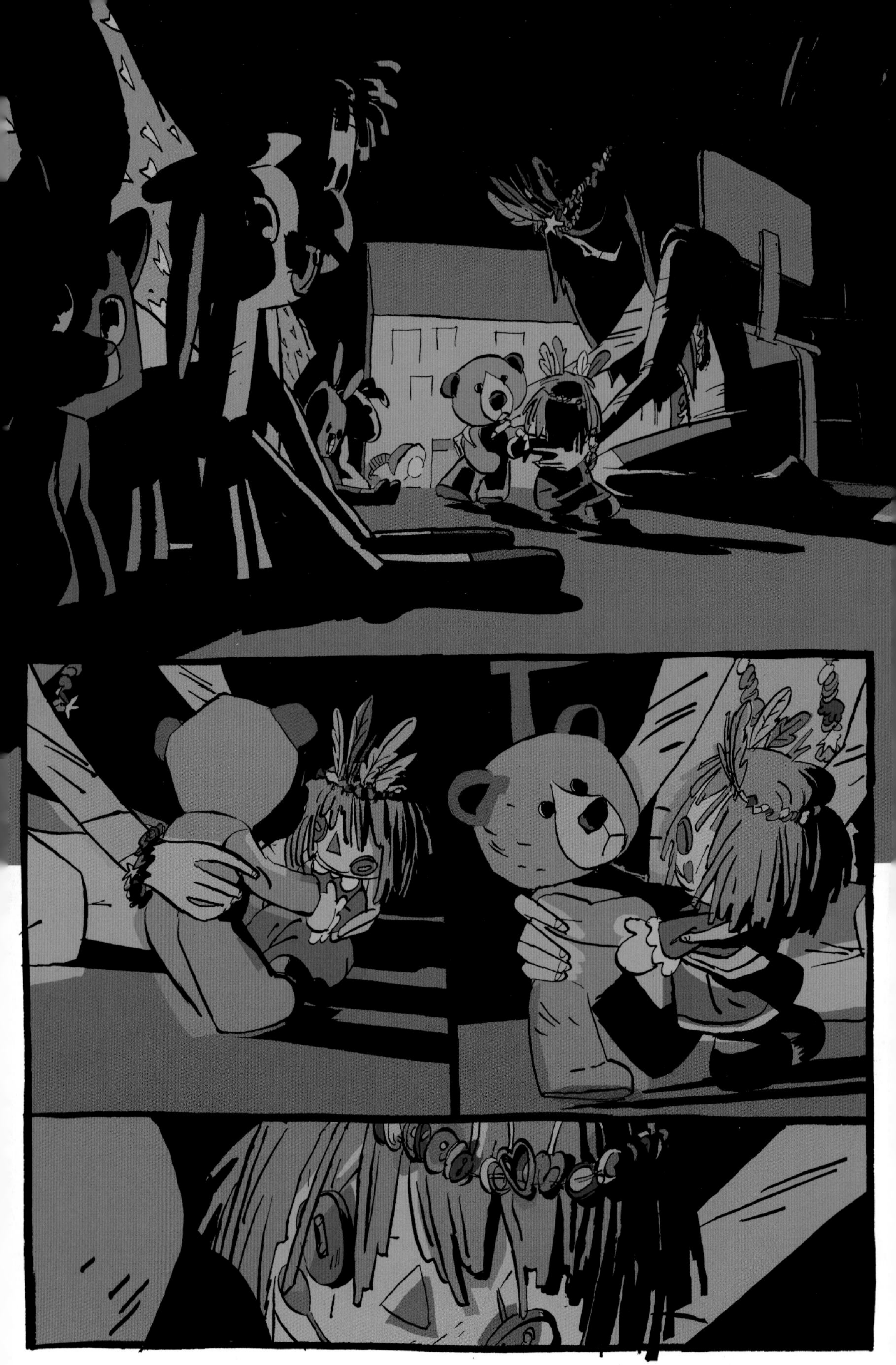

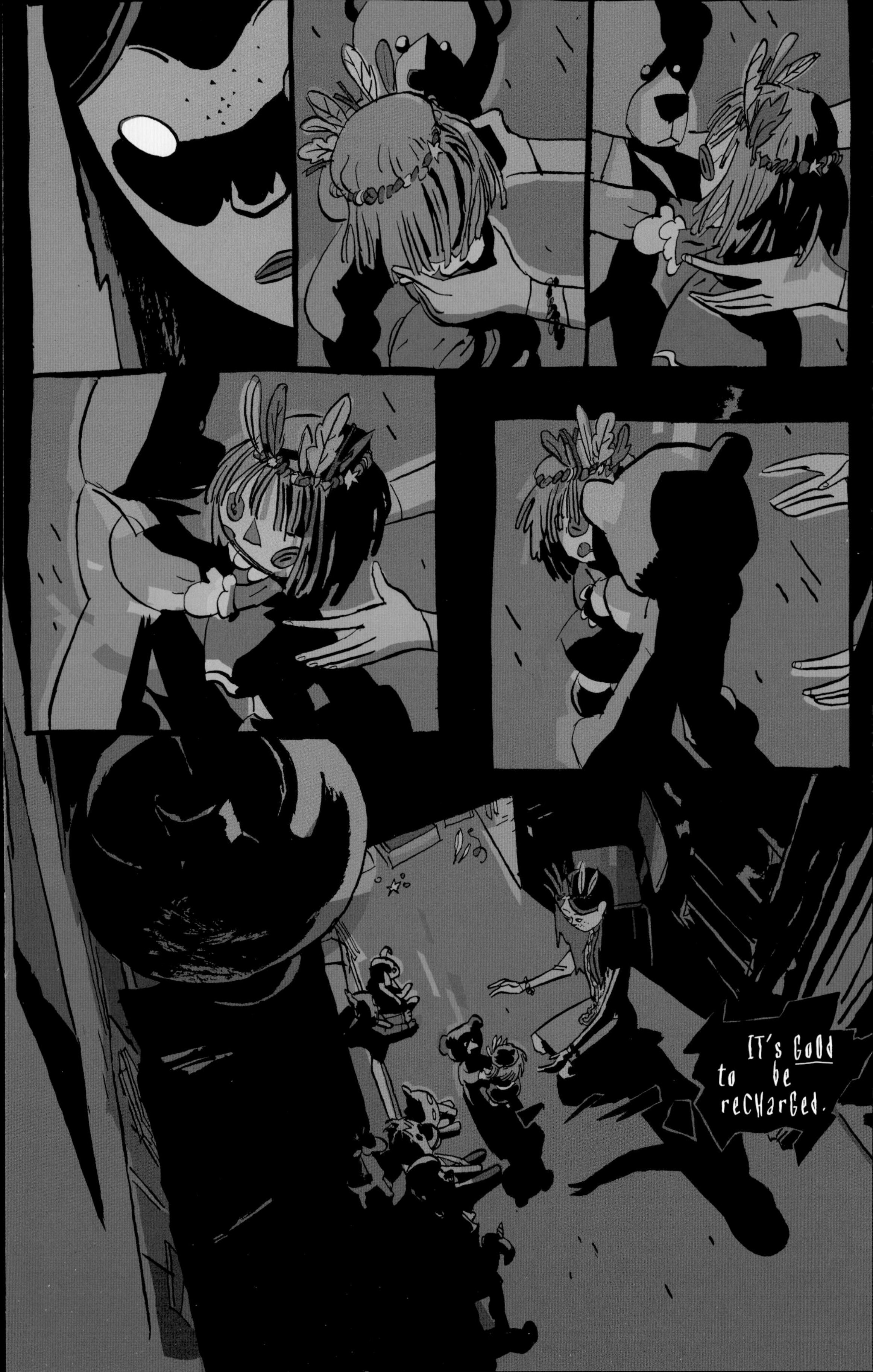
IT's GOOD to be reCHarGed.

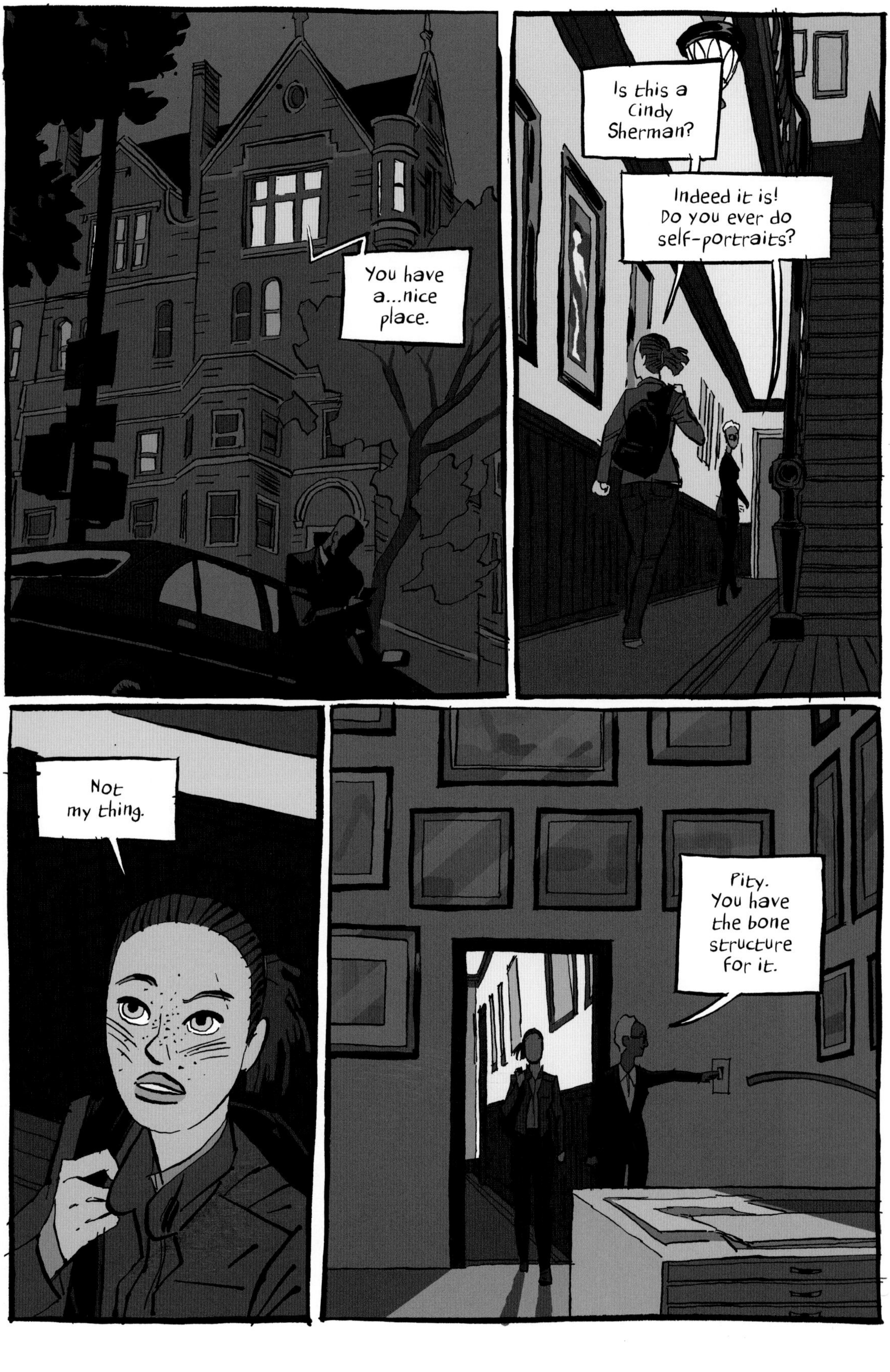
You have a...nice place.
Is this a Cindy Sherman?
Indeed it is! Do you ever do self-portraits?
Not my thing.
Pity. You have the bone structure for it.

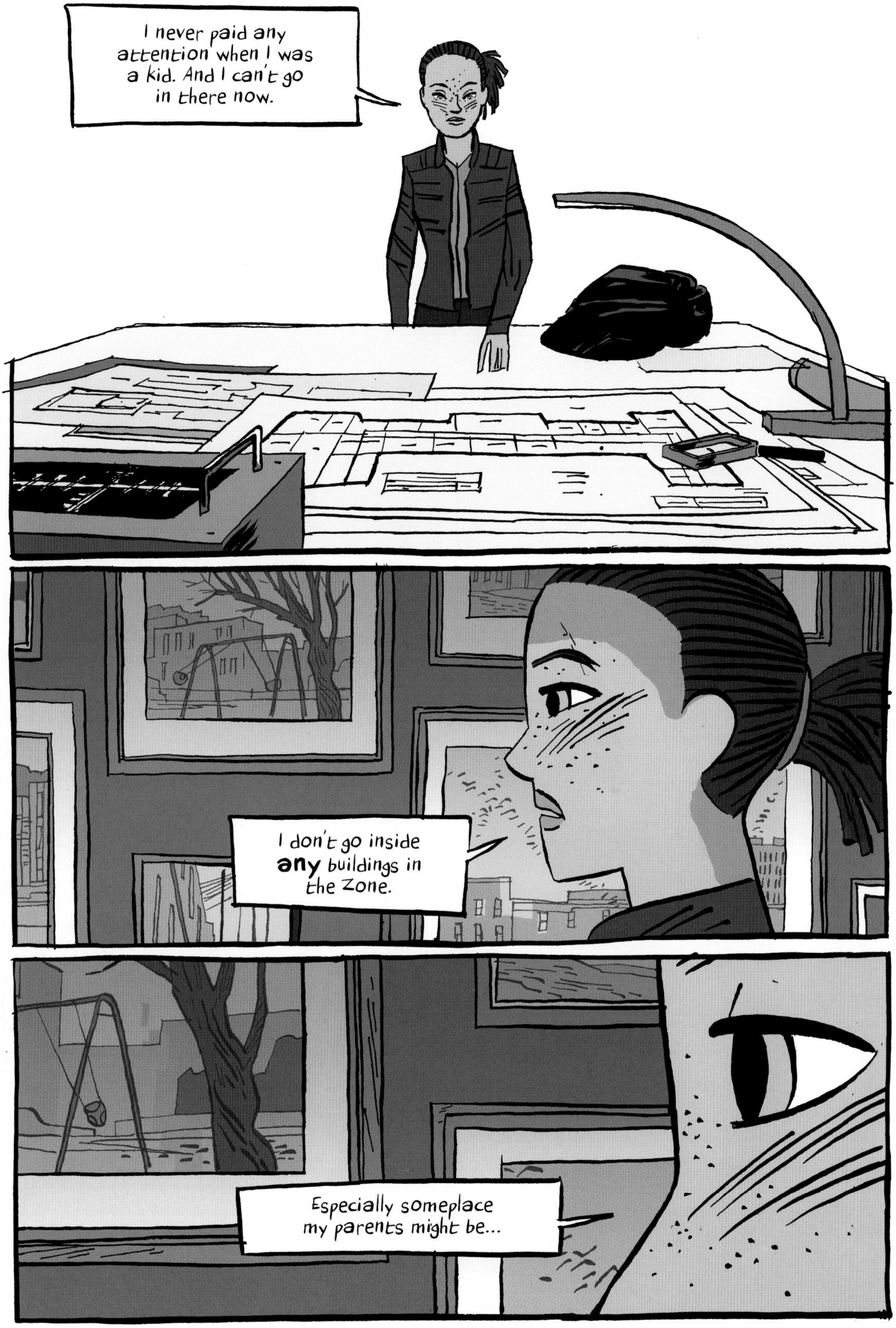
I never paid any attention when I was a kid. And I can't go in there now.
I don't go inside **any** buildings in the Zone.
Especially someplace my parents might be...

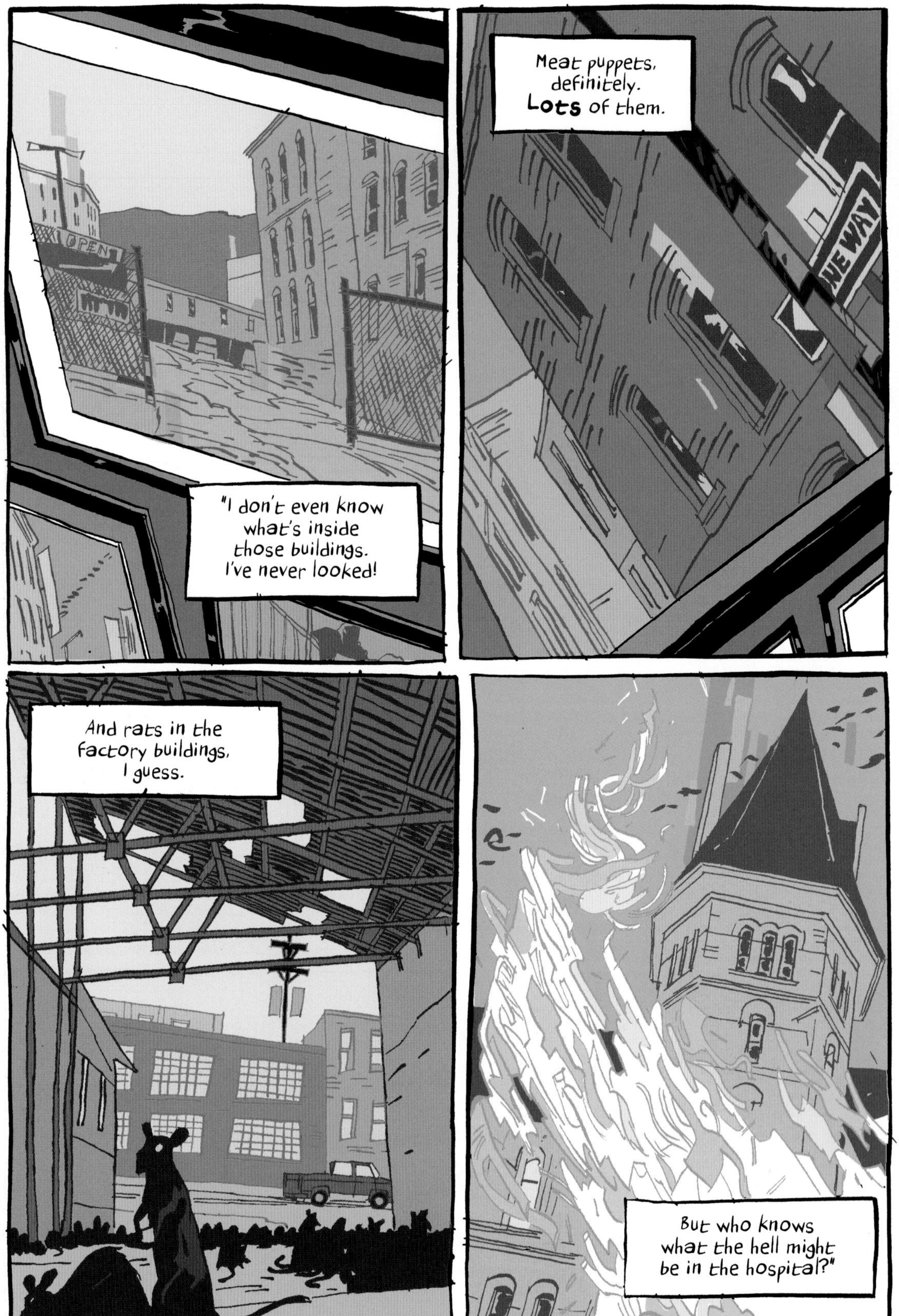
OPEN
"I don't even know what's inside those buildings. I've never looked!
Meat puppets, definitely. **Lots** of them.
And rats in the factory buildings, I guess.
But who knows what the hell might be in the hospital?"

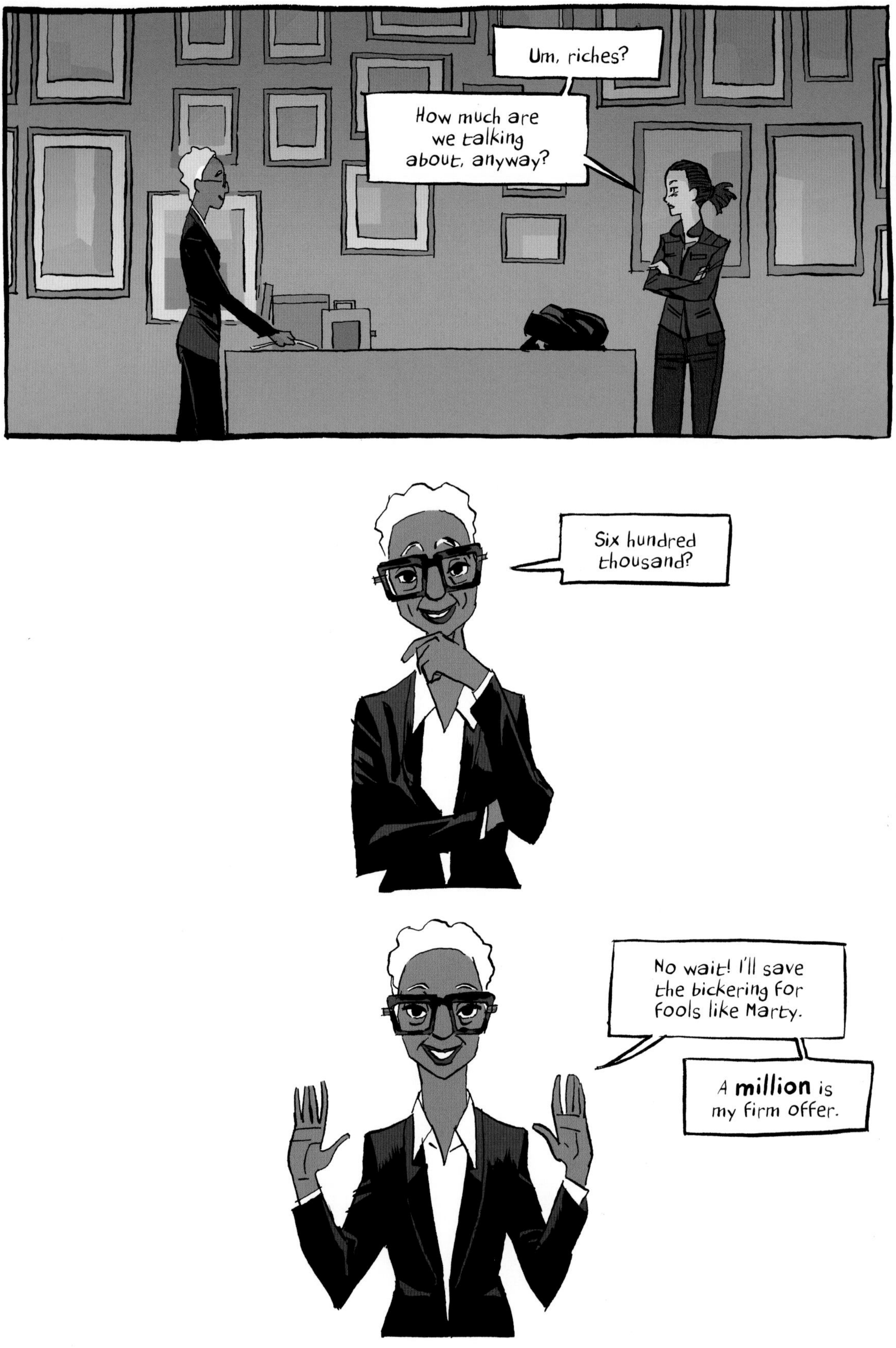
How much are we talking about, anyway?
Um, riches?
Six hundred thousand?
No wait! I'll save the bickering for fools like Marty.
A **million** is my firm offer.

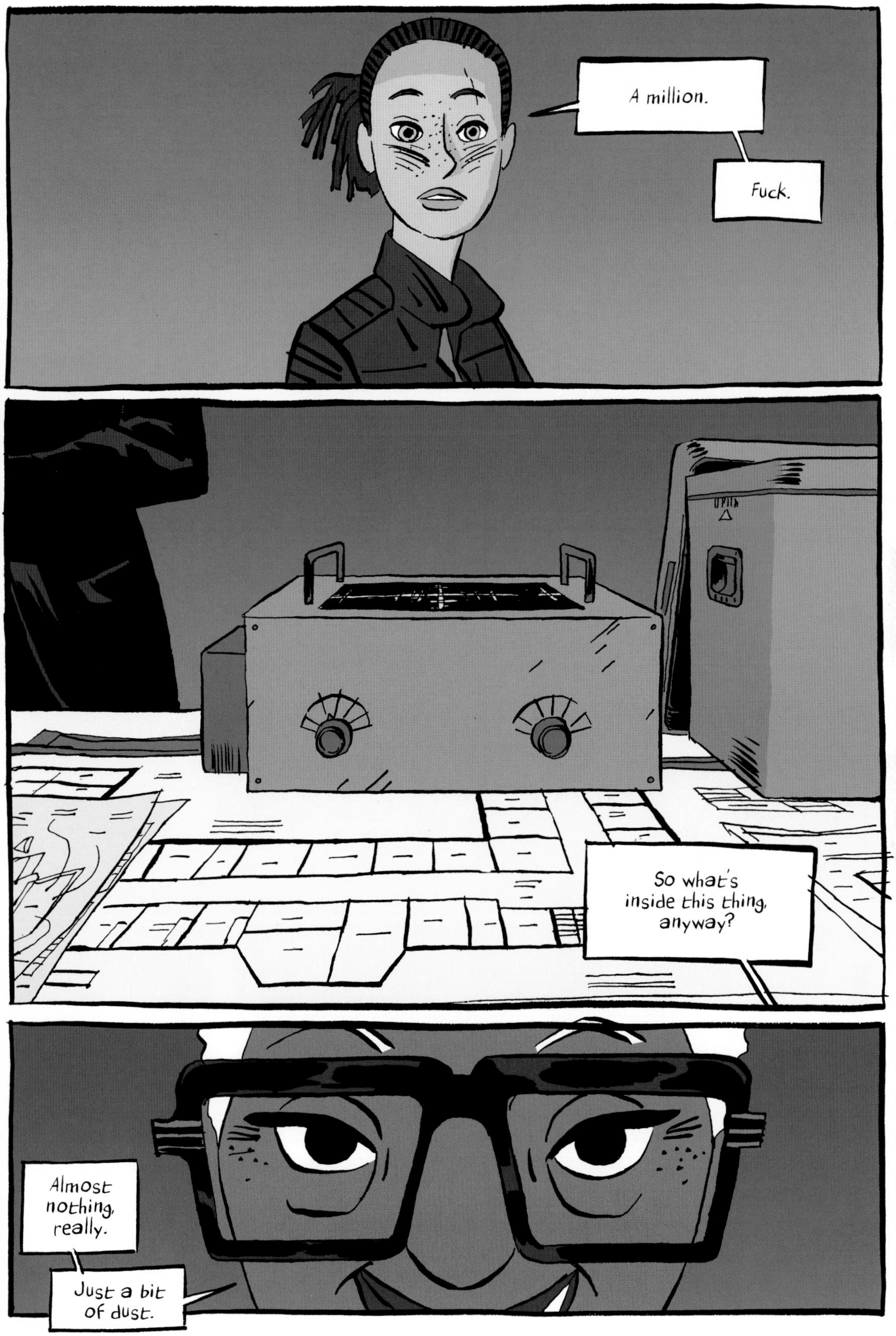
A million.
Fuck.
So what's inside this thing, anyway?
Almost nothing, really.
Just a bit of dust.

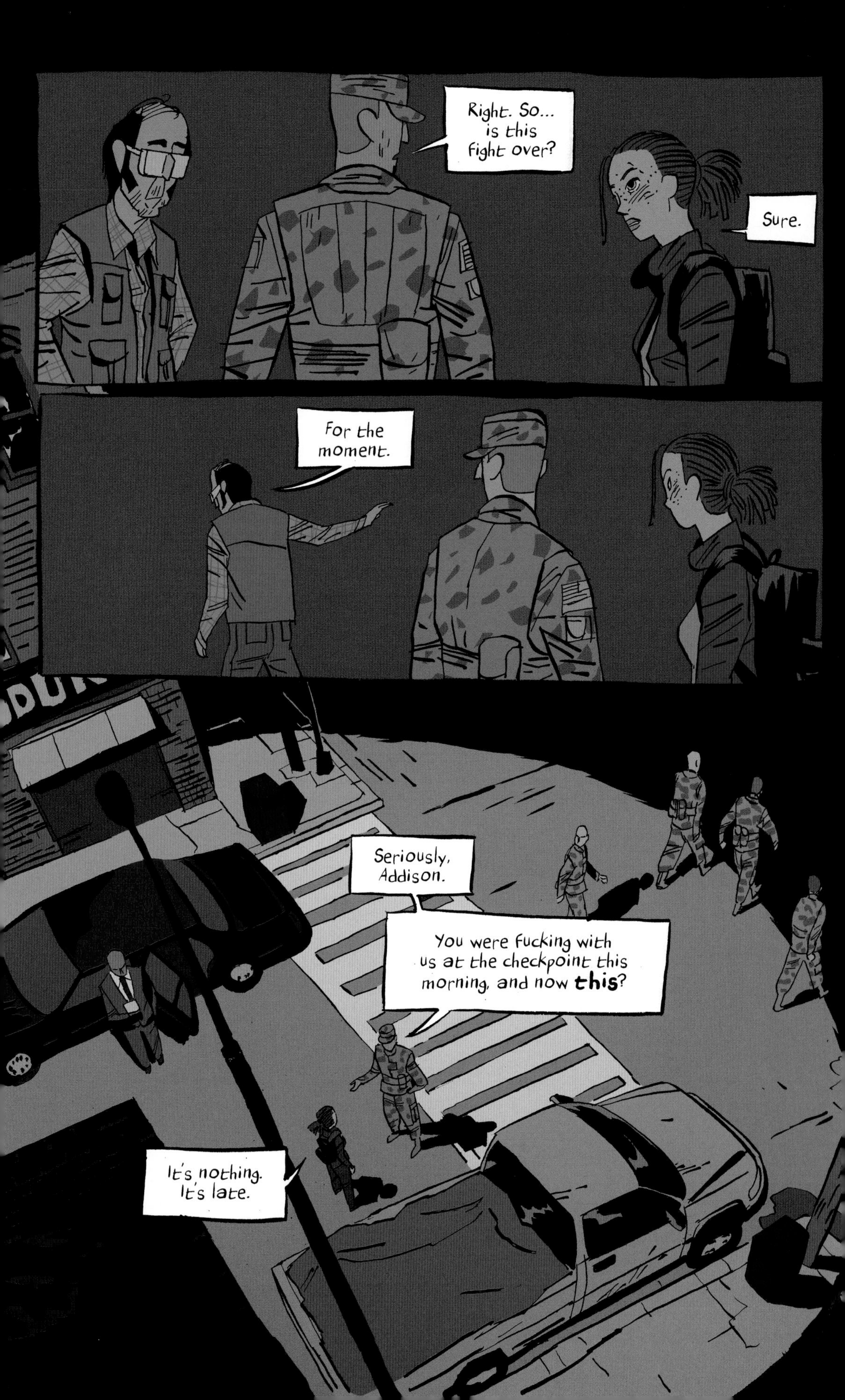
Right. So...
is this
fight over?
Sure.
For the
moment.
Seriously,
Addison.
You were fucking with
us at the checkpoint this
morning, and now **this**?
It's nothing.
It's late.

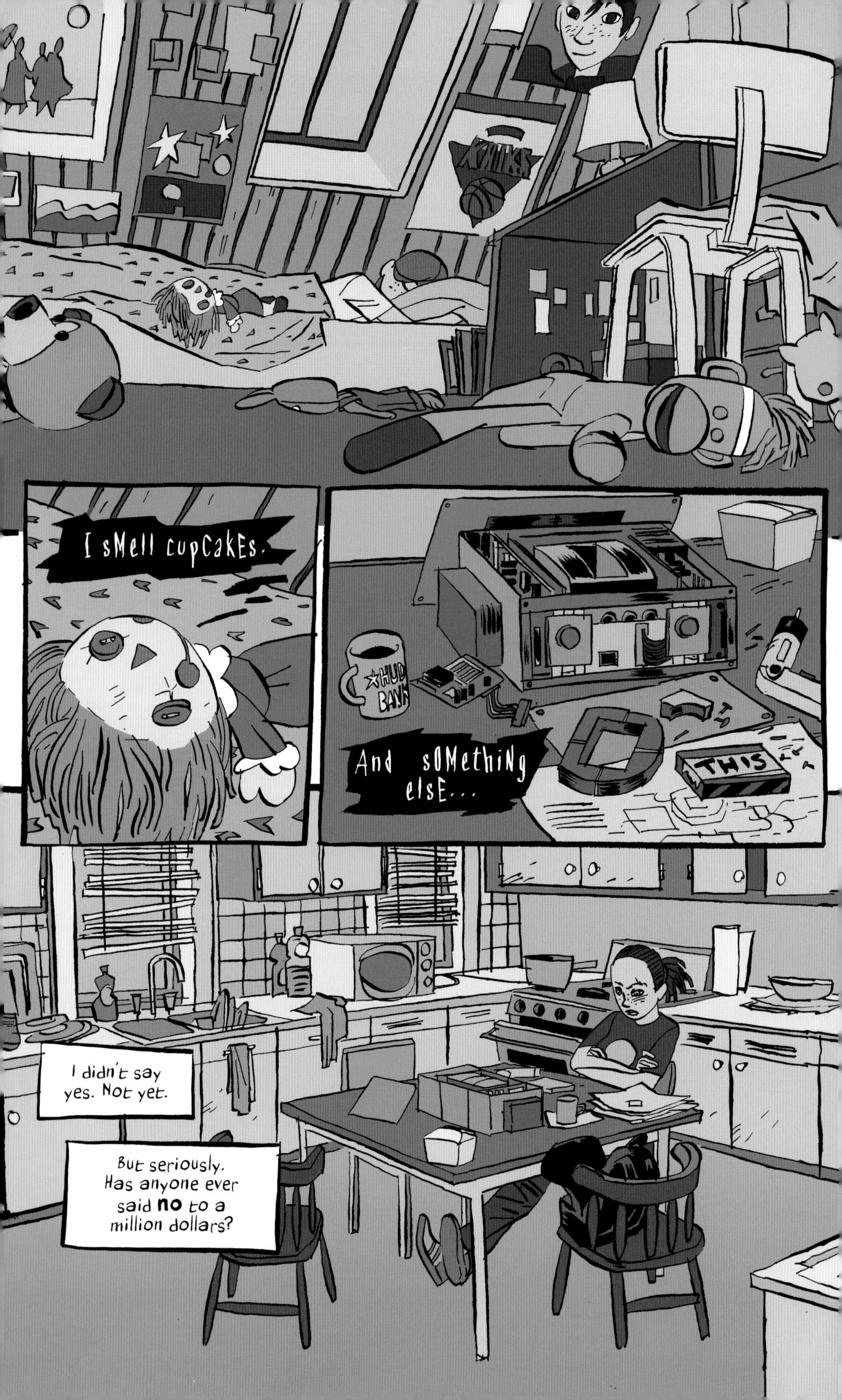
KNICKS
I sMell cupCakEs.
HUD BAY
And sOMethiNg elsE...
THIS
I didn't say yes. Not yet.
But seriously. Has anyone ever said **no** to a million dollars?

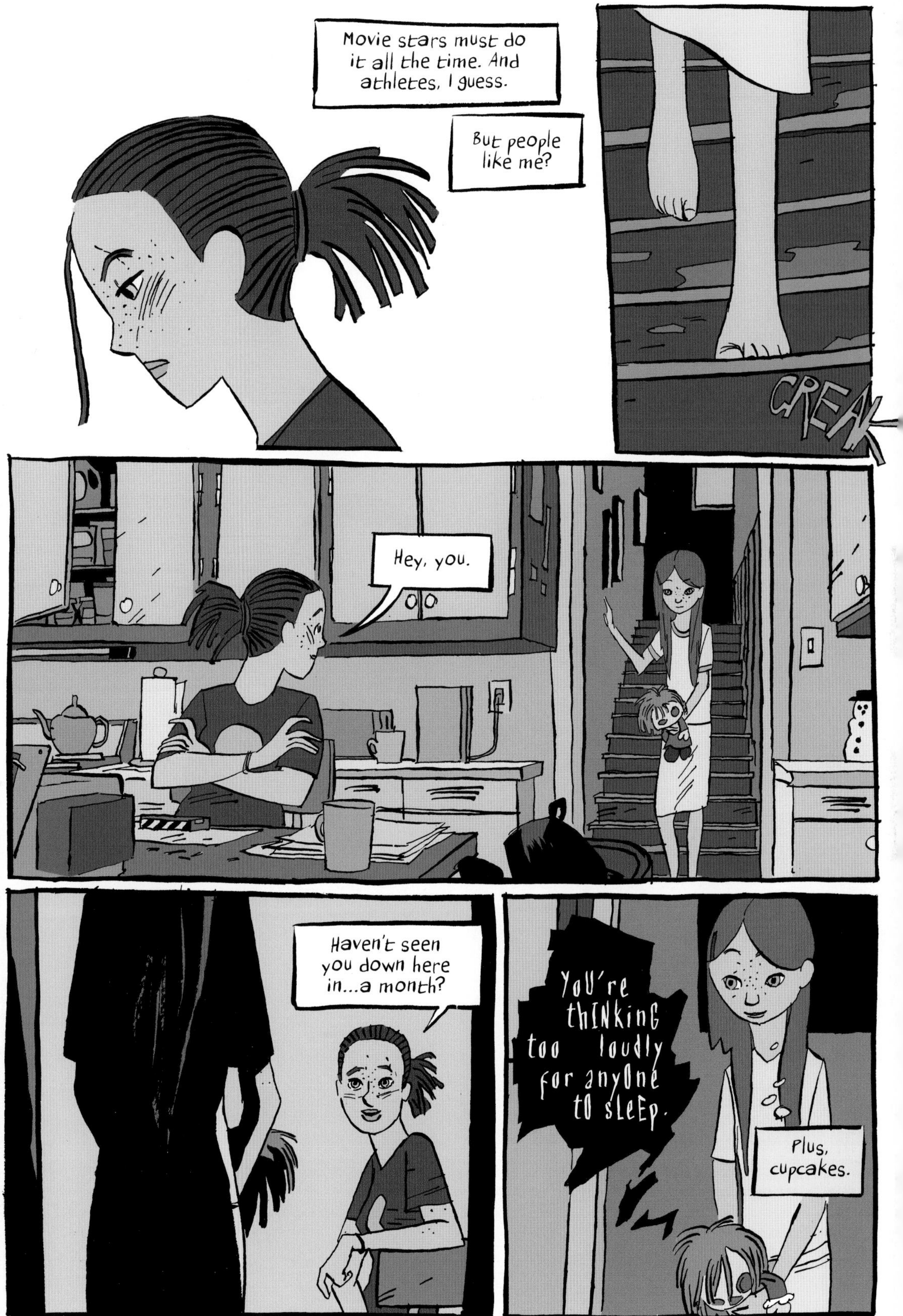

Movie stars must do it all the time. And athletes, I guess.
But people like me?
CREAK
Hey, you.
Haven't seen you down here in...a month?
YOU'RE THINKING TOO LOUDLY FOR ANYONE TO SLEEP.
Plus, cupcakes.

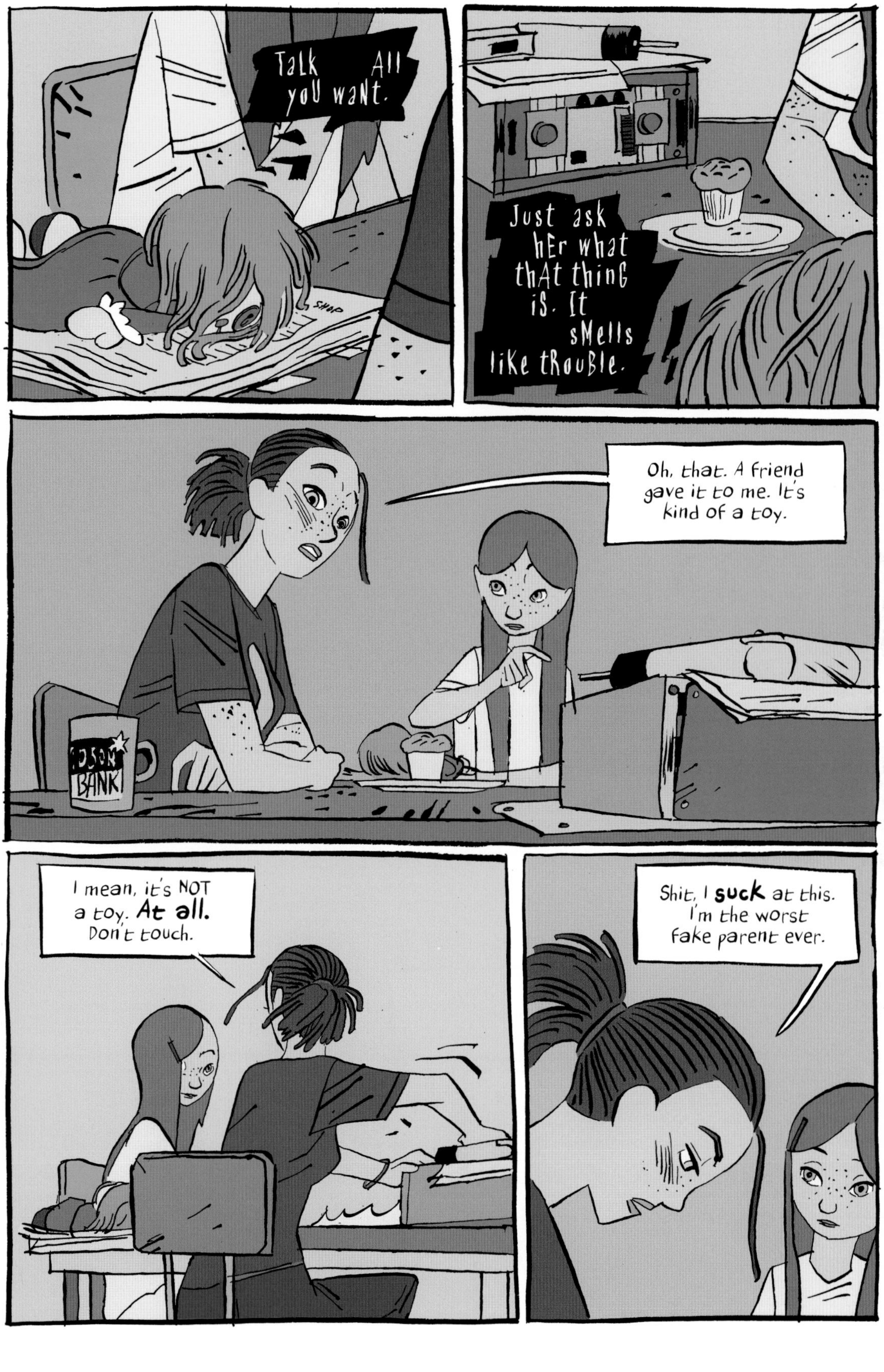
Talk All you want.
Just ask her what that thing is. It smells like trouble.
Oh, that. A friend gave it to me. It's kind of a toy.
I mean, it's NOT a toy. At all. Don't touch.
Shit, I suck at this. I'm the worst fake parent ever.

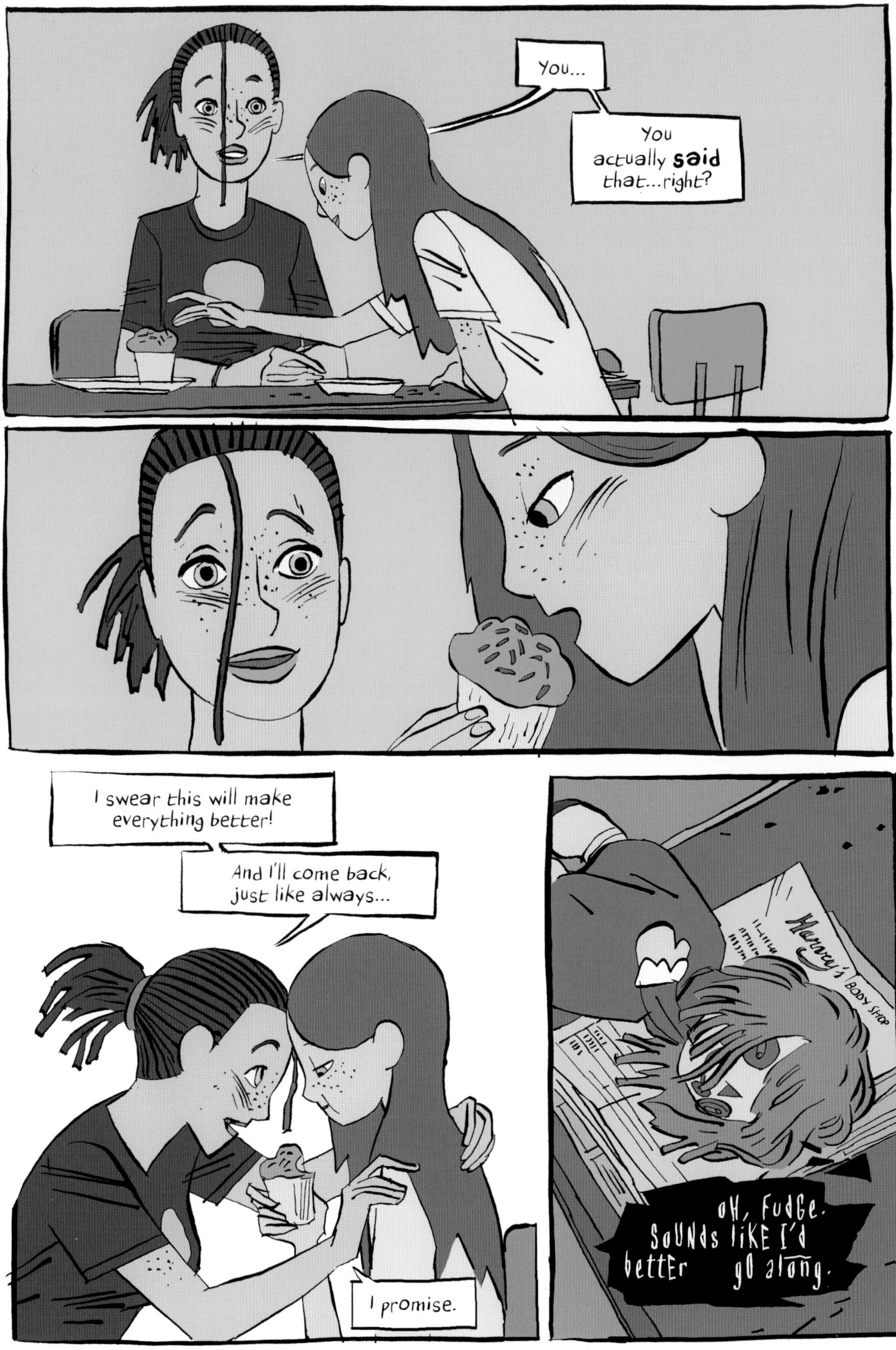
You...
You actually **said** that...right?
I swear this will make everything better!
And I'll come back, just like always...
I promise.
BODY SHOP
OH, FUDGE. SOUNDS LIKE I'D BETTER GO ALONG.

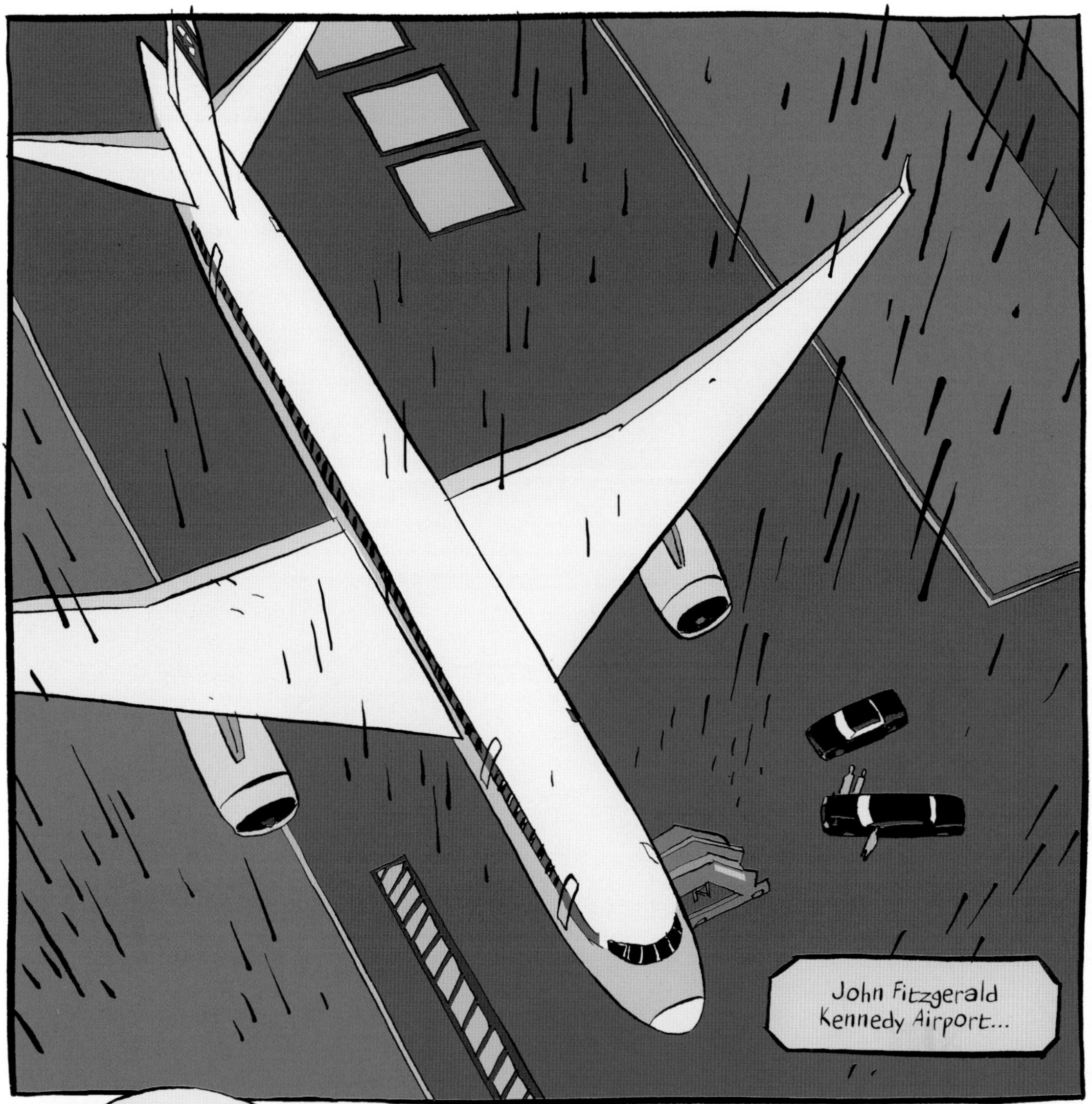
John Fitzgerald Kennedy Airport...

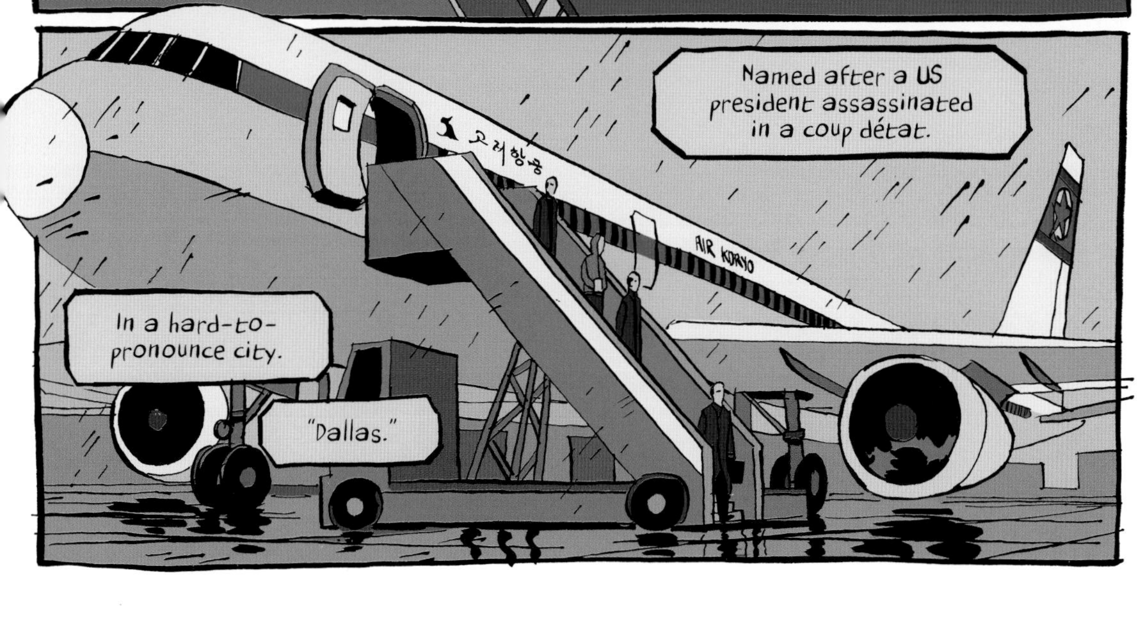
Named after a US president assassinated in a coup détat.
고려항공
AIR KORYO
In a hard-to-pronounce city.
"Dallas."

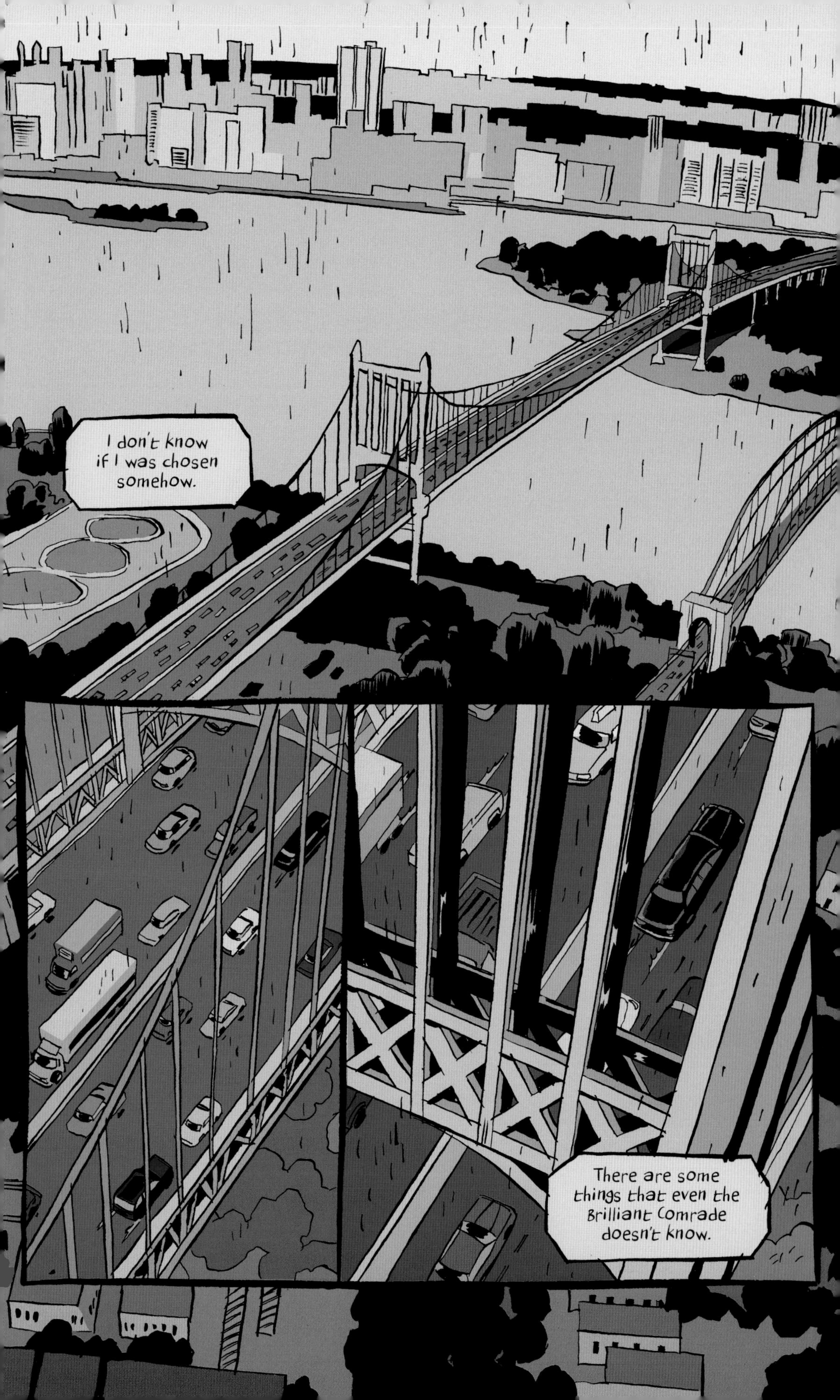
I don't know if I was chosen somehow.
There are some things that even the Brilliant Comrade doesn't know.

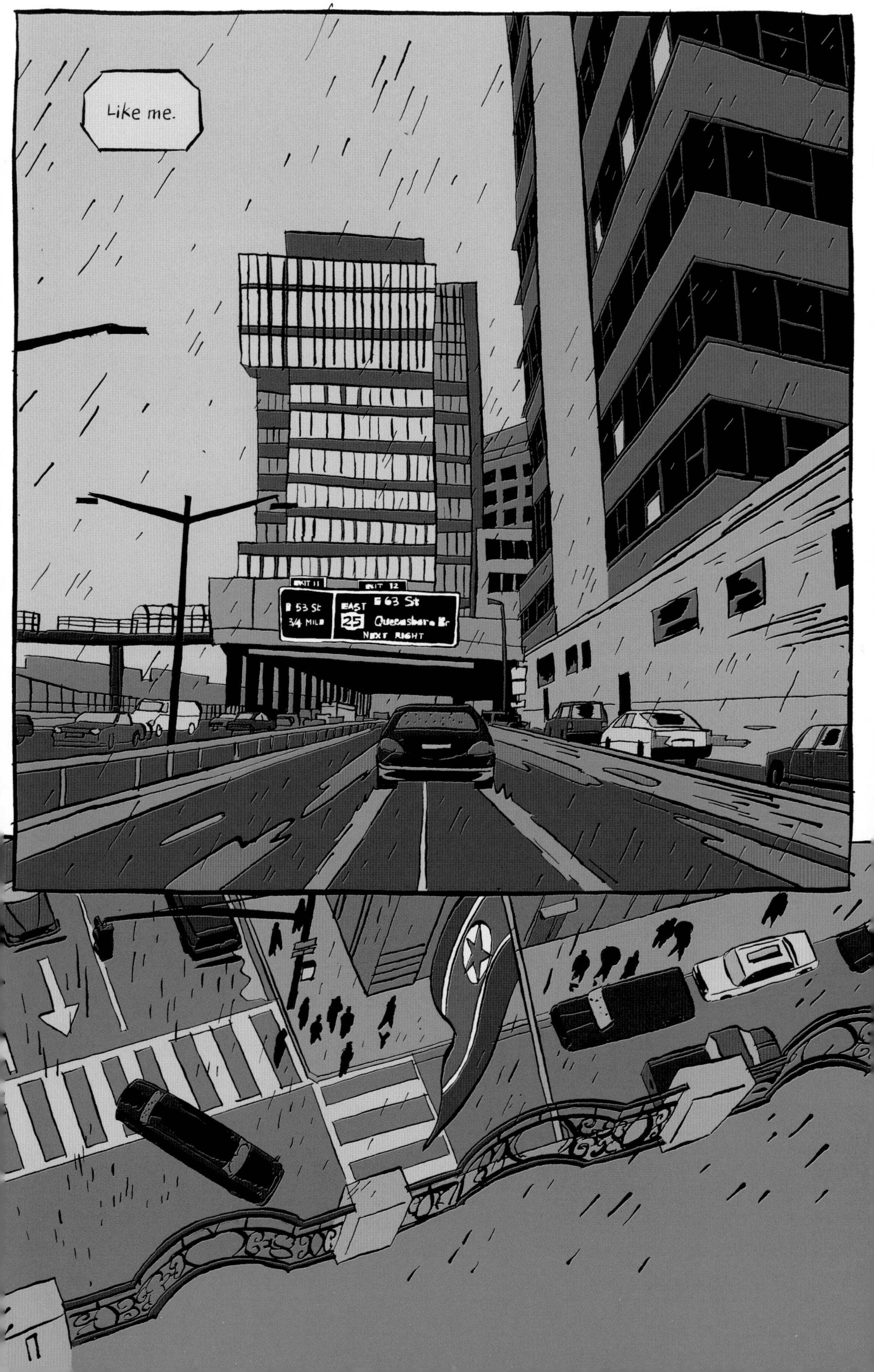
Like me.
EXIT 11
EXIT 12
53 St
3/4
EAST
63 St
25
NEXT RIGHT

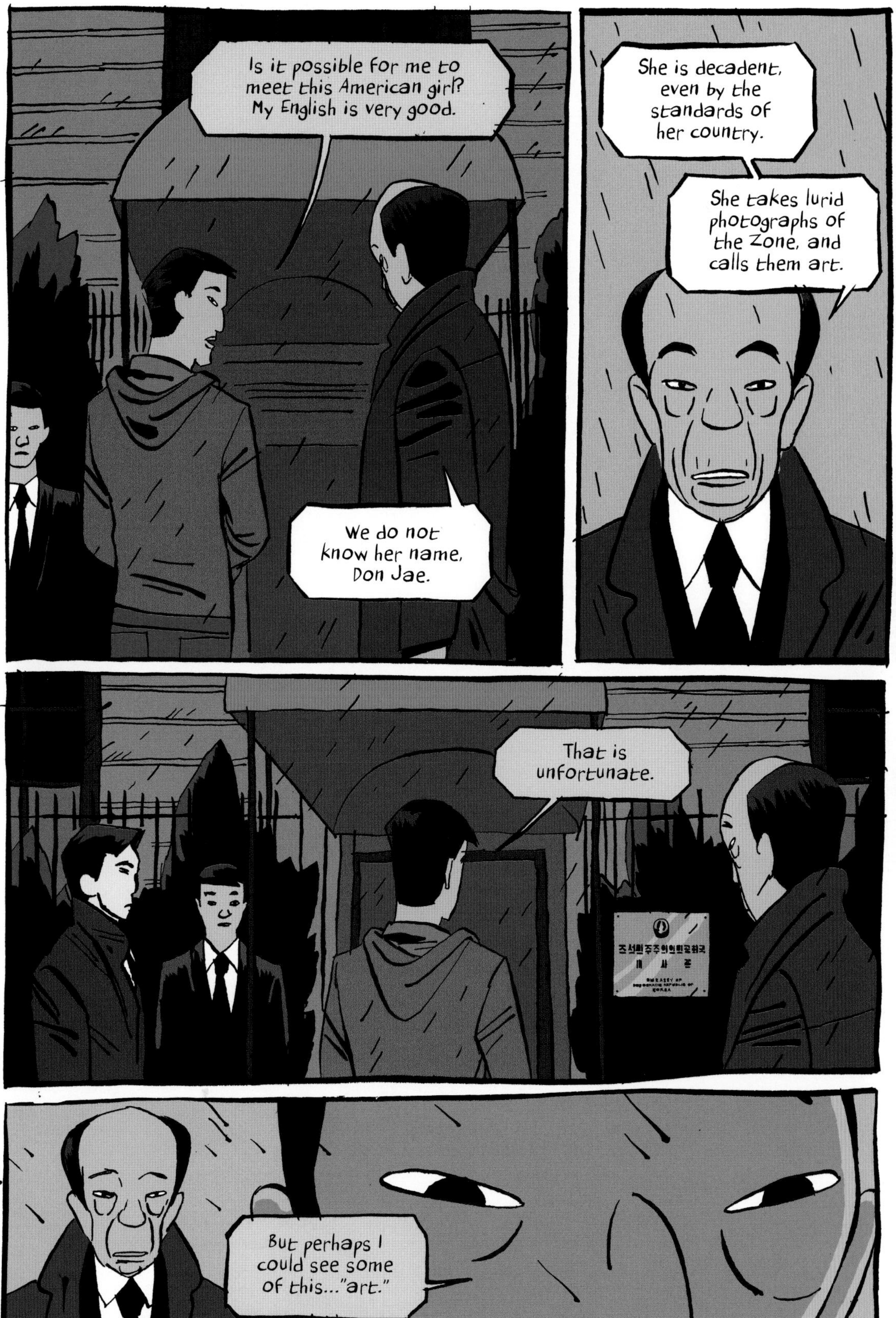
Is it possible for me to meet this American girl? My English is very good.
We do not know her name, Don Jae.
She is decadent, even by the standards of her country.
She takes lurid photographs of the Zone, and calls them art.
That is unfortunate.
But perhaps I could see some of this..."art."

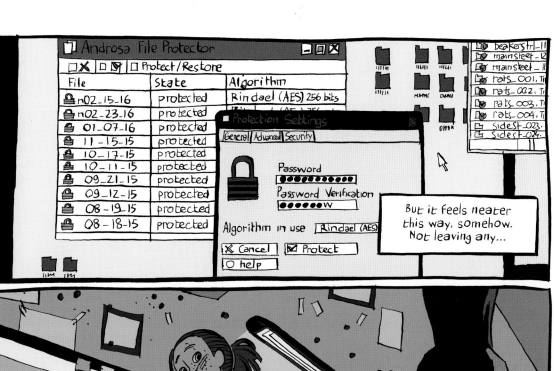

But it feels neater this way, somehow. Not leaving any...

loose ends.

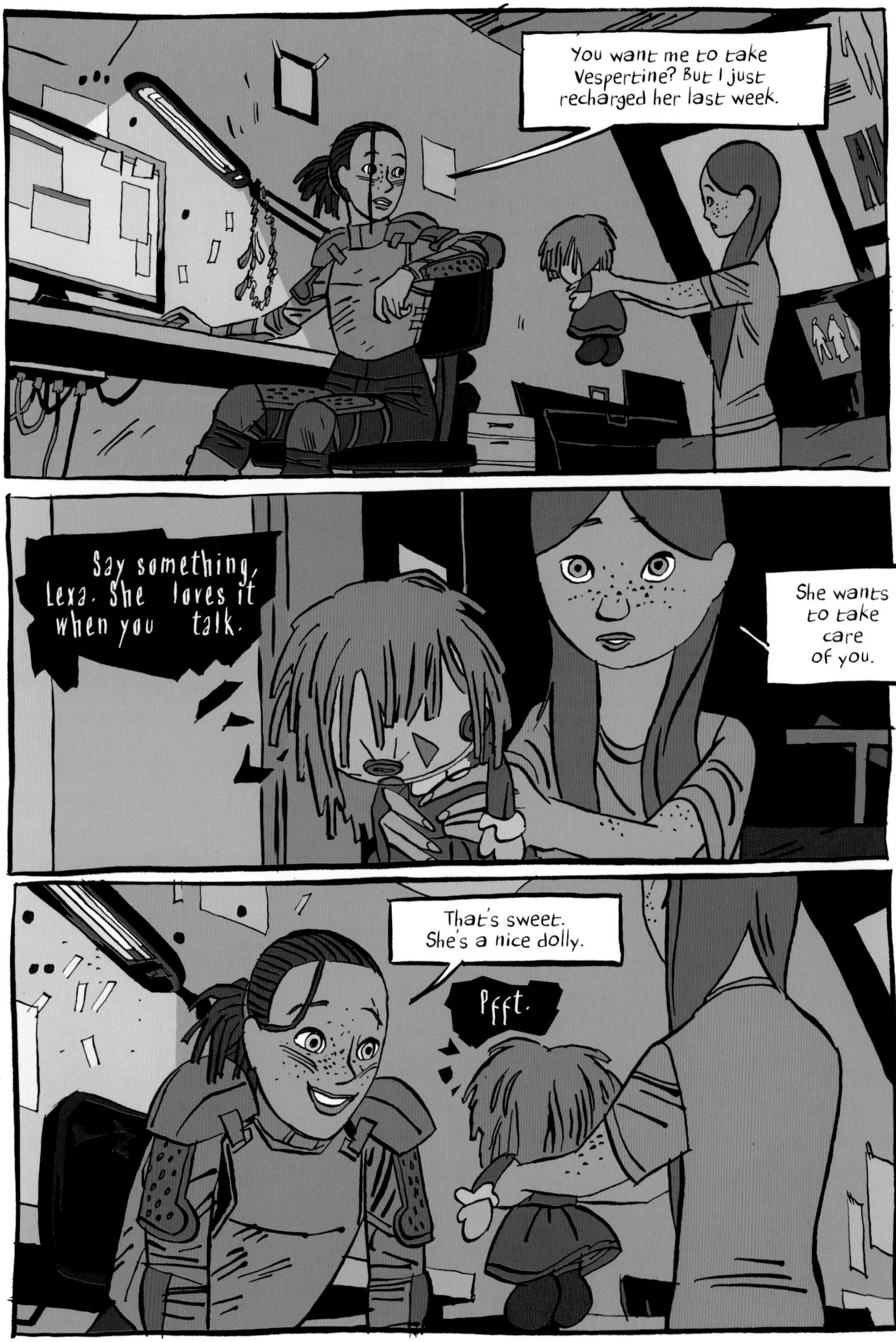
You want me to take Vespertine? But I just recharged her last week.
Say something, Lexa. She loves it when you talk.
She wants to take care of you.
That's sweet. She's a nice dolly.
Pfft.

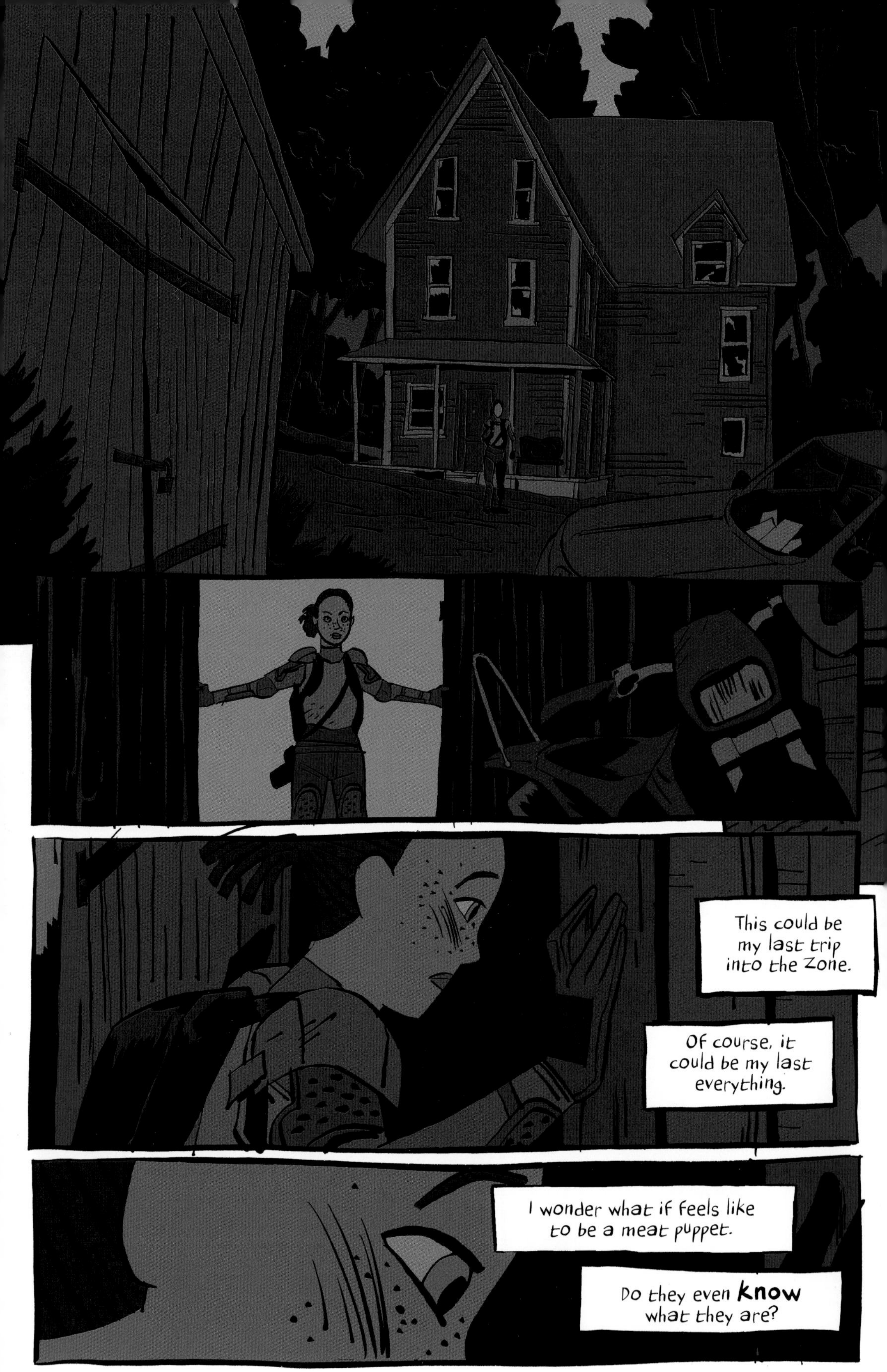
This could be my last trip into the Zone.
Of course, it could be my last everything.
I wonder what if feels like to be a meat puppet.
Do they even **know** what they are?

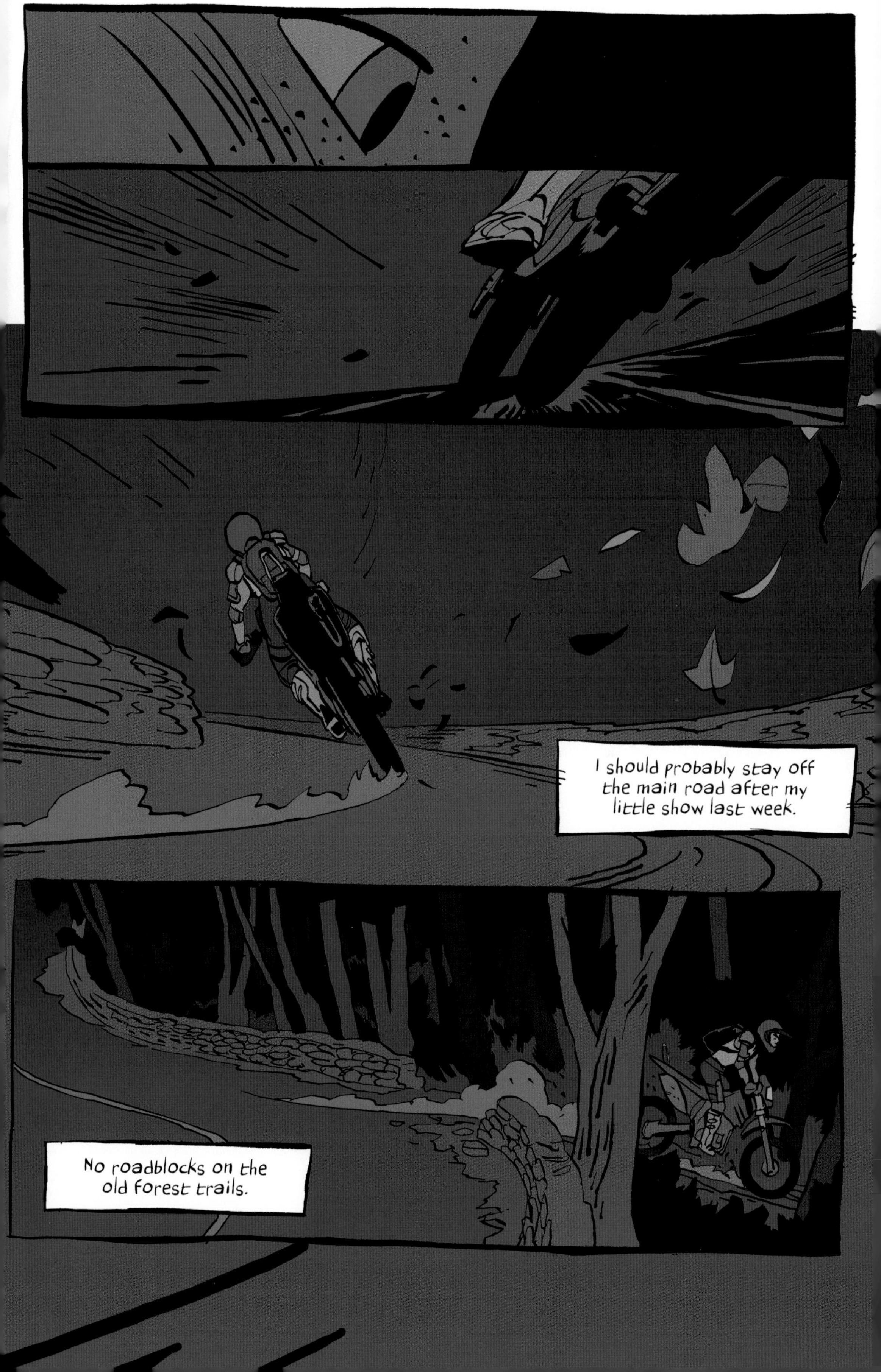
I should probably stay off the main road after my little show last week.
No roadblocks on the old forest trails.

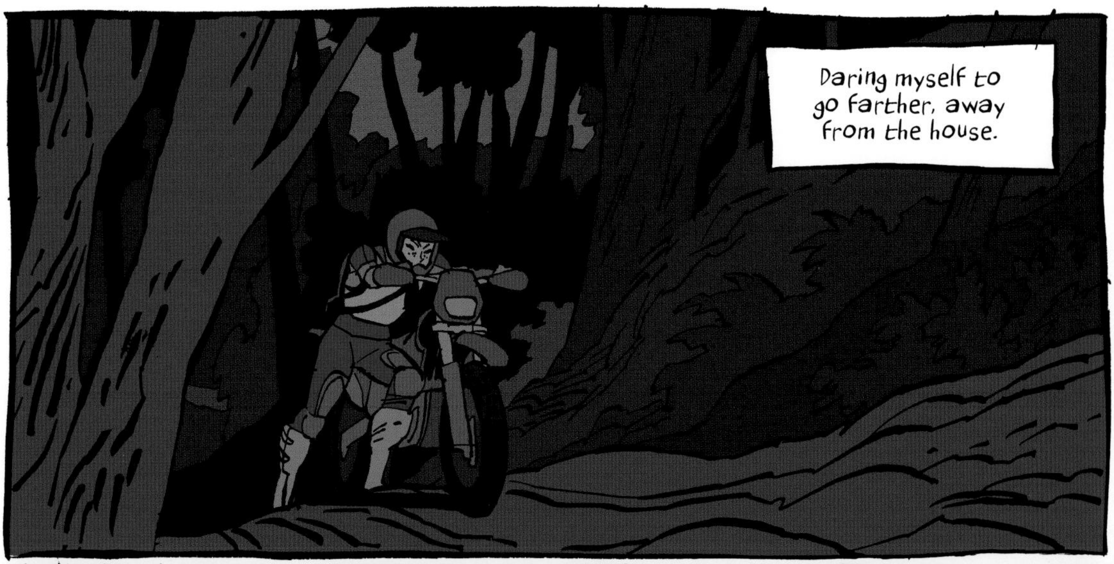
Daring myself to go farther, away from the house.

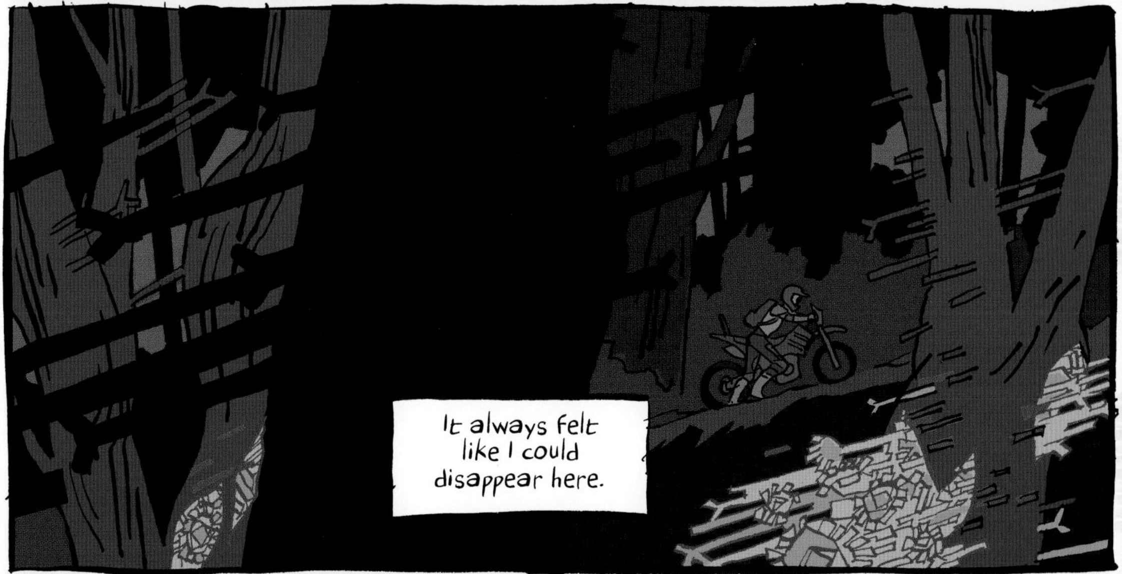
It always felt like I could disappear here.

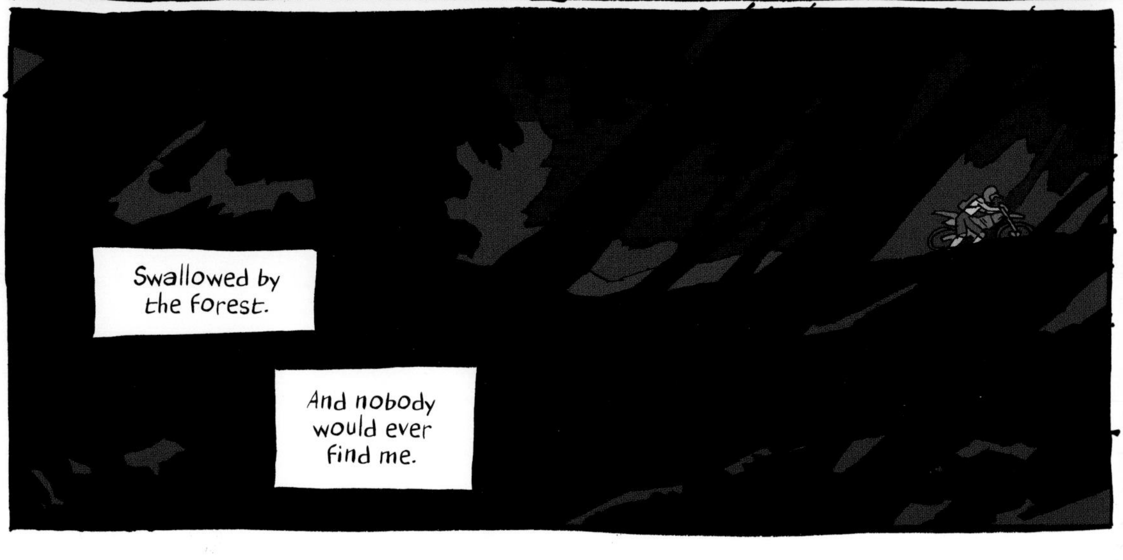
Swallowed by the forest.
And nobody would ever find me.

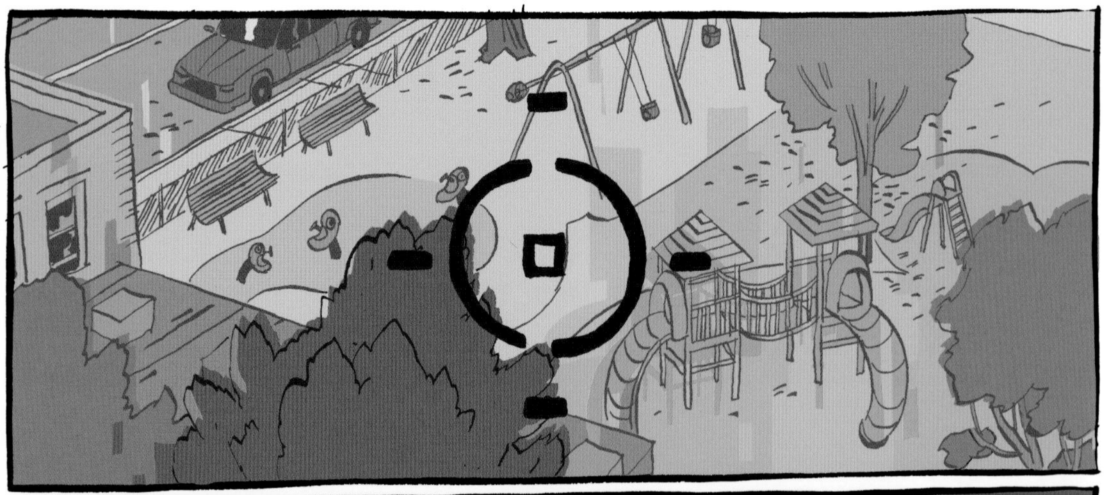

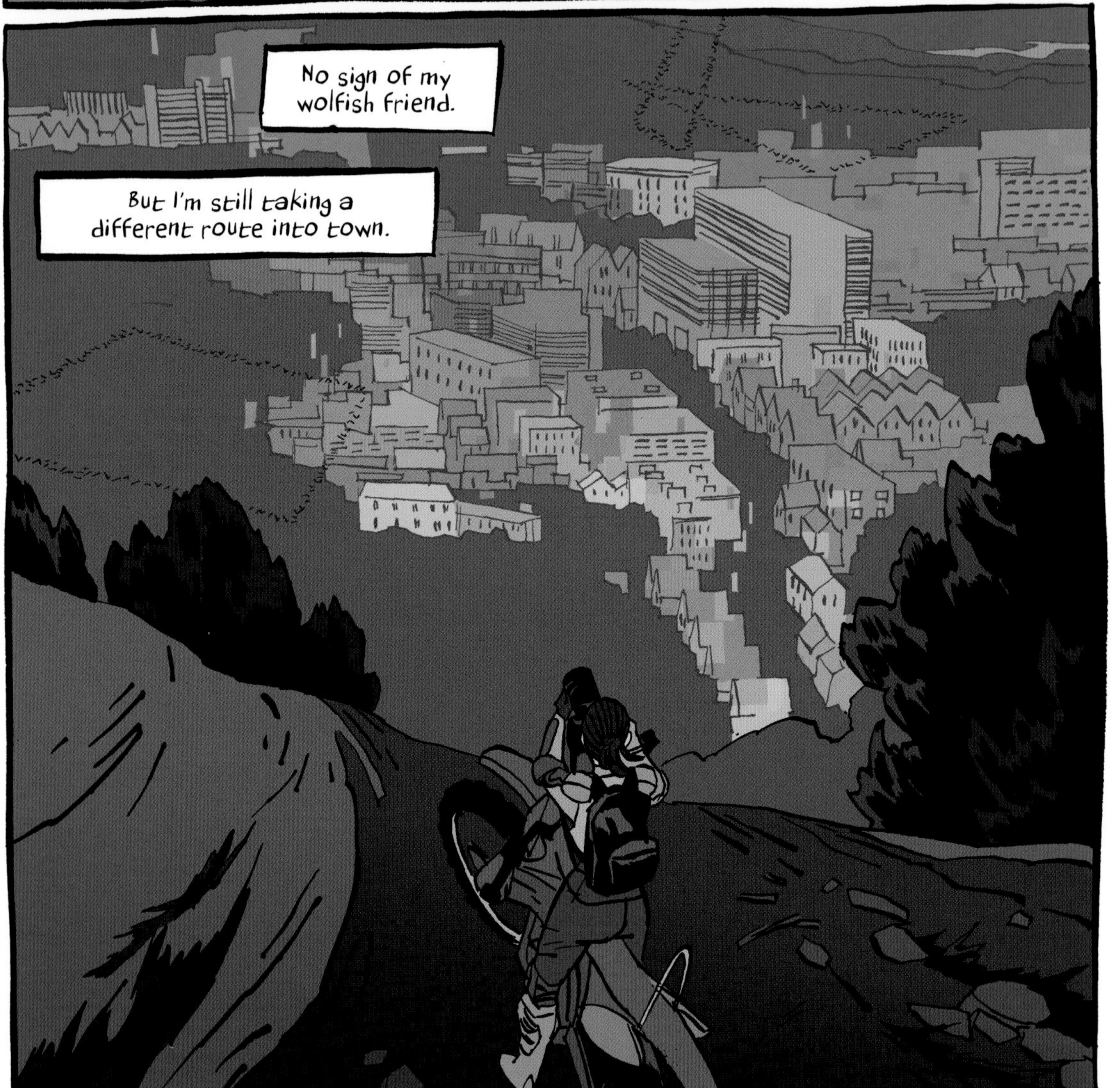
No sign of my wolfish friend.
But I'm still taking a different route into town.

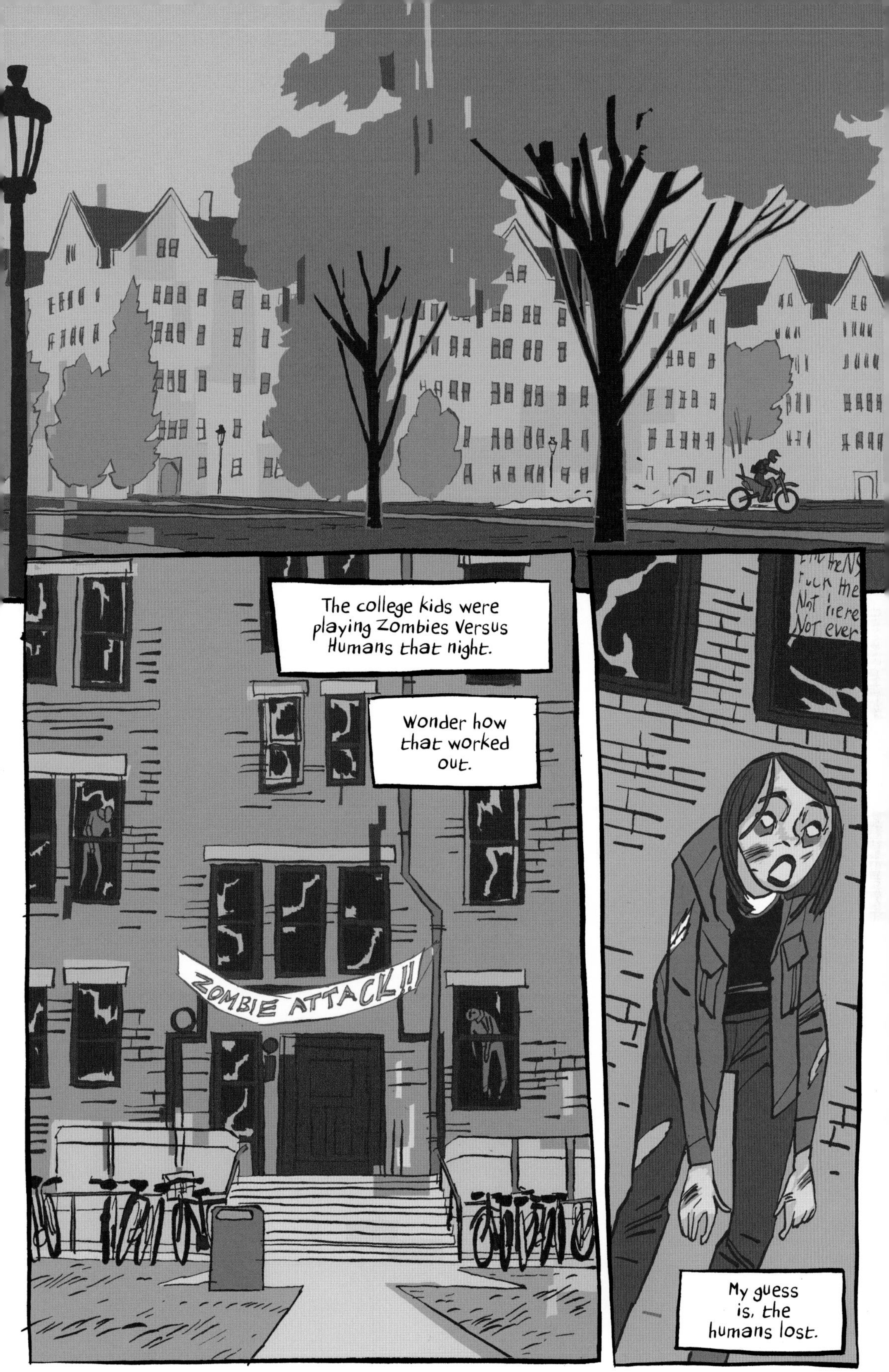
The college kids were playing Zombies Versus Humans that night.
Wonder how that worked out.
ZOMBIE ATTACK!!
My guess is, the humans lost.

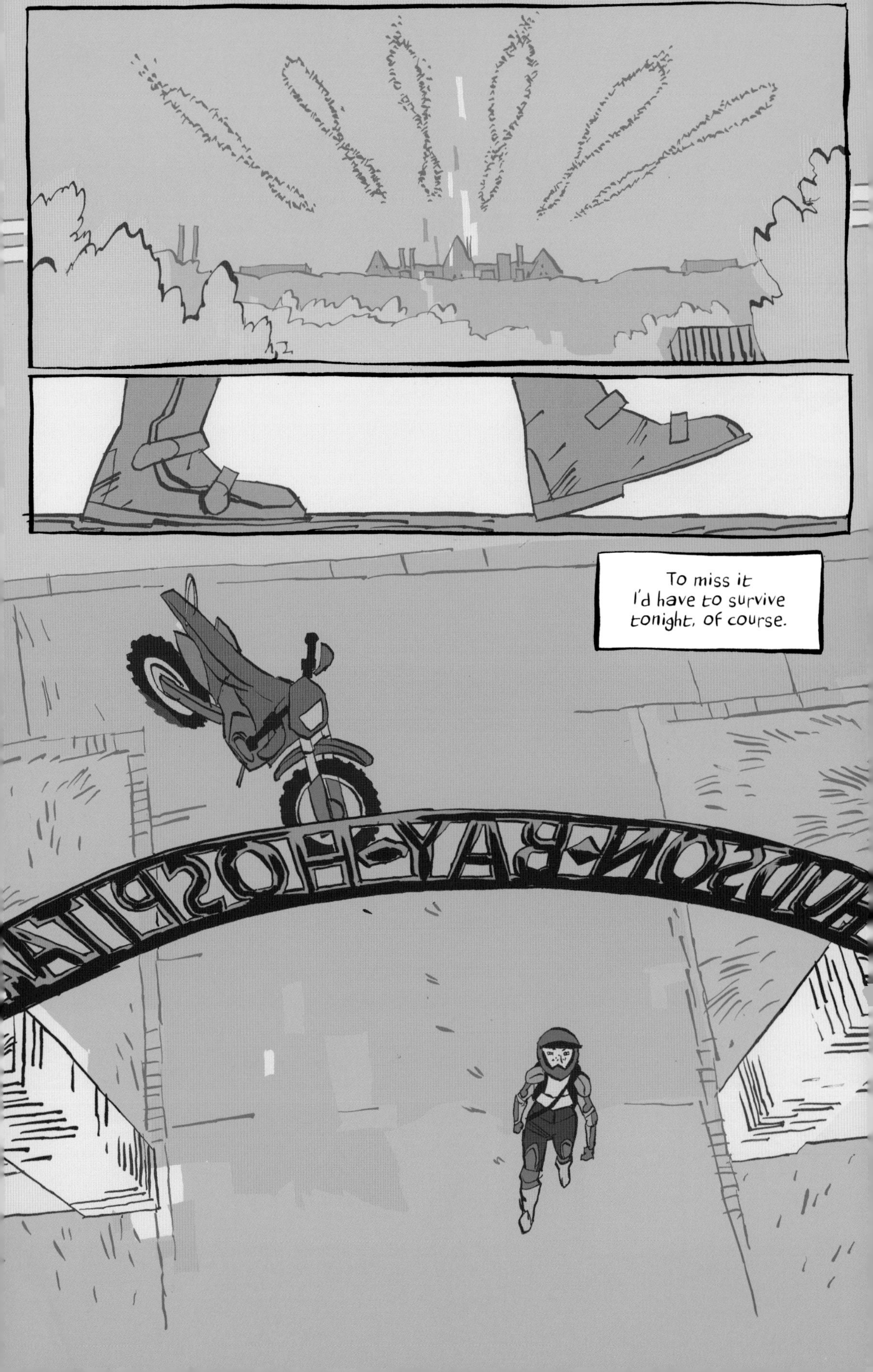
To miss it I'd have to survive tonight, of course.

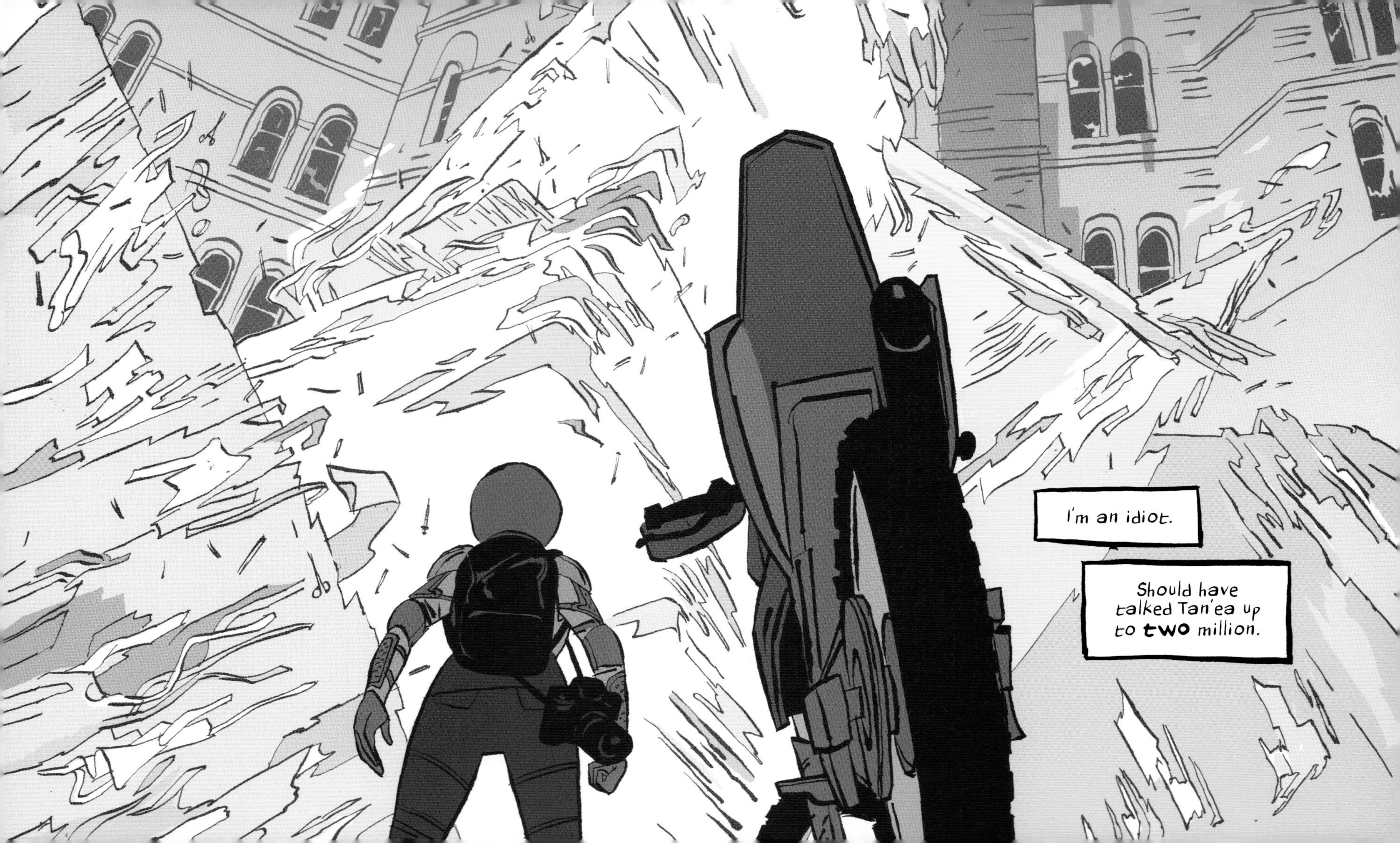
I'm an idiot.
Should have talked Tan'ea up to **two** million.

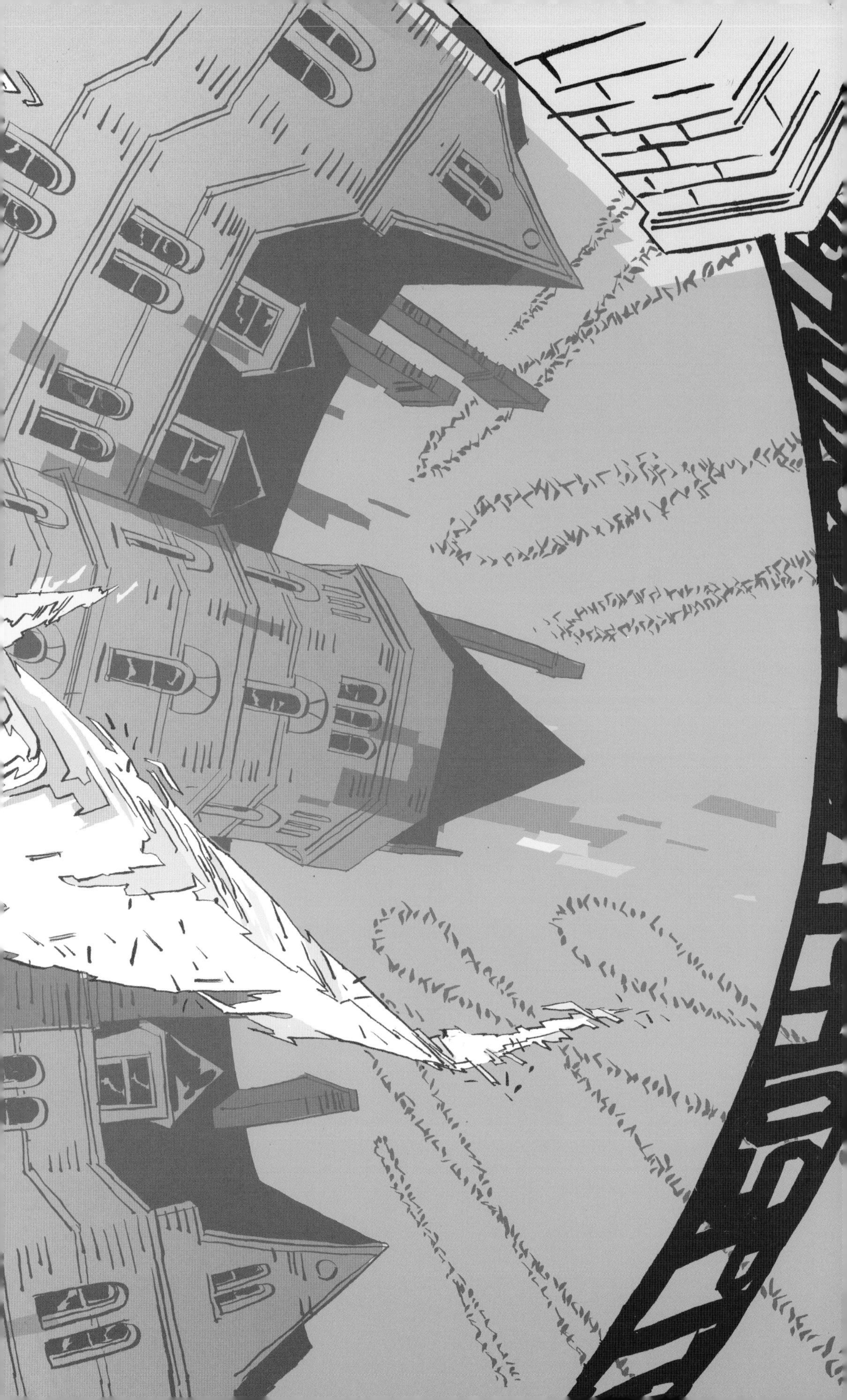

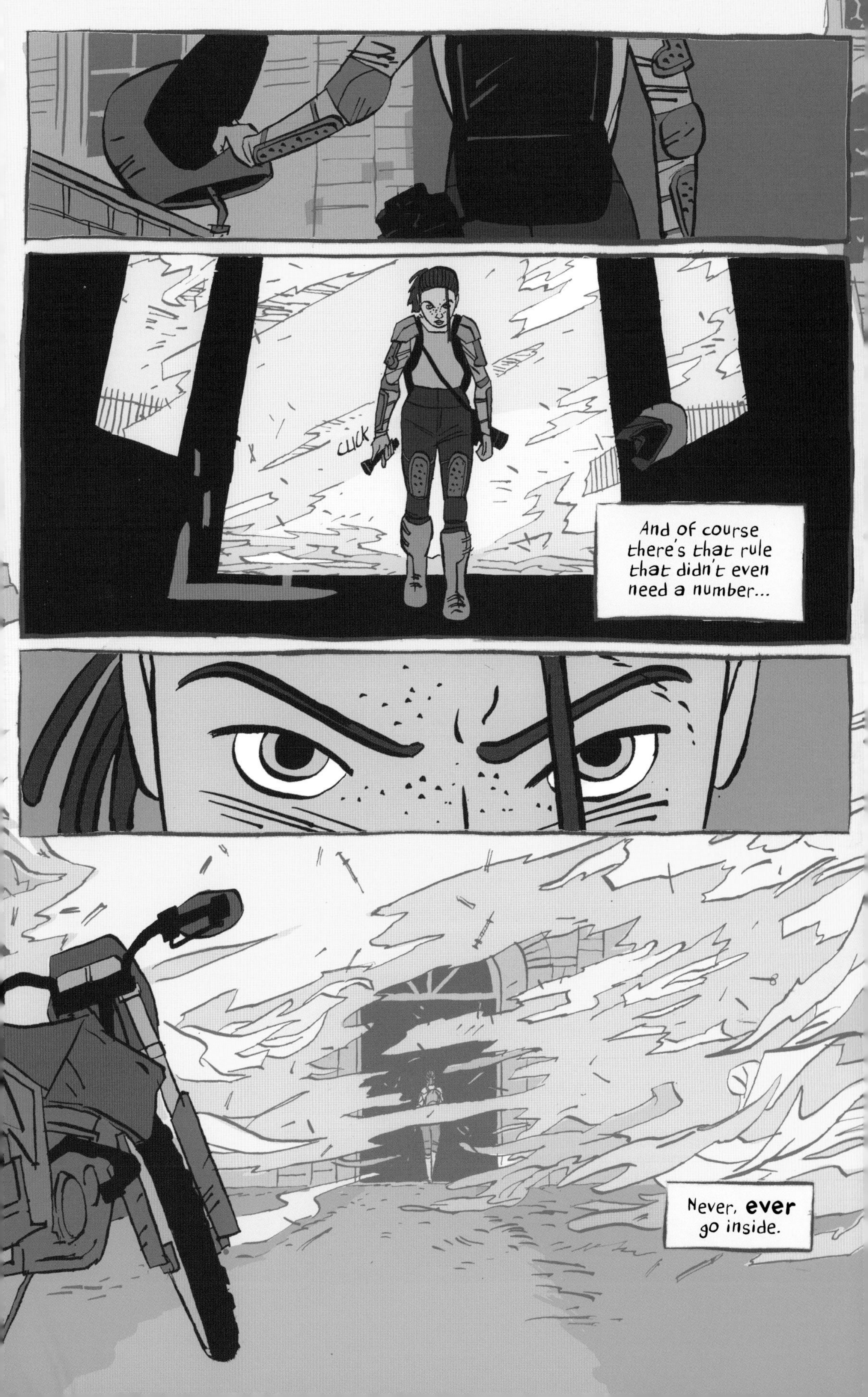
CLICK
And of course there's that rule that didn't even need a number...
Never, **ever** go inside.

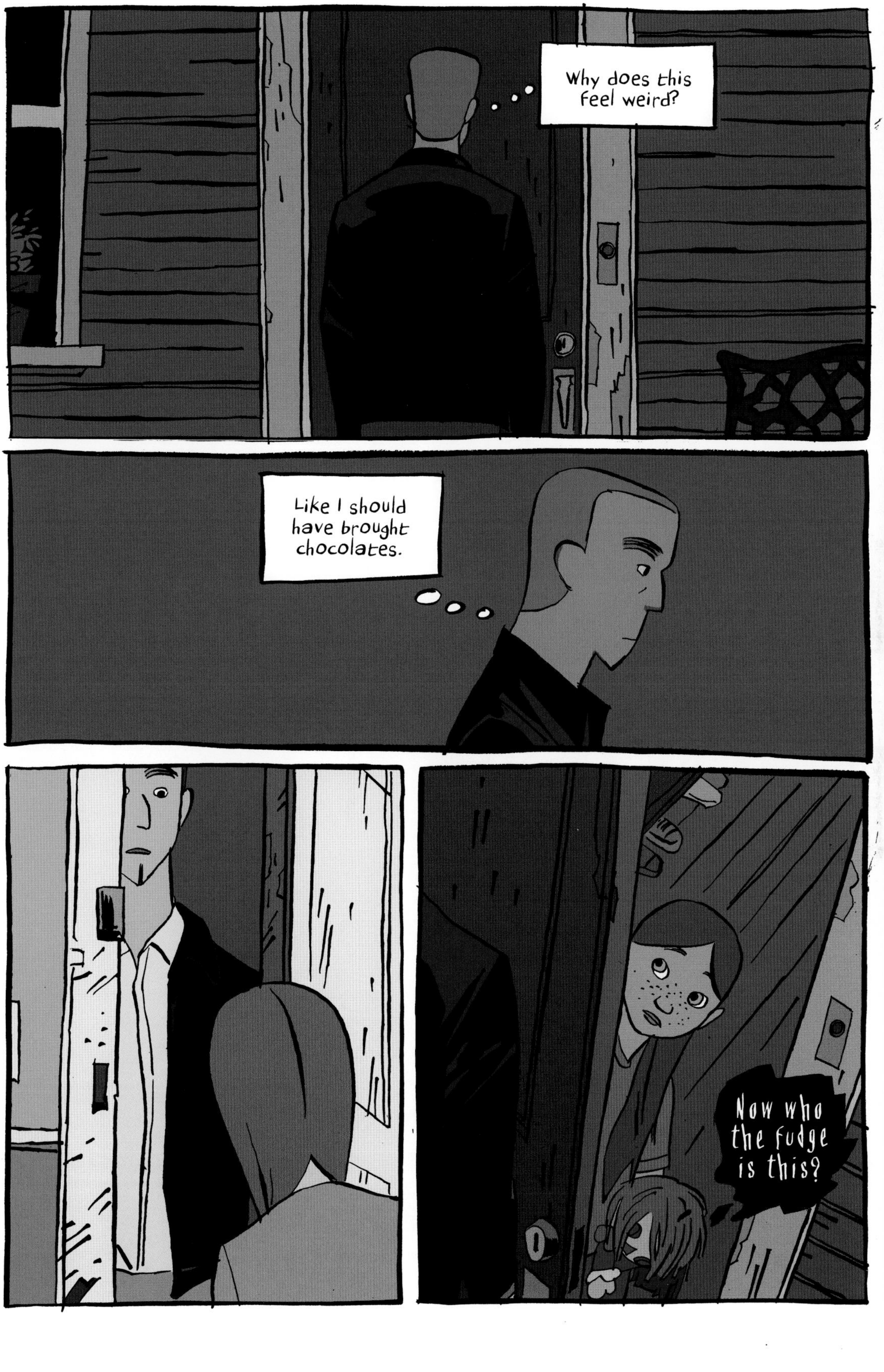
Why does this feel weird?
Like I should have brought chocolates.
Now who the fudge is this?

Oh, um, hi. I'm Corporal Wiley.

You must be...

Well done, genius.

Uh...her little sister.

I told you not to open the door.

Yeah, but **you** were the one who was bored.

And, look. His face is kind of funny.

That's cause he wants to dance with your sister.

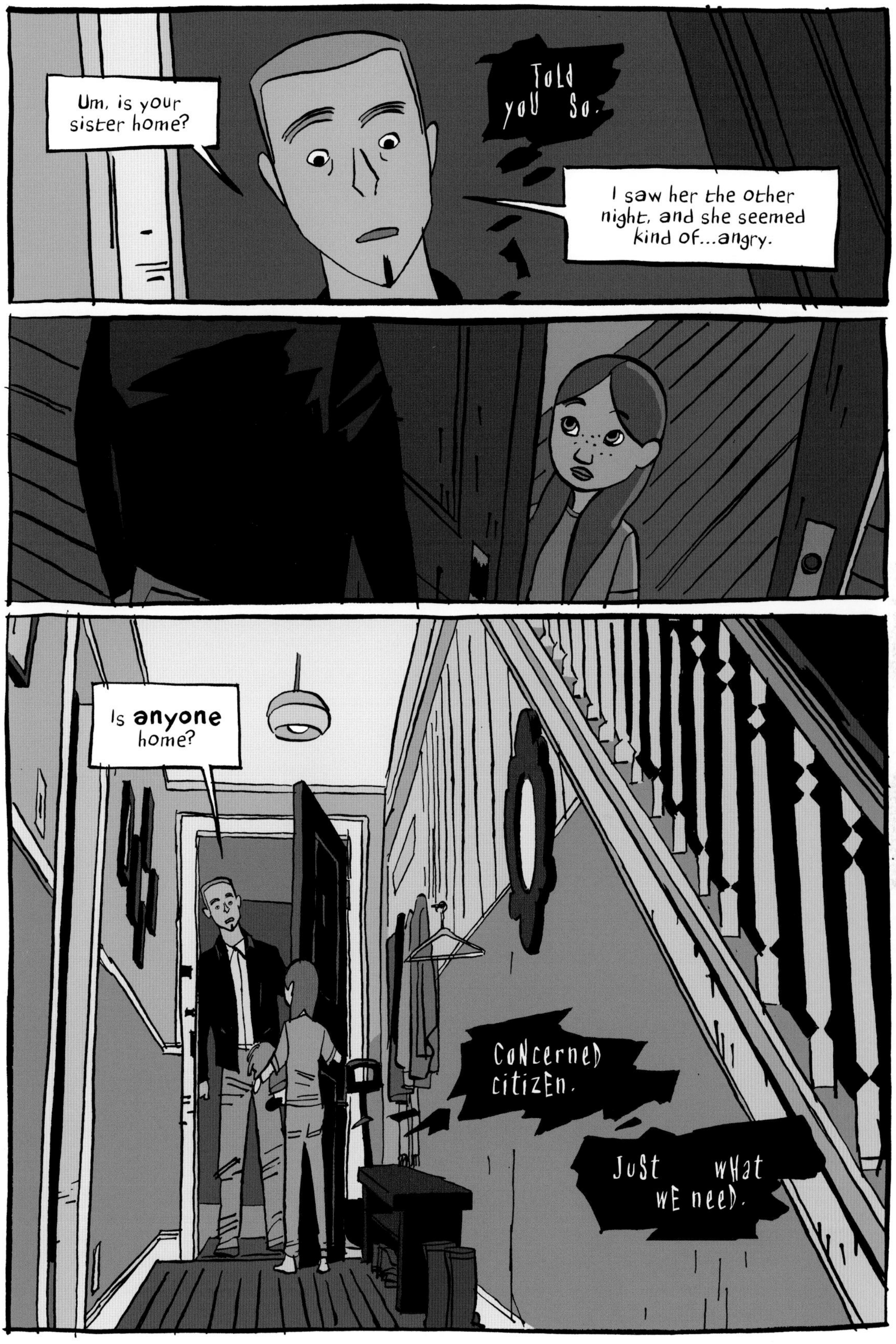
Um, is your sister home?
Told you so.
I saw her the other night, and she seemed kind of...angry.
Is **anyone** home?
Concerned citizen.
Just what we need.

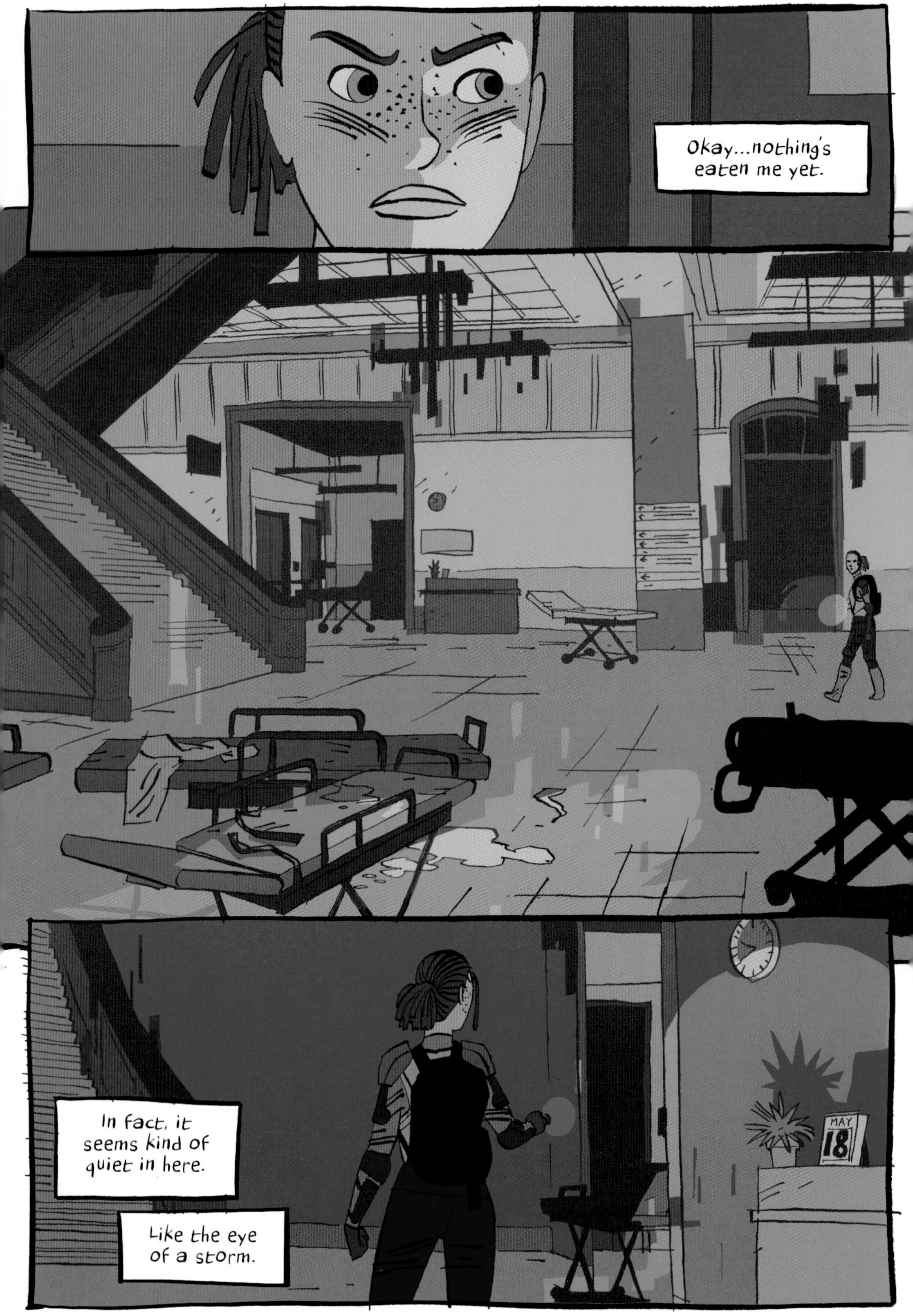
Okay...nothing's eaten me yet.
MAY
18
In fact, it seems kind of quiet in here.
Like the eye of a storm.

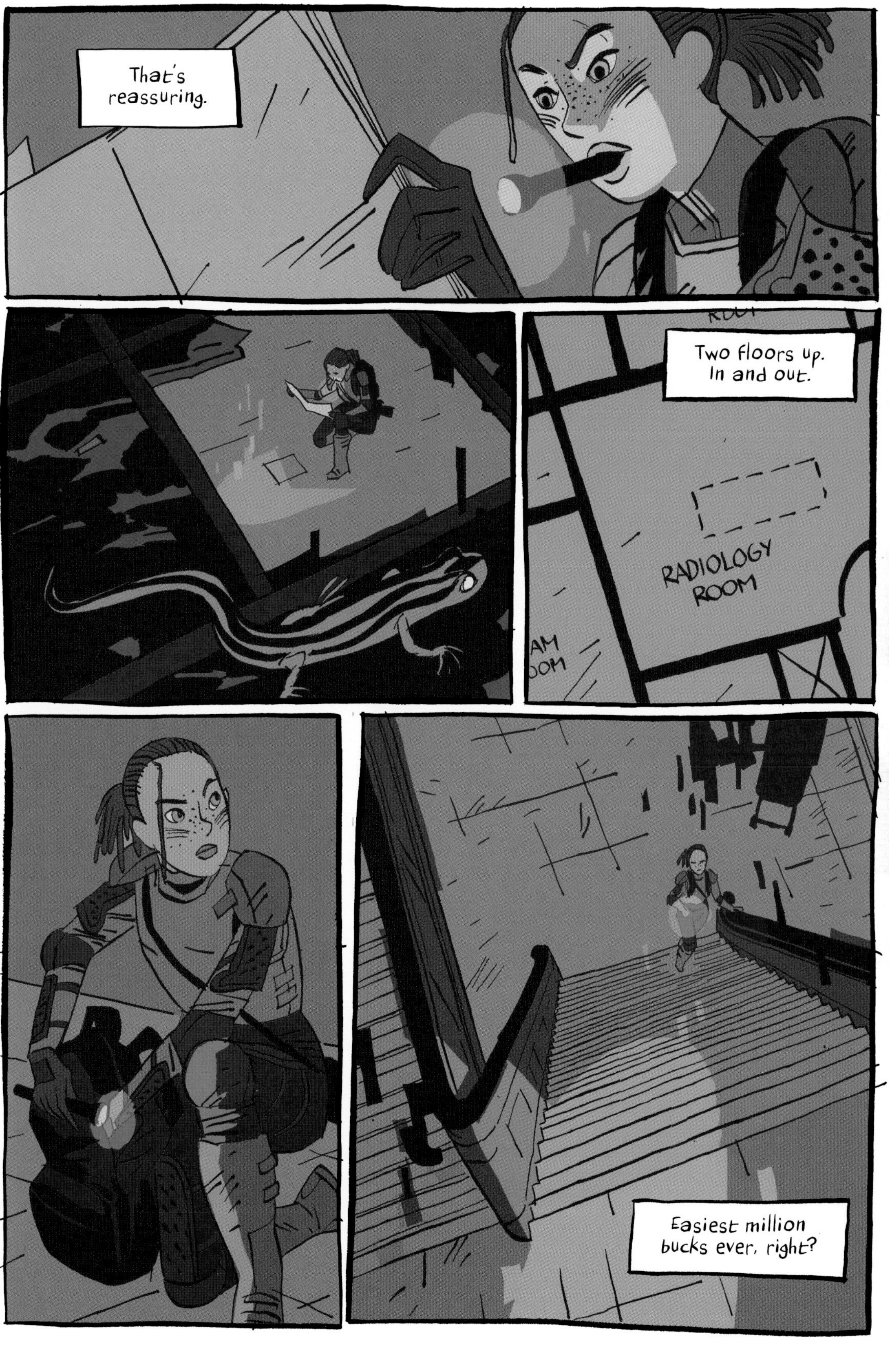
That's reassuring.
Two floors up. In and out.
RADIOLOGY ROOM
Easiest million bucks ever, right?

This almost looks familiar.

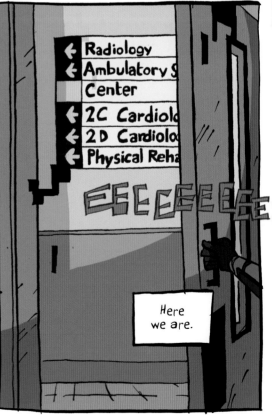

← Radiology
← Ambulatory S
Center
← 2C Cardiolo
← 2D Cardiolo
← Physical Reha

Here we are.

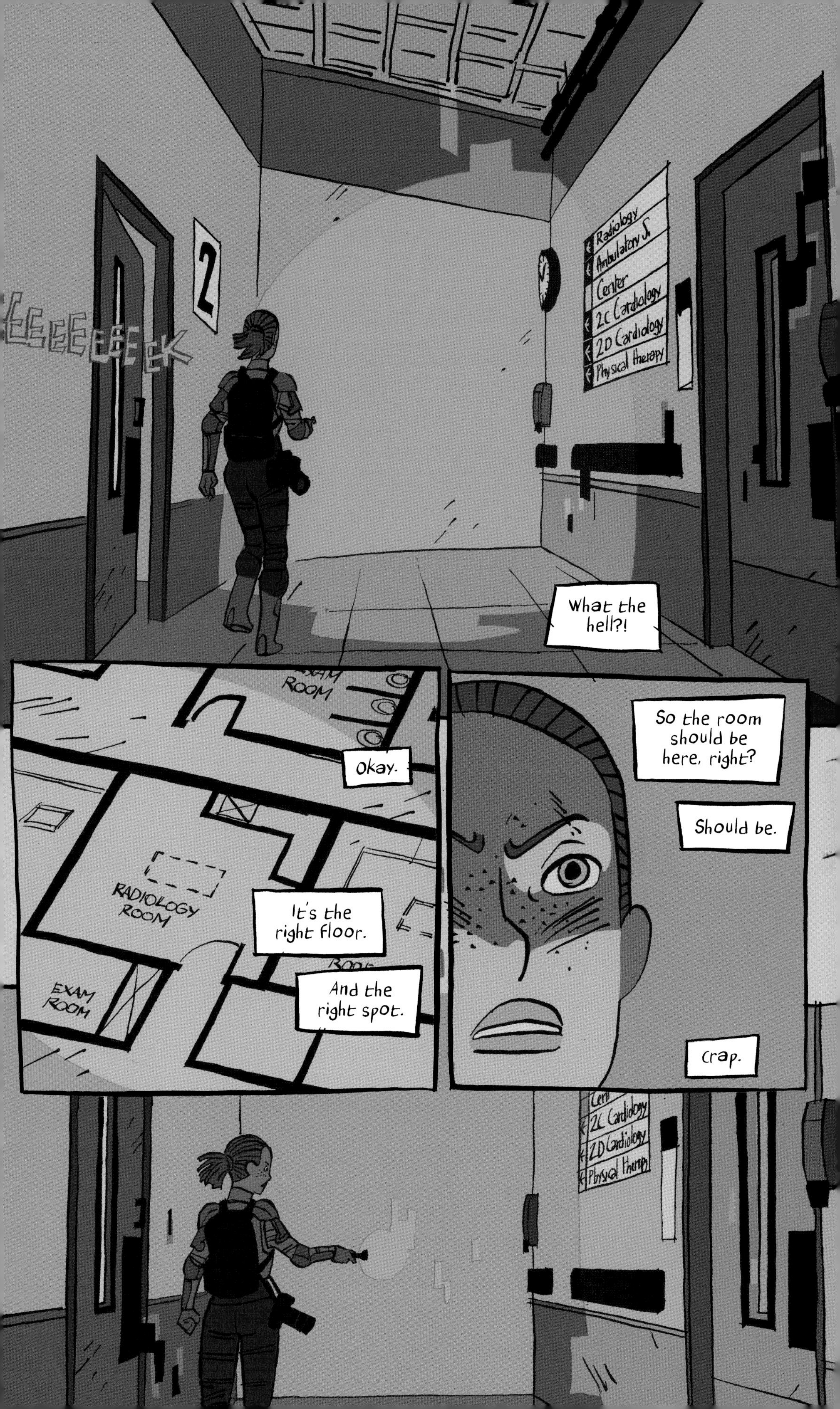
EEEEEEEEEK
2
Radiology
Ambulatory S.
Center
2C Cardiology
2D Cardiology
Physical therapy
What the hell?!
EXAM ROOM
RADIOLOGY ROOM
EXAM ROOM
Okay.
It's the right floor.
And the right spot.
So the room should be here, right?
Should be.
Crap.
2C Cardiology
2D Cardiology
Physical therapy

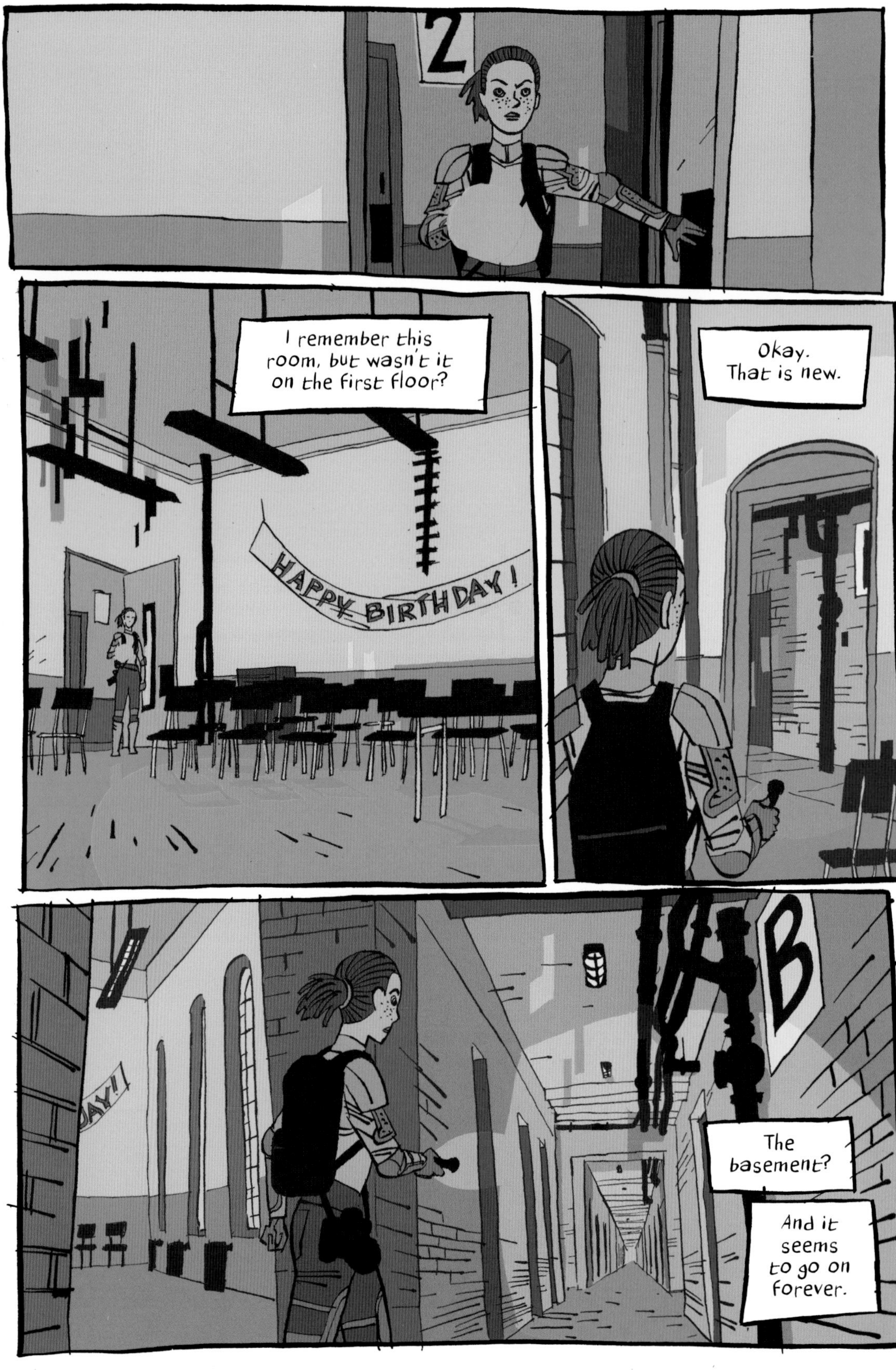
2
I remember this room, but wasn't it on the first floor?
HAPPY BIRTHDAY!
Okay. That is new.
B
The basement?
And it seems to go on forever.

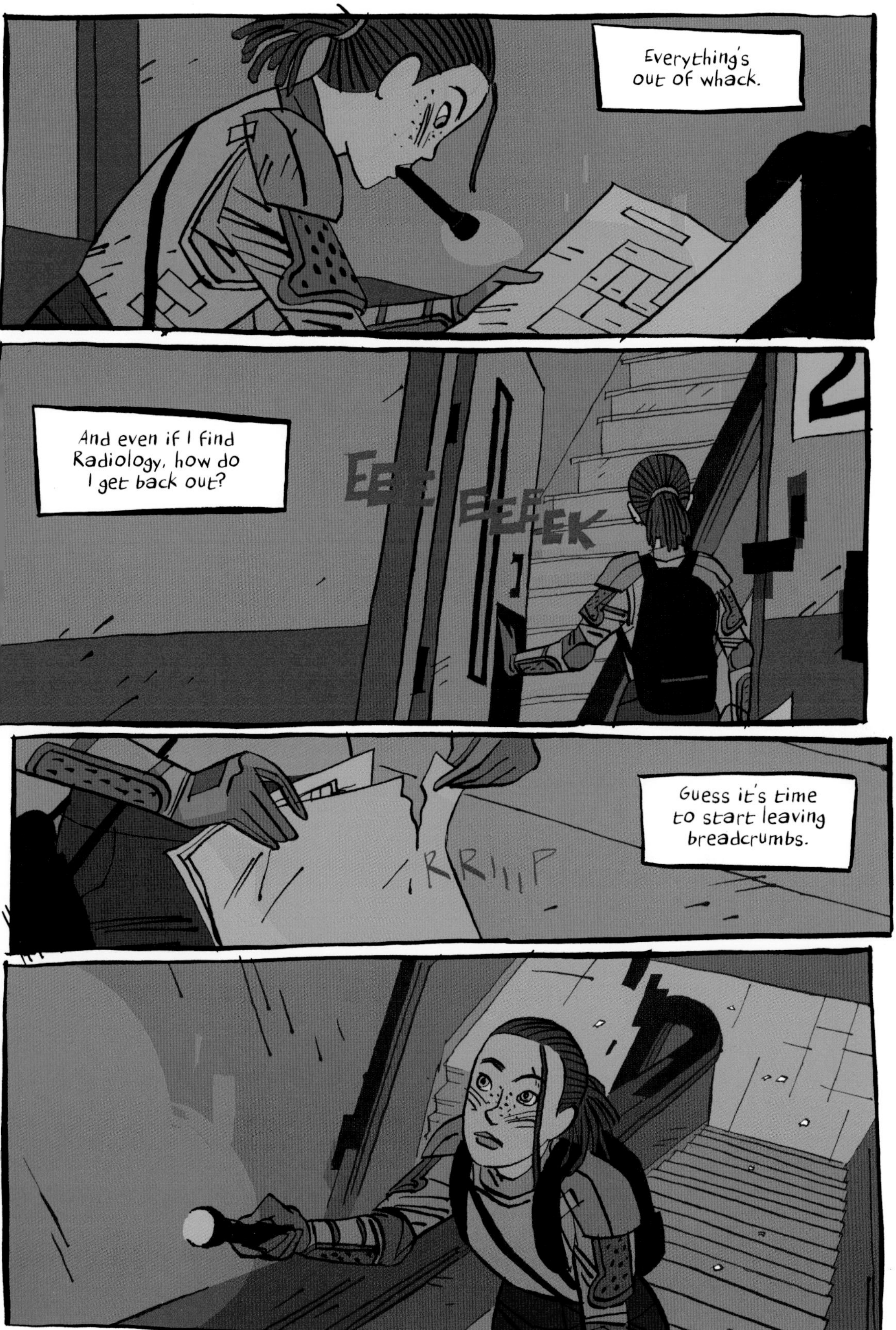
Everything's out of whack.
And even if I find Radiology, how do I get back out?
EEEE EEEEEK
Guess it's time to start leaving breadcrumbs.
RRIIIP

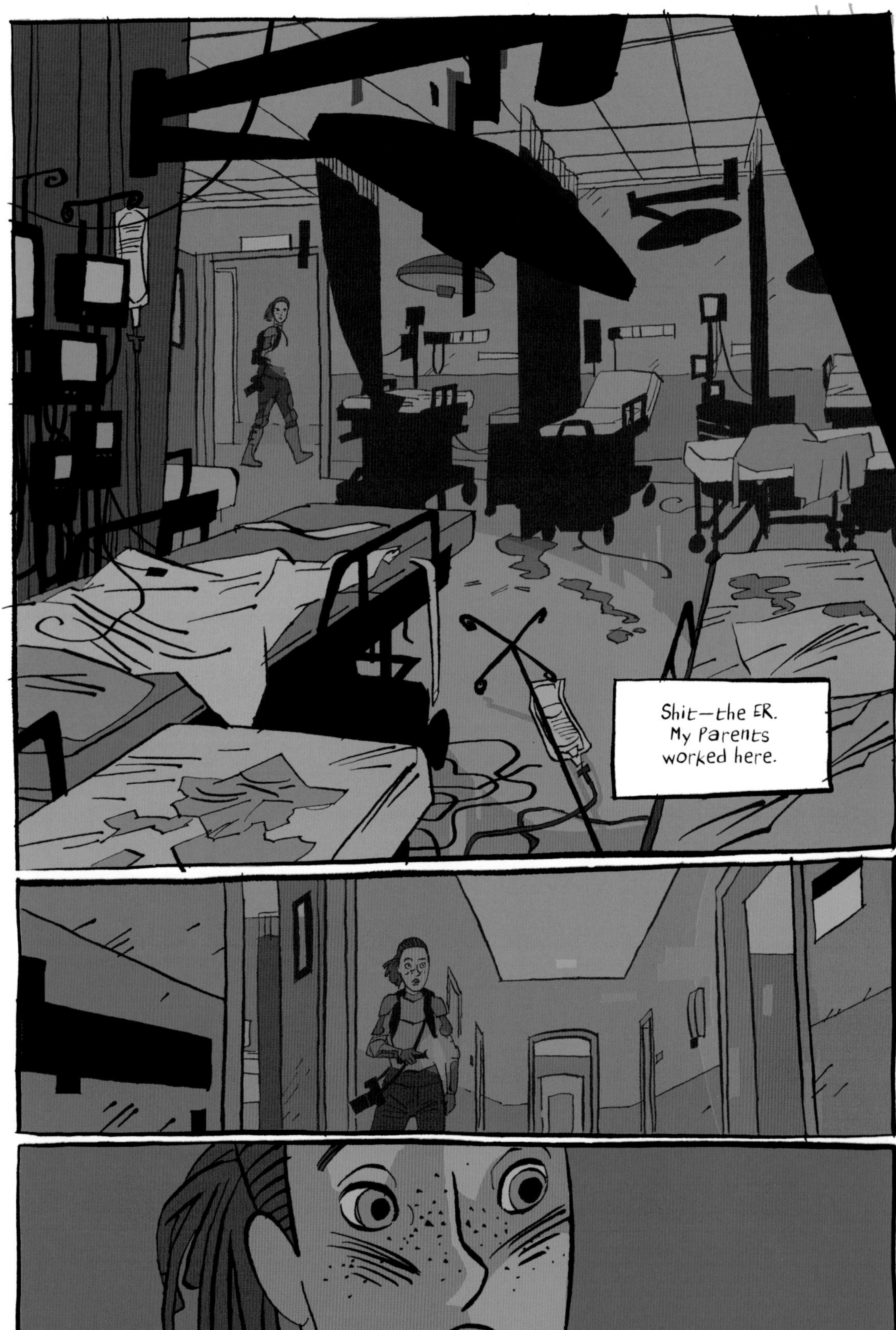
Shit—the ER.
My Parents
worked here.

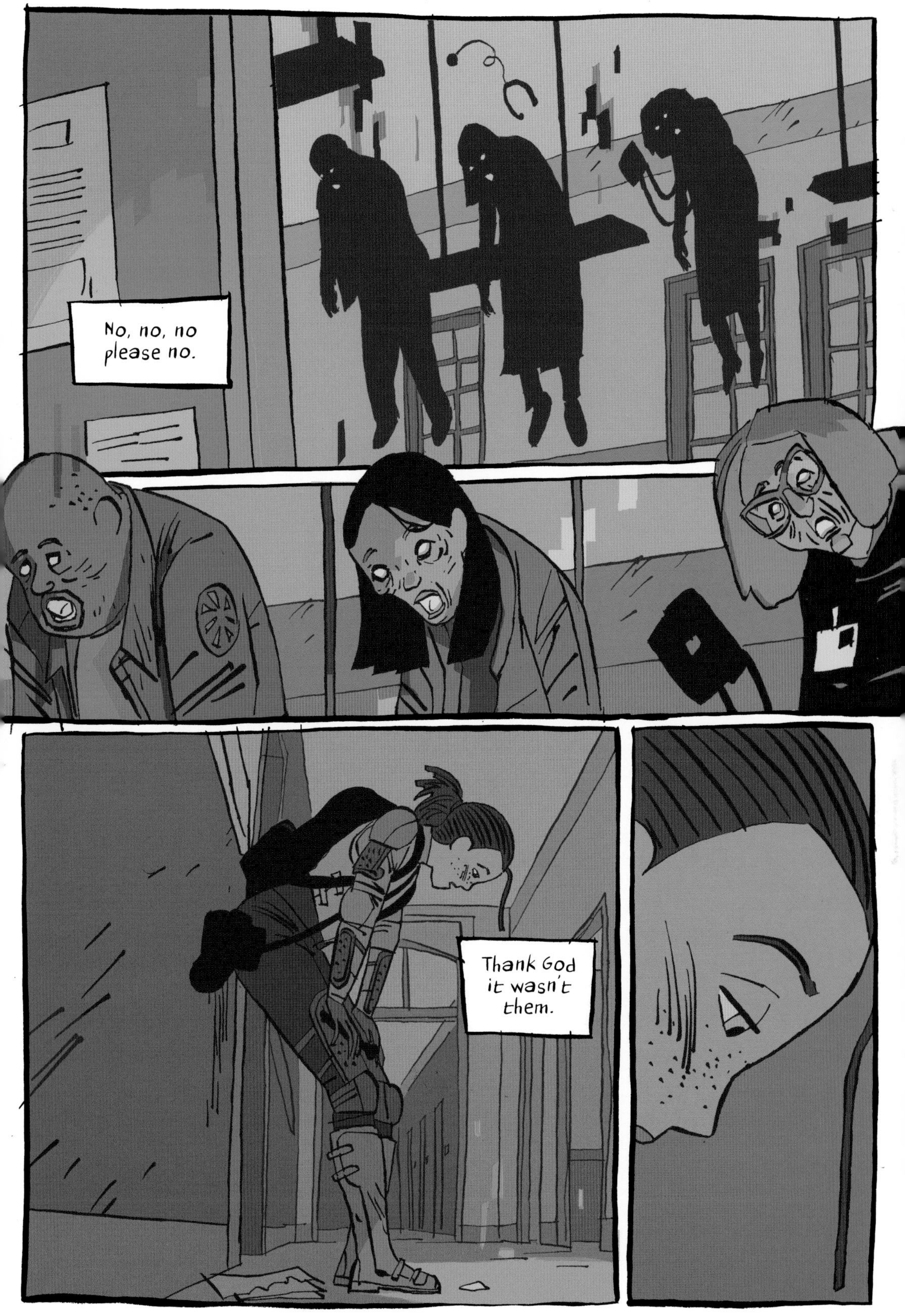
No, no, no
please no.
Thank God
it wasn't
them.

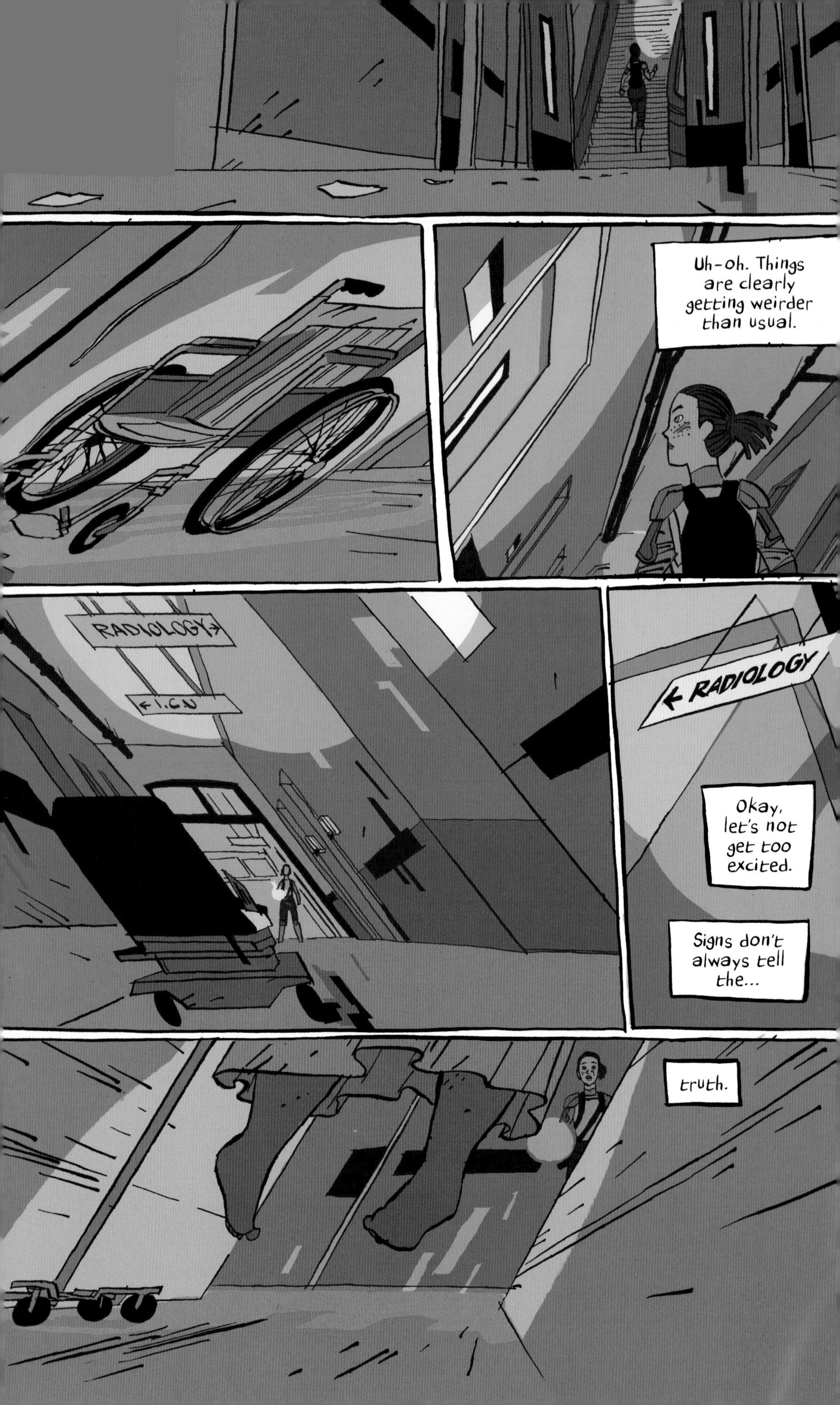
Uh-oh. Things are clearly getting weirder than usual.
RADIOLOGY
I.C.U
RADIOLOGY
Okay, let's not get too excited.
Signs don't always tell the...
truth.

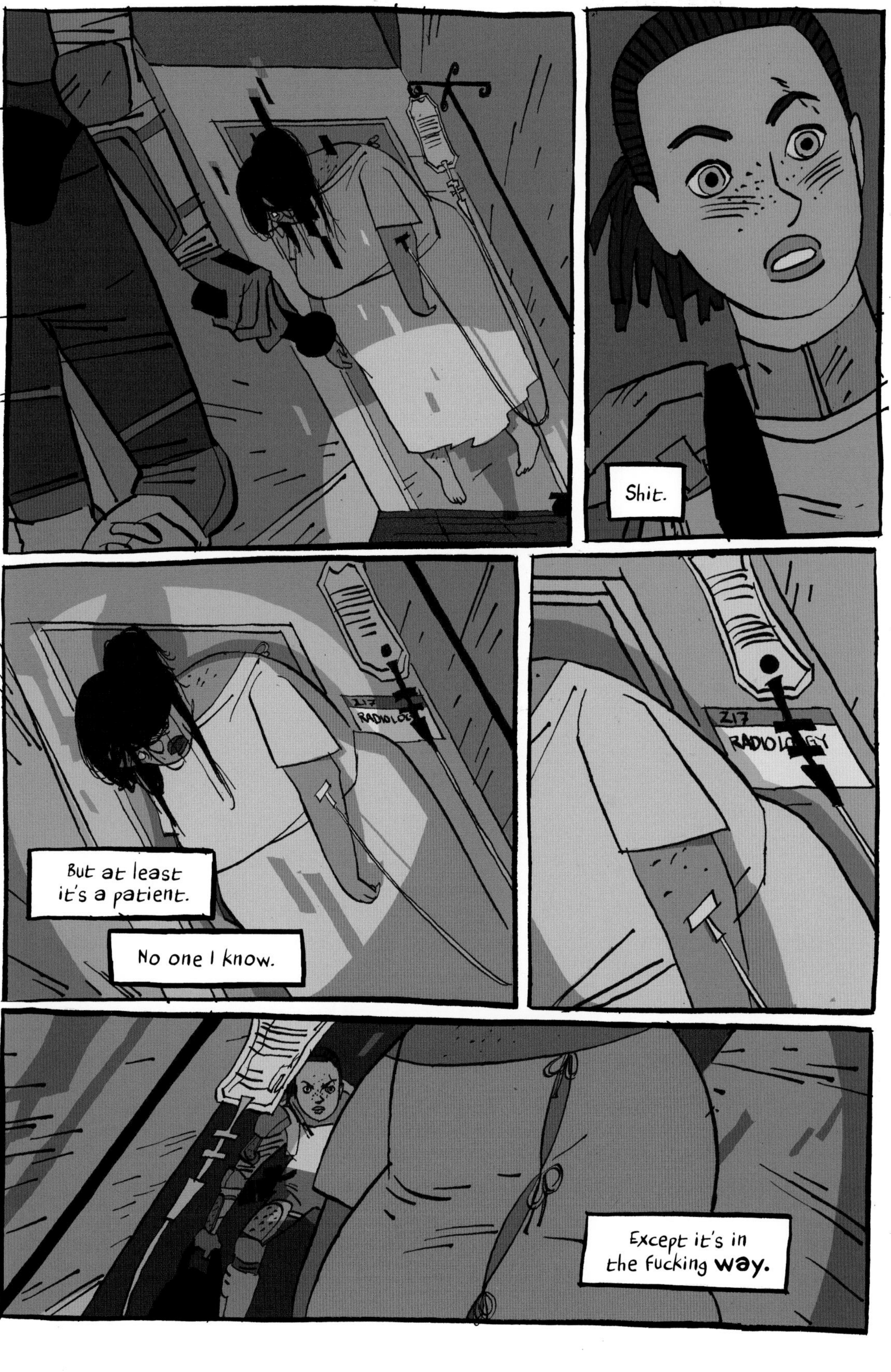
Shit.
217
RADIOLOG
217
RADIOLOGY
But at least it's a patient.
No one I know.
Except it's in the fucking way.

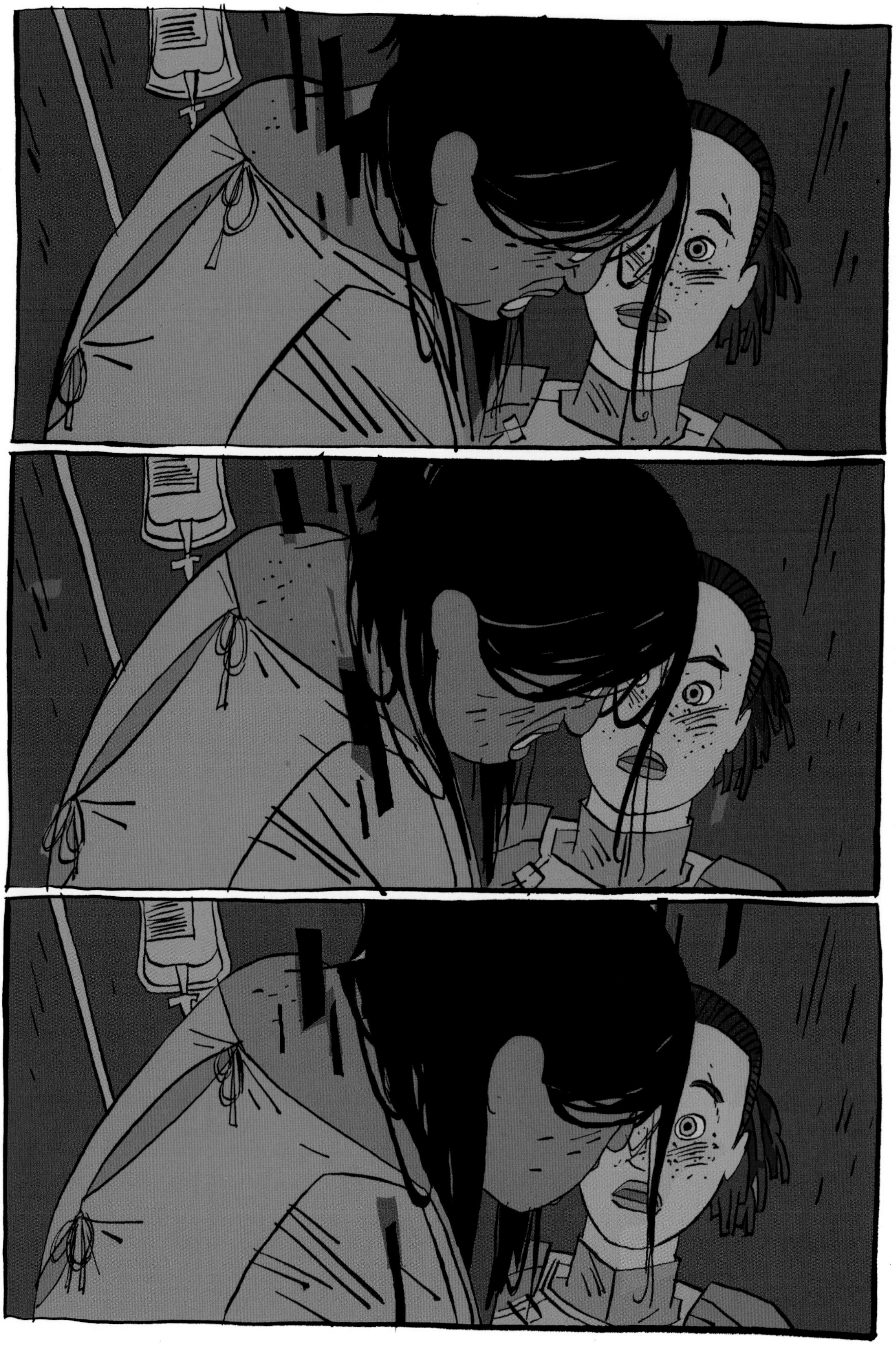

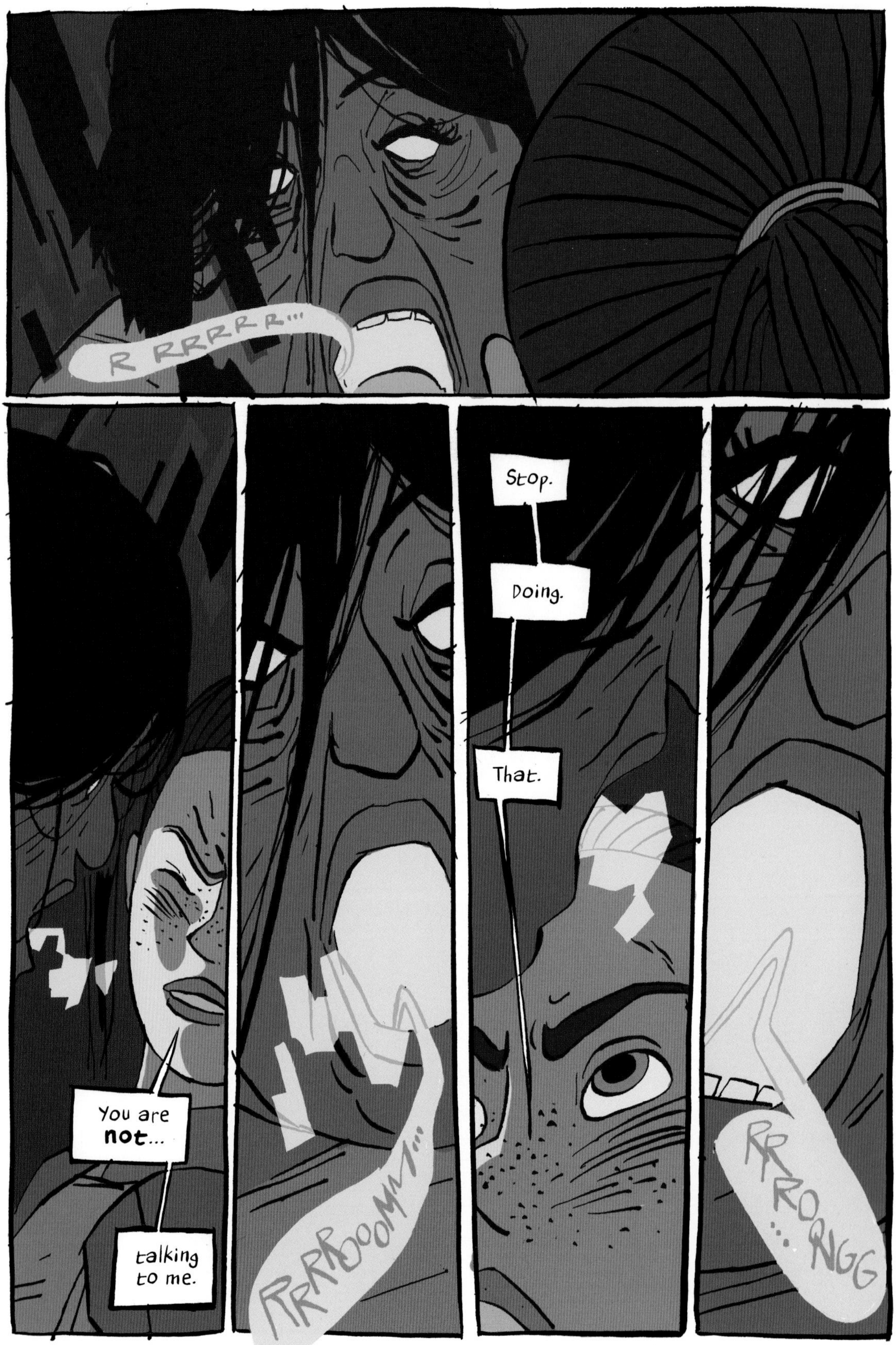
R RRRRR...
You are not...
talking to me.
RRRROOOMM...
Stop.
Doing.
That.
RRROO...NGG

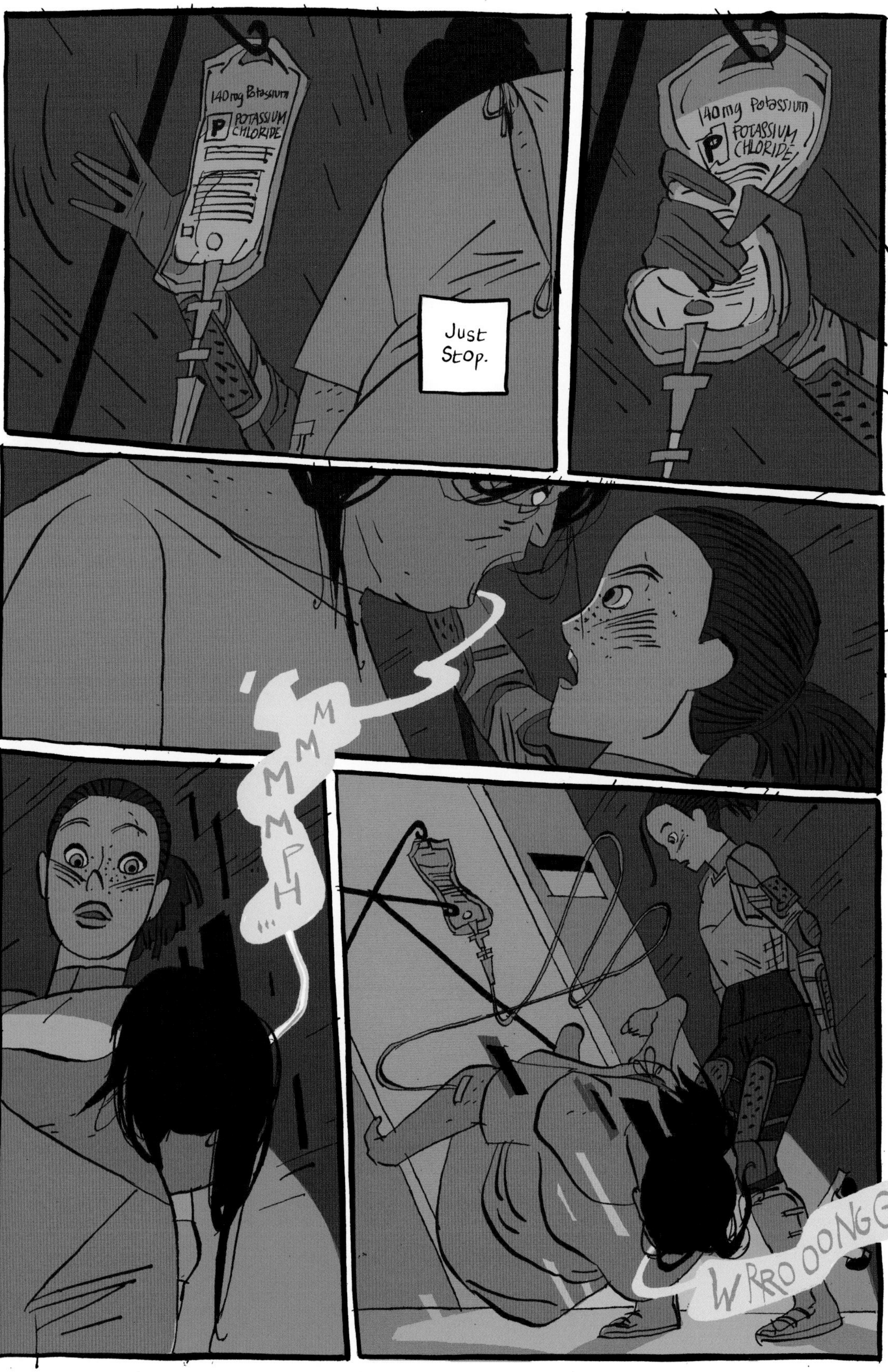
140mg Potassium
P POTASSIUM CHLORIDE
Just Stop.
140mg Potassium
P POTASSIUM CHLORIDE
'MMMMMPH...
WRROOONGG

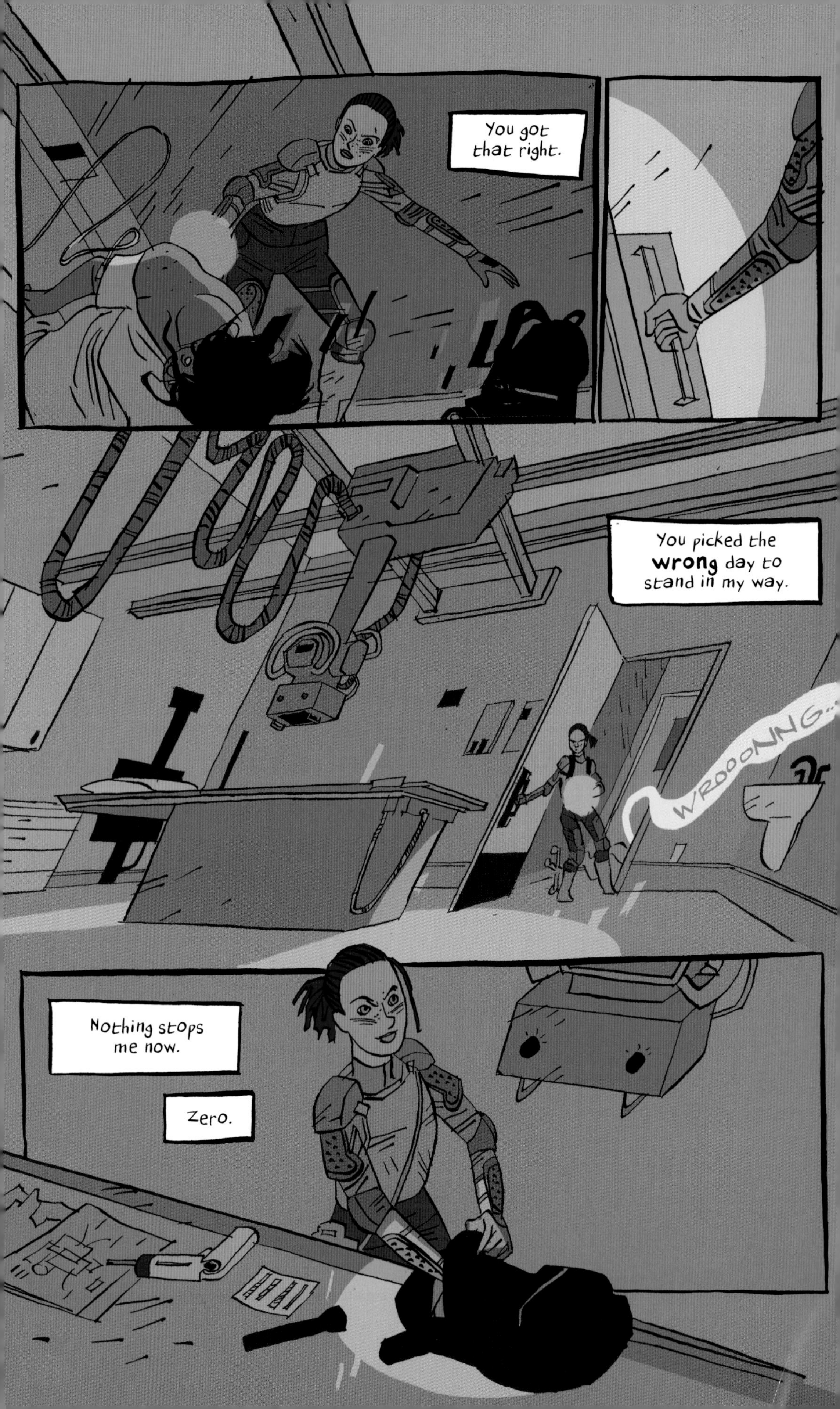
You got that right.
You picked the **wrong** day to stand in my way.
WROOONNG...
Nothing stops me now.
Zero.

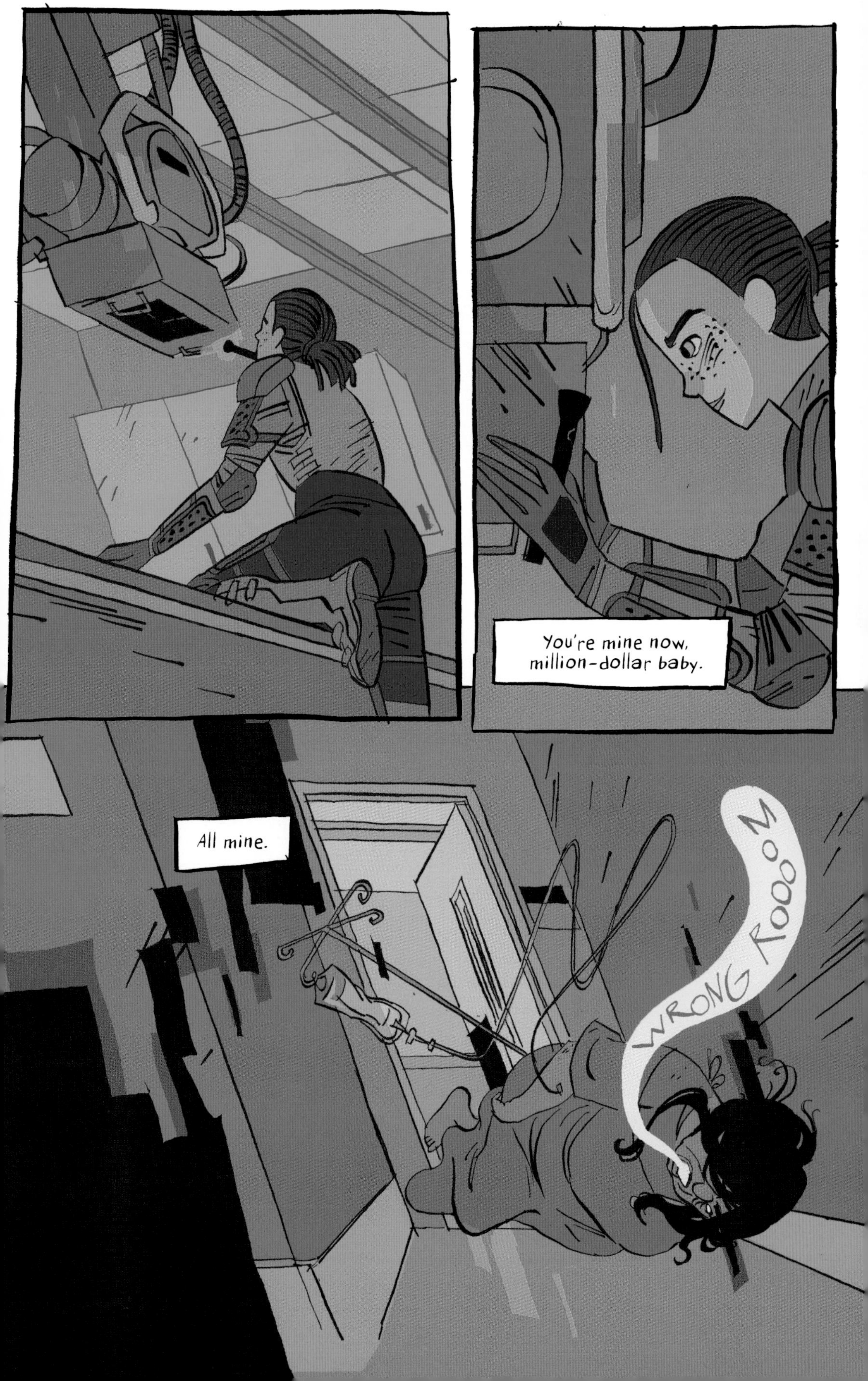

You're mine now, million-dollar baby.
All mine.
WRONG ROOOOOM

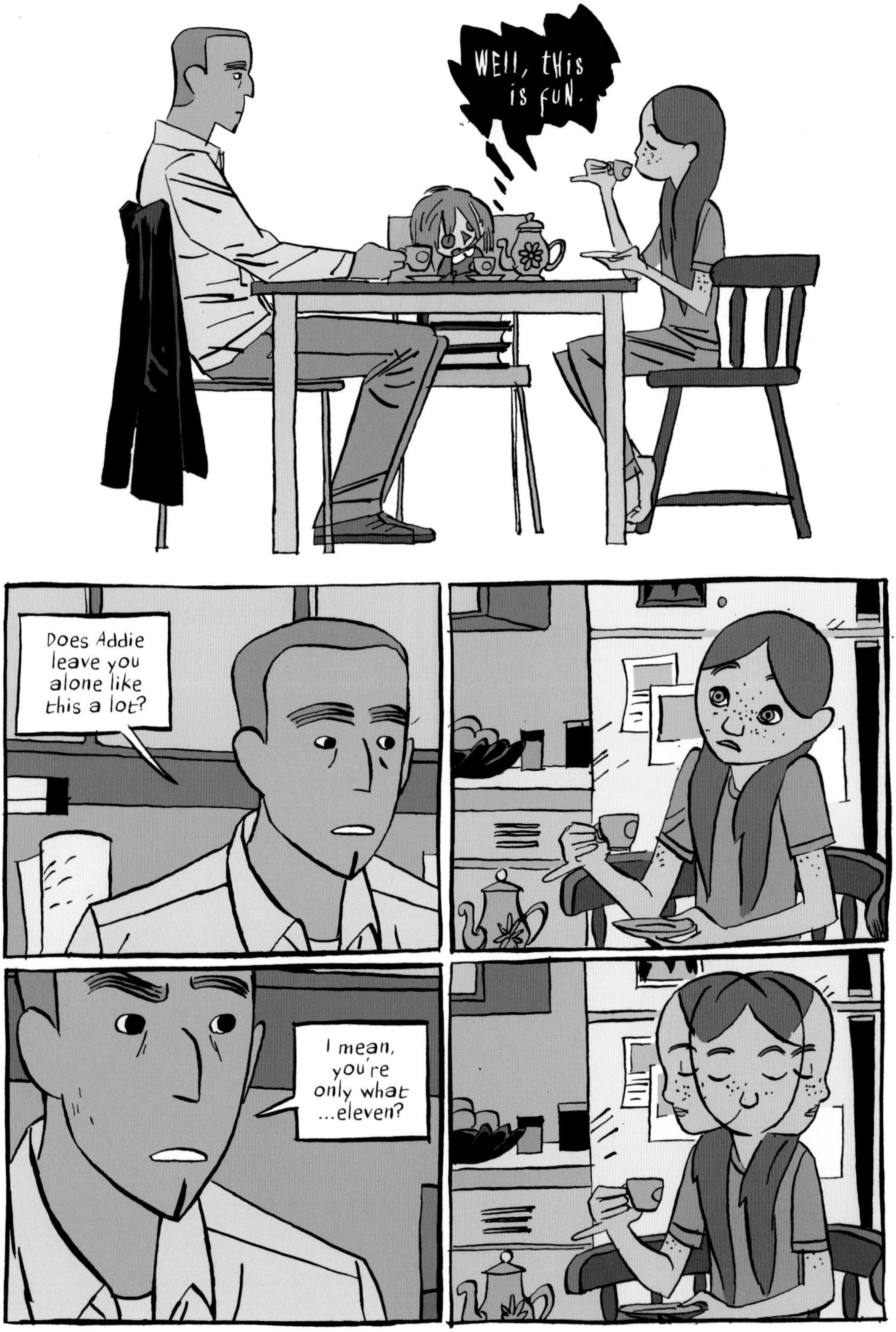
WEll, tHis is fuN.
Does Addie leave you alone like this a lot?
I mean, you're only what ...eleven?

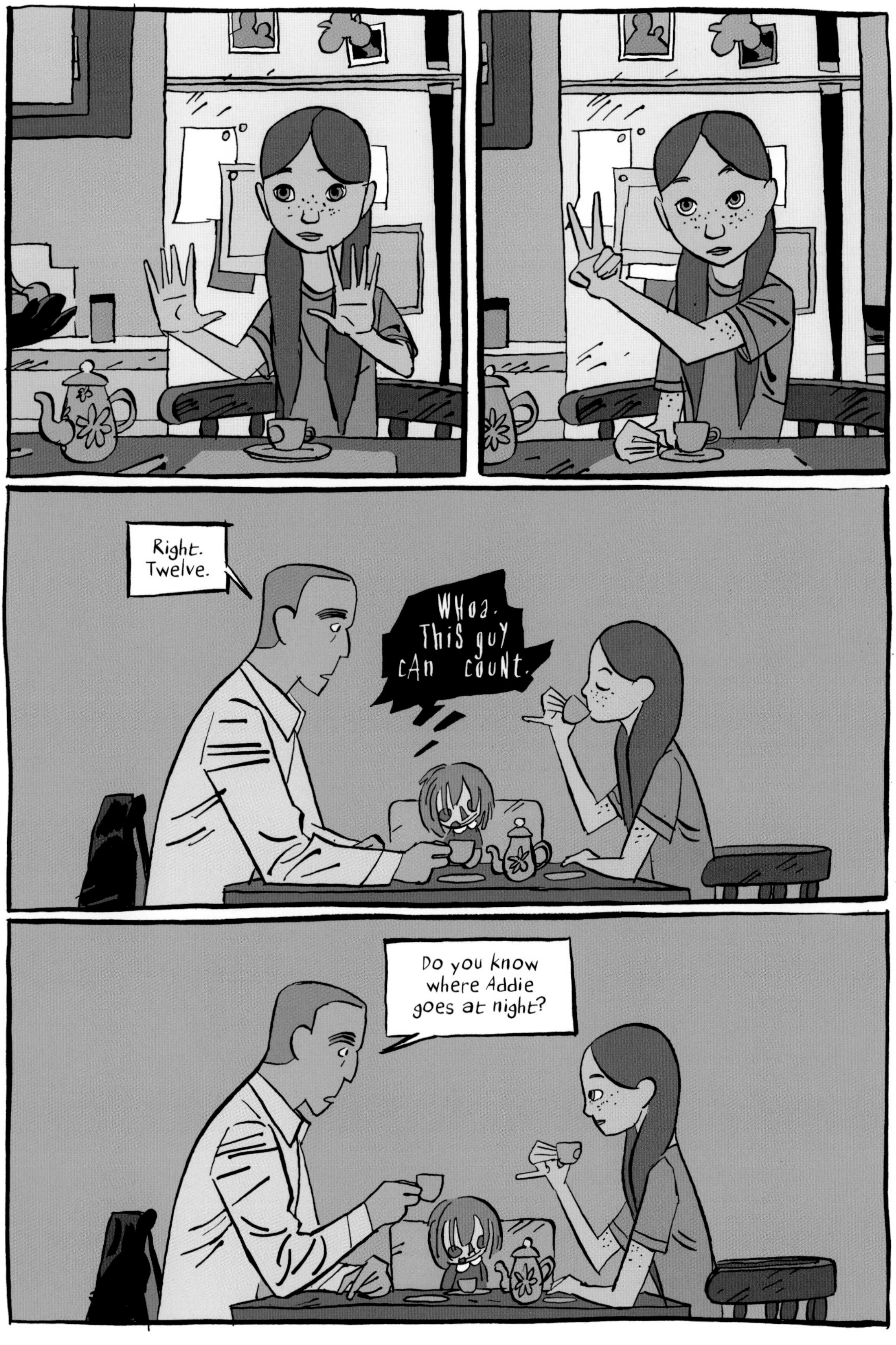
Right.
Twelve.
WHoa.
This guy
can count.
Do you know
where Addie
goes at night?

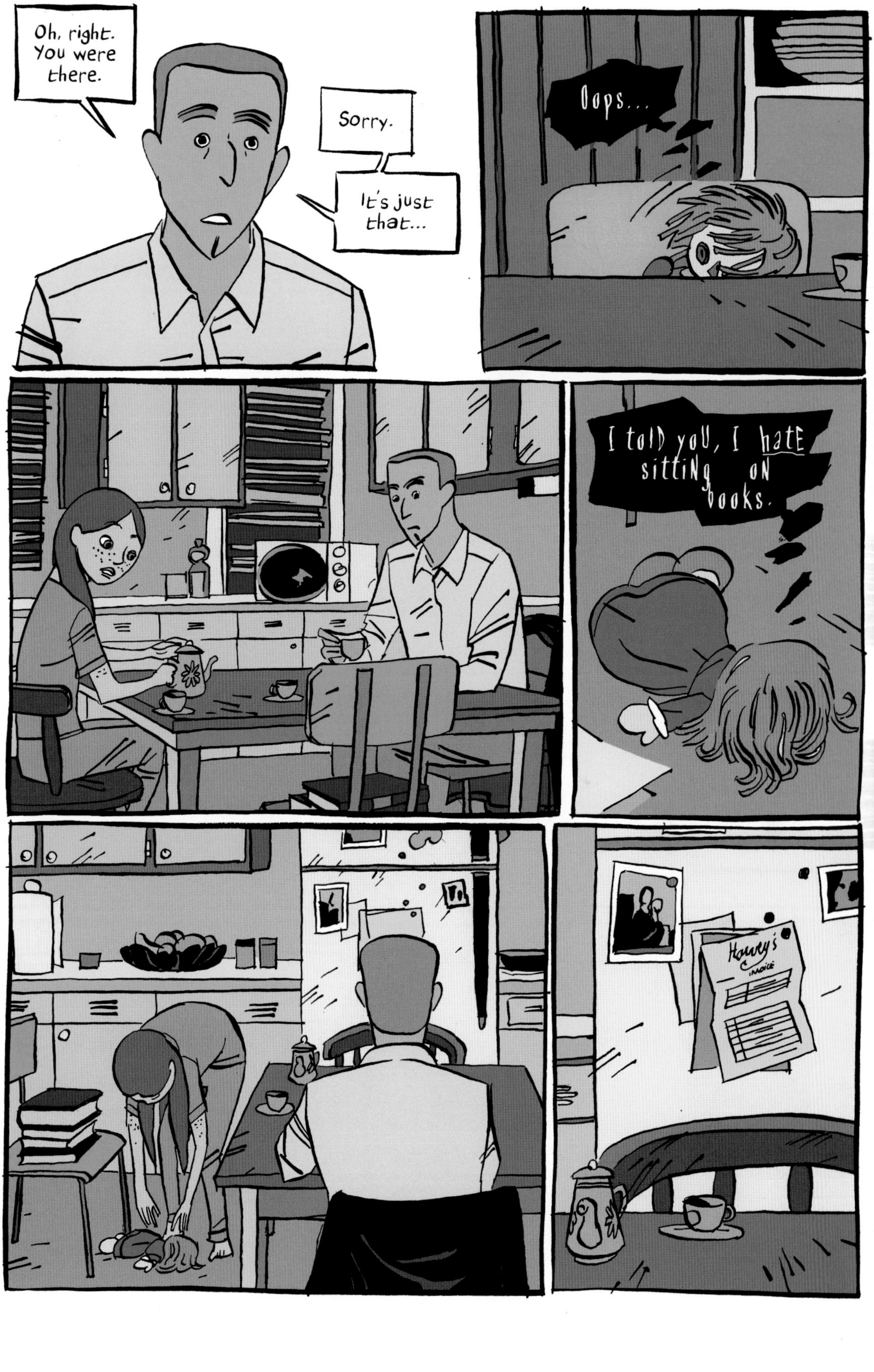
Oh, right. You were there.
Sorry.
It's just that...
Oops...
I told you, I hate sitting on books.
Honey's invoice

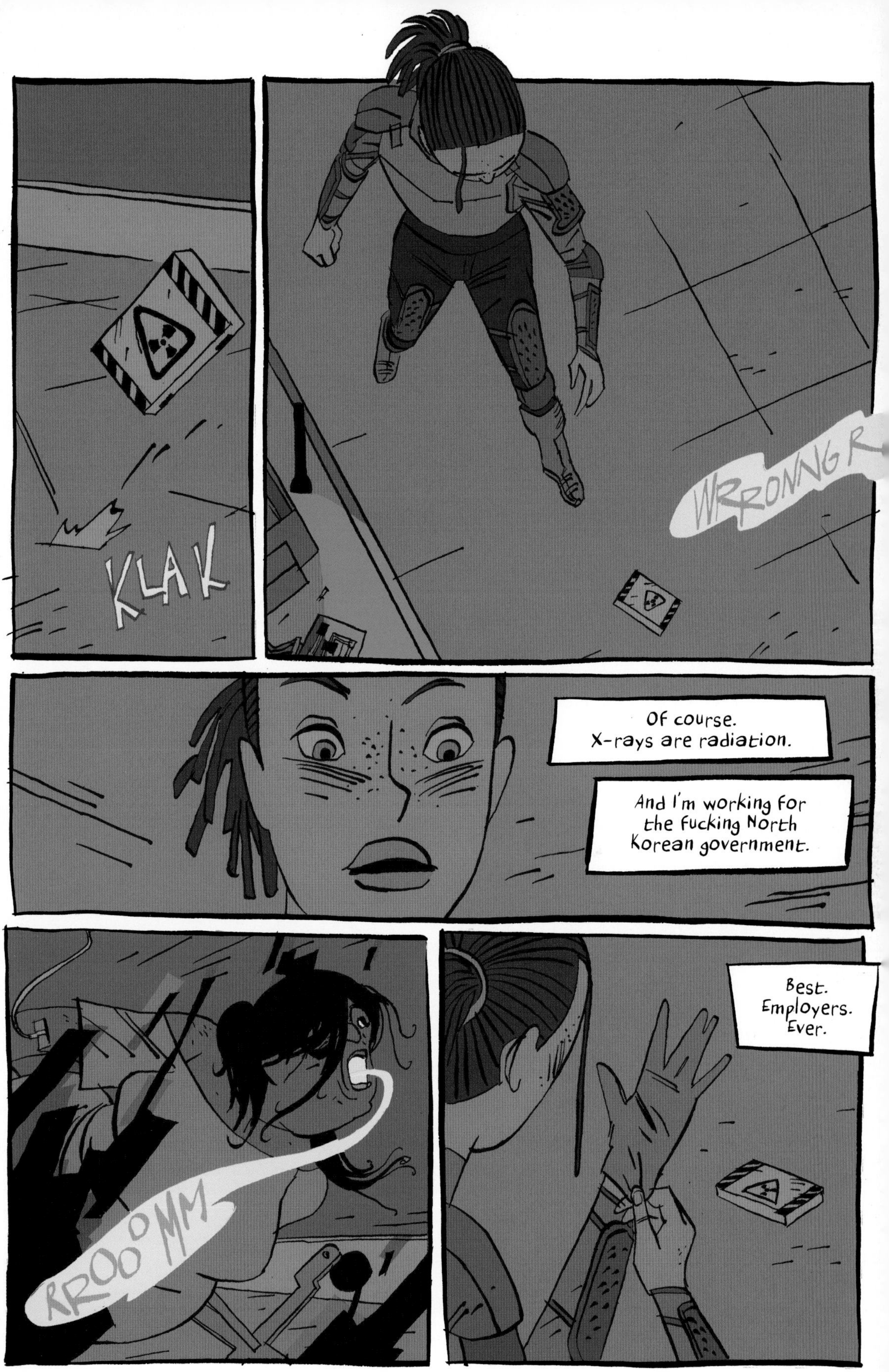
KLAK
WRRONNGR
Of course.
X-rays are radiation.
And I'm working for the fucking North Korean government.
RROOOMM
Best.
Employers.
Ever.

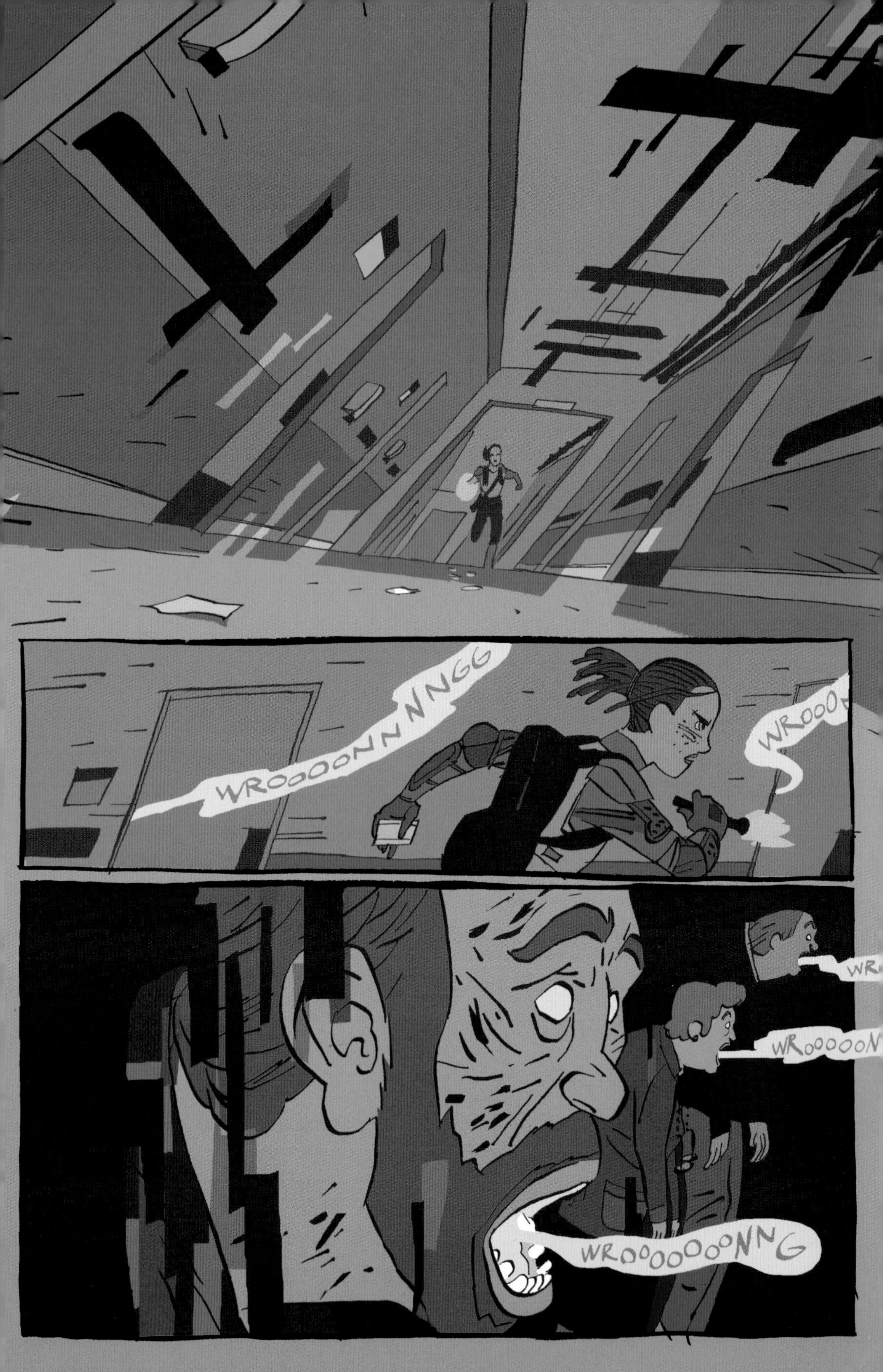
WROOOOONNNNGG
WROOO
WR
WROOOOON
WROOOOOOONNG

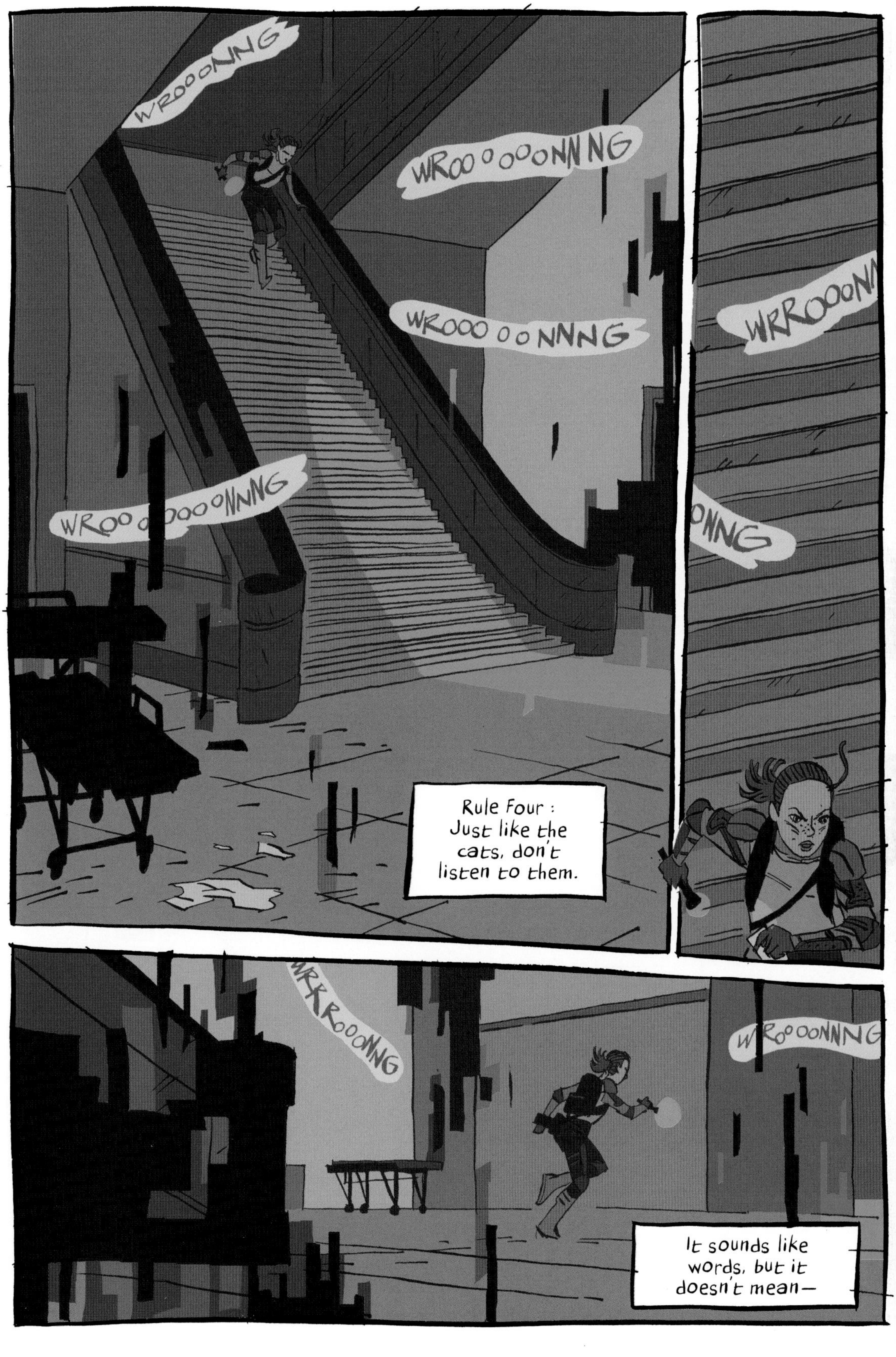
WROOONNG
WROOOOOONNNG
WROOO OONNNG
WROOOOOOONNNG
Rule Four : Just like the cats, don't listen to them.
WRROOON
ONNG
WRKROOONNG
WROOONNNG
It sounds like words, but it doesn't mean—

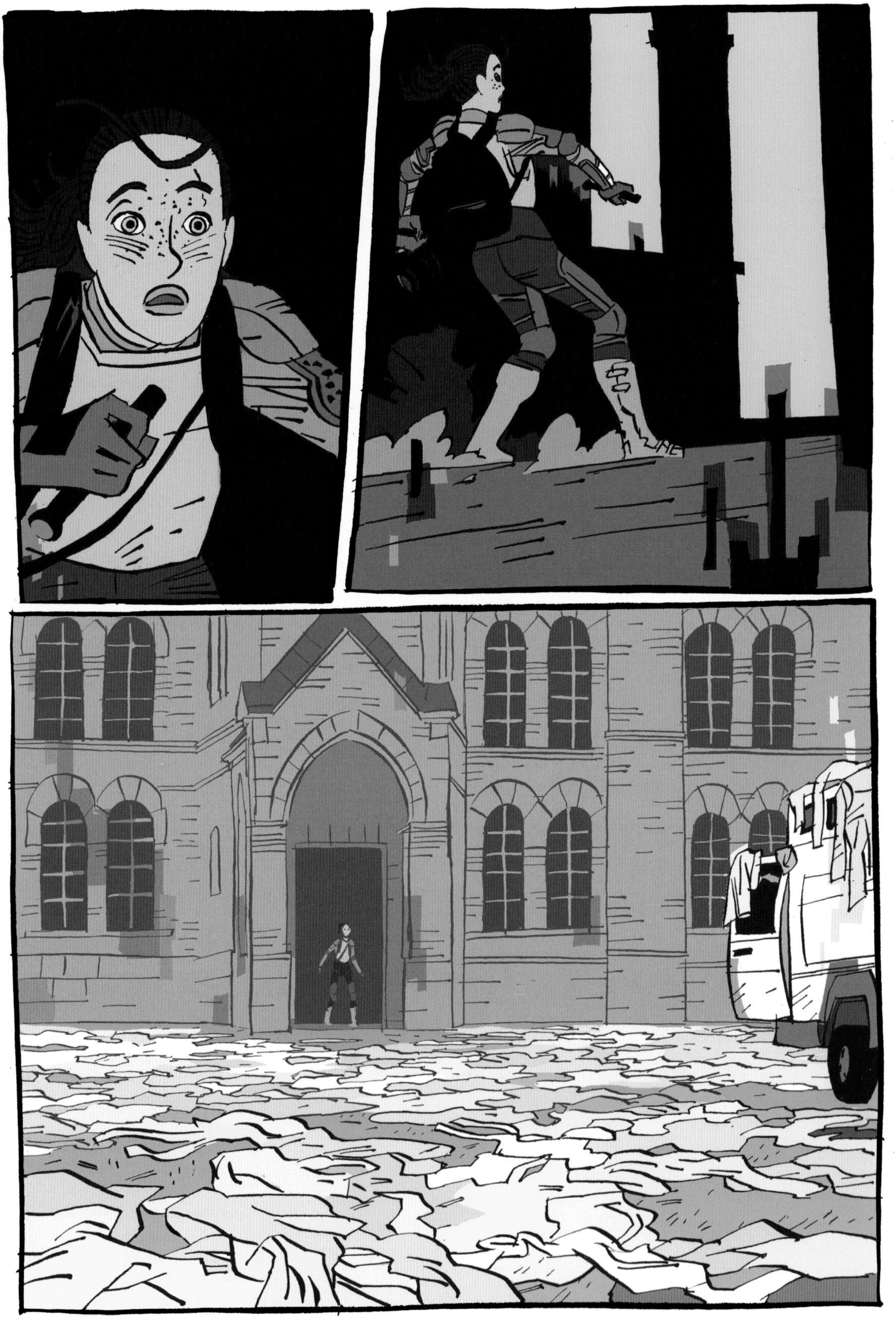

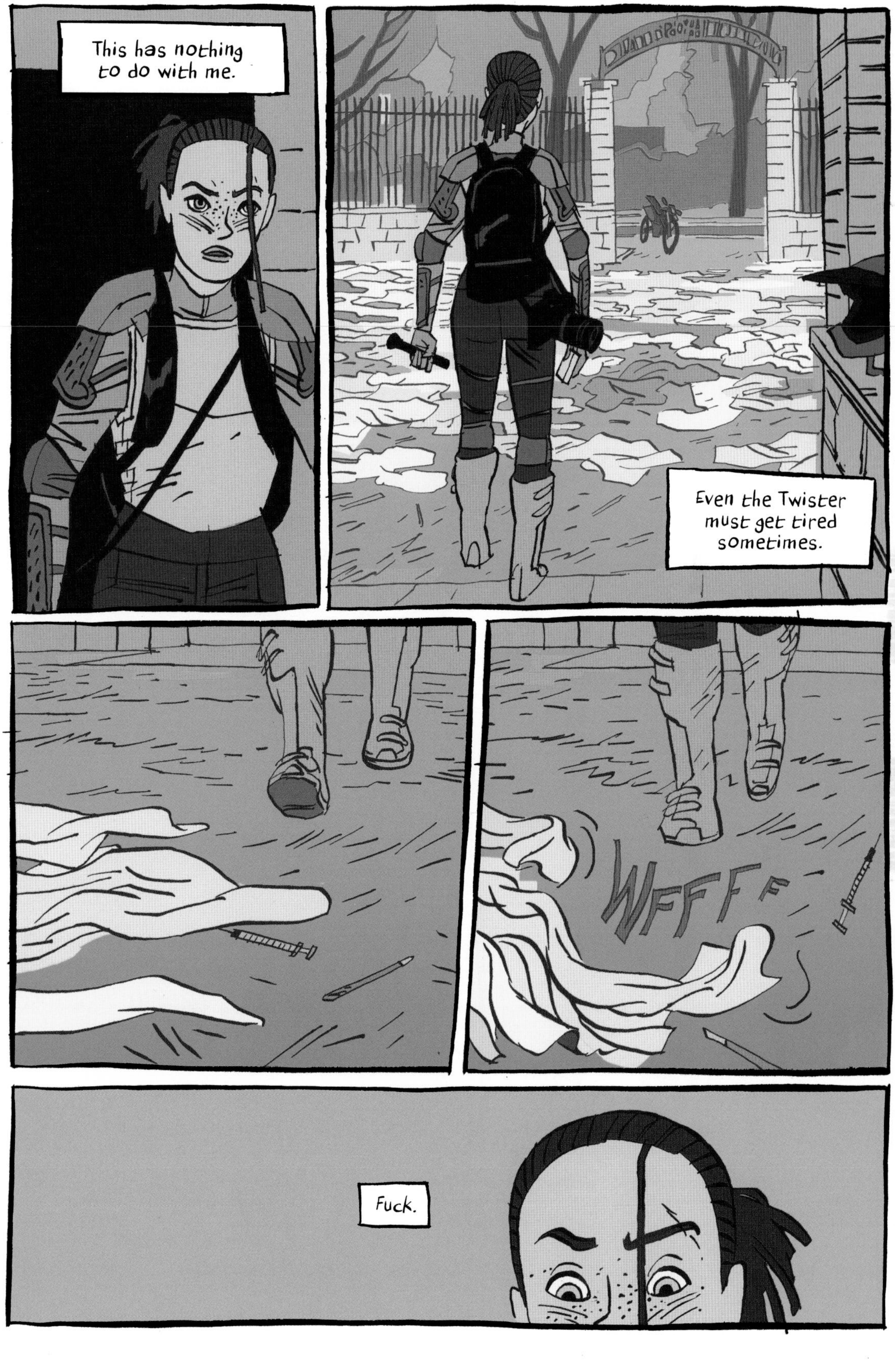
This has nothing to do with me.
Even the Twister must get tired sometimes.
WFFFF
Fuck.

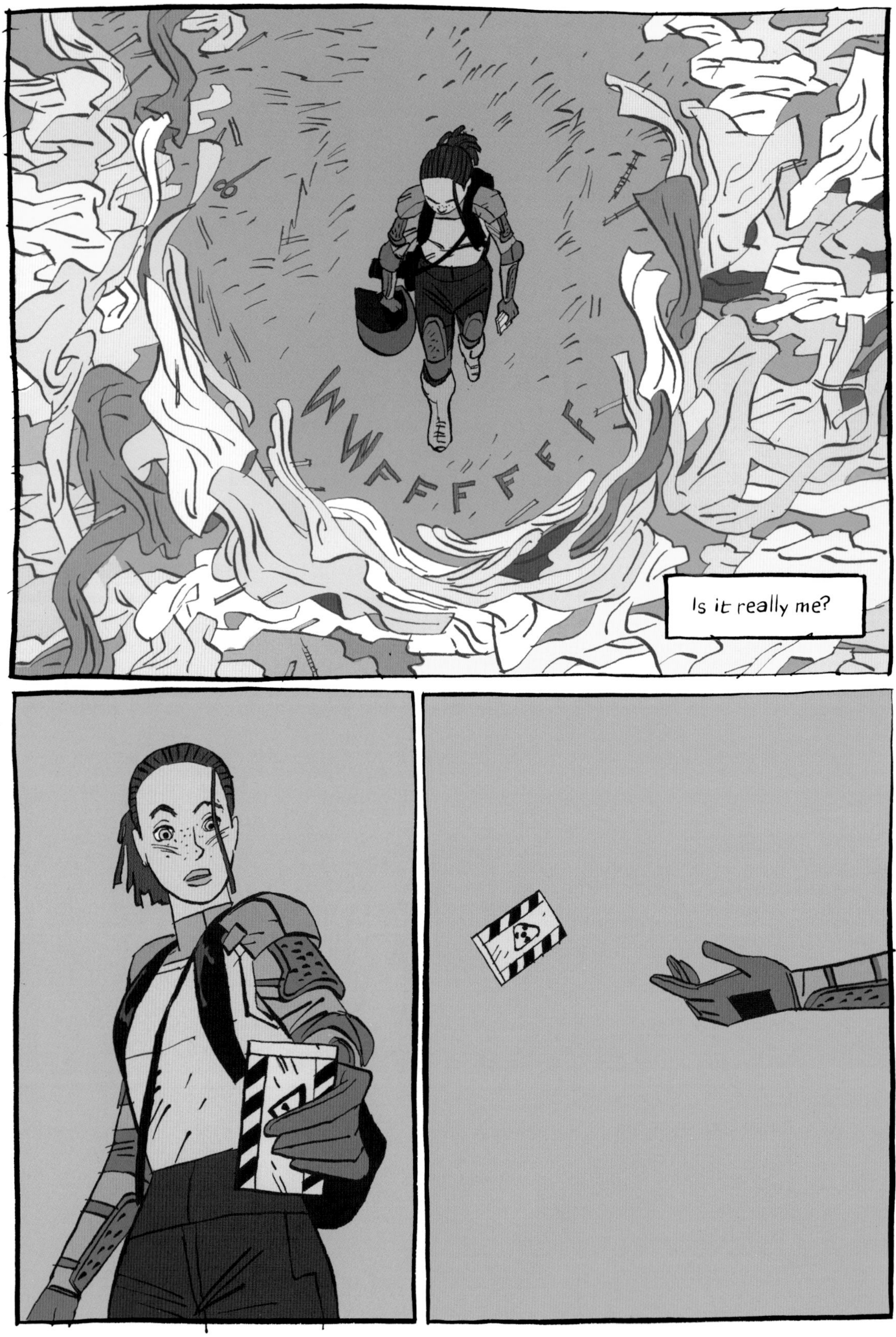
WWFFFFFF
Is it really me?

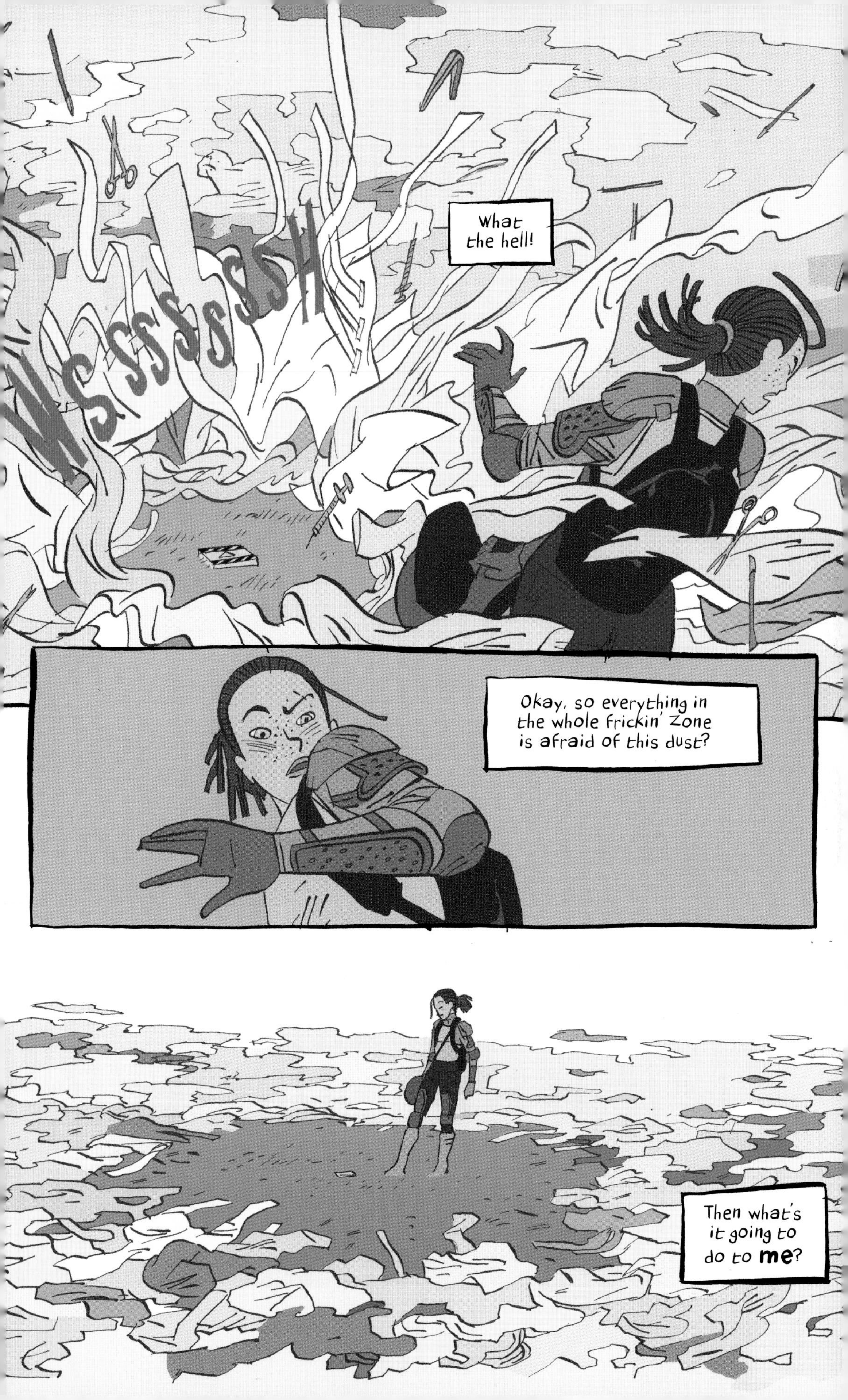
WSSSSSSSSH
What the hell!
Okay, so everything in the whole frickin' Zone is afraid of this dust?
Then what's it going to do to **me**?

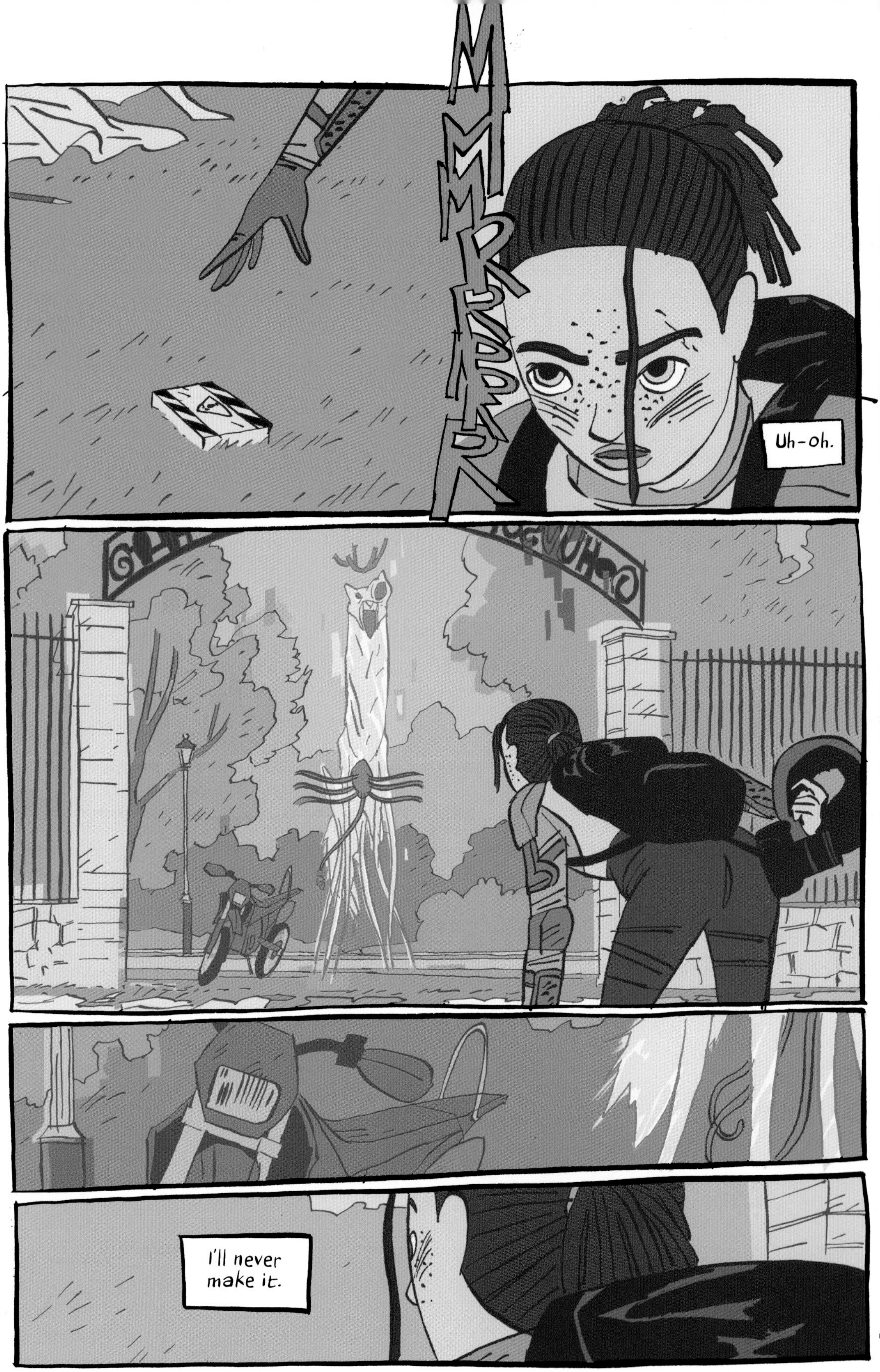
MMMRRRRRR
Uh-oh.
I'll never make it.

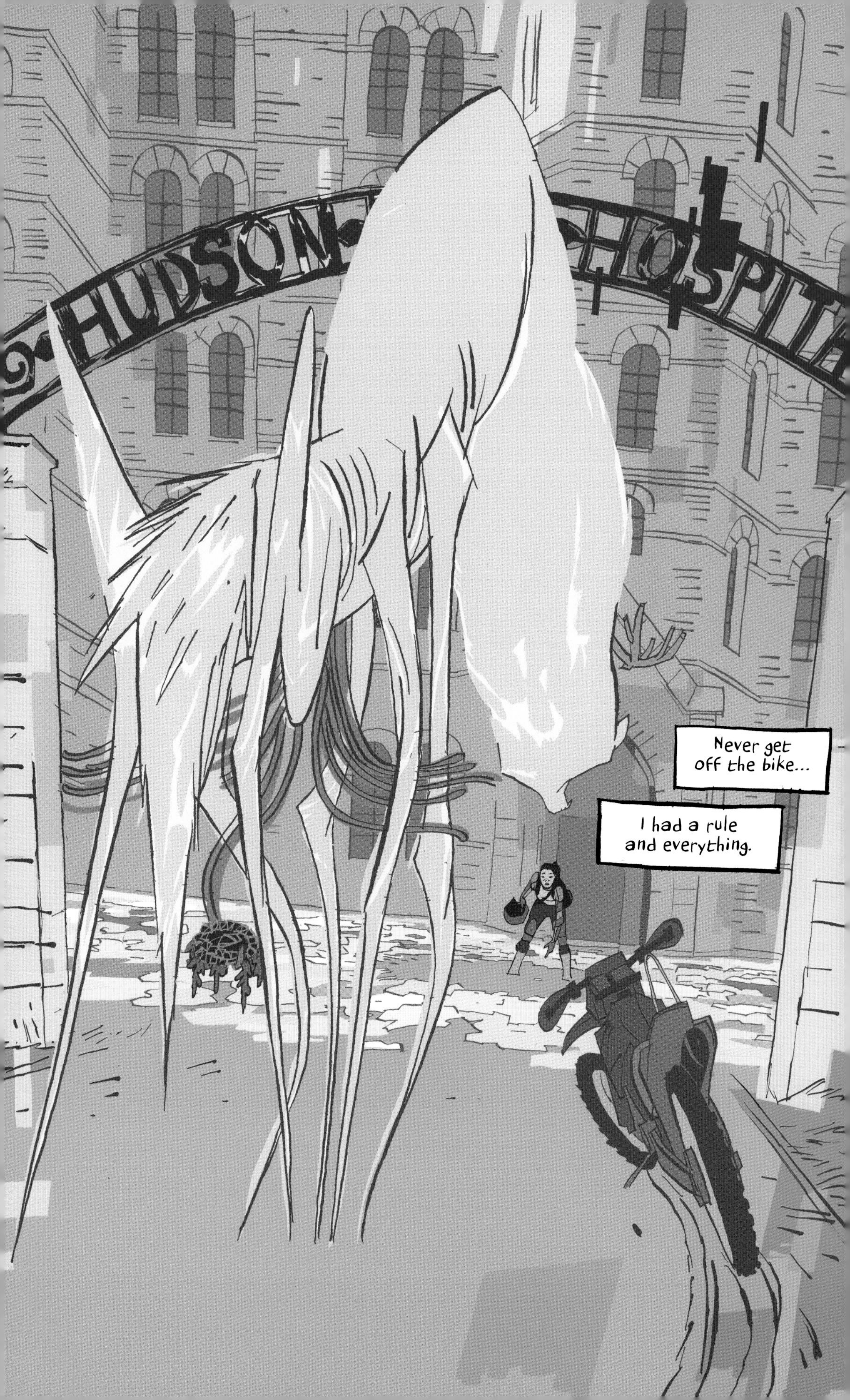

HUDSON HOSPITA
Never get off the bike...
I had a rule and everything.

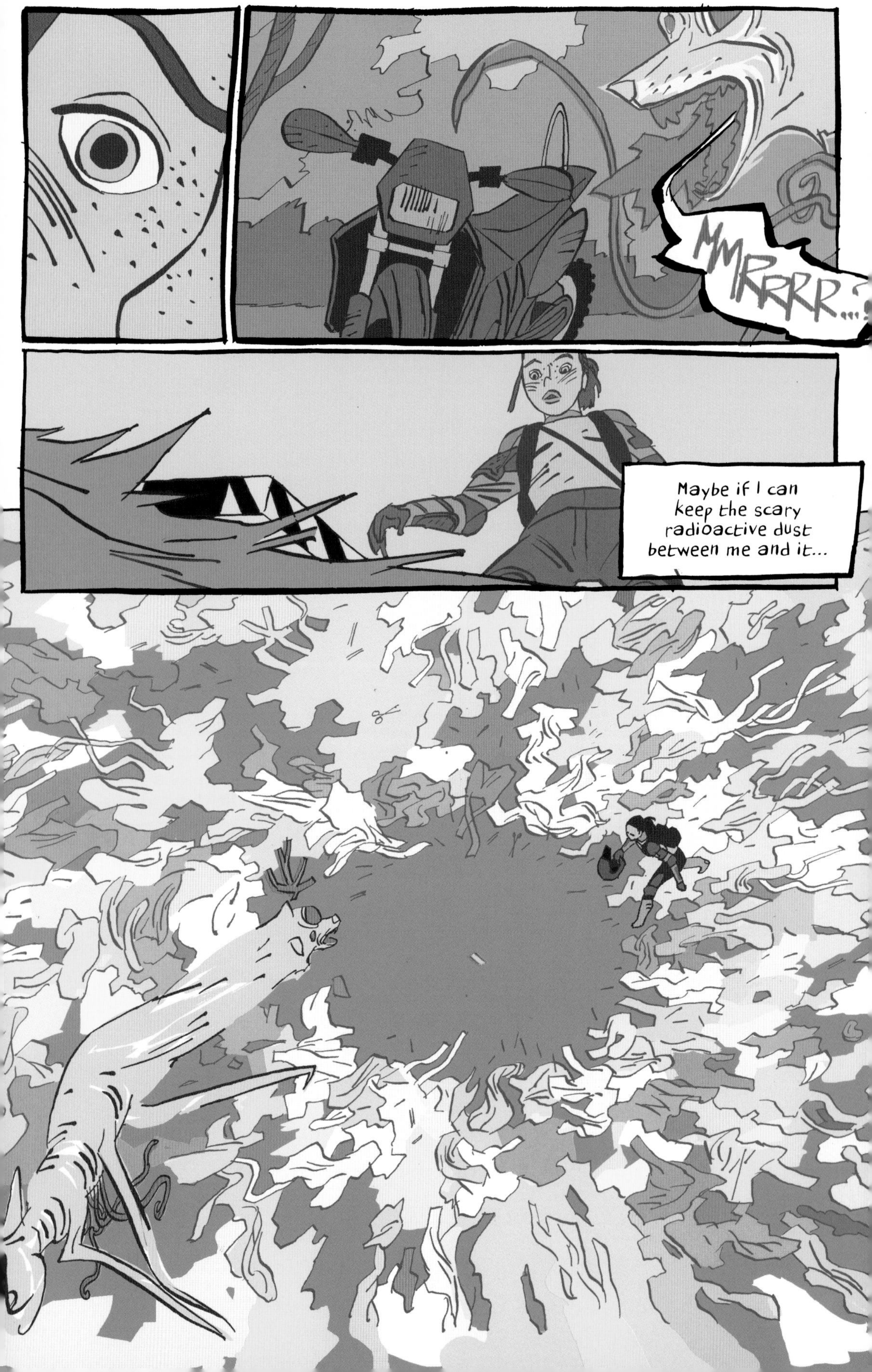
MMRRRRR...?!
Maybe if I can keep the scary radioactive dust between me and it...

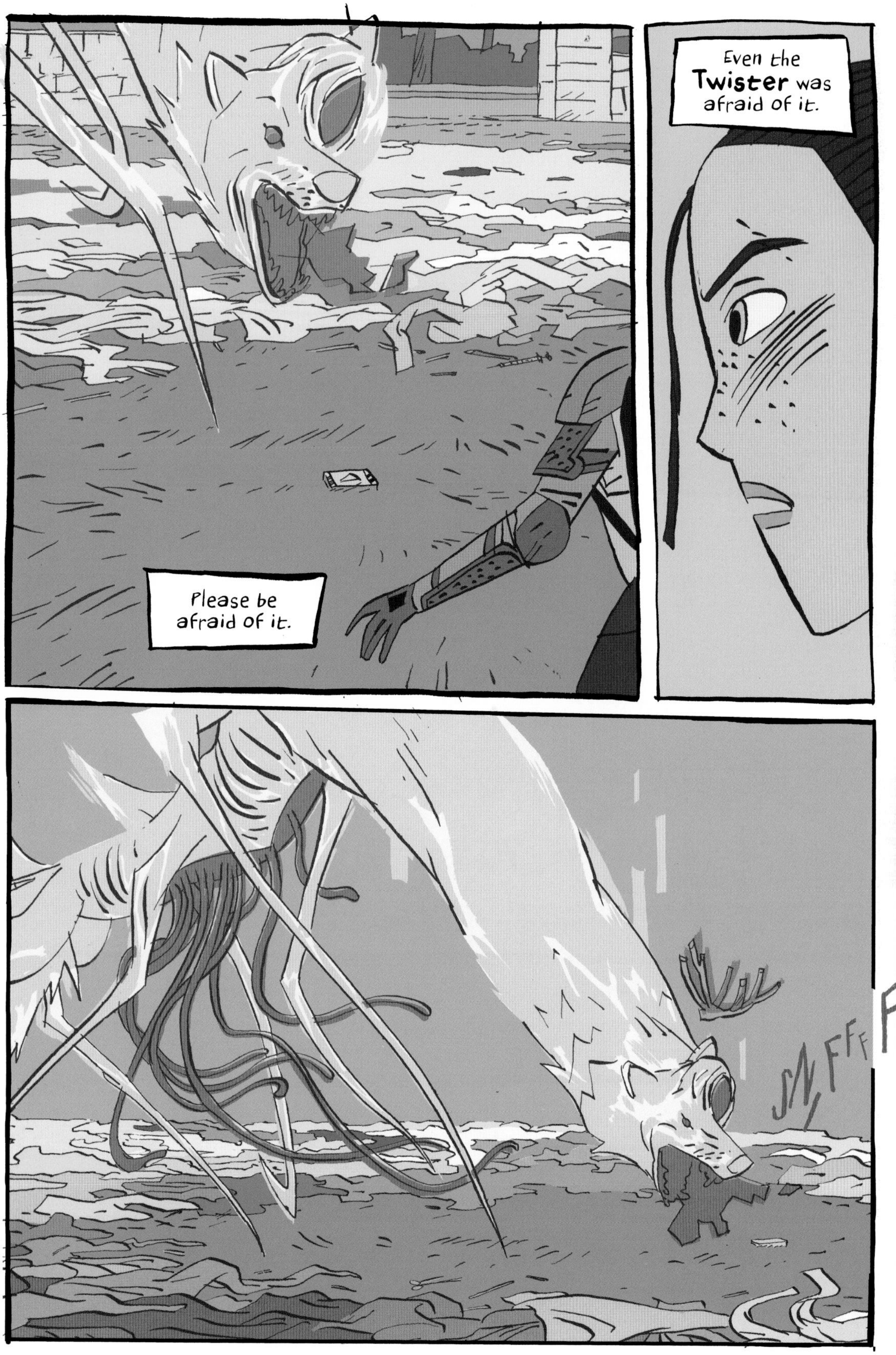
Please be afraid of it.
Even the **Twister** was afraid of it.
SNFFFF

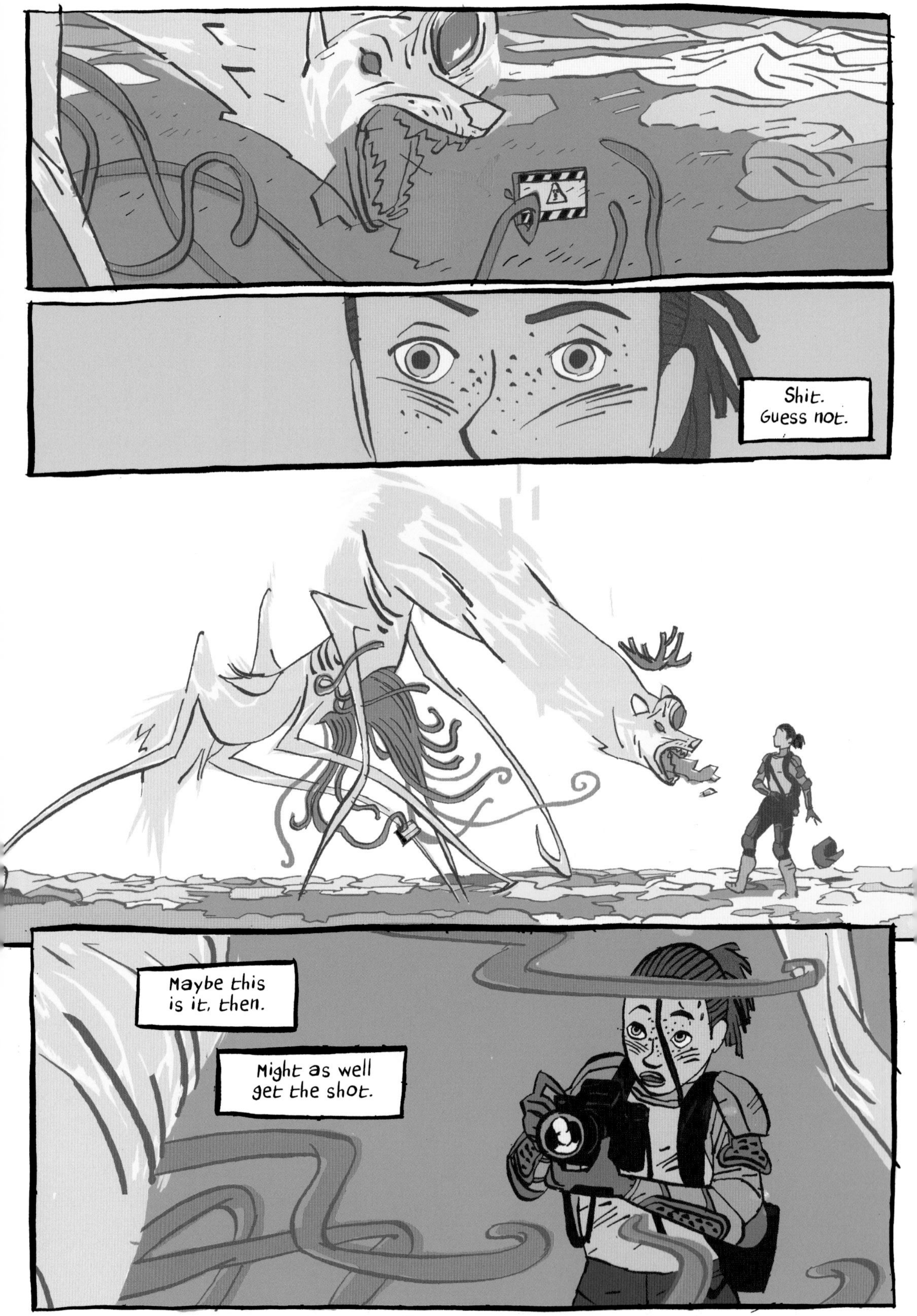
Shit.
Guess not.
Maybe this is it, then.
Might as well get the shot.

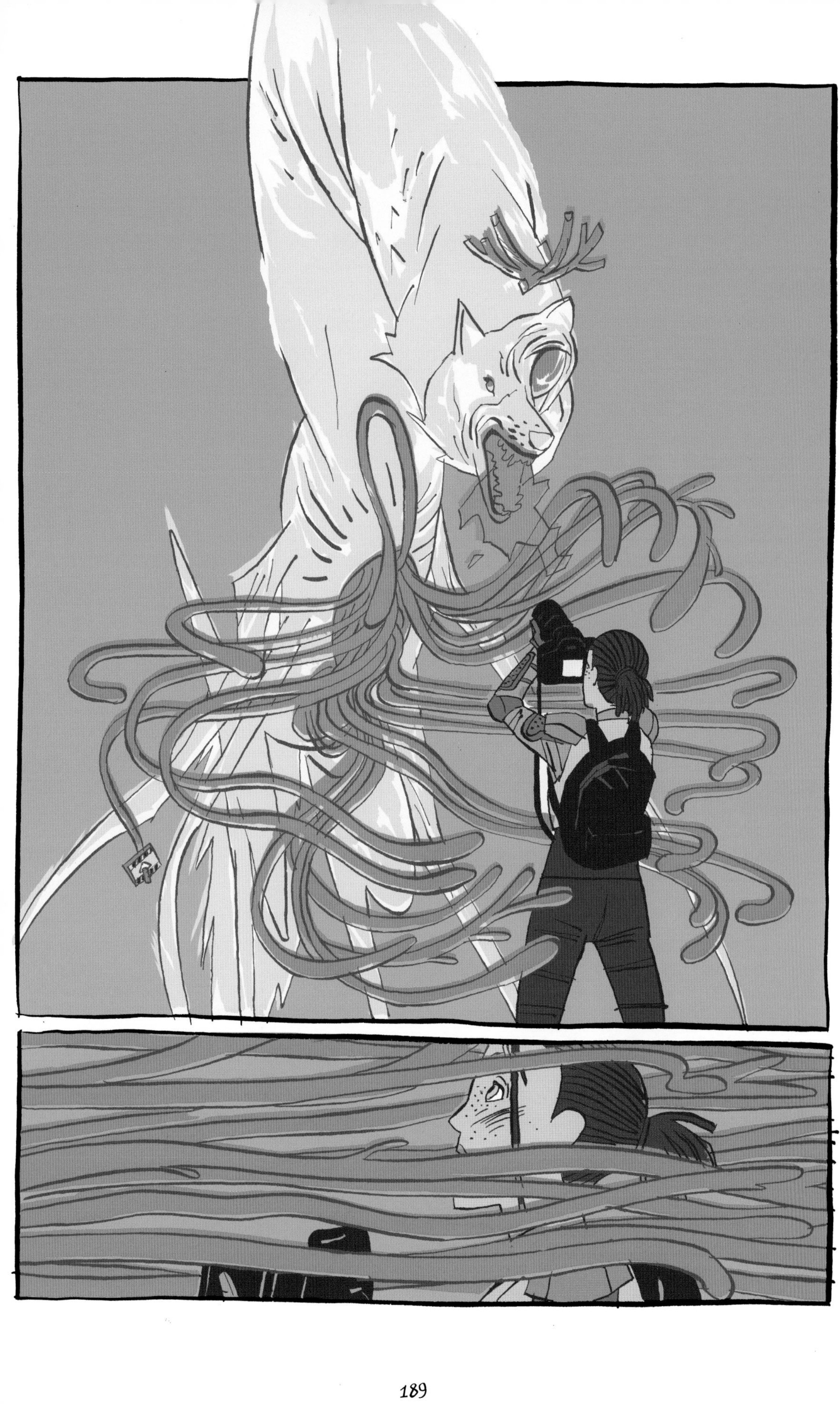

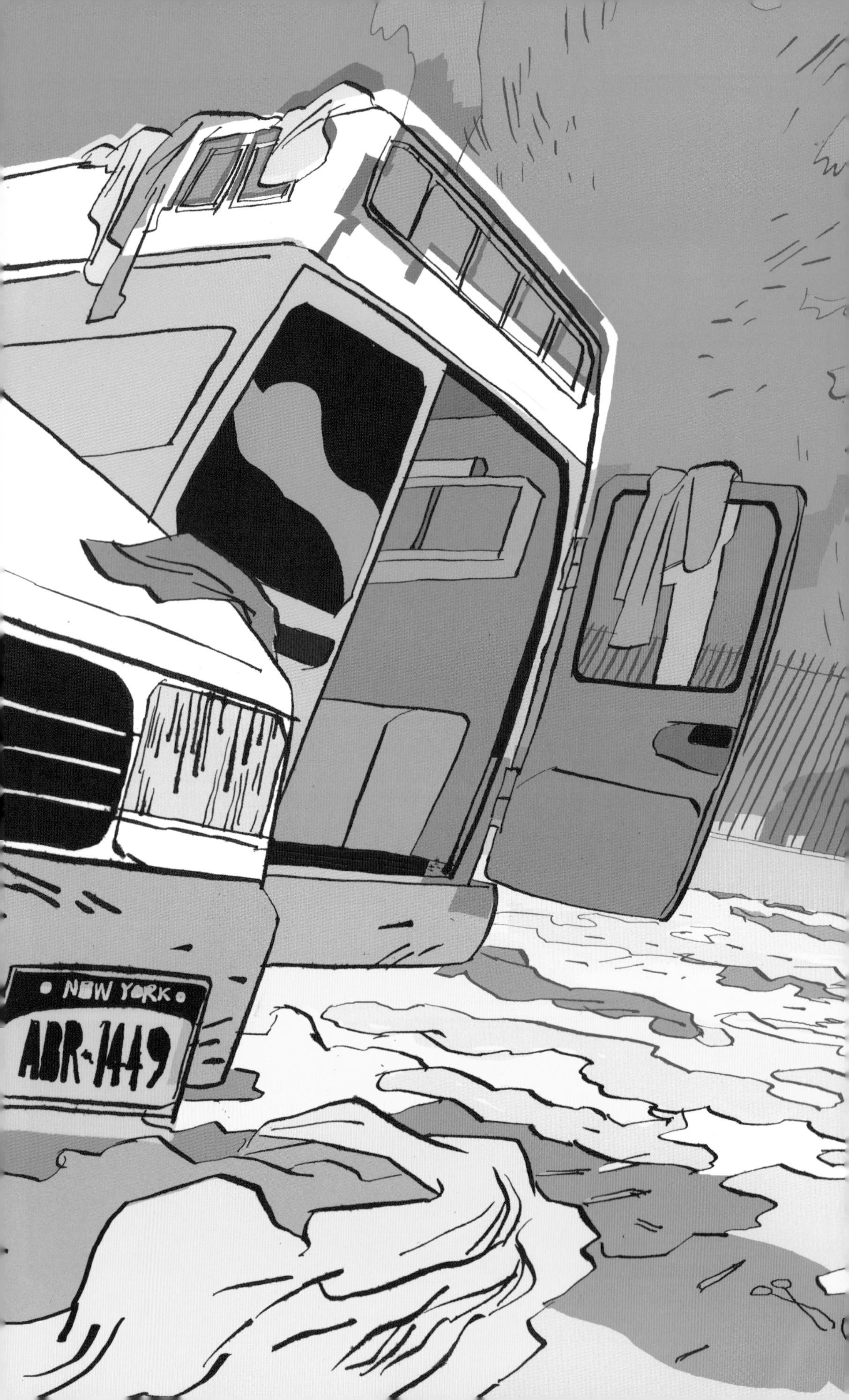
NEW YORK
ABR-1449

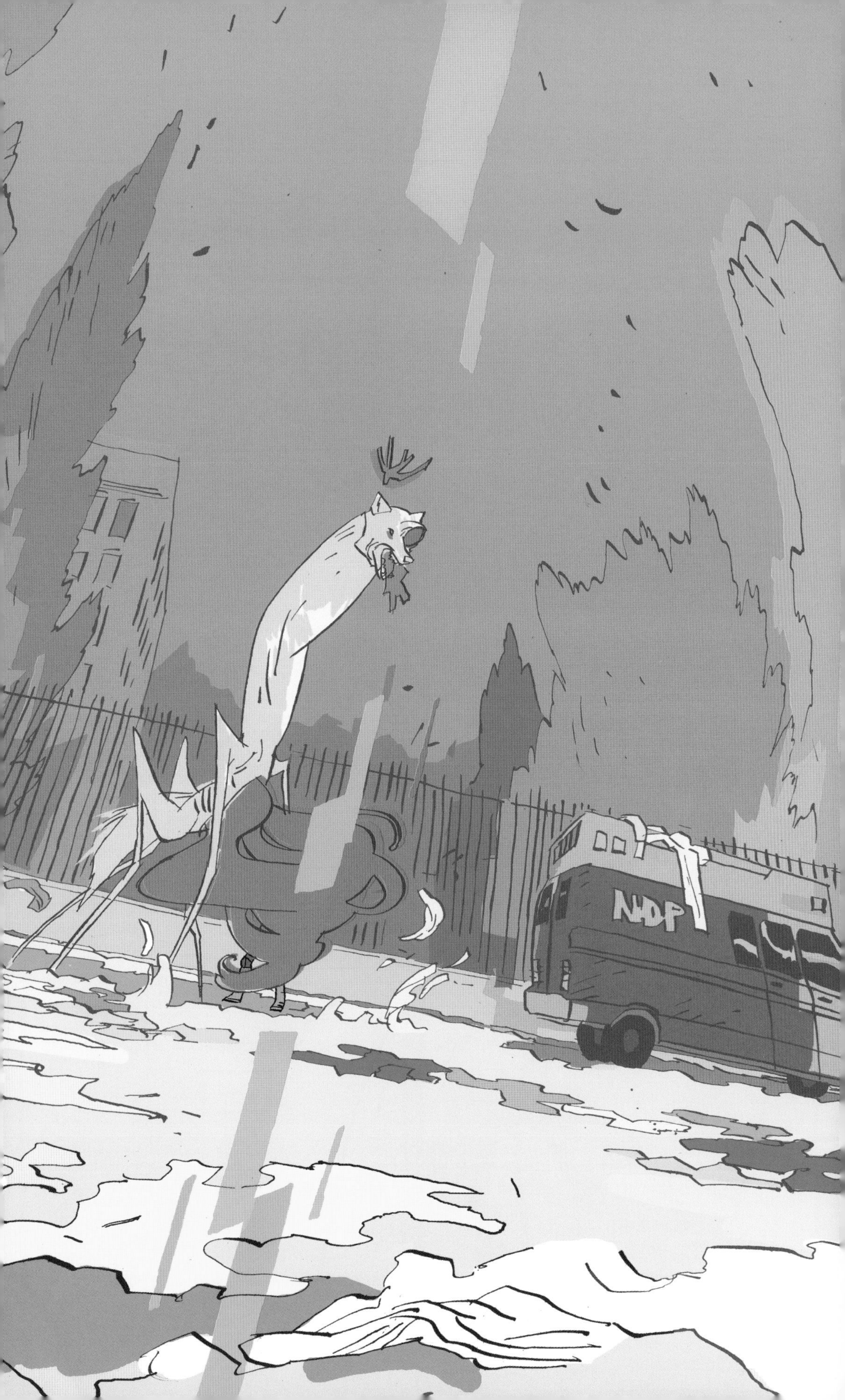
NHDP

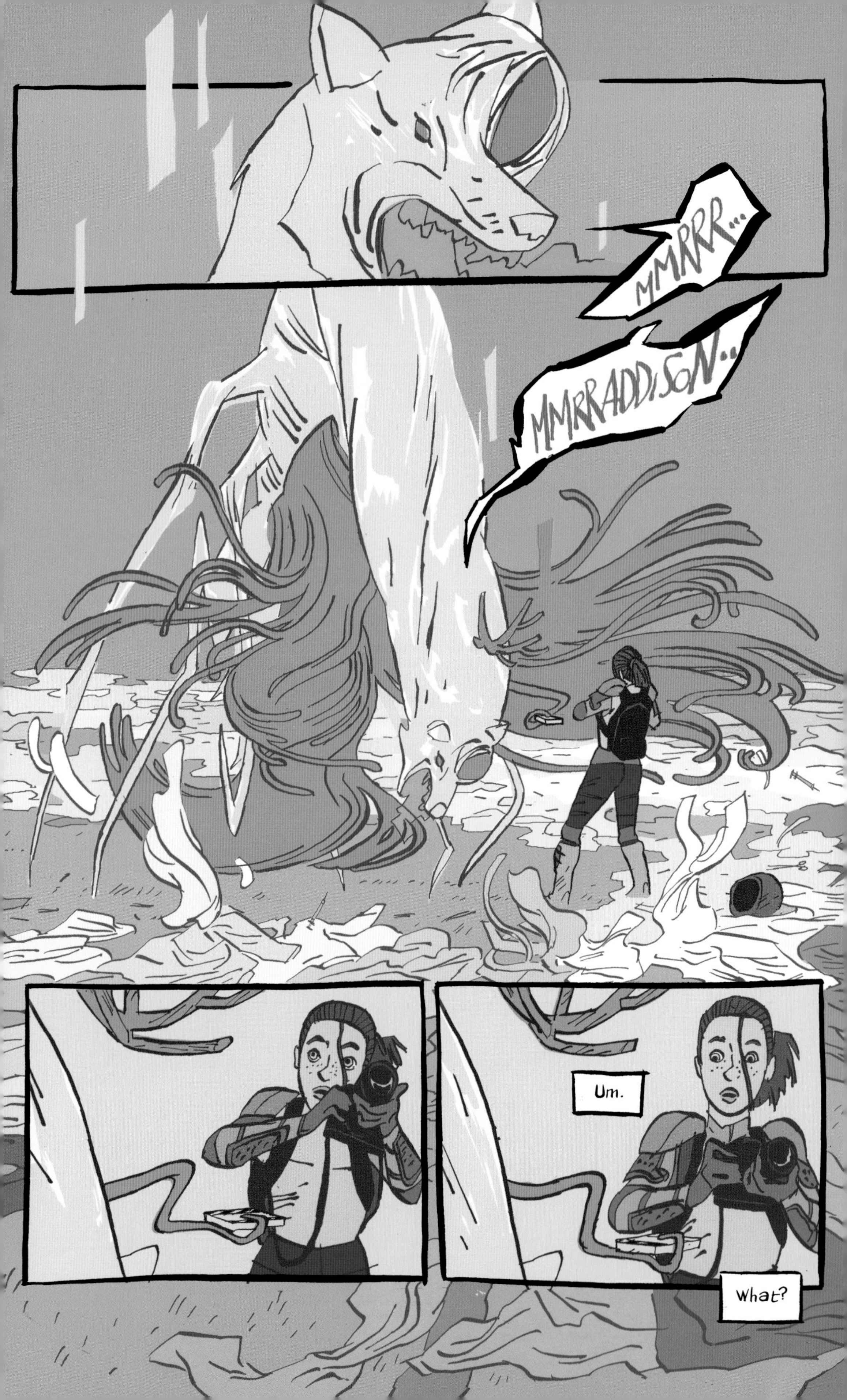
MMRRR...
MMRRADDISON...
Um.
What?

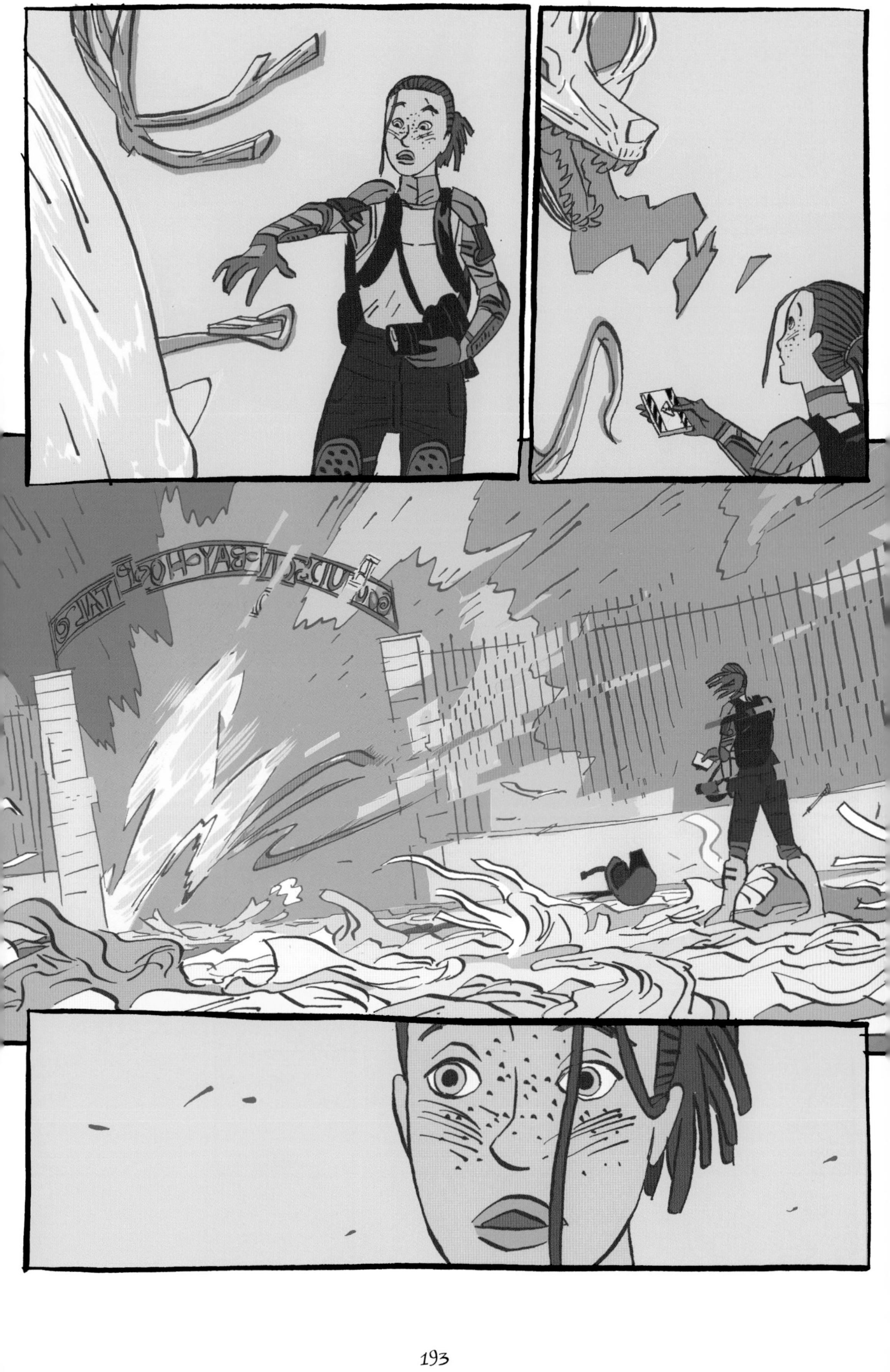

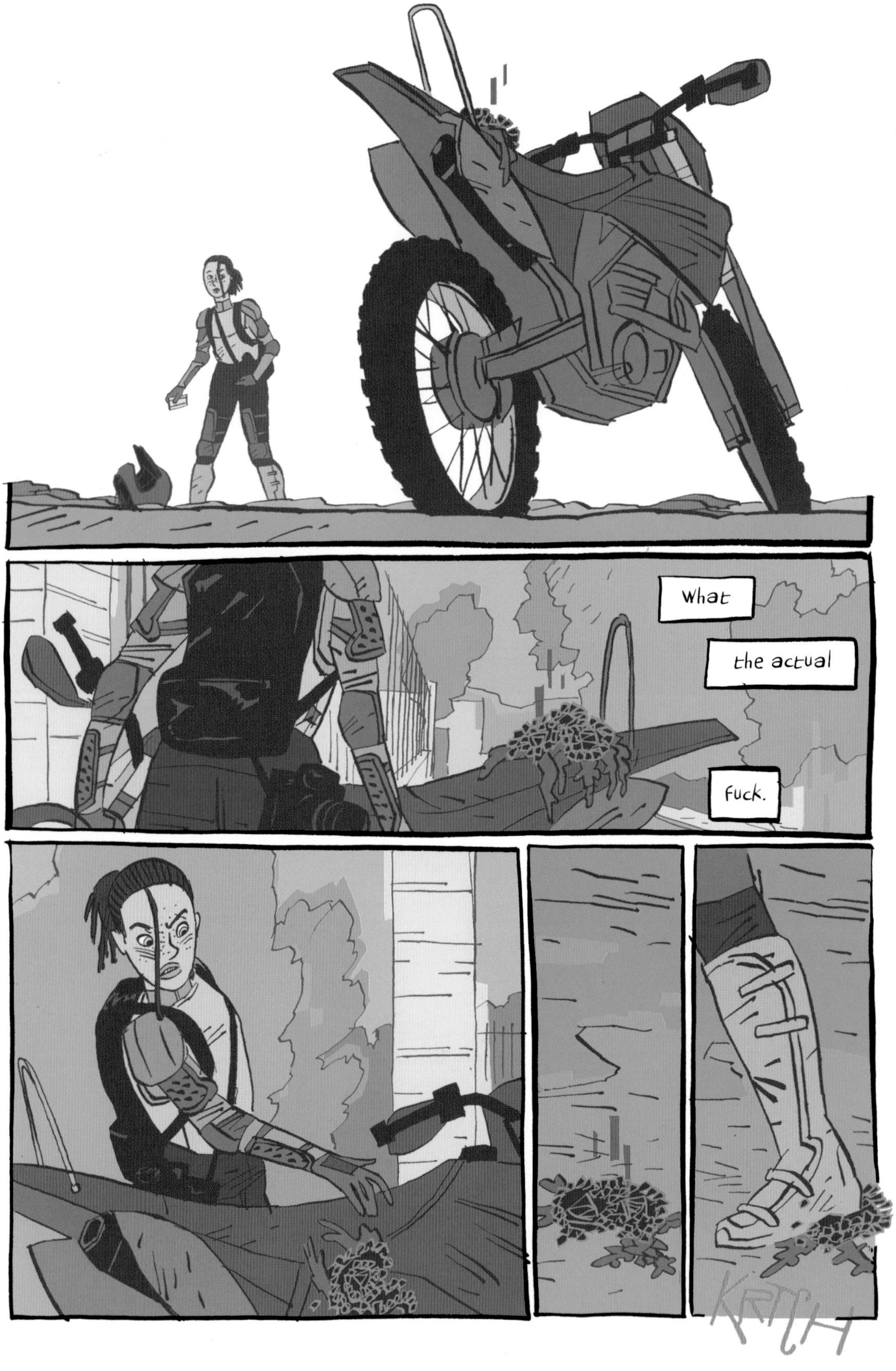
what
the actual
fuck.
KRTCH

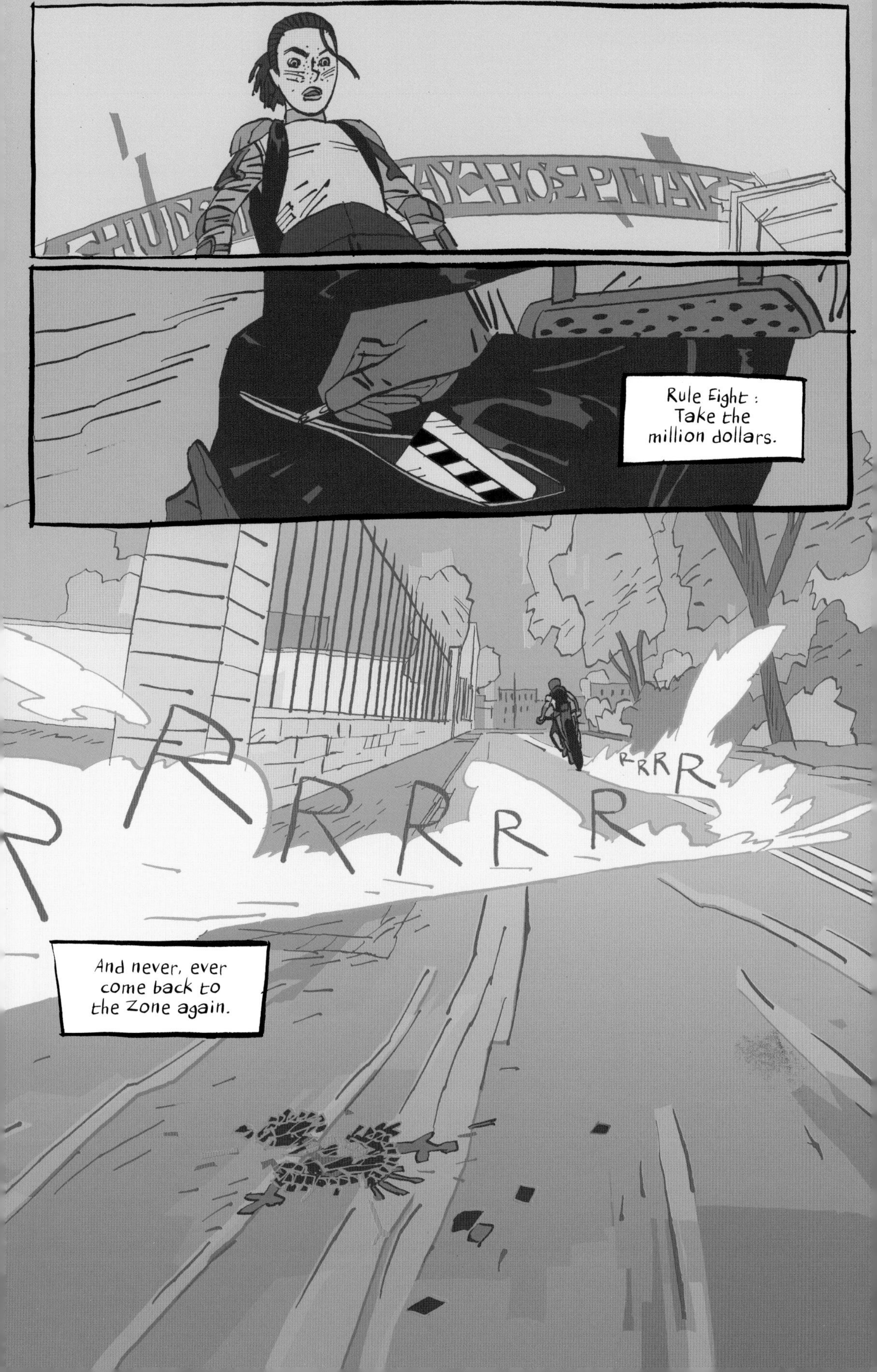
Rule Eight : Take the million dollars.
RRRR
RRRRRR
And never, ever come back to the Zone again.

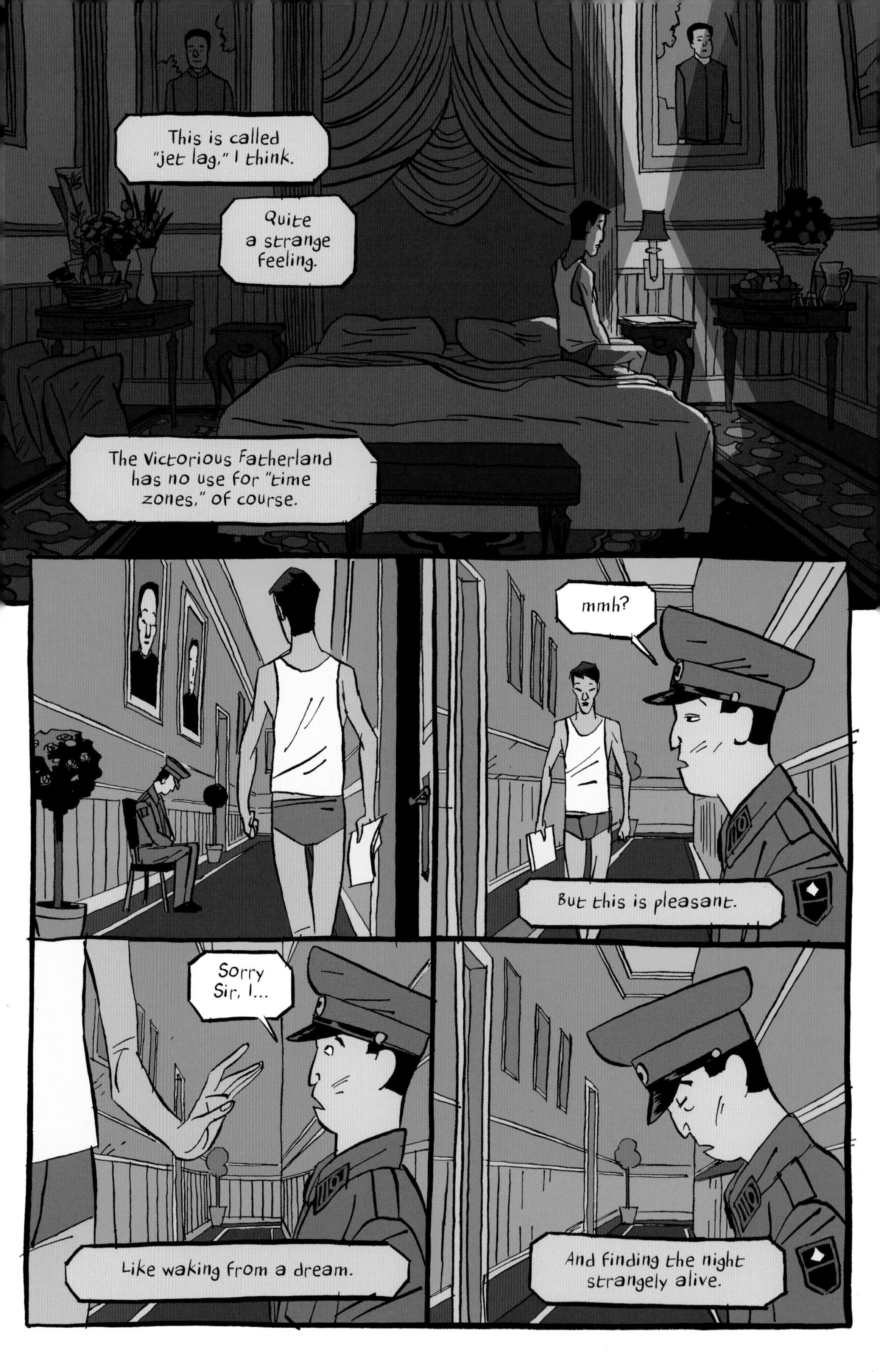
This is called "jet lag," I think.
Quite a strange feeling.
The Victorious Fatherland has no use for "time zones," of course.
mmh?
But this is pleasant.
Sorry Sir, I...
Like waking from a dream.
And finding the night strangely alive.

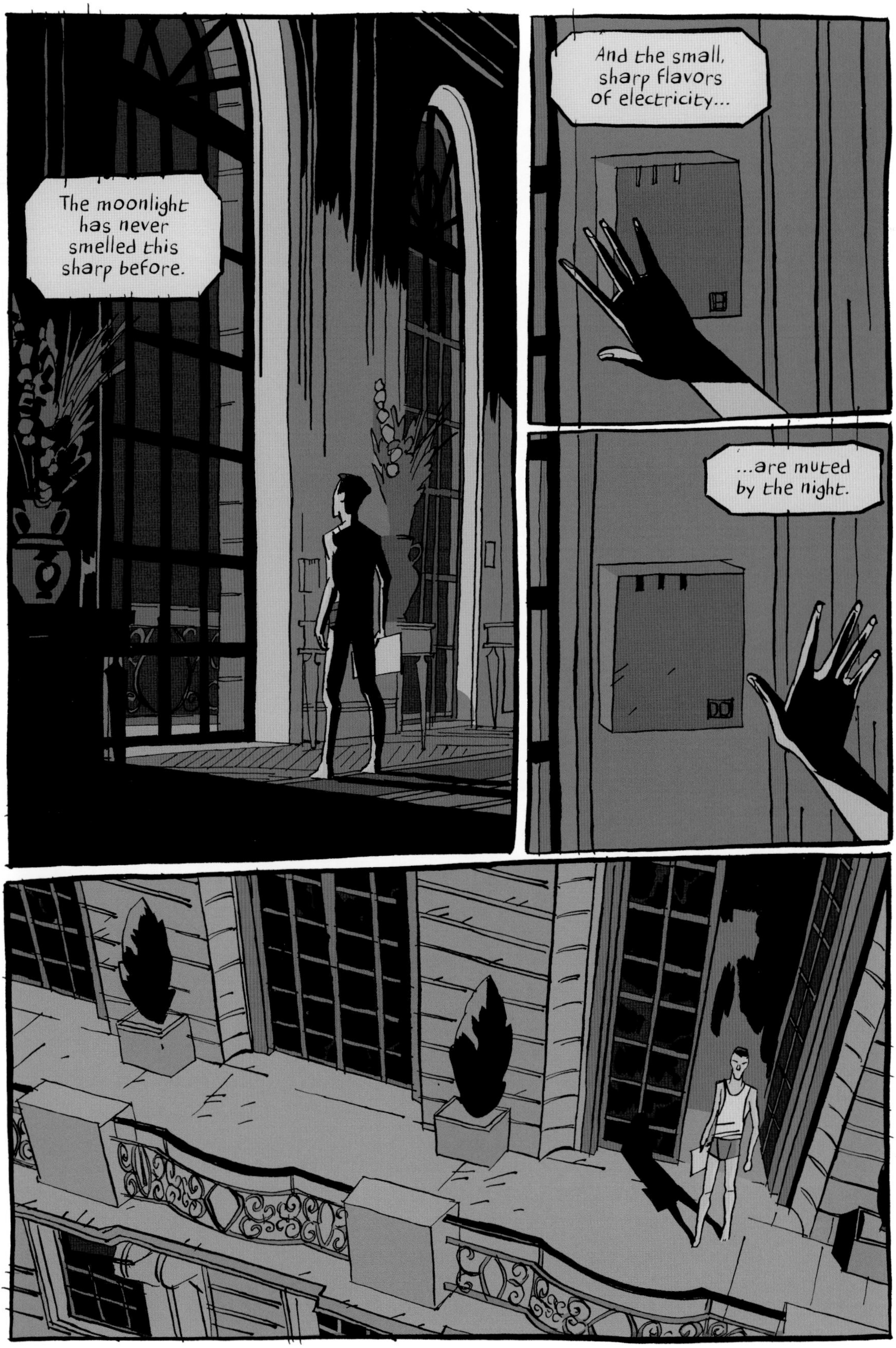
The moonlight has never smelled this sharp before.
And the small, sharp flavors of electricity...
...are muted by the night.

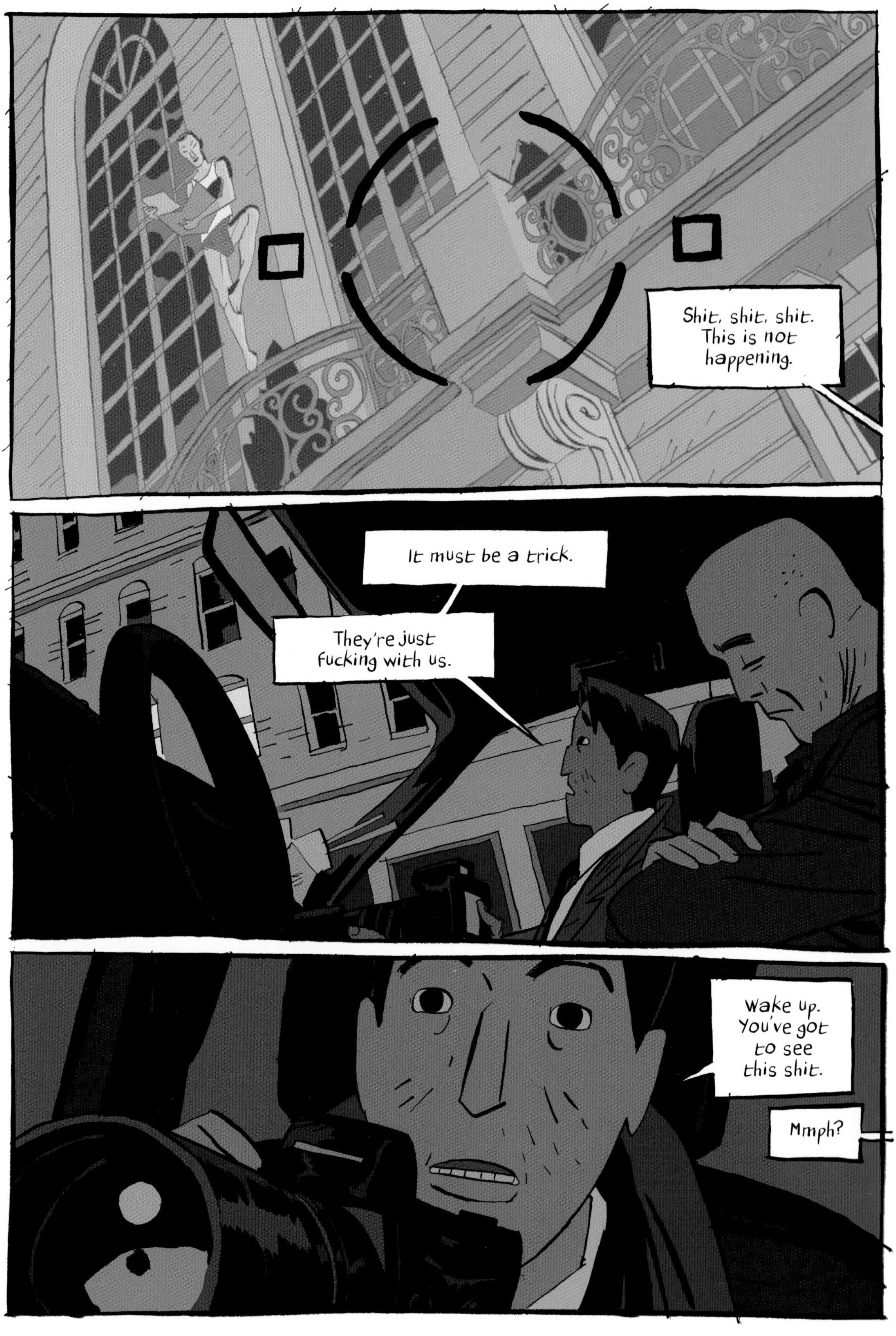
Shit, shit, shit. This is not happening.
It must be a trick.
They're just fucking with us.
Wake up. You've got to see this shit.
Mmph?

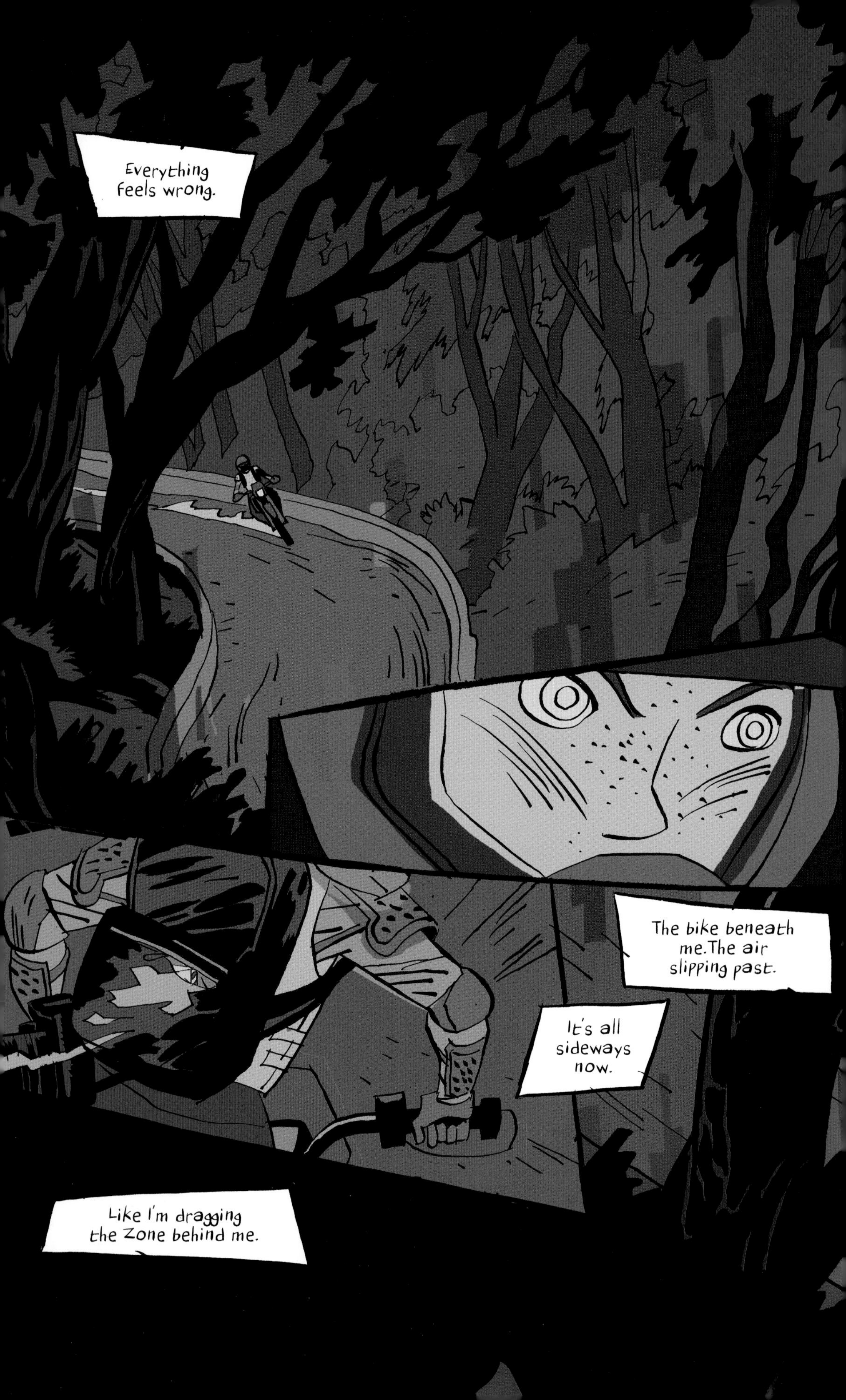

Everything feels wrong.
The bike beneath me. The air slipping past.
It's all sideways now.
Like I'm dragging the Zone behind me.

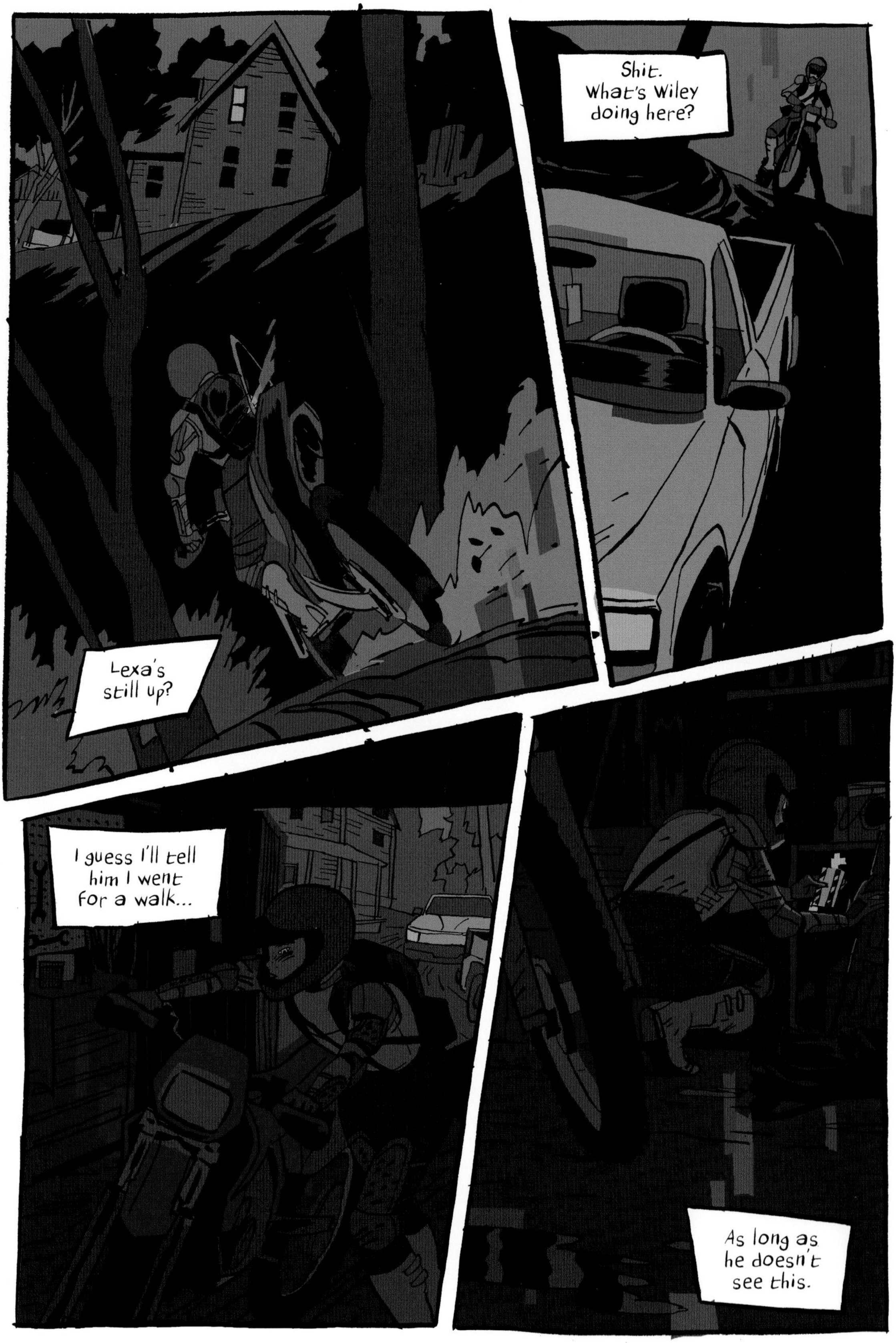
Lexa's still up?
Shit. What's Wiley doing here?
I guess I'll tell him I went for a walk...
As long as he doesn't see this.

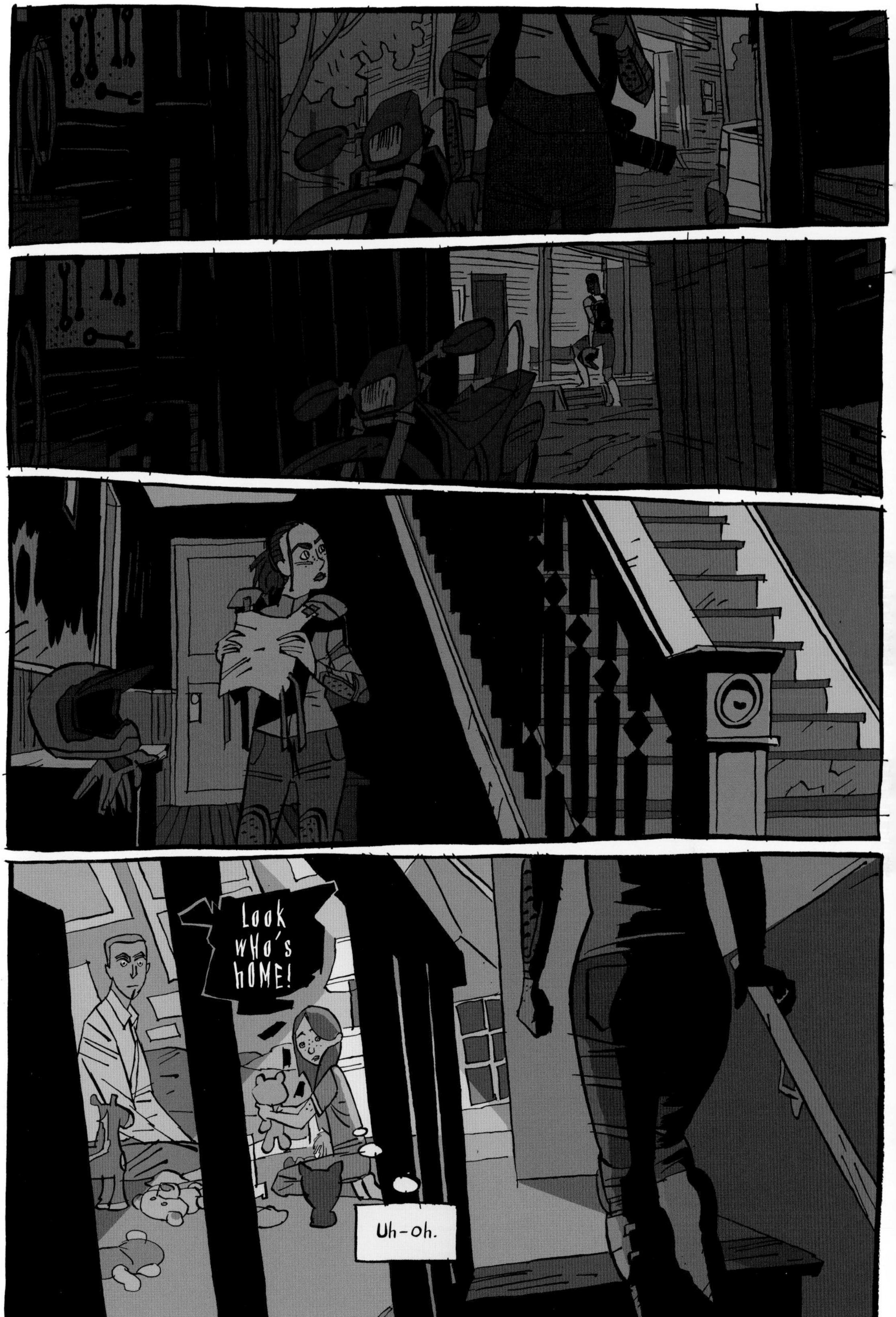
Look who's HOME!
Uh-oh.

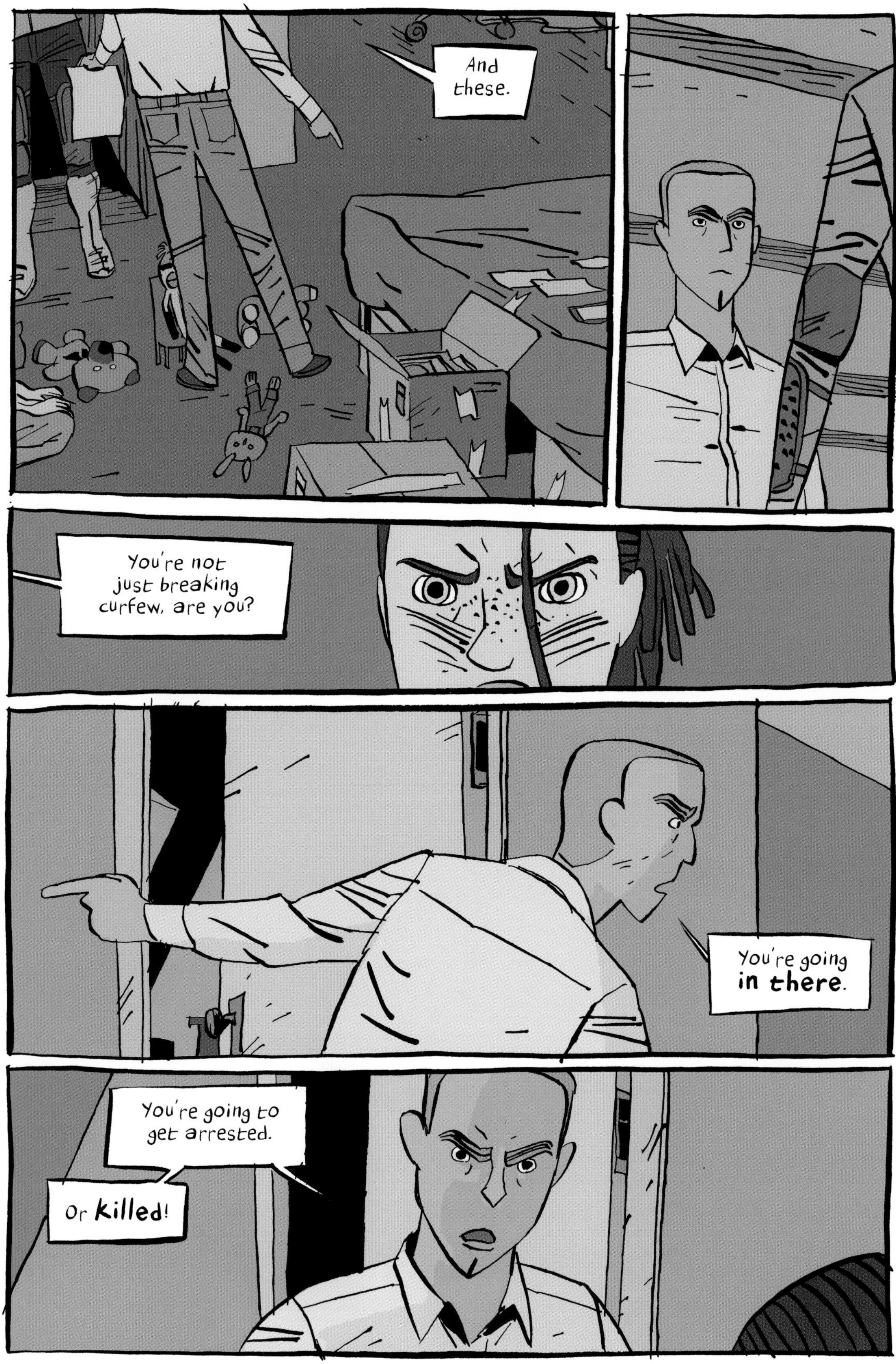

And these.
You're not just breaking curfew, are you?
You're going **in there**.
You're going to get arrested.
Or **killed**!

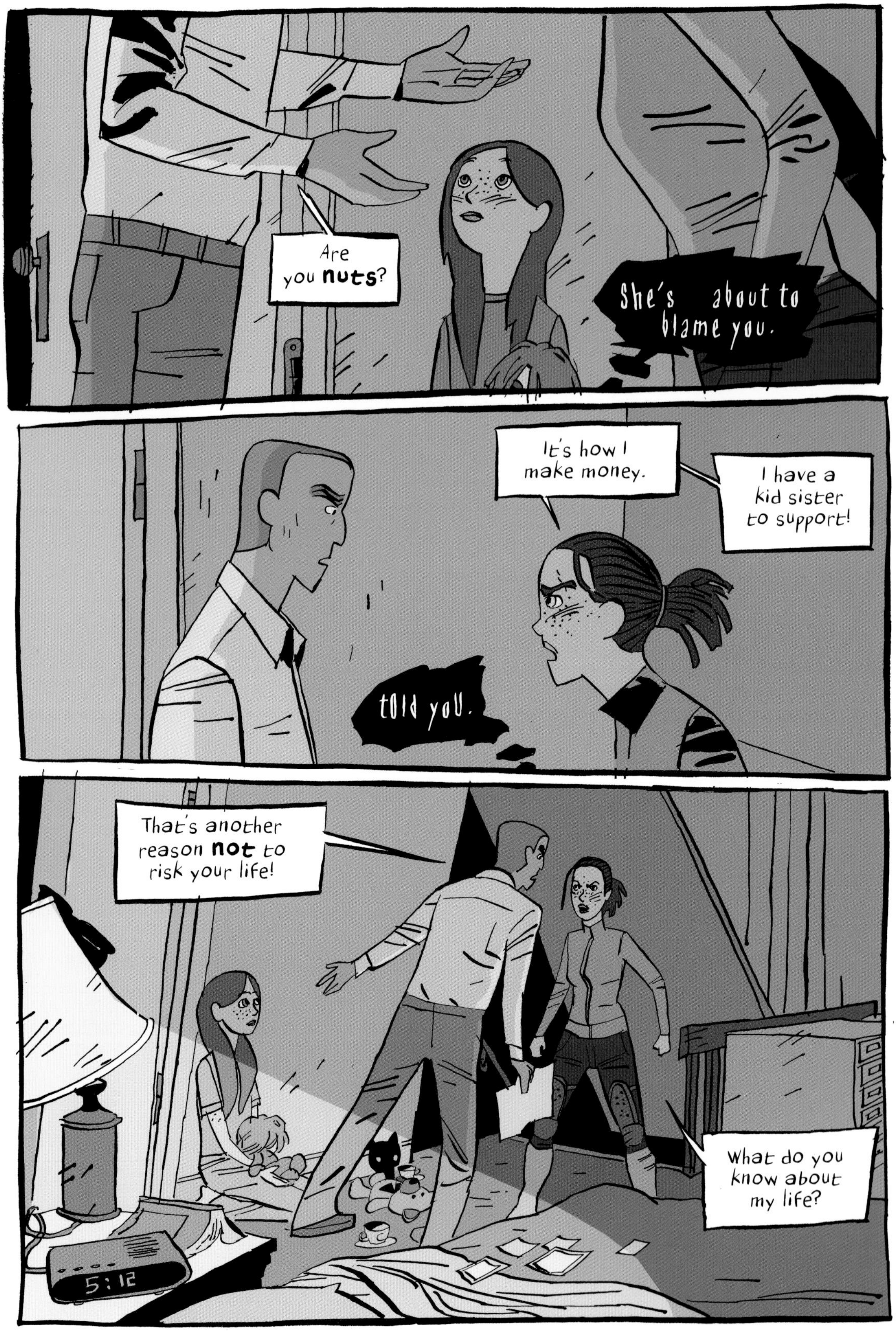
Are you **nuts**?
She's about to blame you.
It's how I make money.
I have a kid sister to support!
told you.
That's another reason **not** to risk your life!
5:12
What do you know about my life?

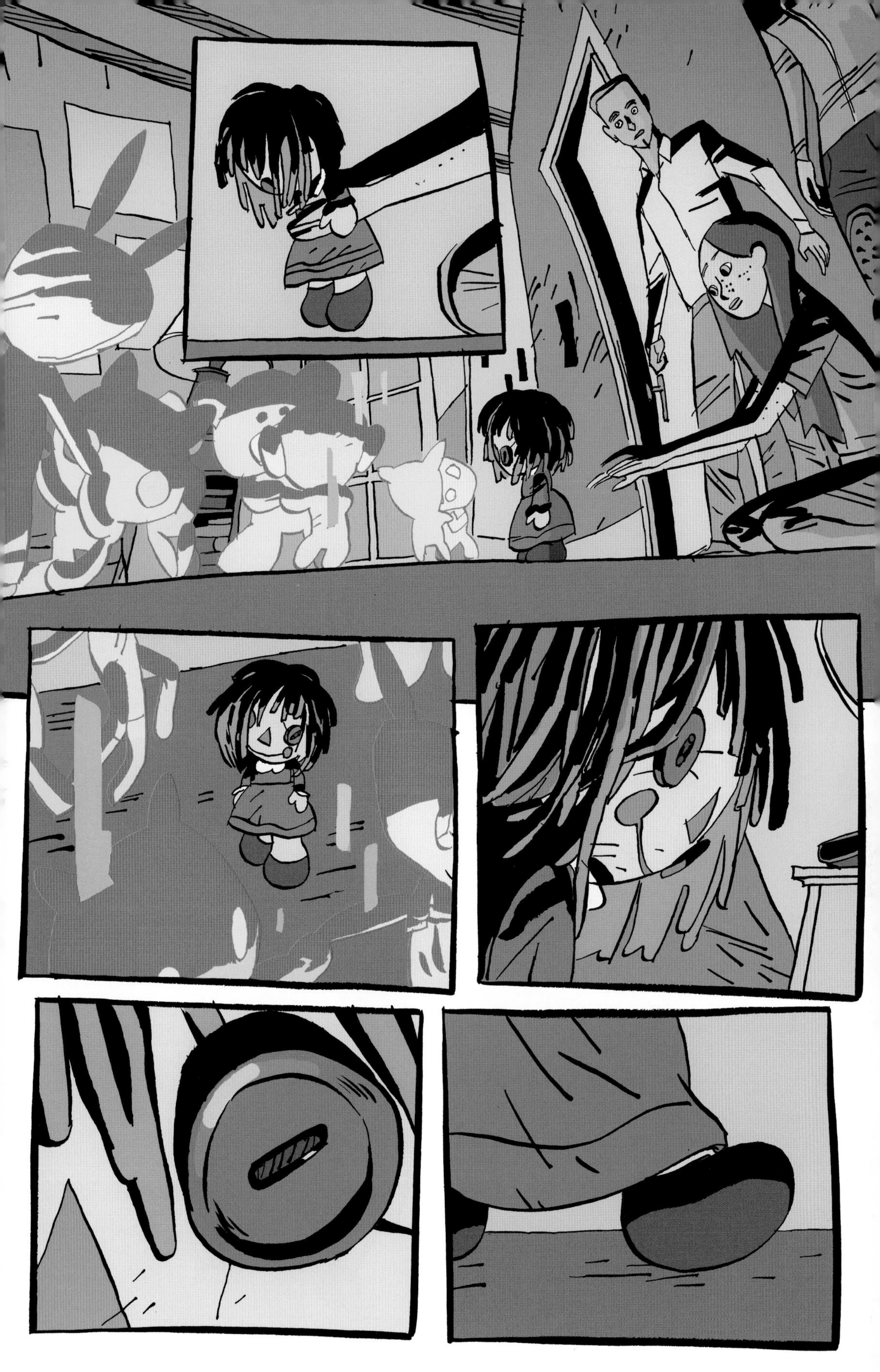

Keep reading for a bonus comic

SPILL NIGHT,

set in the world of

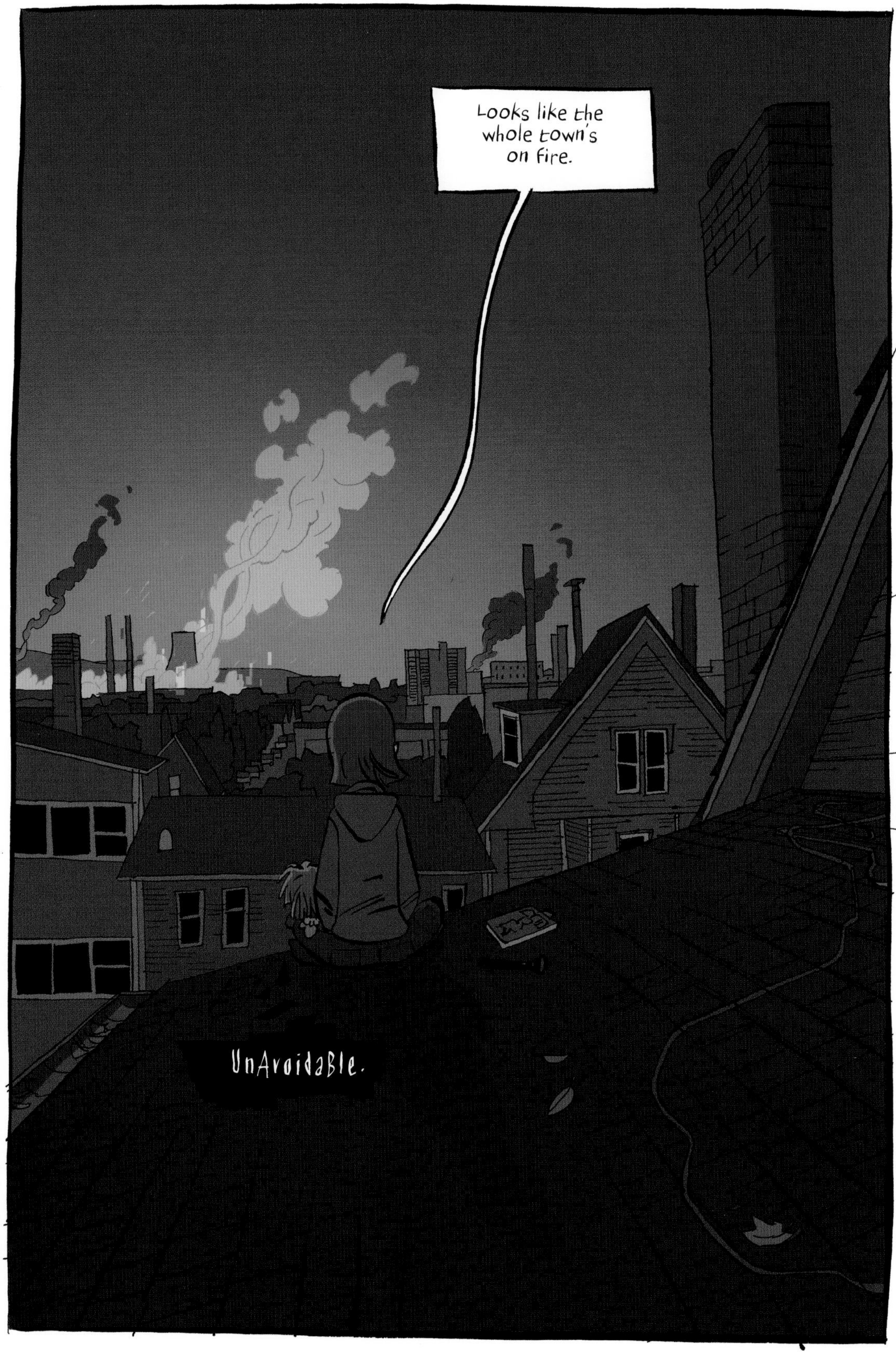
Looks like the whole town's on fire.
UnAvoidable.

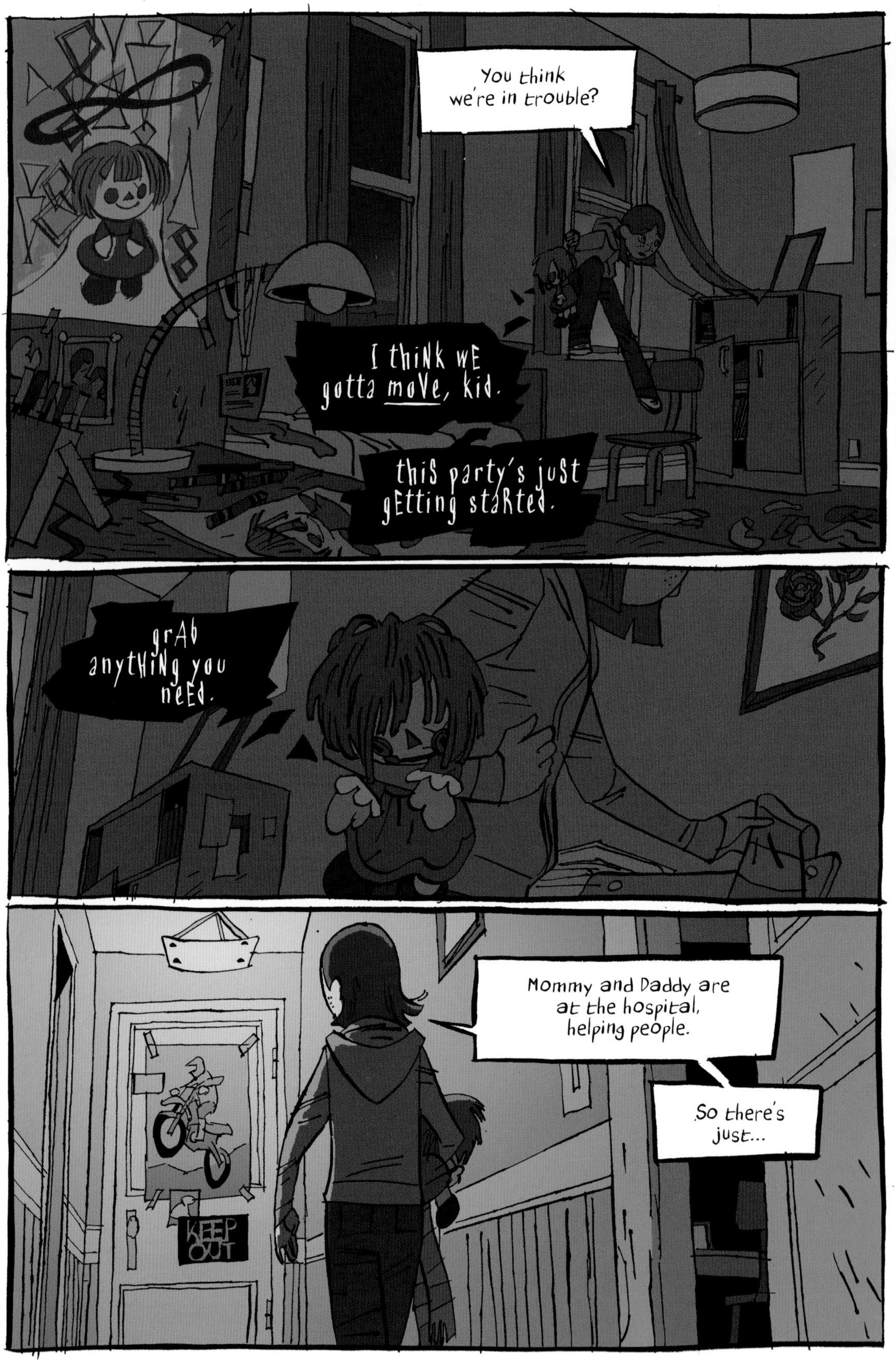
You think we're in trouble?
I think we gotta move, kid.
this party's just getting started.
grab anything you need.
Mommy and Daddy are at the hospital, helping people.
So there's just...
KEEP OUT

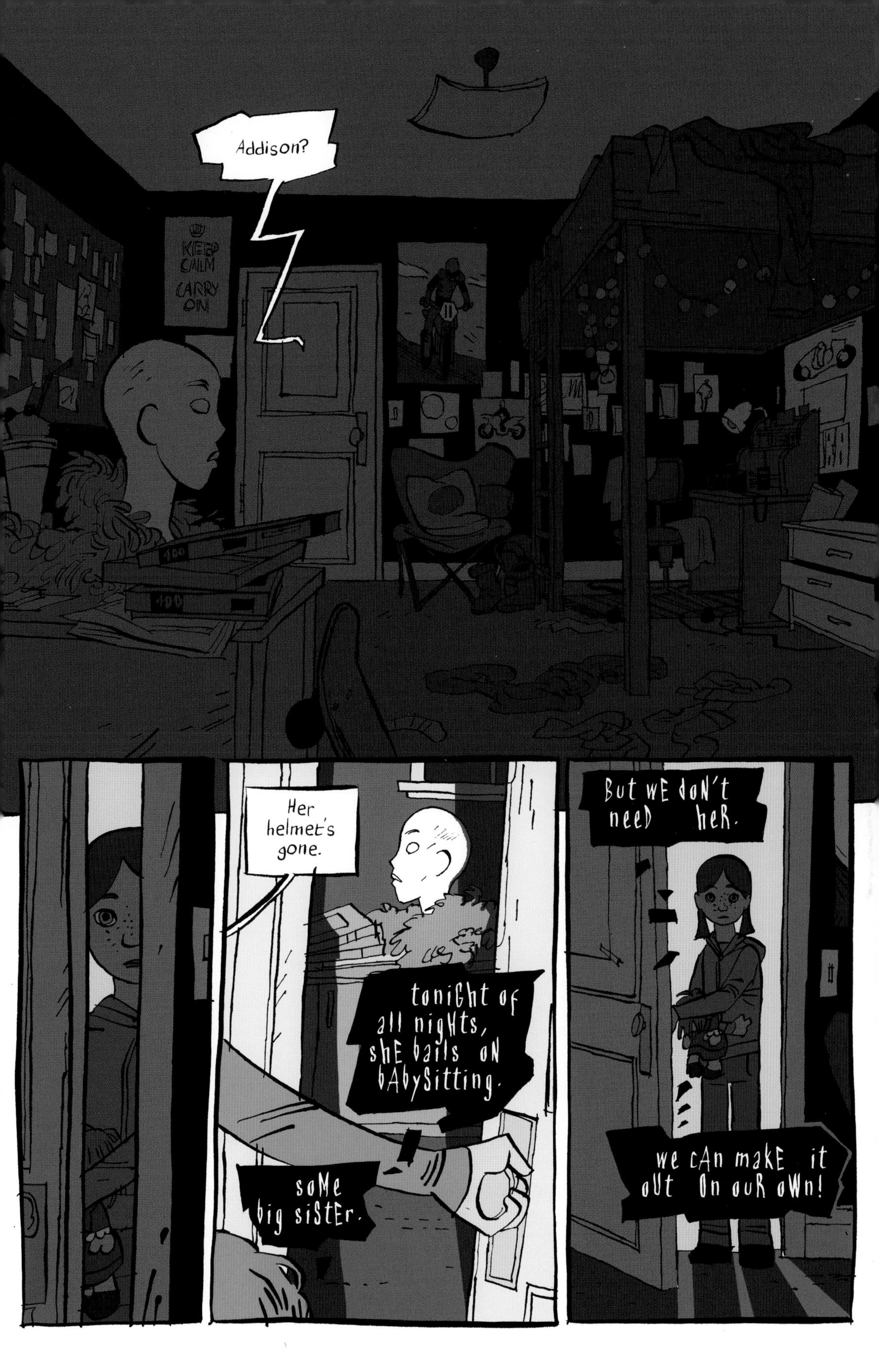
Addison?
KEEP CALM CARRY ON
Her helmet's gone.
tonight of all nights, she bails on babysitting.
some big sister.
But we don't need her.
we can make it out on our own!

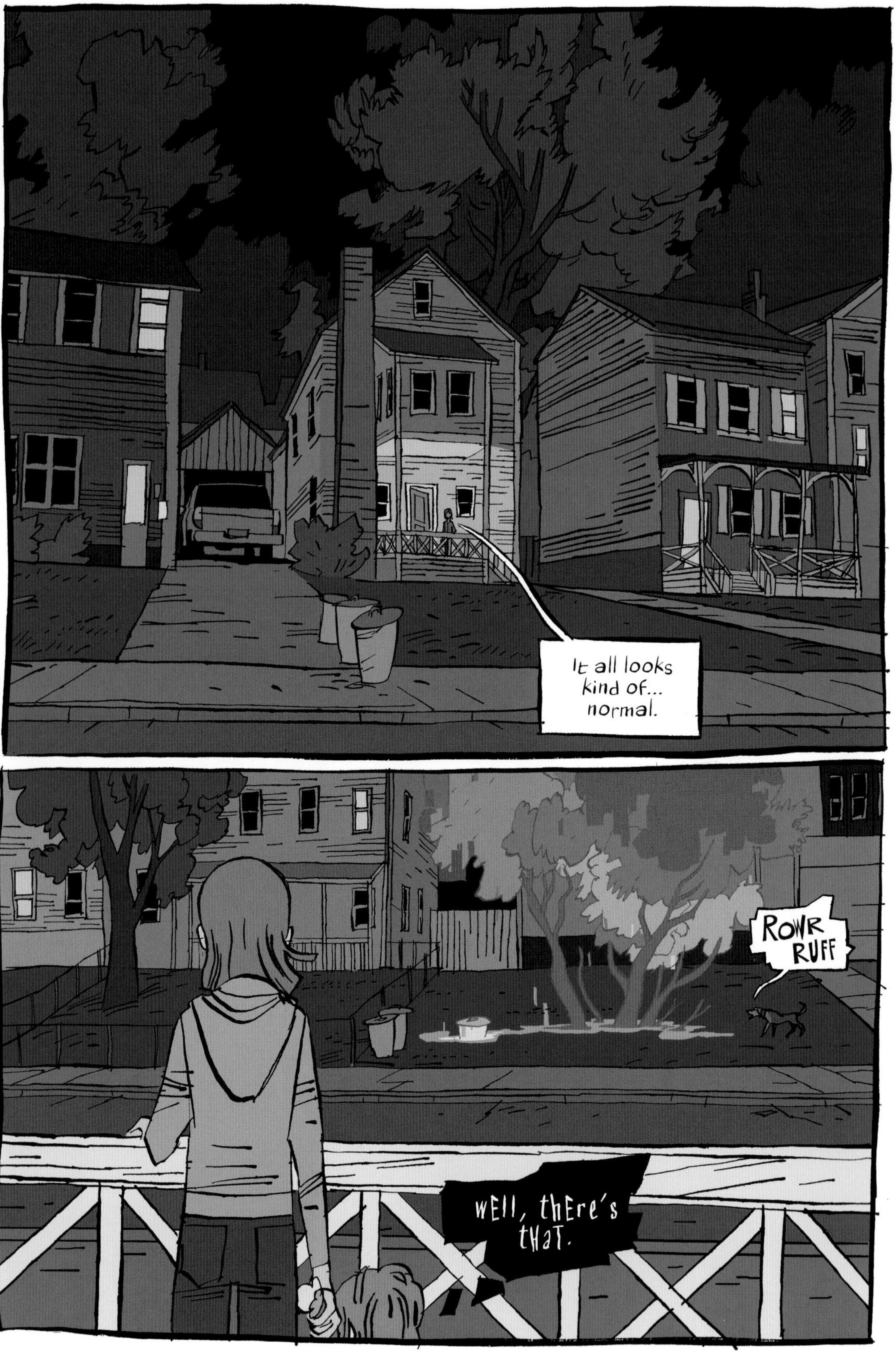
It all looks kind of... normal.
ROWR RUFF
WELL, THERE'S THAT.

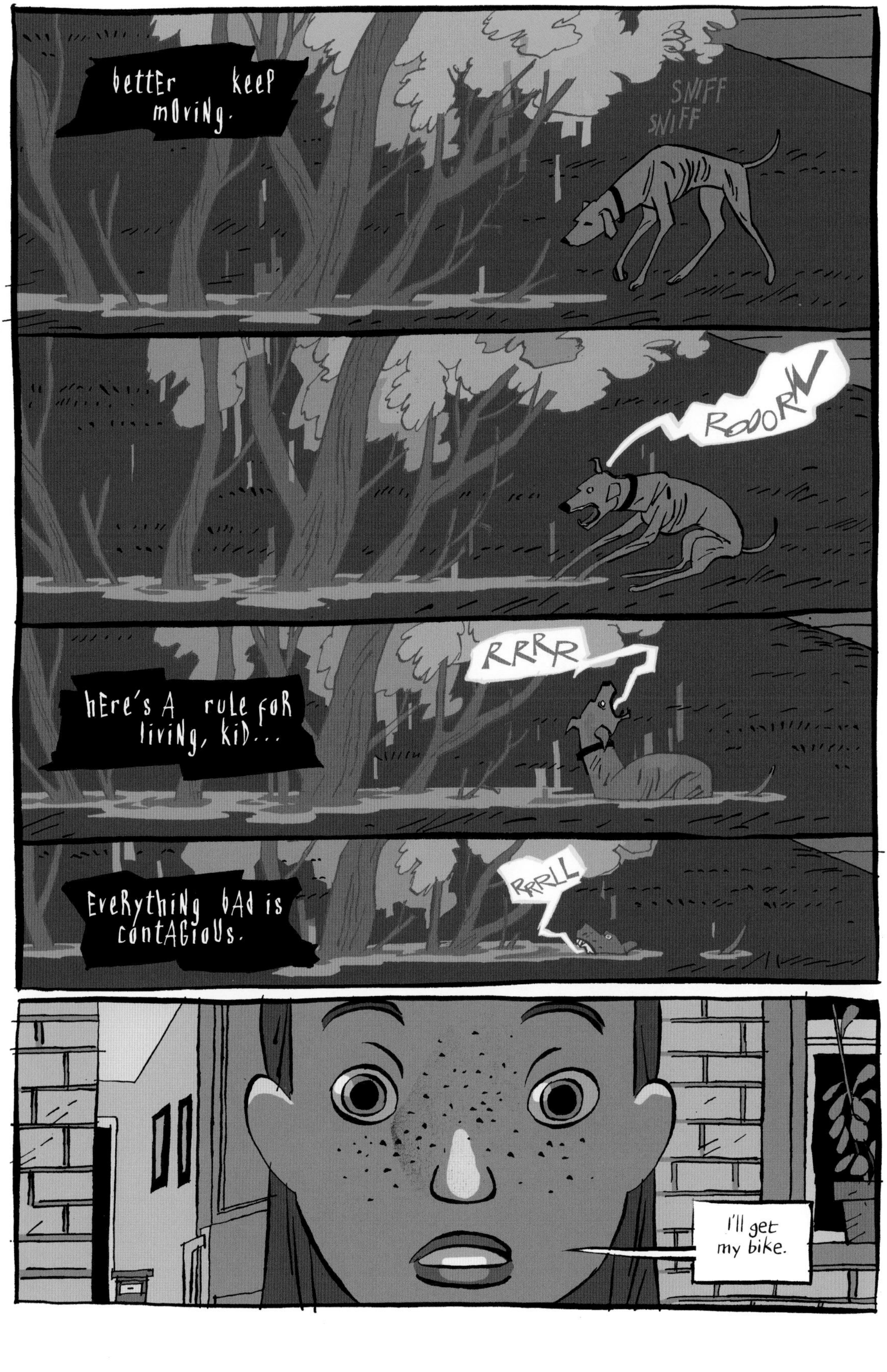
better keep moving.
SNIFF SNIFF
ROOORW
RRRR
here's a rule for living, kid...
RRRLL
Everything bad is contagious.
I'll get my bike.

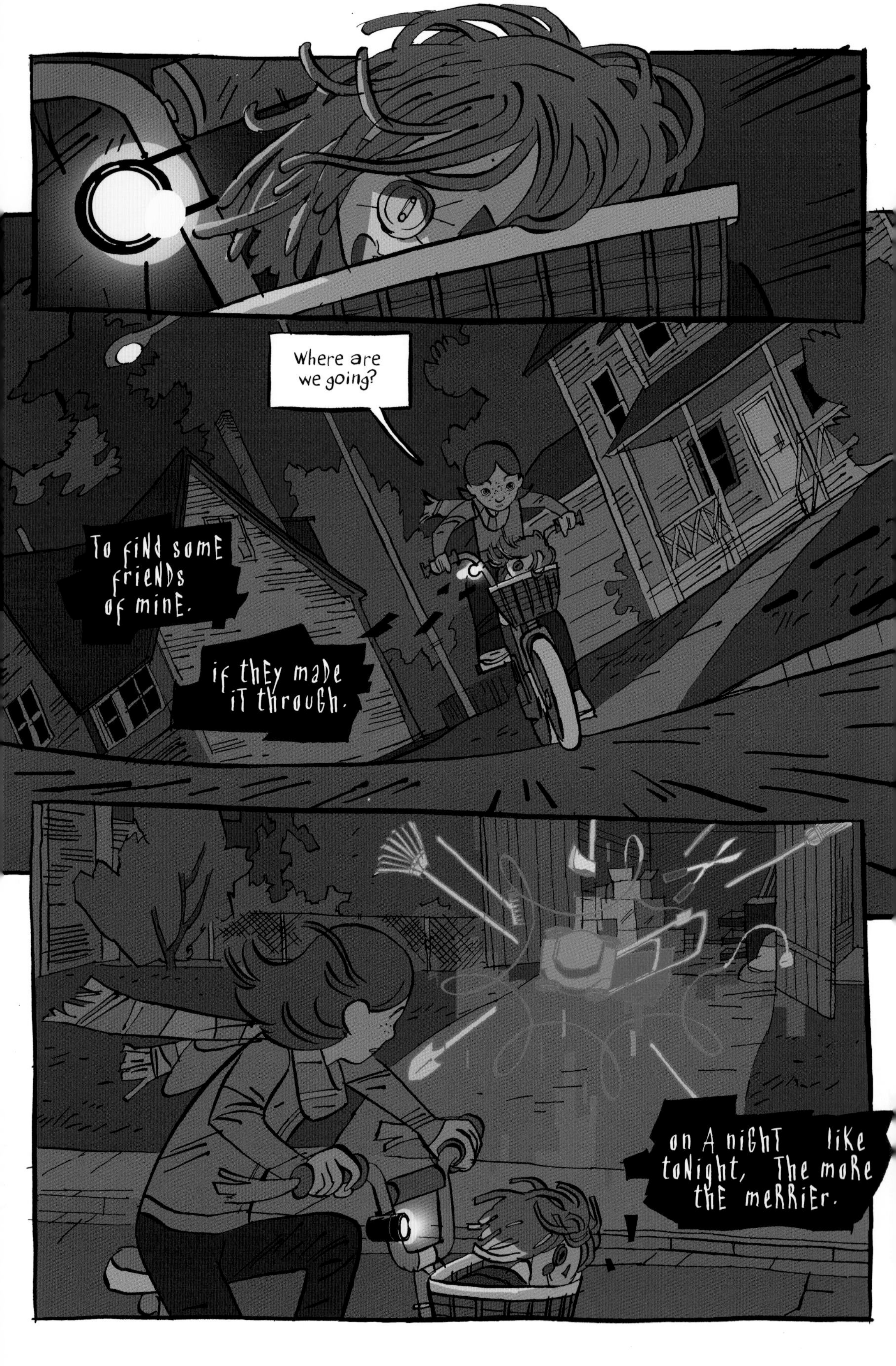
Where are we going?
To find some friends of mine.
if they made it through.
on a night like tonight, The more the merrier.

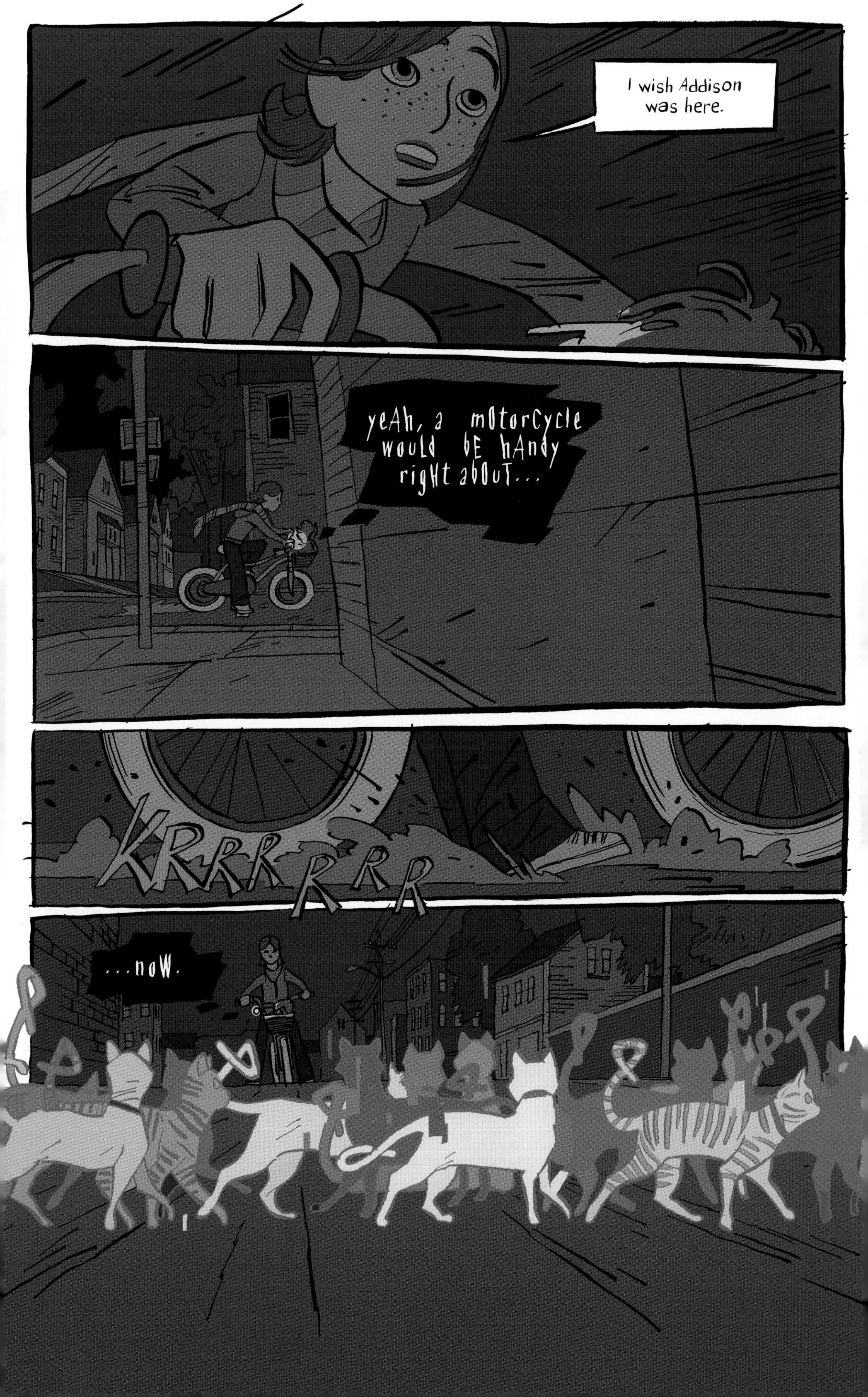
I wish Addison was here.
yeAh, a mOtorcycle would bE hAndy right abOuT...
KRRRRRR
...noW.

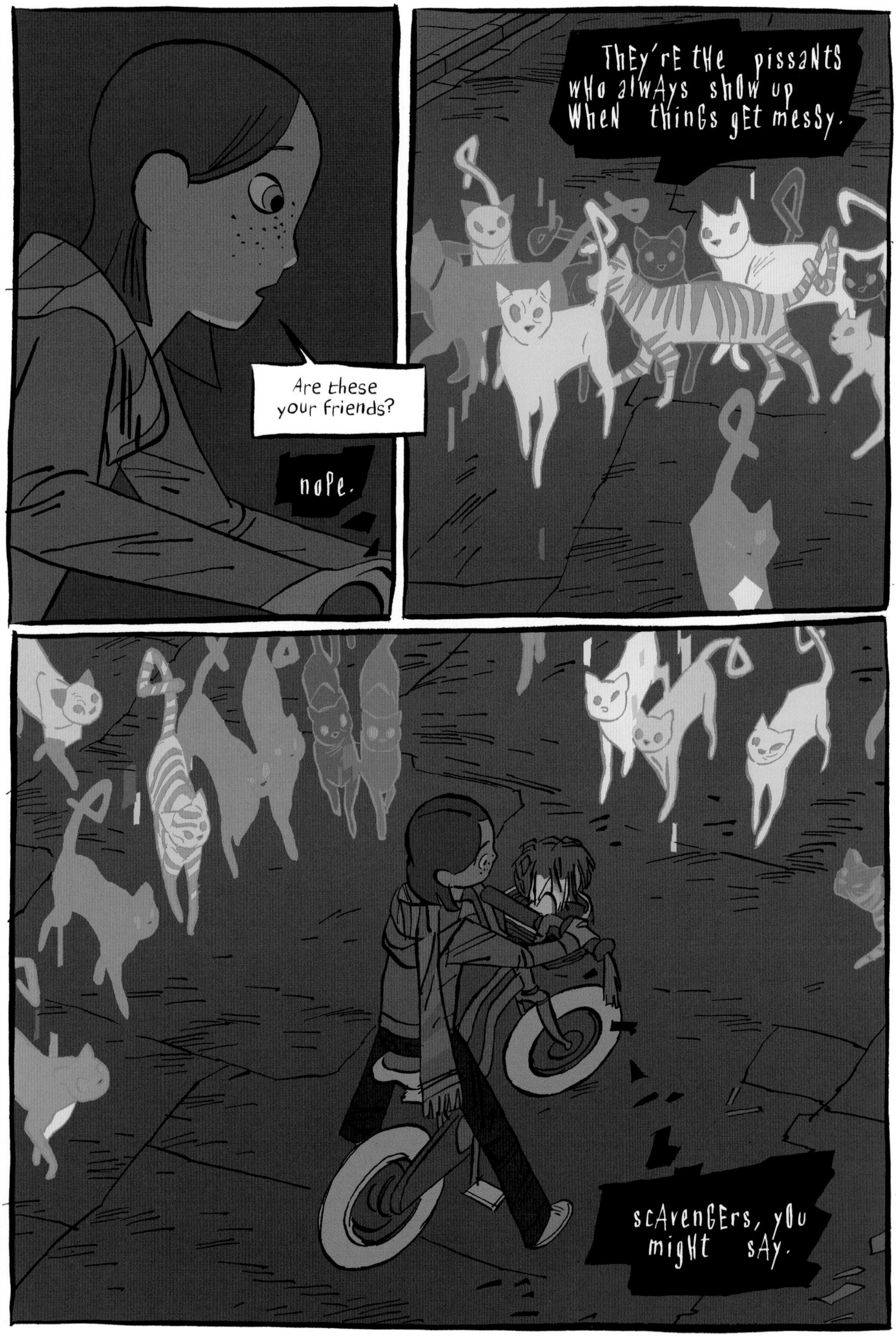
Are these your friends?
nope.
THEY'RE THE pissants WHO always show up WHEN things get messy.
scavengers, you might say.

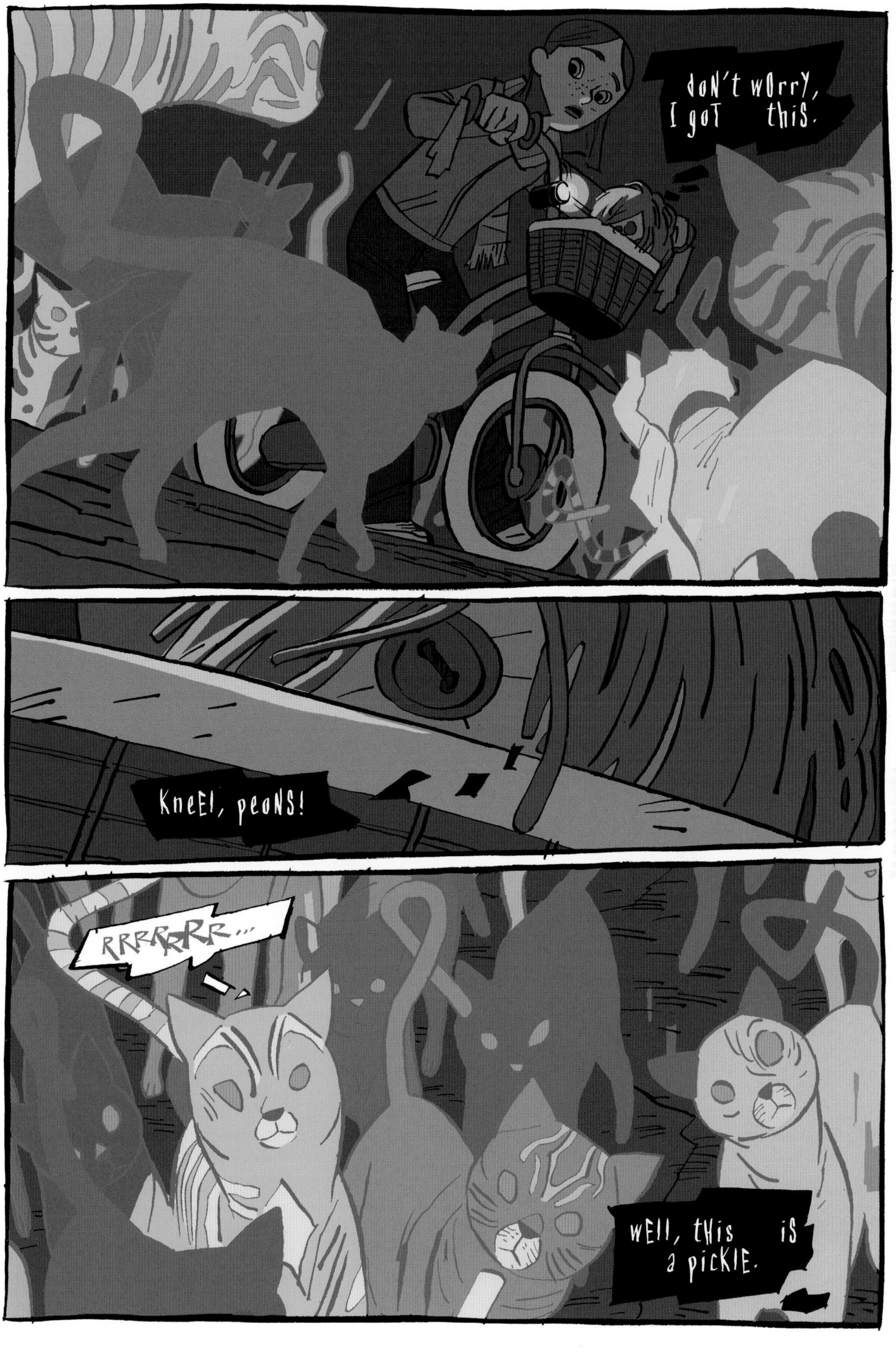
doN't wOrry, I goT this.
KneEl, peONS!
RRRRRRR...
wEll, tHis is a pickle.

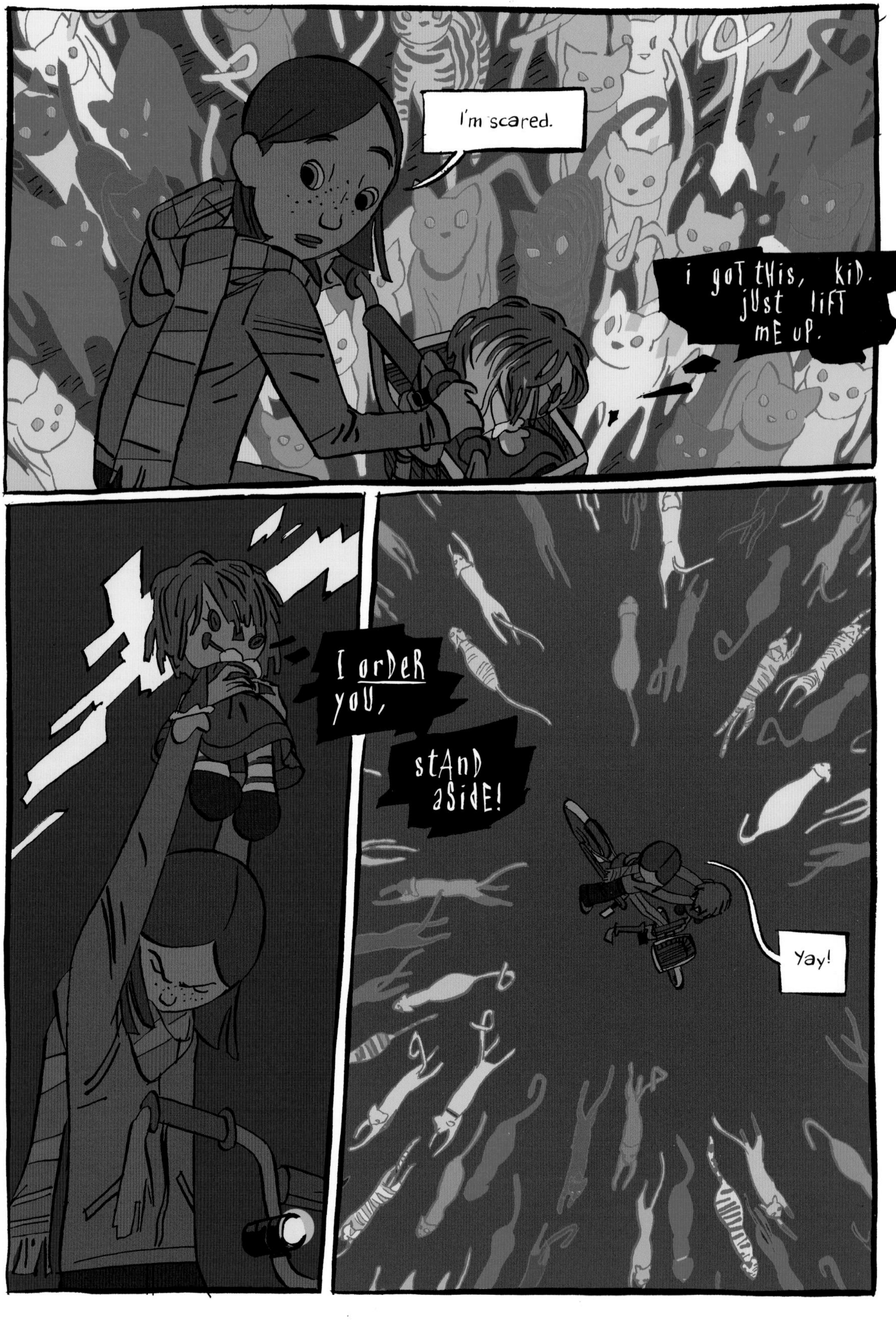
I'm scared.
I GOT THIS, KID. JUST LIFT ME UP.
I ORDER YOU,
STAND ASIDE!
Yay!

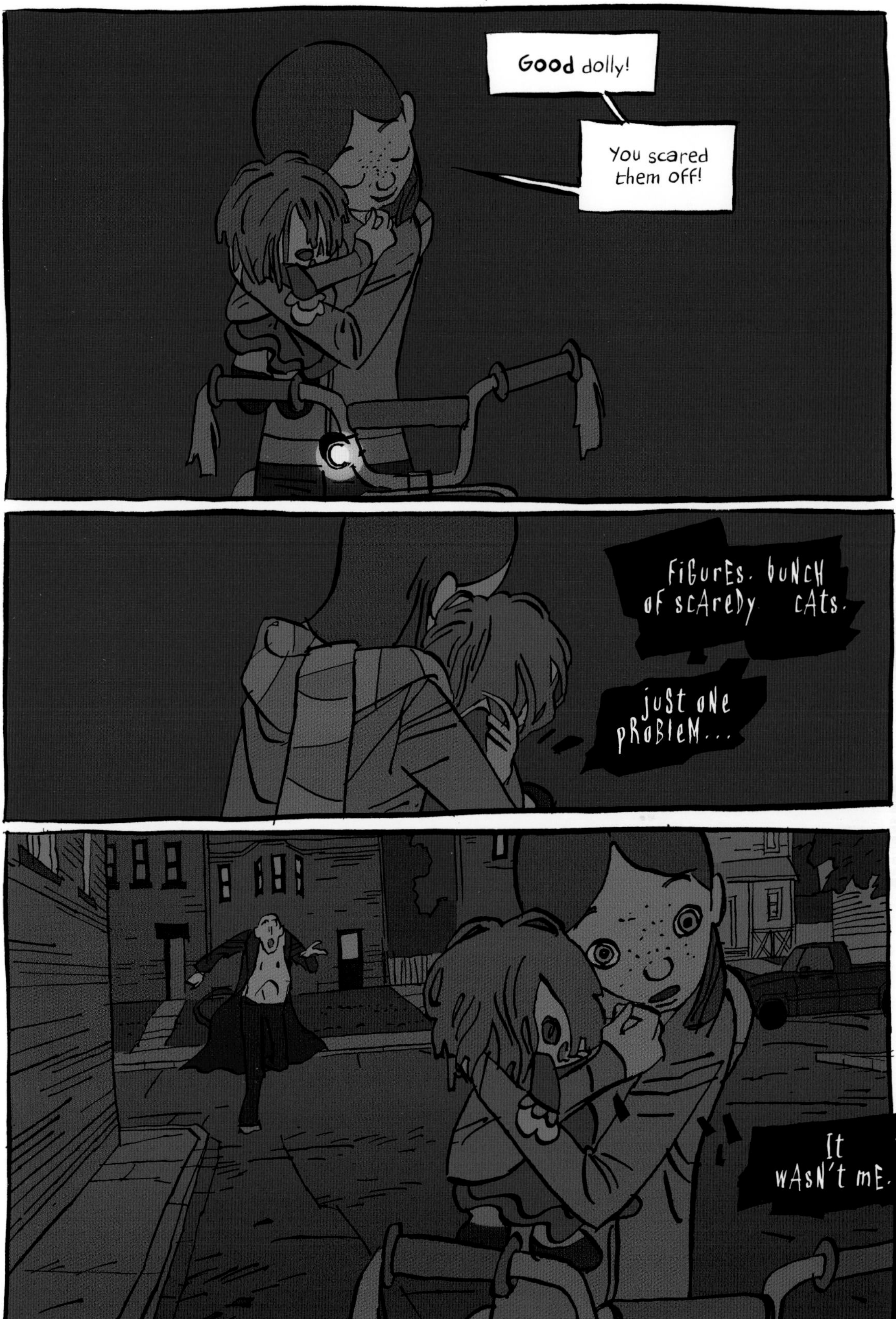
Good dolly!
You scared them off!
Figures. Bunch of scaredy cats.
Just one problem...
It wasn't me.

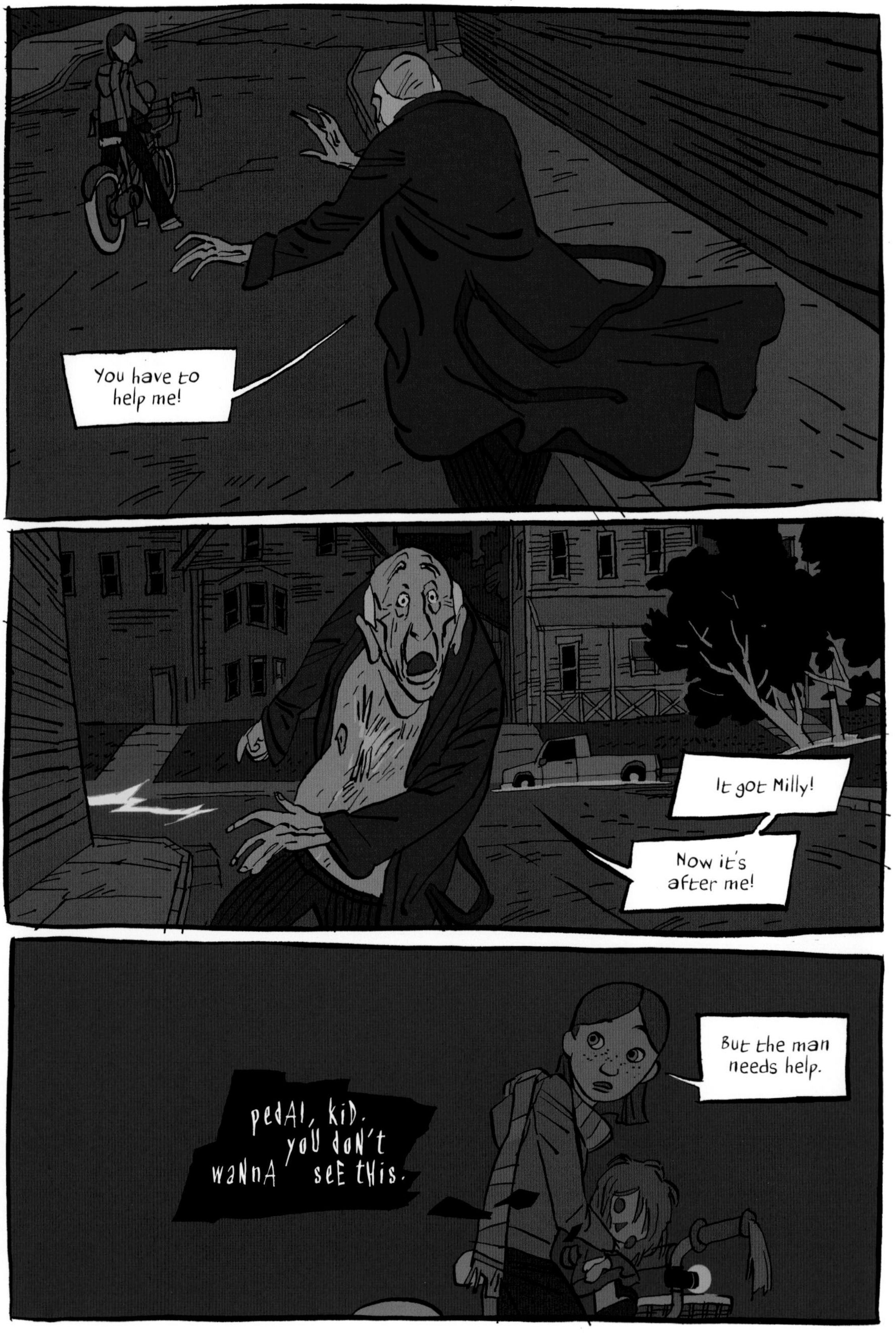
You have to help me!
It got Milly!
Now it's after me!
But the man needs help.
pedAl, kiD. yoU doN't wanNA seE tHis.

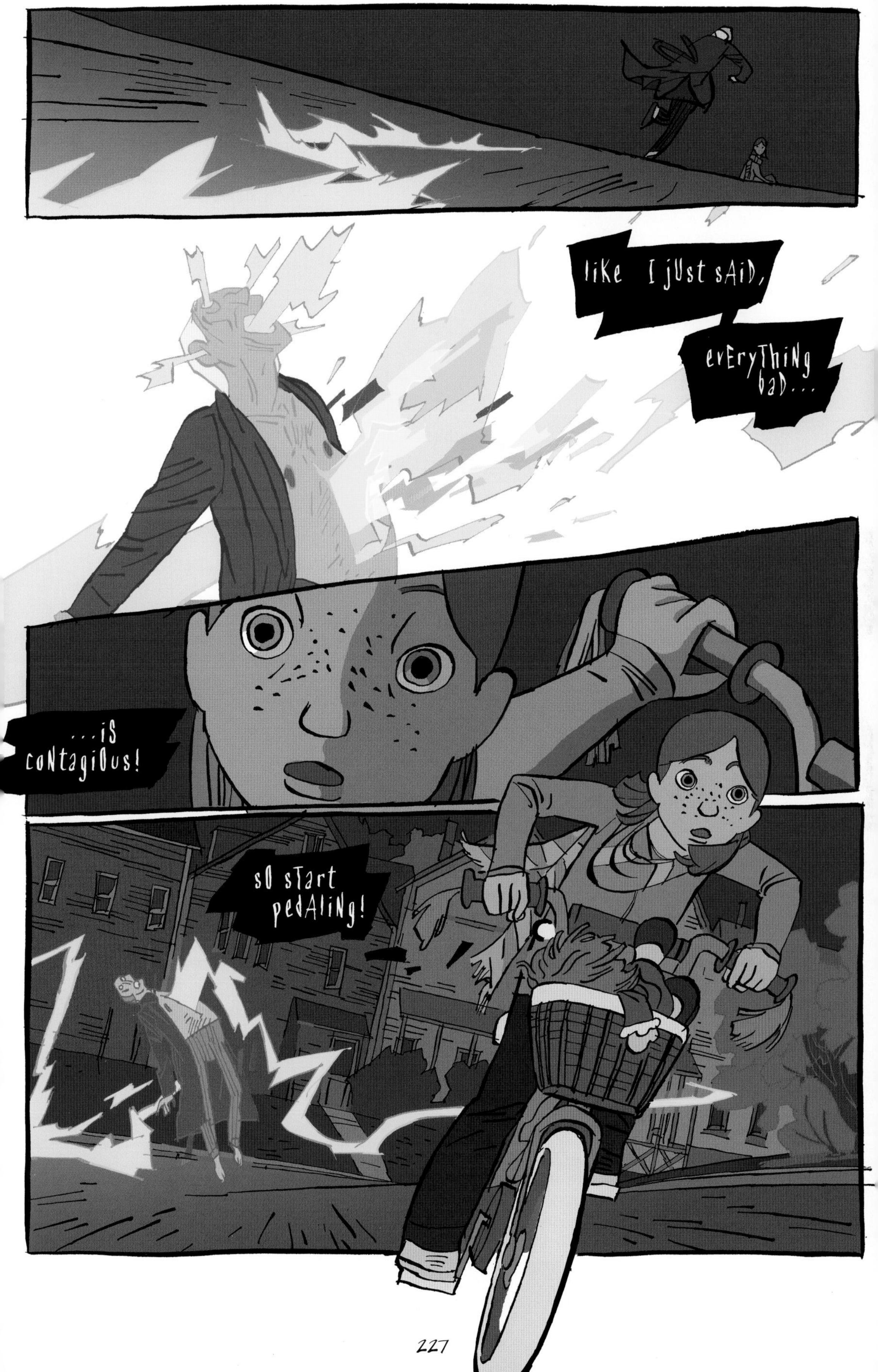
like I just said,
everything bad...
...is contagious!
so start pedaling!

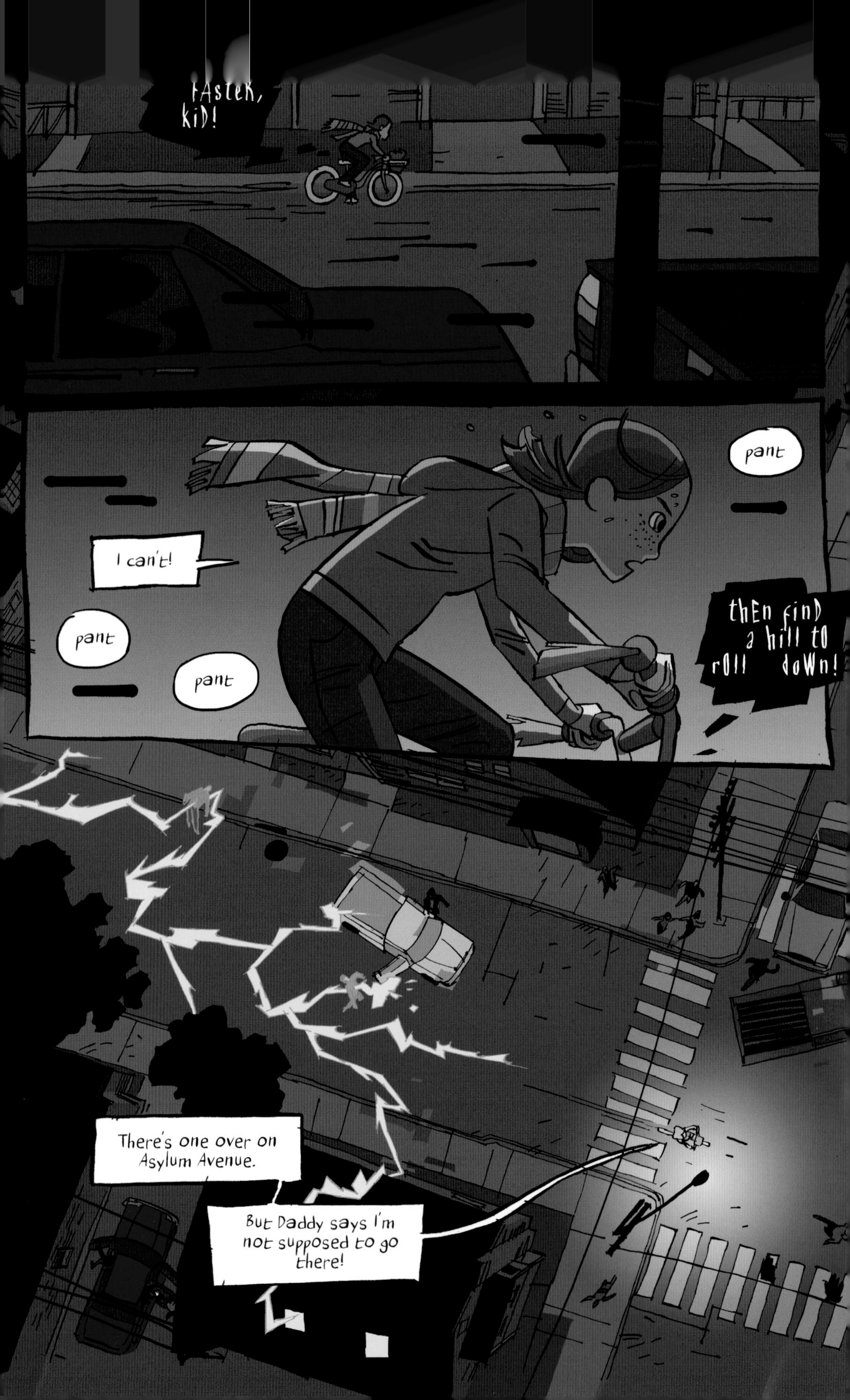
FASTER, KID!
I can't!
pant
pant
pant
THEN FIND A HILL TO ROLL DOWN!
There's one over on Asylum Avenue.
But Daddy says I'm not supposed to go there!

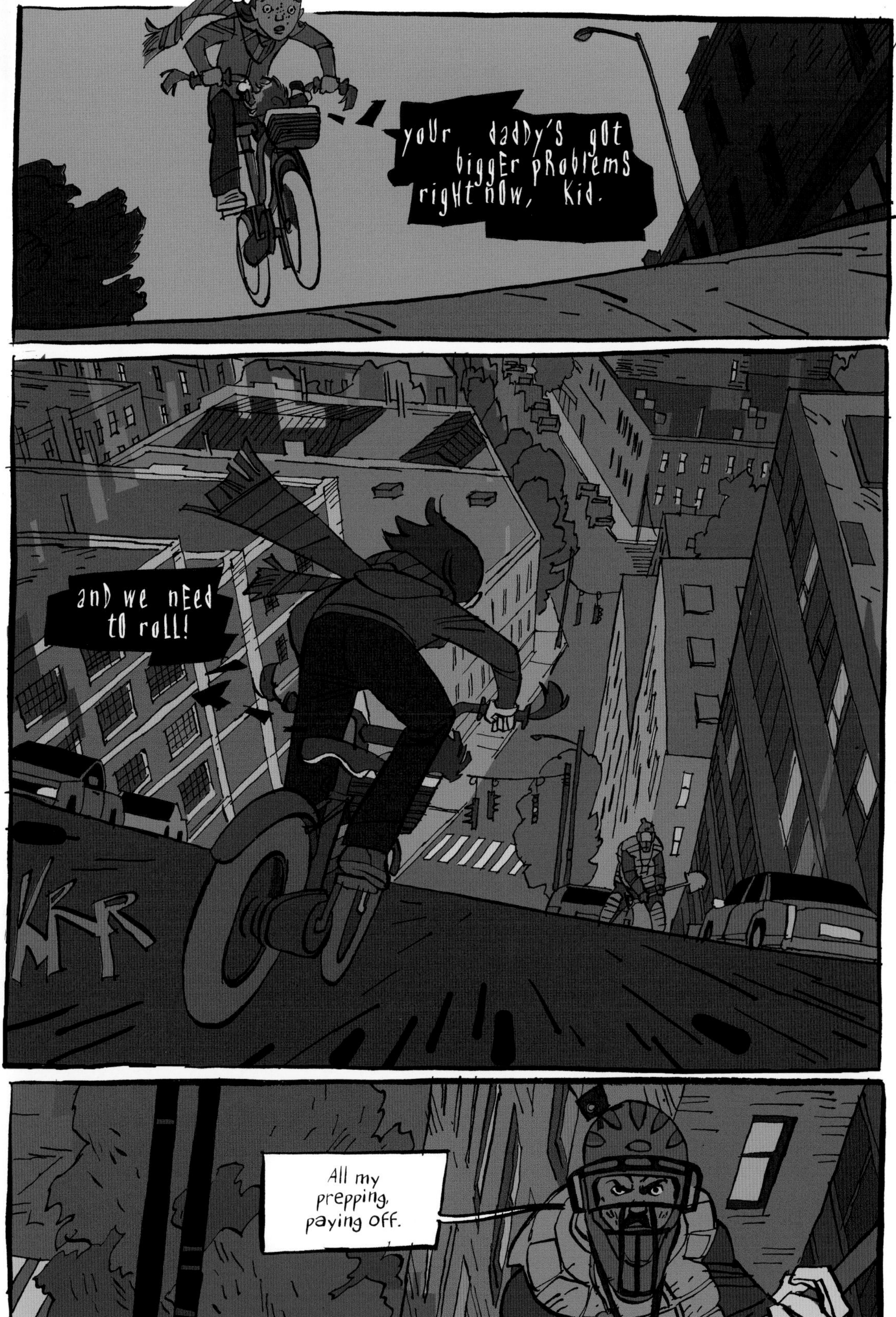
your daddy's got bigger problems right now, kid.
and we need to roll!
KRR
All my prepping, paying off.

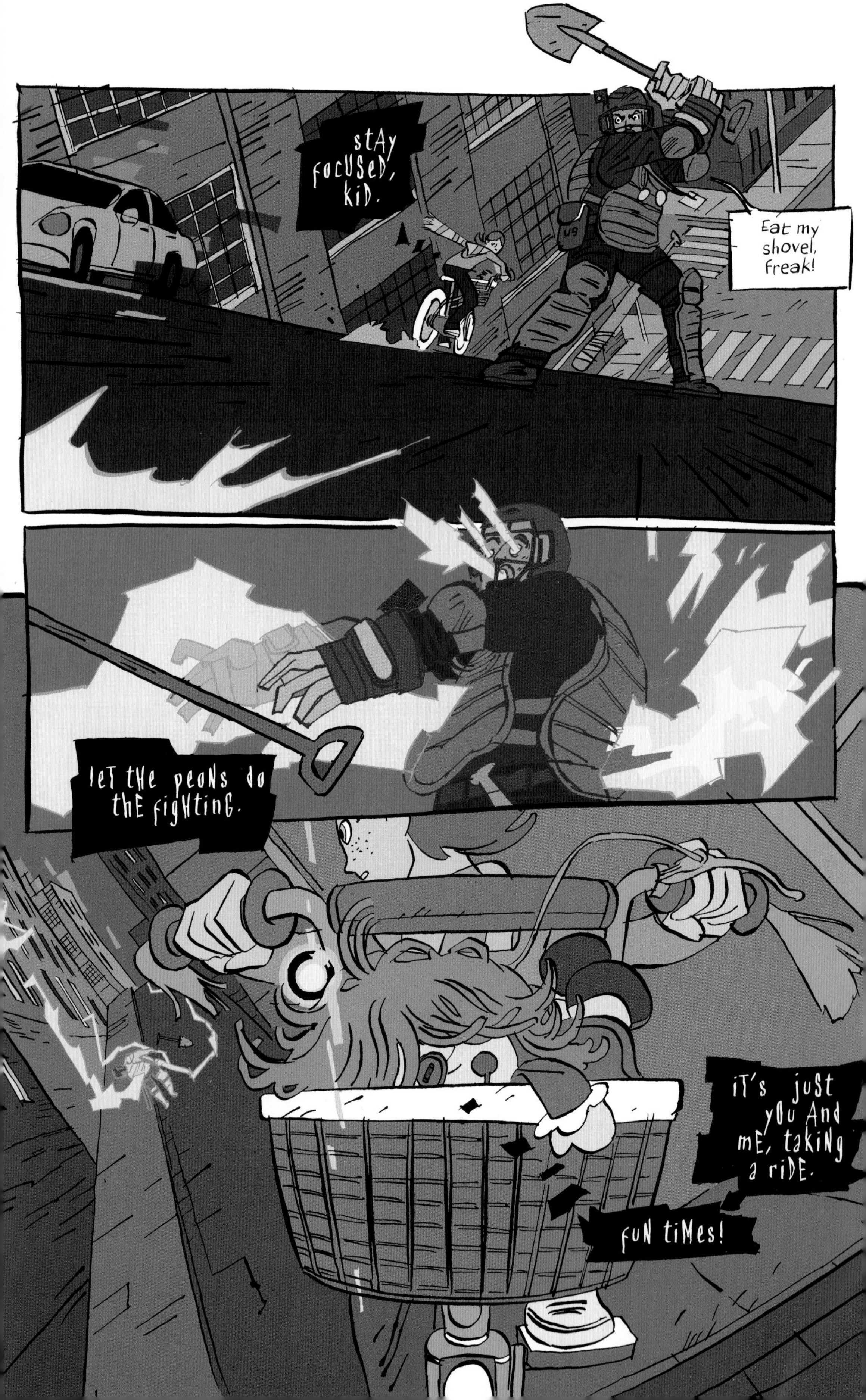
stAy focUSeD, kiD.
Eat my shovel, freak!
let tHe peoNs do thE fighting.
iT's just yOu And mE, taking a riDE.
fuN tiMes!

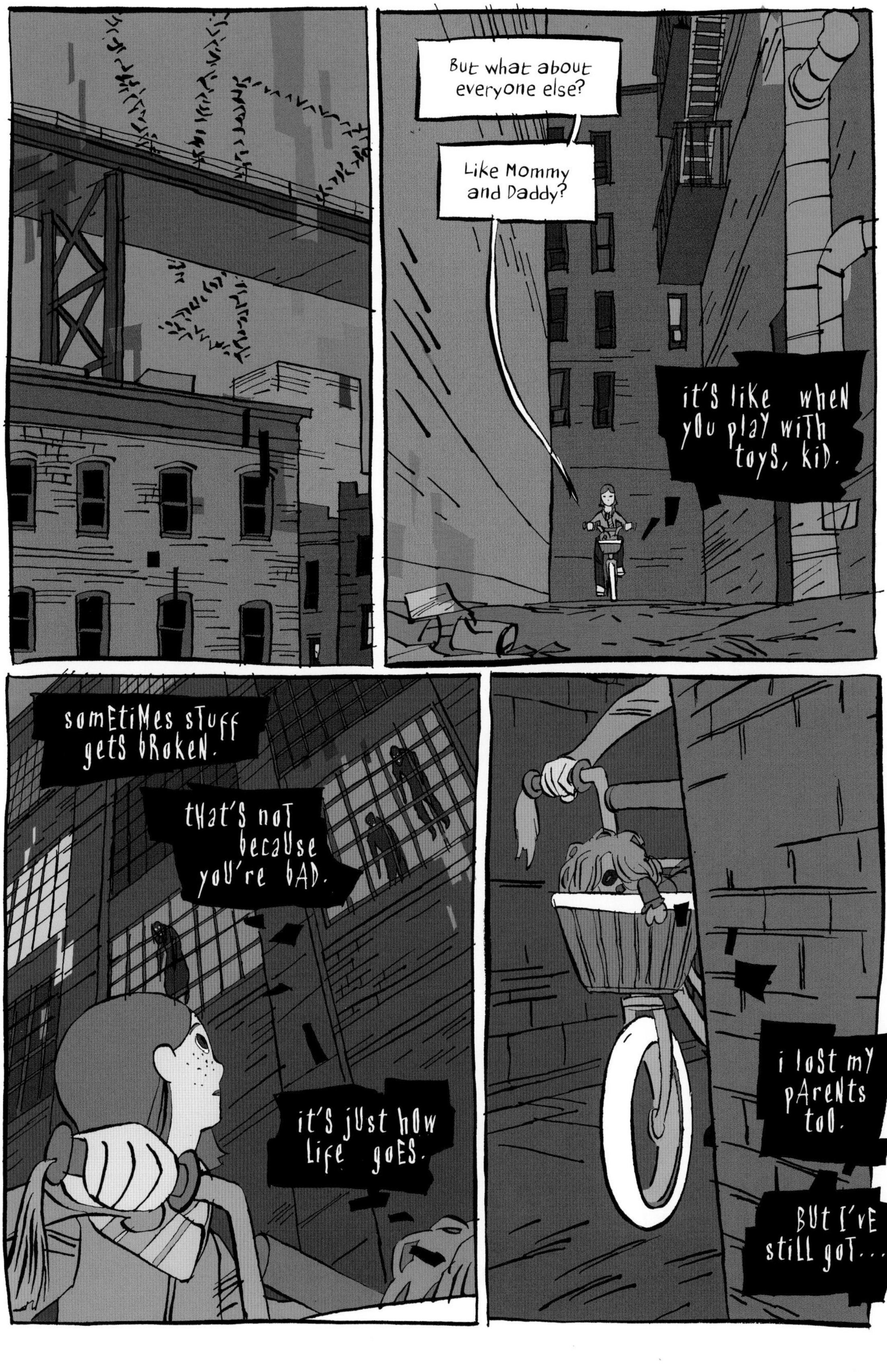
But what about everyone else?
Like Mommy and Daddy?
it's like when you play with toys, kid.
sometimes stuff gets broken.
that's not because you're bad.
it's just how life goes.
i lost my parents too.
but i've still got...

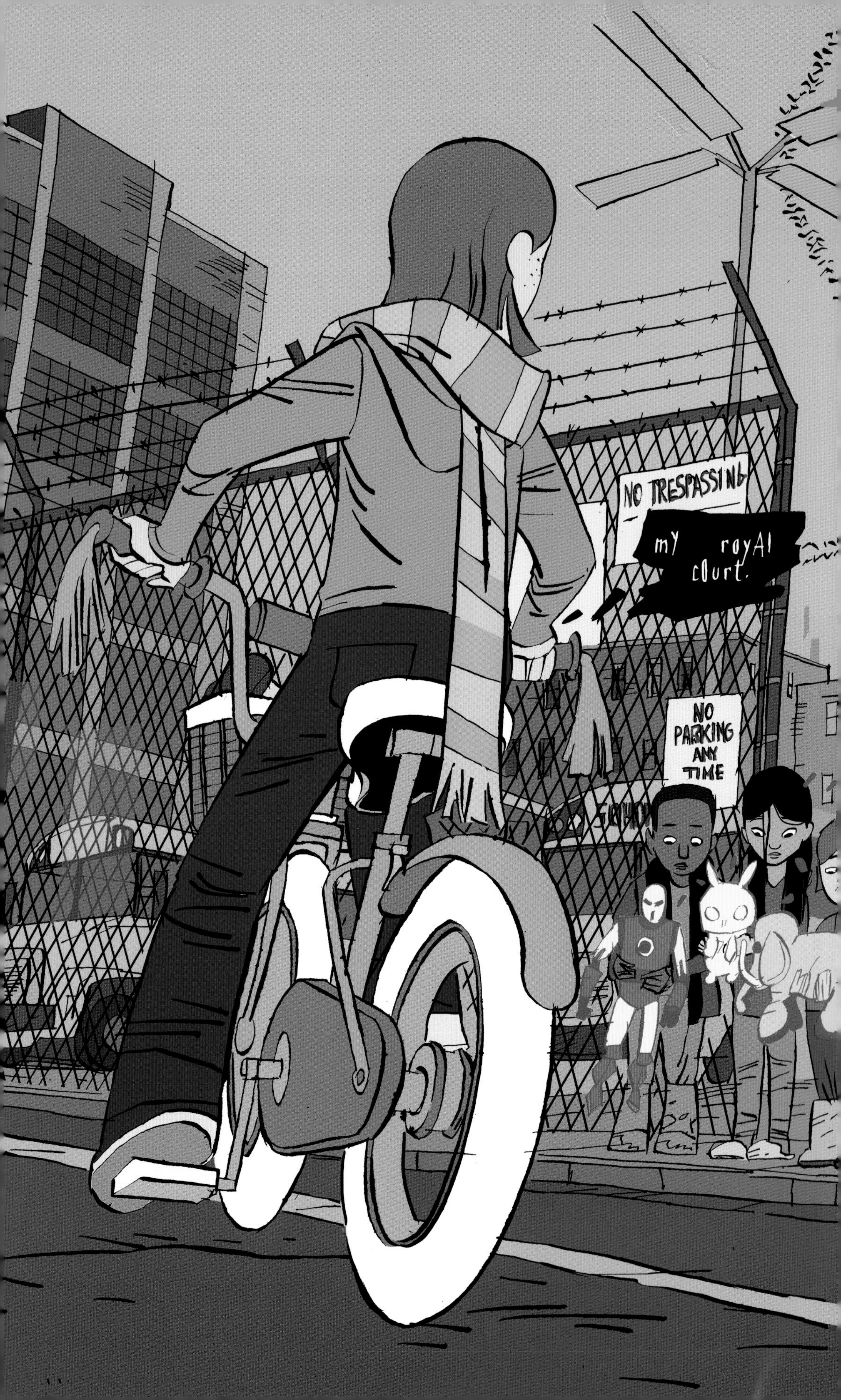
NO TRESPASSING
my royAl cOurt.
NO PARKING ANY TIME

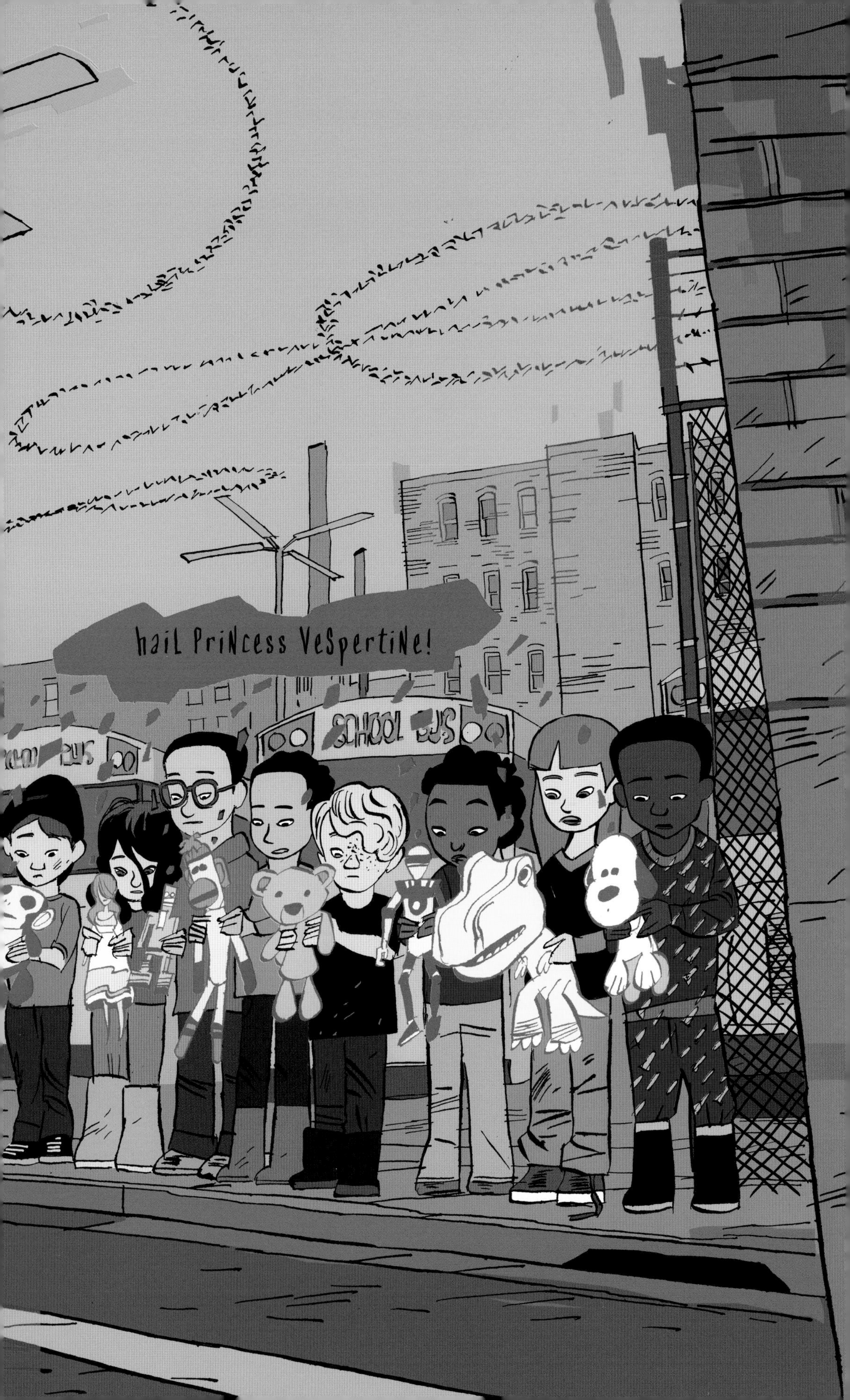
hail Princess Vespertine!
SCHOOL BUS

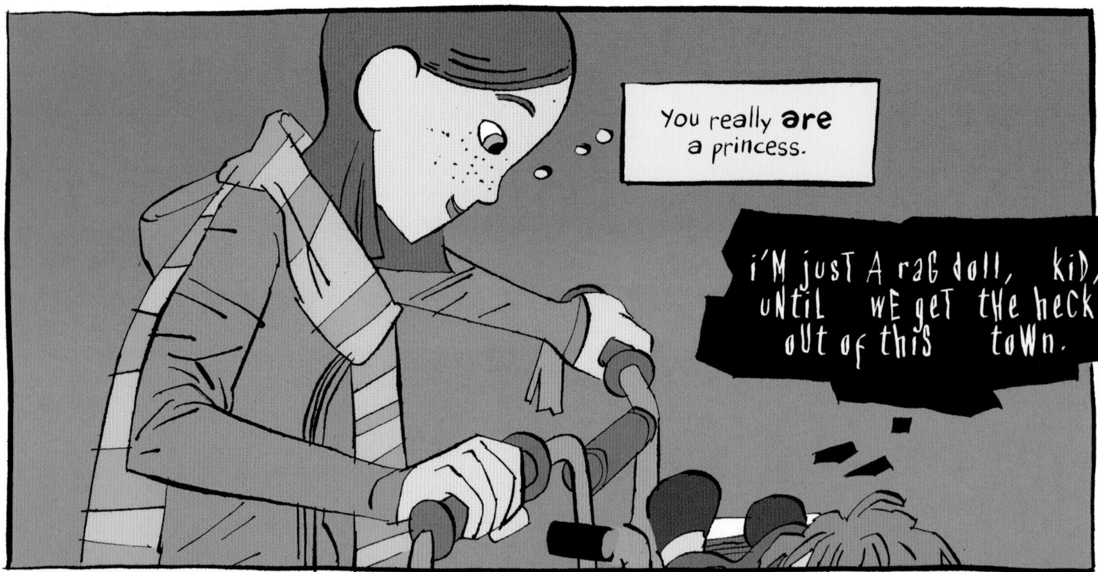
You really **are** a princess.
I'M JUST A RAG DOLL, KID, UNTIL WE GET THE HECK OUT OF THIS TOWN.

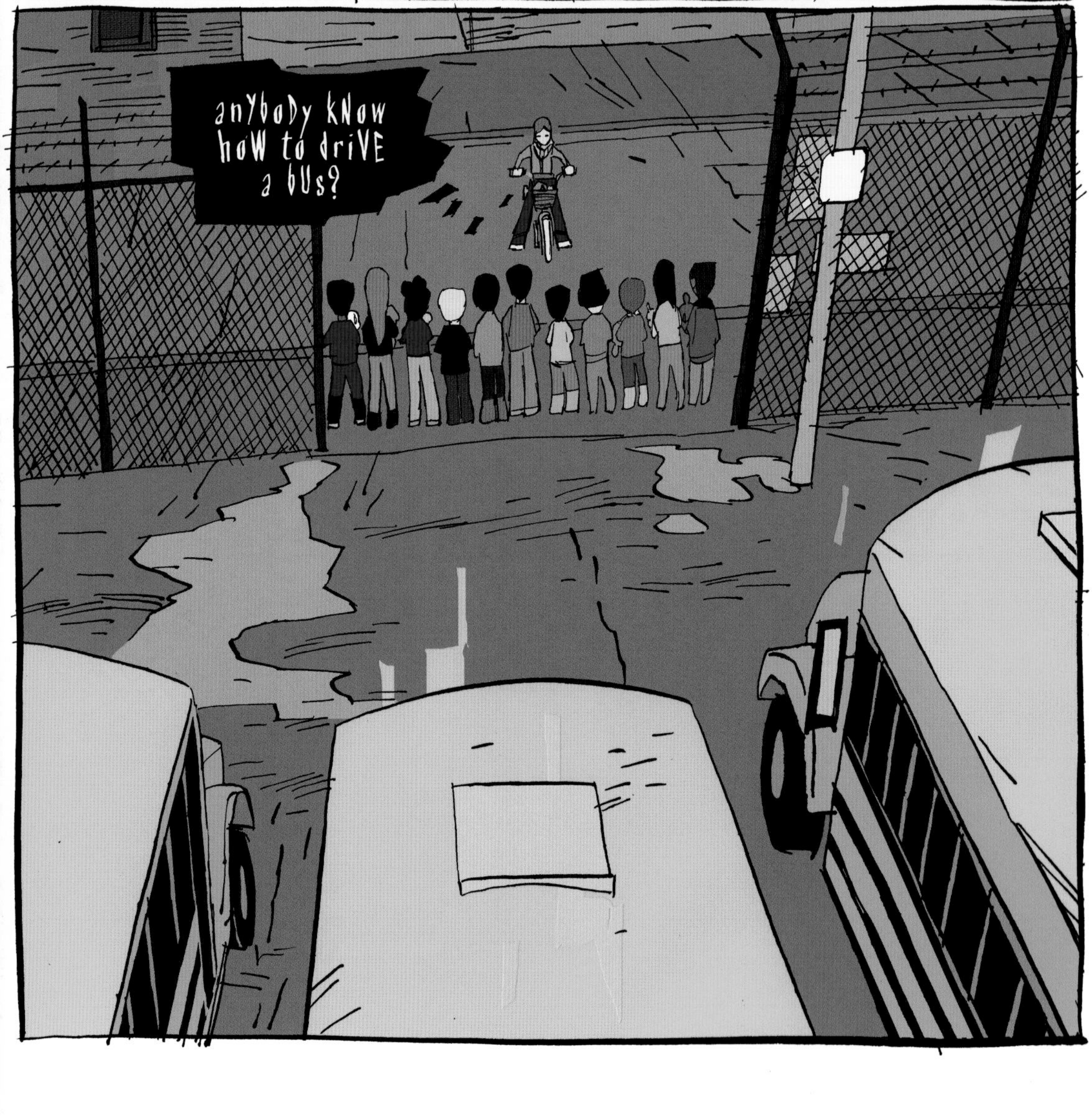
ANYBODY KNOW HOW TO DRIVE A BUS?

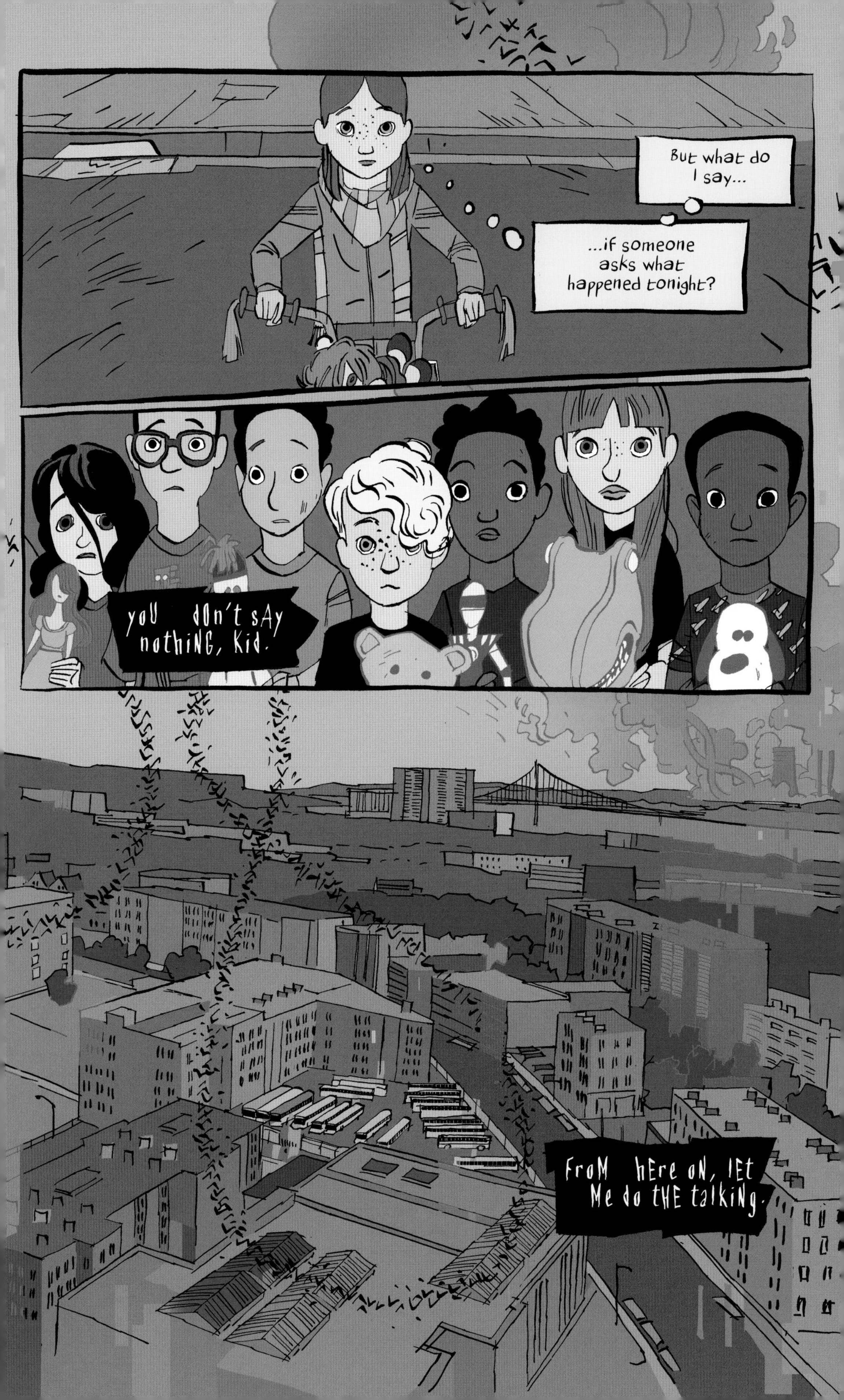
But what do I say...
...if someone asks what happened tonight?
you don't say nothing, kid.
From here on, let me do the talking.

To everyone who creates fan art,
thanks for putting drawing, painting, costuming,
and building at the center of your reading
—S.W.

To my petit nenuphar
—A.P.

First Second
New York

Published by First Second
First Second is an imprint of Roaring Brook Press,
a division of Holtzbrinck Publishing Holdings Limited Partnership
175 Fifth Avenue, New York, New York 10010

Library of Congress Control Number: 2016945565

ISBN: 978-1-250-15872-7 (paperback)

Our books may be purchased in bulk for promotional, educational,
or business use. Please contact your local bookseller or the Macmillan
Corporate and Premium Sales Department at (800) 221-7945 ext. 5442
or by e-mail at MacmillanSpecialMarkets@macmillan.com.

First edition, 2017
First paperback edition, 2018
Book design by Andrew Arnold, Molly Johanson, and Rob Steen
Printed in China by RR Donnelley Asia Printing Solutions Ltd.,
Dongguan City, Guangdong Province

1 3 5 7 9 10 8 6 4 2

Penciled and inked on regular copy paper
with a Speedball pen nib number 103 and a Pentel
brush pen. Colored digitally in Photoshop.